D1210989

ARUNDEL TITLES BY
SHARON LINNÉA
AND
B.K. SHERER:

Chasing Eden
Beyond Eden
Treasure of Eden

BY SHARON LINNÉA:

These Violent Delights

BEYOND EDEN

SHARON LINNÉA
B.K. SHERER

Arundel

ARUNDEL PUBLISHING • 2011

BEYOND EDEN

First Arundel printing April 2011

Copyright © 2007 by Sharon Linnéa and B.K. Sherer.

Cover design and original interior design by Christian Fuenfhausen
Cover images by Evgeny Kuklev, Eddy Lund, and Soubrette
Interior layout by 1106 Design

For information:
Arundel Publishing, P.O. Box 377, Warwick, NY 10990

ISBN: 978-1-933608-03-7

Originally published by St. Martin's Press/October 2007

For Jonathan Scott,
son and godson extraordinaire,
who would certainly lead the escape

CONTENTS

Then the Lord God said, "The man has now become like one of us, knowing good and evil. He must not be allowed to reach out his hand and take also from the tree of life and eat, and live forever." So the Lord God banished him from the Garden of Eden to work the ground from which he had been taken. He drove out the man, and he placed at the east of the Garden of Eden cherubim and a flaming Sword flashing back and forth to guard the way to the tree of life.

—GENESIS 3:22–24

BEYOND EDEN

PROLOGUE

DEPARTMENT OF THE ARMY
HEADQUARTERS, 57TH CORPS SUPPORT GROUP
UNIT #93404
APO, AE 09303-3404

April 14, 2003

Mr. Joseph Richards
234 Garden Street
Terre Haute, IN

Dear Mr. Richards,

     I wish to express my heartfelt concern to you and your family for the deep distress you must feel as you wait for news of your sister, Chaplain (Major) Jaime L. Richards. I know you must be very frustrated, and I promise that I will keep you informed as we continue to search for her.

     Jaime was last seen in the ruins of Babylon near Al Hillah, Iraq. Evidence collected to date indicates she was kidnapped by someone working with the Fedayeen and taken to a farmhouse on the outskirts of Baghdad. A member of the Central Intelligence Agency was able to follow her captor's trail to that point, and his search of the house uncovered many of her personal effects. Those items will be returned to you as soon as our forensic experts have completed their analysis. There were no signs of struggle, or any other indication that she has been harmed. Unfortunately, there were also no further clues as to her whereabouts.

     When I deployed, I vowed to bring home every member of my command. I do not plan to break that vow. Jaime is a valued member of my staff, and loved by all the soldiers. We miss her dearly, and will not rest until she is found.

     I know that there is little I can say to ease your mind as you wait for information about your sister. If there is anything I or any member of my command can do to assist you, please do not hesitate to ask.

Sincerely,

Abraham M. Derry
Colonel, Quartermaster
Commanding

344

ON THE MORNING of the day on which he would be kidnapped, Jimi Afzal cut himself while shaving. It was a small nick, but it bled, and he was unhappy because he didn't want anything to serve as a distraction to the proposal he was pitching at his 9:00 A.M. meeting.

He'd worked hard to earn this meeting. He was an associate editor at one of the few mid-sized independent publishing houses left in London. He had long wanted to do a series of nonfiction books with a brilliant man who had been nominated for a Nobel Prize in physics and was a friend of his parents. When the gentleman was over for dinner, as he had been often at the Afzal family flat, he got to talking about physics, and life, in a way that was compelling and accessible. Jimi just knew there was the potential for a series of books that could become classics. After careful wrangling, he had gotten the agreement of the friend, the support of his mentor editor, and an appointment with the executive editor of the company, whose approval would be needed for such an ambitious project. An appointment that day. December 5, 2005, at 9:00 A.M.

Jimi dressed in his best suit, skipped breakfast, pulled on his gray wool coat, and left his flat in Westbourne Gardens a half an hour early.

The street noise, the people, the winter chill, were all nothing more than backdrop to the presentation he was running again and again on a loop in his head. He was momentarily pleased that he'd reached the platform in the Queensway tube station of the Central Line just as a train was arriving—perhaps the augur of good things to come.

So lost was he in his own thoughts that it took him seconds to realize the air had somehow turned orange. That his eyes were tearing. His throat burning.

Everyone else turning, coughing. Panicking, even, in an oh-so-British, excuse-me-my-good-man, let-me-off-the-train-and-up-the-bloody-escalator kind of way.

His eyes were burning now, but he was in the flow of people heading toward the exits. Emergency services were arriving. A voice of authority over the speaker system. "Stay calm; exit in an orderly fashion."

A young woman next to him was crying. "I can't breathe; I can't breathe," she was sobbing.

He put his arm around her shoulder and said, "Don't panic; you'll suck in more bad air."

But all he was thinking was, *Nine* A.M. *This can't make me late. Damn terrorists.*

Then he was up and back outside. Ambulances, stretchers, constables, arriving news crews.

He dropped off the girl, still sobbing, with emergency personnel and walked through the crowd of terrified people.

Can't be late.

He started walking east on Bayswater, wondering if life was normal a street over.

Behind him, blaring horns, snarled traffic, shrieking people, chaos.

"Are you all right? What's going on?" A woman's face leaned forward.

He looked up to see a black limousine beside him, the back passenger window rolled down.

"Terrorists, I suppose. Chemical attack."

"Horrid! So sorry! You all right?"

"What? Yes, don't know about the others, but I'm fine. Eyes sting; that's the worst, really."

"So sorry!"

"Right. Thanks."

"You need any help?"

"I just need to get to work."

"Well, there I can help." The limo door popped open. "Climb in, then."

"Oh no, don't want to bother . . ."

"Come on. I'll feel I've done my part." The limo's passenger was also dressed for work. Power dressed, black designer suit, black-rimmed sunglasses.

All right. Maybe the day was saved, after all.

"If you really mean it, thanks so much."

He climbed in, and the car snaked forward. It had been past the tube entrance when the evacuation began, and now it was inching out of the area. Seemed it would be free of the mess fairly shortly.

"Where to?"

"Sorry?"

"Where to?" the woman asked, extending a hot cup of tea.

"Golden Rachmann Publishing. It's—"

"I know it," she said, and smiled. She picked up the telephone handset and had a brief discourse with the driver.

"It's not far past my stop," she said. "Not a problem."

"Thanks so much."

Even given the favor the woman was doing him and the tea he was now holding, he again retreated into his head, into the midst of his presentation.

The tea was in a real cup, with a saucer. It was heaven in his throat, which still burned. The woman finished her own tea, put the cup on the small table where the hot pot was, leaned across him, and said, "This is me."

The car rolled to a halt, and she climbed out in front of a chic building.

"Thanks so much," he said again as the car began to move.

Thank you for seeing me, Mr. Rachmann. I believe we have an extraordinary opportunity before us. . . .

The words played again and again in Jimi's mind.

They were beginning to make less sense.

His tea was gone. He set his cup down next to the woman's empty cup.

He looked out the window and was shocked to see countryside. He was confused. So confused. His head was spinning.

"Driver, you've got to let me out," he said, banging on the window. "Driver, we've missed my stop."

But the car kept going. He swayed and lurched back toward the long bench seat. No, this wasn't right. This wasn't right at all. Through the worsening haze in his mind, he tried to open the back door, even though the car was moving. But it was locked. It wouldn't open.

"Let me out! Nine o'clock. I must, really—," he said. And he passed out on the backseat without fully comprehending that he wouldn't make any more 9:00 A.M. meetings for a very, very long time.

NUTMEG AND GINGER. No matter how many pine-scented candles were sold as part of the Christmas season, for Juliet Kettner it was the aroma of baking with nutmeg and ginger that would forever signal to her that the season had truly arrived. She hummed along with the radio station that was playing Christmas songs and peeked in at the gingerbread men in the oven. The kids would be back soon, and she knew they'd all prefer the chocolate-chip cookies, but now they, too, would have ginger-scented memories of the season.

What a great day. The first large snowfall of the season had blanketed Warwick on Friday, canceling school and warming hearts everywhere. By today, Sunday, when the kids from church had planned to go Christmas caroling, the roads were clear, yet the ground was still white. How perfect was that?

The kids had a blast caroling, both at the homes of targeted "shut-ins" as well as up and down blocks where friends and families resided. Finally a group of a dozen or so had come back to the Kettner house for pizza and snow play, ending with hot chocolate and warm cookies by the fire.

The Kettner house was a block from Stanley–Deming Park, a large village park that had a classic sledding hill. The remaining middle schoolers had grabbed saucers and sleds and headed out, promising to be back by 7:00 P.M., since it was a school night. Parents would start arriving soon to pick up their offspring.

Juliet tossed another log on the fire in the great room and headed to the front door. She could see the outlines of the kids trudging back up the final hill from the park. Right on time. They were singing as they approached, another old standard: "Grandma Got Run Over by a Reindeer."

Juliet grinned and opened the door, reminding them to stomp their boots before coming in and shedding snow clothes. Their breath was white, their cheeks were crimson from the cold, but they were in high spirits.

"Everyone into the great room! Popcorn is out; grab a cup of cocoa as you pass through the kitchen. Half have marshmallows; half do not—take your pick! Cookies coming in right away!"

The gingerbread cookies were ready. She used a spatula to scoop them onto a Christmas-angel-shaped platter and waded into the great room, Christmas tree lit and glowing in the corner, room now stuffed with kids, laughing, dropping to the floor, arguing over television channels.

She put down the trays of chocolate-chip cookies first and then looked for her son's friend whom she knew particularly liked gingerbread. Didn't see him first time through.

"Anyone seen Ryan S.?" she asked. They had multiple Ryans and went along with the school habit of differentiating them by first initials of last names.

"Probably in the bathroom," said Ian T.

But a few minutes later, Ryan hadn't reemerged.

"Seriously, guys, where's Ryan?" she asked again.

"He was with us, Mrs. K. He was racing with Jonathan and D.J."

"He wiped out big-time, twice!" added Jonathan enthusiastically.

Juliet had done a sweep of the entire first floor, to no avail. She called her own two kids out of the crowd to see if Ryan's snow clothes were in the pile by the door. They didn't seem to be.

"I'm going to check the park. I'll be right back," she said. She pulled on boots over her stocking feet, wrapped a coat around her, and went out.

In contrast to the house, the outdoors was eerily still. There were no streetlights in the hilly part of the park where the sledding had taken place, so the snow was gray and shadows loomed large. All the sledders were now gone. The park was entirely empty.

"Ryan?" she yelled. "Ryan S.?" she yelled louder. The whistling wind was the only reply.

She trudged by herself along the abandoned hill, seeing the various sledding tracks cut into the snowbanks, worn flat by multiple uses. There were no huddled children left with an unnoticed broken ankle or broken back.

There was nobody.

Maybe a friend from Ryan's neighborhood had offered him a ride home and he had neglected to tell anyone?

That had to be it.

Juliet turned around and headed home. As she got to the top of the hill, she saw something protruding from a couple of well-pruned bushes that made a barrier between the park and the sidewalk. She walked up to it and tugged.

It was a round purple snow saucer. Around the rim, the name "Ryan S." was written in black Sharpie.

Juliet was still clutching the abandoned saucer when the first three parent cars turned onto her block. The second car, a white Prius, was Ryan's mom. She was in the car alone.

Juliet Kettner's heart sank.

Forever after, she would think of this as the day that had ruined the warm comfort of nutmeg and ginger for her, forever.

MING ZHOU FINALLY LOCKED the main office of the Home of Hope orphanage and turned to trudge the distance to his small home just outside the compound. The air was bright, clear, and chilly, and the nearly full moon above the northern mountains easily lit his way.

His wife had been gone for a week now, having meetings with both government agencies and private charitable organizations, hoping to find more funding for the orphanage. There was an unexpected tsunami of AIDS orphans in Henan. Many of the working poor sold their blood for extra income, and for years the local blood bank had reinjected donors with platelets so they could donate again sooner. However, none of the platelets had been screened for AIDS, and consequently tens of thousands had been infected by the platelet injections. That had quickly translated to thousands of orphans.

On top of that, the Central Government had never acknowledged the crisis and, in fact, had been cracking down on people who ran AIDS orphanages. He feared for his wife's safety.

Zhou sighed and slipped into the dark quiet of his own house. The mountains provided a breathtaking backdrop out the window, and he remembered the English saying "too bad you can't eat the scenery." Too bad indeed. They'd feast like emperors on a view like that.

Coming home always comforted him, even with Mei Ling away. He made it a practice to say a small prayer as he entered their home and to leave the cares of the day on the doorstep.

Everything was peaceful. He went to look in the baby's room. The teenage girl who worked as their nanny slept on her mat, a small smile playing at the corners of her mouth. Zhou tiptoed into the room to see his baby daughter. She was nearly a toddler now, he acknowledged wistfully. He came to stand at the side of the small hanging cradle.

But as he reached down to kiss little An Bao, he stood momentarily confused. The covers were askew, and the cradle was empty.

He looked on the floor, in case she'd fallen out, but there was nothing. Had she crawled away?

Trying to remain calm, he went over and shook the teenager awake.

"I heard nothing, Master Zhou," she said. "Bao was asleep; she was fine; I would have heard if she fell!"

It took them less than fifteen minutes to search the small house, including any space in which a toddler could crawl or hide.

Fifteen minutes for Zhou to realize that his baby was gone.

She was gone.

"HELLO, MEGHAN? Patsy. Listen, sorry to do this to you on a Sunday, but I just got a call from work, the urgent one I mentioned I was expecting. Could you be here in five? . . . Thanks, you're a doll."

Patsy Covington hardly listened for the sitter's response before hanging up the phone. Part of the deal of being the Covington child-care professional was that you were available when needed. Period.

Patsy smiled at her toddler in his high chair and finished giving him the last two bites of the organic peas and carrots she'd just mixed herself. Patsy prided herself, above all things, on being a good mother. The Good Mother. It was a stereotype she'd created for herself in her late teens, and with effort, she'd managed it as an adult.

Oh, sometimes she had to work on Sundays, but it was rare. She certainly had chosen her profession wisely and gotten the most bang for her buck. Or, more precisely, the most buck for her time. She only worked part-time, but her fees were astronomical. She was able to provide well for herself and her two young children.

She pulled the cotton bib off of Bartlett and unstrapped him from the chair. She spun him around gently and kissed his chubby cheek, eliciting the requisite gurgle/giggle.

"Where's your sister, big boy?" she asked. She plunked him down into his bouncer and pulled a frozen teething ring from the freezer, which he accepted happily.

Patsy had last left four-year-old Portia reading in the den of the upgraded fifties ranch house. She stopped on her way in and looked in the bathroom mirror. She wore casual black slacks and a black top with white collar. The jewelry at her neck was short, so that Arty couldn't reach it, yet expensive and well chosen. It would do for today. She freshened her lipstick and sealed it. Attractive urban matron was what she was going for—it was a ubiquitous look, and she believed she'd caught it.

"Where's my future leader?" she asked now, swinging into the den. The only thing that remained from the previous owner was the golden shag carpet in the den. It was in pretty good shape and it cracked her up, so she kept it.

She glanced at the sofa but didn't see the little girl anywhere.

"Portia?" she asked. "Portia, where are you?"

There was silence.

"Portia, answer me!"

"Here, Mama," said Portia, looking up from the carpet behind the reading chair. She held a hard-backed illustrated edition of *Black Beauty*. Whoever said four-year-olds can't be taught to read? "I'm sorry; I was in the book."

"Want to come help your mama work today?"

"Oh yes," said the girl, her eyes lighting. She gently replaced her bookmark and stood up. She was wearing a small baby blue sweat suit with a yellow headband across her dark brown hair. Her eyes were large and sparkly.

"Go get your shoes on, then, and meet me at the car. Meghan will be here any minute to take care of Arty."

"Yes, ma'am!" she said.

Patsy unconsciously picked up the book and straightened the pillows. As she did so, she heard the housekeeper/nanny's car engine as it pulled into the driveway.

Portia gave Meghan a small hug as they passed her in the hall.

"I'll drop her back in about an hour," Patsy told the young woman in her mid-twenties. "Then I'll be gone until Tuesday. I assume that's no problem?"

"No, of course not, Ms. Covington," said Meghan.

Patsy hummed as she strapped her daughter into the child seat and heard the buckle click into place. She knew that bringing Portia was a sign of great confidence. She would never work with her daughter in public unless she knew for certain that they'd never be noticed. Well, that they'd never be noticed *and* that the victim would ultimately be killed. Those being kidnapped for this job had been carefully chosen and carefully taken. She'd been the front on several of the riskiest ones herself, which she would never do if there was any chance at all that those brought in would live to describe her.

Let alone her daughter.

But today's kidnapping would be in broad daylight, in a well-populated place. No one would look twice at a mom and child out shopping. No one, of course, except the victim, this one named Daniel Derry, a 15-year-old who would undoubtedly be happy to help two females in distress, especially when one was so adorable. Once he was taken, and out cold, Patsy would drop her daughter home and continue the trip.

"You ready, missy?" Patsy asked her daughter as she pulled out of the driveway and headed for the Pentagon City Mall.

THURSDAY

JAIME RICHARDS AWOKE under a fiercely blazing canopy of stars. The air around her was chilly and still. She was under a coarse woven blanket, with another blanket beneath to shield her from the dusty ground.

She had dreamed of a land of shimmering colors, deeply intense in their hues. It was a land she'd come to know well. She was back now in what they called the Terris world. Even as she awoke, it felt uncomfortably unfamiliar. But she was back for an urgent purpose, and she had to get her bearings. She tried to sit up.

The landscape swam, and vomit lurched in her stomach.

"Don't worry. I know you're in a hurry, but it will take less than half an hour for the drug to wear off. You're safe, and your guide is coming before dawn." The voice was male, the accent Farsi. "Relax. Let yourself drift. You can't hurry the process, but if you don't fight it, you can make it more pleasing."

Jaime willed herself to relax, to close her eyes. And in her mind, she went back to Eden. She was sitting on a mountainside terrace, outside the Operative training school. She loved sipping her tea, overlooking the verdant valley growing lush with bougainvillea, roses, morning glory. She loved the colors glistening off the rooftops, the jewels shining in the sun. She loved that she was in a very intense training program and yet she'd been taught to relax, to breathe, to appreciate every opportunity presented.

She stretched her legs; even though it was February, she wore a colorful summer robe, with bare legs and sandaled feet. She could have been barefoot if she wished.

"You feel at home here."

Jaime looked up to find the master of the school, a fit man with olive skin and white hair, standing beside her with his own cup of tea. "May I?"

"Of course."

He sat on the other carved chair and looked at the world of paradise spread before them. "This feels like home to you?" he said.

"Yes. More than anywhere I've ever been."

"Ah. I'm glad. It means the decision was right to bring you in."

They sat companionably, sipping their tea.

"I've come to ask if you're ready to go back."

Jaime sat straight, knocking the table in her surprise. "Back? But I've only been in training for two years!"

No one was ever given an assignment as an Operative of Eden back in the Terris world until they'd completed the five-year initial training course.

"Special circumstances require special actions," Clement said. "The identities of some of our people in the Terris world have been compromised. We must send in an Operative whose identity we know has not been compromised—someone new. It is early for you. You would be taking a chance. We would be taking a chance. But I wouldn't be asking if we didn't think you were up to it, that the odds are in favor of your success."

He carried a small pouch of pretzels and offered her one. "What do you think? Are you ready to return? If so, things will move quickly."

Was she ready?

Now here she was, two days later, on the ground of the desert of western Iran, if things had gone as planned.

Jaime heard an odd noise, like the tinkling of small tinny bells, and opened her eyes again, giving them time to adjust to the dark. This time, she felt much better. She realized someone was sitting beside her.

"Here. Would you like a drink?" He held out a canteen. "Don't worry. The water is pure. It arrived here with you."

She sat up slowly and took the canteen gratefully.

The man beside her was strapping and tall, with the dark leathery skin of a nomad, who spent his days outside. He wore loose pants, a shirt, and a vest and a hat, although colors were hard to discern at that hour. He also had a thick, curly beard. She looked beyond him to the large herd of animals just below them on the landscape.

"There are over twelve million goats in Iran," he said conversationally in Farsi. "Almost every home has one or two. They're easier to keep than sheep—goats can find food almost anywhere."

"How many have you got?" she asked, also in Farsi. If her reentry story was that she had spent time with Iranian goat herders, she would have been expected to speak with them. So over the past year, she had learned.

"One hundred and forty-six," he replied. "It's a communal flock, belonging to our extended family, many of whom are now sleeping in those tents over the hill. The goats are nearly all female; their breed is Tali. We use them for milk. They drop one kid per year. We let the kids grow up; then we sell the males to the market."

"All of the males?"

"No. We keep a couple to father the next year's kids. And we also castrate a few. Those are the ones you're hearing. They become the 'guide goats.' They get to wear tassels and bells so they're easy to spot, and they keep the herd together." He smiled. "God save me from tassels and bells."

"Someone is coming for me?" she asked, also conversationally. Neither of them would ask the other for any kind of identification. When she left, it would be as if she'd never been there.

"By the time the comet has disappeared."

"The comet?"

He used his whole hand to point in an arc from the top of the sky down toward east southeast, to the horizon. "Follow a line from the sliver of the moon, down past Venus . . . there . . . do you see? Just above the horizon?"

She sat still, letting her eyes adjust to the celestial lights in the far sky. And there, hanging just where he'd shown her, was a small fireball blazing sideways.

"A welcome back," he said.

She let her hands run across the homespun blanket beneath her and breathed again of the silent night air. She was back; she was here in the Terris world, with its sand and stars, pollution and wars.

She'd been sent back on an urgent mission. But was this home anymore?

"How long does the comet blaze?" she asked.

"Only half an hour a night," he answered. "You will go soon. Are you feeling all right?"

She nodded. Then she said, "Thank you for your hospitality."

"It's all right," he said. "I'm up anyway."

They sat silent, side by side, two friends who knew nothing about each other.

And Jaime's new adventure began.

COMMAND SERGEANT MAJOR Zack DeCamp was not having a good day. He commanded a five-vehicle convoy that served as the personal security detachment for the 5th COSCOM commanding general who was based in Balad, Iraq. If the CG, the Commanding General, had to get somewhere by ground, it was DeCamp's responsibility. Many American soldiers in Iraq prayed they didn't have to ride in a convoy very often. Between IEDs (improvised explosive devices), civilian traffic, and the cramped, stifling interior of the new "improved" up-armored Humvees, traveling outside the confines of a Coalition base was both exhausting and dangerous. But convoys were DeCamp's way of life.

Today the five vehicles had done a test run along the road from the COSCOM headquarters in Balad, an hour north of Baghdad, down to Tallil, which was four hours south of Baghdad. It hadn't been easy. Waiting for the engineers to defuse two improvised explosive devices, coping with small-arms fire, and fixing a plain old flat tire had put the convoy three hours behind schedule. And now he was monitoring a very interesting conversation on his SINGARS radio that threatened to delay him even more.

"Checkmate, this is Earthpig Five, over," came the initial call over his headset.

"Go ahead, Earthpig; this is Checkmate." DeCamp knew that "Checkmate" was the quick reaction force that patrolled this portion of the route between Scania and Tallil. He figured that "Earthpig" must be the large convoy that just passed them on the other side of the divided highway.

"Checkmate, there is an LN female who just tried to flag down our convoy. She was right along the shoulder waving and signaling to us. It looked very suspicious."

"LN" was the term for "Local National." DeCamp knew the convoy commander was concerned that she might be a suicide bomber or trying to set them up for a trap farther down the road. "She is currently located one kilometer north of checkpoint Delta. Over."

Command Sergeant Major DeCamp looked at his map and clenched his teeth around the unlit cigar stub dangling from his lips. Guess who would be coming up to the position in a matter of minutes? He sighed heavily and then spoke into his radio. "Checkmate, this is Outlaw Seven."

"Go ahead, Outlaw Seven."

"We are one klick from location reported by Earthpig Five. Will check it out."

"Roger, Outlaw Seven. Call if you need backup."

"We ain't gonna need any," he growled to himself. His personal security detachment was its own damn backup. It consisted of five fully up-armored Humvees, each with a rotating turret and gunner with automatic weapon. Compared to the old canvas-sided Humvees, these machines looked like Brinks trucks.

If Earthpig, barreling in the opposite direction, had just passed the woman, she should be right about here . . . and indeed, it wasn't long before DeCamp spotted her, standing alone on the opposite side of the highway. Her head was covered with an ivory-colored scarf, and she wore a long green tunic and matching pants. She waved at them as she had at the convoy before.

Speaking over the convoy's internal communication system, DeCamp laid out the plan. "Outlaw One-One and One-Three, cover my right and left. I'm going straight up the middle. Outlaw Eight and Five, take up blocking positions on the highway."

His driver cut the wheel to the left and bounded across the median, heading straight for the woman. He skidded to a halt 25 meters directly in front of her, kicking up an immense cloud of dust that sent her into a coughing fit. The next truck pulled off to his right about 30 meters, as if to cut off her escape path to the south. The third did the same to the north. The last two held back to stop any traffic that might approach along the highway. Every turret gunner, while pointing his large automatic weapon toward the ground, kept a close eye on the woman in case she made any sudden or threatening moves.

The only feature DeCamp could make out was her eyes, and they were understandably wide-open and fearful. It seemed she grasped her disadvantage in the current situation. She slowly raised her hands in the air as if to say, *I surrender.* He muscled open his door, unsnapped the holster strap on his 9mm pistol, and took a few steps in her direction. He knew he painted a very imposing figure, despite his short five-nine stature. His swarthy skin and stocky frame, combined with a tanker's helmet and body armor that included extra shoulder protection as well as knee and elbow pads, gave the impression of a Storm Trooper from *Star Wars.*

The woman was of medium build, slim, and an inch or two shorter than he.

By now, the command sergeant major was close enough to tell that she was carrying no weapons. Nor could she be hiding any bombs. He decided to take a chance and approach her. He dug into his pocket and pulled out a special card written in Arabic that the Civil Affairs team had given him to help communicate with the Iraqis. He held it before her eyes and saw her brow furrow.

"What? I can speak some Arabic, but I can't read it very well," she blurted out.

He jumped back, startled. "You speak English!"

"Yes, of course. I'm an American!"

"What do you mean, 'of course'? What the fuck are you doing standing along the side of the road in local dress waving at convoys?"

The woman struggled to suppress a smile at his rather crass answer. "It's a long story, and one I will gladly share with you, but do you suppose that we could find somewhere more, uh, conducive to a civil conversation?"

"Oh yeah, sorry." He reached out his hand and shook hers firmly. "I'm Sergeant Major Zack DeCamp, 5th COSCOM. Who are you, some sort of reporter working with the locals?"

"No, I'm an American soldier. My name is Jaime Richards. I was with 57th CSG under V Corps. I may be listed as MIA." She reached up and removed the head scarf, allowing her blond hair to fall freely to her shoulders.

DeCamp had thought he was past being shocked by anything. Nothing surprised him anymore. But . . . *holy shit.*

Chaplain Jaime Richards had been missing since Operation Iraqi Freedom 1. The early days of the war. Very few people knew of the incident, because it had been classified "Top Secret." The only reason DeCamp knew was because his general—the Commanding General of the COSCOM in Balad—was senior commander over the unit to which Jaime had belonged.

Jaime Richards. DeCamp squinted and studied her more closely. Blond hair obviously bleached lighter by the desert sun. Skin tanned, but not unhealthy. The thoughts behind her green eyes seemed curious rather than traumatized.

"Do you have any I.D.?"

"No, I lost all that when I was kidnapped three years ago."

No I.D. But the woman was clearly American and had divulged information already that very few people knew.

Jaime Richards.

Holy shit.

His voice remained calm and detached, but he added a tone of reassurance as he spoke quietly. "Most of my team will not know who you are, because your situation has been kept close hold. But my CG is going to want to see you ASAP. Climb in my Humvee. We have a long trip to Anaconda."

"Sergeant Major!" yelled his driver as Jaime tried unsuccessfully to open her door. They weren't the same Humvees they'd had when she disappeared. "Checkmate is asking for our status."

"Let me handle it," DeCamp called to his driver as he pushed past Jaime and popped open her door. "And bring our passenger your Kevlar."

As the young driver handed Jaime a helmet and helped her get buckled in, DeCamp was spitting orders over the radio, first to the rest of his own convoy. "Outlaw One-One, this is Outlaw Seven."

"Outlaw One-One," came the reply.

"I need fuel status on all Victors. Change of mission. We head to Balad."

"Does this have anything to do with your blond-haired passenger?" was the response from Outlaw One-One.

"Don't ask," growled DeCamp into his microphone. "Just get the convoy ready. We pull out in 5 Mikes."

And the command sergeant major did something else that he very rarely did on the road.

He grinned.

BRIGADIER GENERAL Elizabeth Culver had spent the better part of an hour trying to wade through unread e-mails. As Commanding General of the 5th Corps Support Command she was allowed unlimited space in her in-box, which was not necessarily a good thing. There were times when she had thousands of e-mails waiting for her attention.

But today she didn't mind. Anything to keep her occupied while waiting for her personal security detachment to return from their mission south of Baghdad. Earlier that day she had received a cryptic message from her command sergeant major via the mobile tracking system. It had been a direct send for her only and stated simply: "Jaime Richards found. Returning to HQ."

Had someone discovered the woman's body? Culver wondered. Of course Richards was dead; they all knew that was the most likely outcome . . . the only outcome that made sense after this amount of time. Although Culver faced so many deaths in a war zone, it never got easier.

And this wasn't an ordinary situation. It was going to have to be handled.

Culver stood up from her desk and walked around it to stare at the wide-screen television hanging above a large mahogany conference table. She was a slim five-eight with light brown hair that was slightly graying at the temples. The general was wearing the new Army combat uniform with a digital pattern and carried a 9mm sidearm strapped in a black holster on her right hip. She unconsciously snapped and unsnapped the safety catch on the holster as she observed the CNN Headline News ticker scroll silently on the screen.

Jaime Richards's disappearance and death had been classified Top Secret, because of extraordinary circumstances that even the general didn't fully understand. News of the missing officer had been successfully kept out of the public eye. Now, on Culver's watch, was it going to break wide open?

At that moment Command Sergeant Major DeCamp appeared in her doorway. He carried his helmet and had not bothered to remove any of his body armor or other protective gear—not even his Wiley goggles. He looked tired and needed a shower and shave—and yet there was a strange glint in his eye. She nodded him into the room. Before this got any further, she needed to know where they'd found the body and how they'd made the identification.

But rather than entering the general's office, he said, "Ma'am, I found her. Or better yet, she found us."

As the general struggled to process what he meant, the sergeant major stepped aside. He pulled a woman in a green tunic into the doorway with him.

"Ma'am, I would like for you to meet Chaplain Jaime Richards."

"You're freakin' kiddin' me!" burst out of Culver's mouth as she stared, dumbfounded, at the young woman. Culver quickly regained her composure and stepped forward, offering her hand to Jaime and saying, "Chaplain Richards, I'm Liz Culver."

With a firm handshake the general drew Jaime into the room as her sergeant major disappeared, closing the door behind him.

General Culver placed her left hand on Jaime's shoulder and gave her a searching look. "How *are* you?" She didn't let go of the hand or shoulder but continued to fix her gaze as if willing her to respond more deeply than the typical "I'm fine."

"Physically I feel pretty good. Emotionally I'm not sure. I really haven't had a chance to process everything that's happened."

Culver motioned for Jaime to sit down at the table and sat also. She ran her hands back through her hair as she sat down on the edge of her seat, leaning her elbows on the conference table.

Chaplain Richards looked tan and healthy. Her eyes were alert, and she seemed fully engaged with the current situation. No point in beating around the bush.

"Where have you been for the past three years?"

"I'm not sure. In fact, it doesn't seem like three years. I remember being kidnapped in Babylon. I think I remember being beaten and left for dead along a dirt road somewhere. The rest is sort of a hazy blur until I 'woke up' again about a week ago. I was living with a family of goat herders somewhere just across the border in Iran."

"That's incredible! How did you find your way back?"

"A cousin of my host family smuggled me across the border and arranged transportation to the highway. This seemed the best way to get me back to my people without bringing notice or harm down on my host family."

"Do you think you could locate where you were on a map?"

"Ma'am, I'm not sure I want to try. I don't know how I got there, but these people took me in and protected me. I don't want to return the favor by bringing trouble down on them."

Culver ran a hand back through her hair again and relaxed into her chair. "Abe Derry was a War College classmate of mine, and when he heard I was bringing the COSCOM on this rotation to Iraq, he told me to keep an eye out for you," she said, referring to the man who had been the commander of Jaime's unit when she had been kidnapped. "I didn't want to burst his bubble with my assumption that you were most likely dead. But he never gave up hope for your return." She shook her head, chuckled, then slapped the table. "But here you are! The question, of course, is what now?"

The one-star general stared at the chaplain. What would she ever have expected if she had been told that Jaime Richards would return? She'd never met the woman, had only seen her I.D. photo. With everything Culver had been told and had thought about the Jaime Richards situation, nothing had prepared her for the vibrant woman who now sat before her.

"First order of business is to make sure you have no lasting effects from this ordeal. I'm going to have one of my captains get you settled over at the theater hospital. They'll want to do an initial checkup while I find out what other requirements we must meet before sending you to Landstuhl. You've been missing for three years, and needless to say, there's a certain repatriation protocol we've got to follow." The general held her hand to her head, as if willing some deeply buried information to surface. "Certainly there are CID interviews, intelligence debriefings, and who knows what else. But for the time being, try to relax."

There was a knock at the door and the general's aide stuck his head in the door. "Ma'am, you have the BUA in 5 minutes."

"Mike, I'm skipping the battle update. I need to speak on a secure line with the corps commander as soon as we can get through. Then call Lieutenant Colonel Grindstaff and ask him to send over one of the female captains from his office for an escort officer." She thought for a moment, then continued, "And go dig up a PT uniform for our guest so she doesn't have to walk around in this costume."

A physical training uniform consisted of shorts and a gray Army T-shirt, which would allow Jaime to blend in without being identified.

General Culver stood, smiling, and Jaime followed suit.

The general shook her head again at the unexpected turn of events. "Welcome back to civilization!" she said, putting one arm around the chaplain's shoulder.

Culver didn't see the wry smile on Jaime's face at her use of the term "civilization."

JAIME UNLATCHED her seat belt and removed her Kevlar and body armor. The crew chief, clad in a gray-green jumpsuit, had just indicated it was safe to move around the Air Force C-17.

Taking off from Balad Airfield was an adventure, because the threat of surface-to-air missiles from insurgents made combat landings and takeoffs necessary. This meant the airplane would initially maintain a steep rate of climb and make quick turns and the passengers and crew would be required to wear full protective gear until a safe altitude was reached.

Except for the flight deck itself, the bulk of this plane's airframe was dedicated to a massive cargo hold that had been converted into a flying hospital. Tonight's destination was Ramstein Air Base in Germany. The plane was currently filled with wounded and ill service members bound for Landstuhl Regional Medical Center for further evaluation and stabilization and then follow-on flight to the United States. During the wild ride that was takeoff, even the ambulatory injured soldiers and Marines had been strapped down on cots, which were linked together and secured to the floor of the cargo bay.

Along the wall opposite the chaplain was an assembly of metal scaffolding that had been erected for insertion of litters, giving it a bunk-bed effect. Some of the more seriously wounded patients were strapped in there. One of those patients seemed to be the main focus of attention of a flight nurse and medical technician who were busy trying to make him comfortable.

Jaime wrapped her body armor around her helmet and put it on the floor next to her seat, which was fixed to the outer wall of the cargo hold. The woman next to her also removed her protective gear, which had been layered over a crisply starched linen shirt and highly creased Dockers. She had introduced herself as Ms. Kay Clarke from the State Department earlier that evening when she swooped into the Air Force Theater Hospital to collect the chaplain.

State Department. Jaime hadn't expected that. She knew she faced a physical examination before she left Balad, as well as inquiries by an intelligence officer. Even less pleasant, Jaime was sure, would have been her chat with CID, the criminal investigation division, who would need to make sure she hadn't done anything illegal, like go AWOL or join the insurgency.

But none of those people had made it to her because she'd been co-opted by the woman beside her. Not that it had been an easy feat to accomplish.

Kay Clarke was about five and a half feet tall, medium build, athletic, with short brown hair. She had shown up at the patient administration department of the Air Force Theater Hospital wielding State Department credentials and high-level orders to escort Jaime immediately to Germany. The doctor in charge of Jaime's case had no intention of letting her go. There were many tests to be run, and protocol demanded the S2 and CID interviews before she be moved anywhere. Ms. Clarke had replied that all would be handled at Landstuhl.

The doctor assigned to Jaime, an Air Force major, flatly refused to comply with the request. He finally called on the Hospital Commander to back him up. When the commander, Colonel Resnick, showed up, Kay Clarke went toe-to-toe with him, not backing down for a moment. Observing the exchange and the woman's unflappable manner in handling these officers, Jaime couldn't help but think, *This woman is like a pit bull with lip gloss!*

Ms. Clarke and the commander disappeared down the hall. While waiting for their return, Jaime had marveled that after more than three years of operations at this location the hospital complex had not been upgraded from an interconnected series of tents pitched over concrete pads. But it was obvious from the constant flow of patients, translators, unit liaisons, hospital staff, and even Iraqi families that this complex of tents was a vital nerve center for medical treatment in Iraq.

A short while later Ms. Clarke and the commander reappeared. Colonel Resnick pulled Jaime's doctor aside and said a few things the major obviously did not want to hear. At the same time, the woman had walked to Jaime and said, "Come on; let's go." And they had left to board the C-17 in which they were now flying to Ramstein.

Jaime was ready to handle whatever was thrown at her during her repatriation. But someone from the State Department with orders high level enough to snatch her from the Army—this was a curveball. It was possible this was a new trajectory, one she wasn't supposed to be on. But obviously, she couldn't bolt. In fact, she couldn't do anything to call attention to herself.

Kay Clarke must have read her thoughts. She was looking straight ahead when she said in a voice loud enough to be heard only by the chaplain, "Jaime, relax. I'm your third and final guide for this reentry."

Jaime laughed, relieved, and shook her head. She should have guessed.

The flurry of activity around the critically wounded soldier across from Jaime had ceased. Falling into her old pattern, Jaime stood to go talk with him. Recognizing her purpose, Ms. Clarke put a restraining hand to Jaime's arm.

"I don't think it's a good idea to mingle. We don't want to draw attention to you."

"I'm incognito in this PT uniform. Besides, I am a chaplain. It's why I'm here." And she continued across the cargo bay to visit with the patient.

A couple of IV bags were attached to the metal bar above his litter. One arm, lying on top of the blue-flowered flannel blanket covering him, was heavily bandaged. She looked in his eyes, could see he was in a lot of pain, but he smiled.

"Who you with?" she asked.

"101st. FOB Speicher." "FOB," or "Forward Operating Base," was the term given the numerous camps spread all over the country. Speicher was located in northern Iraq, vicinity of Tikrit, and home base for the 101st Airborne Division.

"Oh, a Screaming Eagle?" She smiled.

"Air Assault!" he responded.

And that is how it started. For the next 15 minutes she just let him talk. He told her about his family, his girlfriend, and the "band of brothers" he had left behind. Then, when he spoke of his Humvee crew, he broke down. He had been the turret gunner and had taken the worst of the IED blast in his legs. The driver had walked away unharmed, but the TC in the right front seat had been killed.

"I should have seen that bomb along the road. I should have fired it up. But I was looking the other way."

Saying nothing, she gripped his good hand in both of hers while he cried. Then they quietly prayed together. After that she returned to her seat and buckled in. For the first time since her return, even though she was flying through the night sky she felt she had her feet on the ground.

Ms. Clarke nodded, then turned her attention back to a notebook where she was furiously scribbling comments. Jaime, now completely exhausted, leaned back to collapse for the remainder of the flight.

"ABE, WHAT THE HELL is going on here?" Brigadier General Culver had managed to reach Abe Derry by secure line to his office in the Pentagon. "I have a hospital commander foaming at the mouth because a former MIA has been jerked out of his grasp without following the repatriation protocol. I've got to admit, I'm baffled as well. Sure, she looks good, but she has been gone for three years! Do you have any G2 on this?"

"Liz, if I had anything to tell you, I would," was Derry's reply. "I don't know much except someone with a lot of pull wanted her kept under wraps and expedited through the system. I assume, with your position and clearance, you have seen the files about her disappearance?"

"Yes, I was read on when I took command here."

"Then you know we were ordered to keep the situation quiet. Now senior leadership is adamant that her return not be publicized. I think they want Chaplain Richards somewhere they can control access to her. I guess we have to trust that the interviews and tests required will all be handled appropriately."

"Well, it really makes me curious about this woman. How well did you know her? She was so calm, healthy, so *balanced*, for someone who was just picked up along the Iraqi roadside!" Which translated politely: *Obviously there's more going on here than I've been privy to.*

"That's my Jaime!" Liz could hear him smile even across the phone line. All of which translated, politely: *I'm not concerned, and you don't need to be. You're also not learning anything else on this phone call.*

"You're a big help!" she threw back at him, chuckling at his reaction.

They talked for a few more minutes, comparing notes about the difference between his deployment in 2003 and her current tour.

Finally, Abe said, "Liz, I hear good things about your work downrange. You've built up a great rep here in the building. Keep it up, but be safe, OK?"

"Thanks, my friend. And lift a cold one for me, will you? This 'near-beer' shit doesn't quite cut it!"

He laughed hard at that, said his final good-byes, and hung up.

Yes, what I wouldn't give right now for a real beer. And she turned back to her computer and the endless string of e-mail.

FRIDAY

JAIME RICHARDS SAT STARING through the large picture windows of Il Cappuccino Manuel Caffé at Landstuhl Regional Medical Center, a major American military hospital in Germany. The fog outside was thick, typical for a winter's day in southern Germany, and she marveled at the extreme contrast between the snowy, dark greens of this landscape and the dusty browns of the desert she had just left behind.

She still wore the gray Army t-shirt and black shorts they'd given her the day before in Balad. She'd added a pair of black running pants over the shorts and was carrying a gray running jacket because it was a lot colder in Germany than it had been in Iraq.

For the last six hours she had been poked, prodded, trapped in a claustrophobic's nightmare of a CT scan machine, wired up for an EEG, had multiple vials of blood drawn for HIV and blood chemistry work-up, had a full physical exam, and been checked for parasites. She thought Kay Clarke had been doing her a favor by expediting her arrival in Landstuhl, but now she was not so sure.

Upon their arrival at Ramstein Air Base, a large black Ford Expedition had been waiting just off the tarmac. Jaime and Kay Clarke had climbed in the back and been transported directly to the hospital. Once there, Jaime was introduced to a young sergeant who had been tasked to serve as her escort and help find her appointments. Satisfied that everything seemed to be moving smoothly, Ms. Clarke had said good-bye and disappeared.

Now, six hours later, her NCO escort had left Jaime at Il Cappuccino Caffé while he checked on the status of her tests. As she waited, she savored a foamy hot chocolate with lots of whipped cream—which she felt she more than deserved—while technicians reviewed her results to make sure they had all the data they needed and the pictures were clear. She was thankful she'd rested for those few hours on the flight, because there'd certainly been no time for rest since she'd arrived.

It was the price of resurfacing into the military. She'd known to expect it; she had willingly submitted—which still hadn't made it fun.

In times past Jaime would have been drumming her foot in irritation or pacing manically in front of the window as she waited for others to complete their work, especially since time was of the essence. But over the last three years she had learned patience and the art of relaxation. With a few deep breaths she centered herself and brought her awareness to the room around her. The television in the corner was muted, but a radio behind her blared old rock-and-roll tunes. A young couple sat in the corner, surrounded by potted plants meant to give the café a tropical look, as their young son tried to climb on a chair to bat at giant silk moths suspended from the ceiling. On a stool by the window, a young soldier was working desperately to master a game on his Nintendo DS.

As Jaime took another healing draught of the hot beverage, she heard footsteps approaching through the doorway from the food service area of the café, an assured gait, not a doctor or nurse, but a gait she recognized. The dress shoes halted a few paces behind her.

Jaime stood, turned, and smiled broadly. Before her stood her former commander and mentor, Colonel Abraham Derry. A tall, muscular African-American, Colonel Derry was one of the officers on her most admired list. Jaime had been his unit chaplain when he commanded the 57th Corps Support Group in Hanau, Germany. She'd been assigned to the unit only a couple of months before they deployed to Iraq three years earlier, but she did have the opportunity to get to know Colonel Derry, his wife, Eirene, and their three children there on the base in Germany. They'd had an instant bond.

Jaime soon had discovered Abe Derry was a veteran of Desert Storm and was held in highest esteem by all the men and women who had served under him. He led with a quiet confidence. He had been the one to whom Jaime had appealed in Tallil when she needed to get to Babylon three years before. He'd let her go.

She hadn't seen him since.

His dark brown hair, although close-cropped, was showing a little more gray along the temples. And in spite of his dark skin, she could see the hint of circles under his eyes. He was tired, but he returned her smile and wrapped his arms around her, easily picking her up in a tremendous bear hug. He slowly lowered her to the ground and she stepped back, holding him at arm's length.

Suddenly her eyes widened. "You're kidding me!"

He was wearing dress green pants with a black zip-up jacket rather than a dress coat, and on each shoulder was pinned a single star. "A *general?* They made you a general?"

"Can you believe it?" He laughed. "It must have been a slow day at the Pentagon." Then he sobered quickly. "How about we go for a walk?"

Jaime nodded and tossed her now-empty cup into the trash as they left the restaurant. They spoke quietly as they walked up a long, sloping hallway. The walls were plain beige, dotted with framed posters of famous watercolor paintings.

"I don't need to ask how you knew I was here," stated the chaplain. "General Culver, right?"

"She called me the moment you left her office. As a matter of fact, we've spoken twice since you reappeared."

"She said you'd told her to keep an eye out for me. But did you ever really expect me to turn up?"

"Normally, given the circumstances, I'd have said no. But knowing you like I do, I gave it even odds."

"You really thought so, even after three years?"

His voice dropped. "Only because I was fairly certain I knew where you were. And if I was right, you were safe, and all we could do was wait to see if you might reemerge."

Jaime paused in mid-stride, confused by his answer. "But how could . . . where would I . . . what would make you think . . . ," she ventured, treading lightly, trying to put the pieces together.

He stood stock-still and waited for her to come to the realization on her own. Only when her eyes widened did he nod.

"You knew where I was? That I was . . ."

"In Eden," he said quietly.

"You *knew*?"

"An educated guess, although I hear it wasn't an uneventful journey." He paused, letting his words sink in.

She dropped her voice to a murmur. "How do you know about Eden?"

"I was born there," he said simply.

Their stroll had brought them to the end of the hallway. General Derry nodded toward the exit door that led to the stairwell beyond. They went down one flight and found the entrance to a small courtyard with a covered porch. It was chilly outside but seemed to be the only place that afforded some privacy. Jaime donned her jacket, zipping it full up as she sat in one of two straight-backed chairs on the porch. Abe, in one of his signature moves, spun the other one around and sat down, his arms across the chair back.

He was silent, letting her begin to process what he'd just told her.

Jaime's first feeling was one of overwhelming relief. She had spent three years in the most extraordinary place, one whose people and lifestyle had marked and changed her forever, yet she was expected to keep it a secret once she resurfaced, to never talk about it or even acknowledge it existed. Now here was this man, one of her own mentors, who was telling her he knew, he understood. He'd been there, too. The weight of the secret was decreased by half.

Three years ago, when she was invited to enter Eden, her guide, Yani, had explained to her that what the world calls Eden was the one place on earth that exists for the good of its neighbors. She still remembered his exact words: "There is not much coming and going, but former citizens of Eden are at work bringing peace and healing throughout the world. It also is very technologically advanced, because many of the world's great thinkers, teachers, and scientists have come to lend support to this altruistic society." So Abe Derry was one of those agents of Eden, using his talents and gifts to work toward peace and healing in the world.

"I can't believe I worked for you all that time and you never said anything!"

He chuckled quietly at her exasperation. "You know I couldn't."

"Of course not," admitted Jaime. "Is there anyone else? I mean, anyone else you can tell me about?"

"Well, of course there's Eirene." Abe's wife of 23 years was a beautiful, petite woman of Greek descent. She was an outstandingly talented sculptor and taught art at a university in Washington, D.C. Jaime had always admired Eirene's calm sense of purpose.

"But your children were born here?"

Abe nodded but was no longer smiling. It was only then that Jaime began to sense that the redness in his eyes was more than jet lag. He was worried and had probably spent many sleepless nights before his trip to Landstuhl.

"Sir, what's wrong?" she asked, afraid to hear the answer.

"It's Daniel. He's . . . missing." Abe Derry almost choked on the second part. His eyes began to tear, and he stared off into space rather than meet Jaime's concerned expression.

At first Jaime was thrown by this revelation. Her closeness to the Derry family and her fondness for Abe's son Daniel made it difficult to think logically about the situation. As she processed this new information, she began to reach some not-so-happy conclusions about her friend's teenage son.

"He didn't run away," she said. It was a statement rather than a question.

Abe Derry shook his head.

Jaime was thunder-struck. "He was taken. He disappeared very suddenly, in broad daylight, in a public place. You have received no ransom note, and the police have absolutely no leads," she continued.

"Yes." He was astounded at the accuracy of her description. "There have been others?"

"Four we know of. Each the Terris-born child of a gardener." The residents of Eden chose to refer to themselves simply as "gardeners."

"But who would do this, and why?" His anguish was apparent.

"That's why I'm here. The sooner we can answer that, the sooner we'll find the captives, to include Did." Did was Daniel's nickname, earned when his friends and siblings recognized the relation between his initials and how often he took the blame—fairly or not—for screwing up. "Did it" became the standard phrase when any accusation was made.

But Daniel Isaac Derry was a good kid—not the athlete/scholar that his older brother was, nor did he have the academic brilliance and strikingly good looks of his younger sister. He was the classic "lost" middle kid, who didn't seem to be notable for anything, at least in comparison with his stellar sibs.

"When did he disappear?" Jaime asked.

"Almost two weeks ago. Sunday, February 12. He was at the Pentagon City Mall with friends. I wondered if the timing of this might have something to do with your reappearance," mused the general. "But how could it? You can't be an Operative . . . you haven't trained long enough!"

All former gardeners who chose to live in the Terris world were considered agents of Eden, working to effect change in the world. Those known as operatives of Eden were intensively trained and called upon to intervene in specific situations.

"These are special circumstances, and I have certain qualities others don't."

"No, this is too dangerous. I can't afford to lose any more people in my life."

Jaime took his hand and connected directly with him, eye to eye. "You're not going to lose me." She did her best to convey confidence that she was not sure she felt. "And now that I know Daniel is with the group, my resolve is doubled. I swear to you, I'll do everything in my power to bring him home safely. Besides, with his presence, I'm encouraged about the captives' ability to survive this ordeal, whatever it may be. Do you recall the story 'Ransom of Red Chief'?" She hoped to make her mentor laugh.

"So you think the bad guys might ultimately pay us to take him back?" He managed a half smile at her joke.

"I wouldn't be surprised." She smiled back. "But before I can do anything to help the captives, I have to get out of here. I understand most returning POW/MIAs are subjected to quite an extensive debriefing before being released into the 'real' world."

"Leave that to me." He had become, once again, the man in charge. "I have a meeting with the hospital commander in 20 minutes, who is probably, as we speak, getting ready to convene the Repatriation/ Reintegration Committee. I'll make sure your medical tests are expedited and you are placed on leave as quickly as possible, with the promise you'll return after leave to complete any outstanding requirements. Have they told you what tests remain?"

Now it was Jaime's turn to laugh ruefully. "I can't imagine they can think of anything else. Although I'm told I still face a psych exam."

"You're on your own there," he said. "That's the one person who will have the power to hold you here, if deemed necessary. So don't act suspicious."

"Don't worry," she said. "As you know, I haven't spent the last three years communing with the enemy or being brainwashed. In fact, I feel great. Although, speaking of being brainwashed, I can't help but have noticed that no one from the intelligence community has swooped down here to 'debrief' me. Is that your doing as well?"

"Well, not directly. I believe Ms. Clarke may have used some of her rather significant influence—but I did make a few calls. And the most I can promise about the debriefing is that it is put off until after you have enjoyed a relaxing four-day pass."

Jaime smiled at the irony of the idea she'd be spending a restful four days.

"Where did you wake up?" Abe asked.

"Just across the Iranian border. With a family of goat herders."

That finally brought the chuckle Jaime had been waiting for. "Gardeners move in mysterious ways," he said.

"Apparently," she agreed. "And, as I found out, so do goats."

"So true," he said, still smiling. "So true."

"Sir," she said, "one of the first things we need to discover is the link between the kids that were taken, other than the fact their parents were from Eden. Let me ask you if any of these names are familiar: Ming Zhou, Paul Mikelti, Ankar or Mary Afzal, or Rebekah Marsdotter, now Rebekah Stevens."

"Yes," Abe Derry said without hesitation. "Those were the people—the gardeners—who traveled with Eirene and me. We all exited during the same door opening, twenty-three years ago. Mary Afzal was expecting at the time."

Jaime took a deep breath. "Was that your entire group?"

"Wait; no, there were eight. One's missing." Abe closed his eyes and again went over the names. "Jorgen Ravenson, Terris name . . . um . . . Edders. Jorgen Edders."

"Does he have children?"

General Derry shook his head. "I don't know."

"Wow," Jaime said. "A whole group . . . compromised."

"And with such horrific results," agreed her mentor.

They stood and began to work their way toward the door. "Can we meet for dinner later?" Jaime asked. "Assuming, of course, I haven't been committed to the psych ward."

"It's a date," he said as they stood and hugged each other once again. "Chaplain, I'm glad you're back." She smiled as they broke contact and watched as he turned and headed off to his meeting with the hospital commander.

"So am I, my friend," she sighed to herself. "So am I."

NESTOR ALLENDE clicked the button to turn off his video-conferencing screen on the wall and shook his head to clear his vision. Fernando, his assistant, appeared immediately with a new vodka tonic, whisking away the half-full glass of the last one, into which too much ice had melted.

Nestor was a comfortably large man, not obese by any means but a man whose desires were usually sated. He was in his sixties but seemed 40. His light brown hair was still his own; he looked healthy and vital. He was both.

"Your wife called to find out when you'll return to the hotel," Fernando murmured in a voice that indicated Nestor could choose to hear the question or dismiss it.

"In half an hour," he said.

"Yes, sir," and the assistant was gone.

The content of the recent conference had already completely left Nestor's consciousness. Business had to be attended to; it was a necessary evil; it was what supplied him with the funds he needed. But he chose each of his lieutenants well. He was a results man; he wanted to see the completed projects, not be bothered by day-to-day details. If you couldn't pull it off, he didn't want to hear about it. *Make it happen* was his mantra when talking to his seconds-in-command.

But now many years of work and research had finally paid off. The most important of all his projects had come to fruition. No matter what else he accomplished in his life, this would stand alone as his crowning achievement. It proved again that nothing was impossible, given the know-how, the drive, and the funding.

And given the ability to see the possibilities, the big picture.

The big picture was the birthright, and the responsibility, of the world's princes. Nestor's father, Chiron Allende, had taught Nestor there were two kinds of people in this world: peons and princes. The peons did the work without question; they were easily led. They believed that they had to work hard, five days a week, eight to twelve hours a day, to survive. They started teaching their children this as young as five, when they sent them off to school on nearly the same schedule. Drudgery, day in, day out. They might know there was a wide world out there, but they were workhorses with blinders on, following the same safe path, day after day.

Whereas the princes knew the secret truth: There were no rules, except those you made for yourself. There was a wide world to be savored, a world of fine wine, fine women, good food. The day came with no self-imposed hours, no schedules, no deadlines. All those things were an illusion perpetuated and bought into by great groups of peons. Some days Nestor worked 12 or 14 hours. Many days he slept until noon and didn't work at all. He didn't have to. He had built his empire and trained his lieutenants. He was the prince.

The amazing thing was that the positions of peon or prince weren't assigned you at birth. First, you're offered peon, and if you accept it, it's yours. But if you refuse it, you're offered another choice. Problem was, most poor bastards meekly accepted what they thought was their fate. Go to school at age 5. Start work at 21. Die at 80, never having lived.

But if you refuse to be a peon, you refuse to accept the blinders, you are offered the chance to become a prince, and the world becomes your gift.

A case in point—and, to Nestor, the *only* case in point—his own father had been born a simple fisherman to a long line of fishermen on the small island of Santorini. But Chiron had refused the offered designation of peon.

He had taught his son how to discover what people needed and provide it. Chiron himself had turned one small boat into a fleet of boats. Nestor, following his example, had turned the fleet of boats into a shipyard and from the shipyard launched a fleet of businesses.

Chiron had taught his son how to grab life and enjoy every bit of what it had to offer, to wring every bit of pleasure from the day.

Chiron had also died when Nestor was 15.

That was the one way Chiron had failed Nestor, had failed himself. He'd left his son to care for his mother and young sister at the time he should have been enjoying his youth.

Nestor leaned back in his ergonomic leather chair in his London office and reached for his drink. Outside, the city went on, full tilt. The drones had no idea that humankind's greatest aspiration was becoming reality. For the princes, of course, the only ones who could afford it. The peons were, as they always had been, expendable.

Damn! The ice had melted again. The billionaire called again for Fernando, who appeared with a fresh drink, removing the full one he'd set down only 15 minutes before.

"Call for the car," Nestor said. "We fly out in the morning."

SATURDAY

THIS JUST DOESN'T ADD UP, thought Lieutenant Colonel Kathryn Heitoff, Chief of Services at Landstuhl Regional Medical Center. She was looking over the results of the full physical and neurological work-up performed on Jaime Richards the day before and found no evidence of prior head trauma that might have caused the amnesia. Even more puzzling, all of her tests, blood, EEG, CT scan, seemed to indicate a patient approximately 25 years of age and in perfect health. The only problem was this patient was in her late thirties and the medical file the Army had on her was filled with the normal by-products of that many years of living. But now, for example, there was no evidence of the scar tissue from Richards's previous shoulder injury. It seemed to have just vanished. Dr. Heitoff began to wonder if she had been given the wrong test results.

She pulled the EEG readings out of the folder. *Wow,* she thought as she examined the wave patterns for test subject Richards, J. The combination of alpha and theta waves was highly unusual. Either she'd fallen asleep during testing, or . . . the doctor flipped back through the papers on her desk to find Jaime's personal data. She could have been meditating. And the intensity of the gamma waves—this woman must be a phenomenal multi-tasker.

The officer was so engrossed in the test readings, she jumped when someone knocked on her doorjamb.

"Dr. Heitoff," said a woman in an Army gray physical training shirt and black pants. "I'm Jaime Richards. The nurse told me to come on back."

"Yes, please, close the door and have a seat." The doctor motioned to a chair across from her. Without staring, Dr. Heitoff observed her patient. She was fit, tanned, and all of her movements were smooth. She seemed to have good motor control and balance. She took the offered chair.

"Chaplain Richards, I'll be frank," said the doctor, now looking her patient directly in the eye. "Considering the long-term trauma you have experienced, I asked for the opportunity to perform a full battery of psychological tests on you. I wanted to ensure there are no lasting effects from your ordeal. For some reason to which I am not privy, I have been overruled by those in authority over me. However, before anyone signs your leave papers, I have insisted on this interview."

"Sounds fair," responded Jaime.

The doctor expected her patient to seem uncomfortable, ill at ease with the prospect of answering the questions posed by a psychiatrist. Instead, Jaime was calm, sitting comfortably in her chair and waiting patiently to see what this interview would entail.

"What is your name?"

"Jaime Lynn Richards."

And so it began. The questions came rapid-fire: "Birth date?"

"August 16, 1966."

"Marital status?"

"I'm widowed."

"Children?"

"None."

"It says here that you lost both your parents when you were young."

Chaplain Richards gave a deep sigh. "I was a sophomore in high school. They were killed on an outing from a Pakistani refugee camp where my father was serving as a doctor and my mother was a nurse. It was a very difficult time. I've come to terms."

"And your husband, Paul Atwood, was killed by a suicide bomber."

"Yeah, I guess that does spice up the file. He was. He was leading a group to Israel and Palestine when he was killed on Jerusalem's Pedestrian Mall. None of the rest of the group was with him. I guess—he was shopping. So, as I said, I'm widowed."

Dr. Heitoff watched the chaplain's face as she talked. She didn't shy away from either subject and was able to deal with her losses directly. Granted, they had occurred some years ago. It seemed she'd taken the time to process the events.

The doctor moved on to a different line of questions.

"Where are we, and what time and day is it?"

Then came word and number list repetition and simple arithmetic questions. All of these were answered without hesitation by the patient. In fact, the doctor sensed that the woman seemed to be secretly enjoying the experience.

"Who is the President of the United States?"

"Well, I have been kind of out of touch, but I just read in the *Stars and Stripes* last night that it's still George W. Bush."

The interview continued with word associations and short-term memory tests. Alcohol and drug use, sleep, appetite, sex life.

"I've been with *goat herders*," she said wryly. "They treated me like an honored sister."

"So no sex life?"

"None that I recall," she answered, trying not to smile.

Then, "Have you had any extremely terrifying events recently?"

"I'm not sure if this counts, but I really thought I was a goner when those five Army gun trucks surrounded me two days ago. All I could think was, 'One wrong move by me and one of these guys might pull the trigger.' But it's not like that is going to give me nightmares or anything."

"What about your kidnapping from Babylon? That must have been horrifying!"

"Truthfully, I don't remember much. The guy drugged me. I will say the image of his sneering face just before I passed out is imprinted pretty strongly up here." She pointed to her temple.

"Does that image intrude unbidden at times?"

"Not really . . . I just know if I ever had to work with a sketch artist, I could give great detail."

"Tell me about the gaps in your memory. I understand you do not have total recall of the events over the last three years."

"Not yet, but each day, as some small thing jogs my memory, it is like a door has opened to a little corner of my mind."

The doctor smiled. "How aptly you put that! My hunch is you will continue to slowly regain your memory over time, as more and more of your 'doors' are opened. But I can't promise it will all return."

Dr. Heitoff decided to take a different tack. "Do you have any feelings that the world or you aren't real? Any strange experiences you don't tell people?" The psychiatrist had fared well in her profession because of an excellent ability to read the faces, body language, and other nonverbal signals of her patients. She noticed immediately that while this patient's face did not change expression, something passed across her eyes. The doctor had seen that before, when someone was holding something back. Perhaps there was more trauma, deep down, than Jaime was currently able to acknowledge.

"Nope, no strange experiences," said the chaplain confidently. "I will admit things seem a little unreal when I see all the changes that have taken place in the Army in just three years. Especially those new digital uniforms! But I don't think that's what you mean."

"You're right, Chaplain Richards, absolutely right."

Dr. Heitoff drummed her pencil on the ink blotter as she looked back over her notes. This woman was an enigma. She was in perfect physical health but still had some extensive memory gaps. She had excellent short-term memory and normal neural activity but was hiding something. Then again, everyone had some secret part of themselves they hid from others. To be a total open book would be more the concern.

Suddenly the doctor stood, having reached her decision. "Chaplain, I can see no reason to keep you here." She walked around the desk and extended her hand to Jaime. "I am going to concur with your request for leave, with the following caution. If you begin to have any sudden mood swings, changes in appetite or sleep patterns, nightmares, or flashbacks, then see a physician immediately. Do you have any questions of me?"

Returning the handshake with a strong grip, the chaplain smiled and said, "None I can think of. Thank you for your time and support."

Then she disappeared out the door and down the hall.

PLAYING GOD.

That was what her husband was doing.

Geri Allende stood on the terrace of their suite at Claridge's and surveyed the slowly lightening rooftops of London. She had her coat pulled tightly around her but didn't notice the pervasive chill or the wind that blew her straight, shoulder-length black hair behind her.

Her husband, billionaire businessman Nestor Allende, was involved in funding scientific research that his wife found morally troubling. He kept trying to convince her of the importance of the work, but it just never sat right with her.

There were some things humankind could futz with and some things that were beyond their purview. If you were conceived, you were supposed to be born. Then you were supposed to die when God called you home. Not until then. And certainly not after. That's what Pastor Raeburn always said. Geri had tried to convince her husband of that for decades.

Until now she'd been unsuccessful.

But now a new possibility had presented itself. One that made such perfect sense.

Geri felt almost like Esther in the Bible. Perhaps she had been led into her marriage with Nestor. Perhaps he had, unwittingly, been made interested in his field of endeavor. Perhaps they'd been given the finances they had for a reason. Perhaps God had put her here for such a time as this.

She looked again down at the city lights. Nestor was still out at meetings, but in a few hours they'd fly out, this time to a destination of her choosing. To Greece.

She opened the door behind her and stepped back into the spacious parlor. The butler had lit the fire and had brought in Geri's prescribed breakfast of organic yogurt, fresh-squeezed orange juice, and a bran muffin. Geri tossed her coat across a wing chair, grabbed the orange juice, and sat on the long, backless settee in front of the fire. She looked at the open Bible there before it. She had marked two passages.

The first was from the Book of Genesis: *And the Lord God planted a garden in Eden, in the east; and there he put the man whom he had formed. Out of the ground, the Lord God made to grow every tree that is pleasant to the sight, and good for food, the tree of life also in the midst of the garden, and the tree of the knowledge of good and evil* (2:8–9).

The second was from Revelation: *Then the angel showed me the river of the water of life, as clear as crystal, flowing from the throne of God and of the Lamb through the middle of the street of the city. On either side of the river is the tree of life, with its twelve kinds of fruit, producing its fruit each month, and the leaves of the tree are for the healing of the nations* (22:1–2).

Geri shivered, though the fire shot heat through her. Perhaps she'd been put here for such a time as this.

For such a time as this.

JAIME IGNORED THE CACOPHONY of car horns and slid through a knot of traffic on the crowded Athenian street on her rented white Vespa. The motorbike fit her mood exactly. It underscored the idea that she was free, on a four-day pass, directing her own future, the wind in her hair. Well, OK, the wind whooshing past her helmet. That was enough for her.

She loved the sights and sounds—and even the smells—of this ancient city. She loved the expressive local drivers and the frequent squeal of brakes around her. She loved that it was 60 degrees Fahrenheit even in the winter. She loved that she was on leave, had come here of her own volition. Once she reached the city itself, she had taken the long way, along Dionysiou Areopagitou, just because she was in the mood to go past the Acropolis.

She was here for a purpose, of course. She was to meet her Terris-based Operative partner here, as Athens was the last known address of Jorgen Edders. But that was in an hour's time. Right now, in this moment, she was free to drive down any street she wished, free to stop at a local stand and buy souvlaki, free to play anything she wanted on her iPod. Just free. For these moments. She'd take it. She'd savor it.

In fact, she did decide to make a brief stop to purchase food. Jaime wasn't quite sure what she was in the mood for, but she steered steadily to the left of the main boulevard on which she'd been traveling and onto a side street lined with small shops and hole-in-the-wall local food shops. The best kind.

She chose one solely by the colorful painting on its sign and was about to stop when she glanced into her rearview mirror.

Two blocks back, a person on a black motorcycle was idling on a corner. His jacket, pants, and helmet were all black—not unusual of itself. In fact, she wasn't sure what it was about the bike that alarmed her. But something did.

Instead of stopping, Jaime rolled her Vespa off the stone sidewalk and back onto the street, reluctantly dismissing the spicy smell of rosemary, lemon, and pepper. Within two blocks, she was out of sight of the black bike. She breathed a sigh of relief and laughed at her own skittish behavior.

Vassilissis Sofias, a major thoroughfare, crossed at the next intersection, and she made the left, wanting to travel on before looking for another likely lunch stop. She'd gone perhaps five kilometers when she passed the black bike waiting at a cross street.

Her whole body shivered.

No, no, no.

She had no time for this.

She continued straight ahead and put on some speed, heading into the thick of city traffic. Her only thought was to lose him and come out the other side.

And it seemed she did. She stayed on main streets, bobbing and weaving through the most crowded parts of town, until she hadn't seen him at all for 10 minutes or so. Even then, she continued to be cautious.

She took a series of shortcuts on smaller streets, streets from which she could have easily seen anyone who was trying to keep up with her. Nothing.

Maybe it had been her imagination. Maybe the fellow was out to meet his buddies at a bar and had happened to be briefly going her way.

At least the incident had served to focus her and rev her instincts. Her sightseeing was over for the day; that much was clear.

Jaime could now feel the salt in the air, as her twists and turns had brought her into proximity of the port. She continued on, her route now along side streets, until she came to one—sort of a cross between a small street and an alley—that was currently deserted. She parked the bike and took off her helmet, shaking out her blond hair, fairly certain she had helmet hair. Being in the Army, she was used to that, at least. She glanced into one of the Vespa's side mirrors to assess the damage and immediately wished she hadn't.

The man in the black helmet loomed behind her. She spun around with a well-placed hook kick, but he caught her foot and pulled her leg up so quickly that she lost her balance and landed with a thud on the pavement on her stomach. He was instantly on top of her, seated astride the small of her back, and he pulled her wrists back and quickly looped them with a rough length of rope that had been tied into makeshift handcuffs.

No, no, no, no.

He pulled her up roughly, muttering in Greek what would happen if she struggled. He pulled a blindfold over her head—from the feel of the soft fabric, it was a sleep mask. It wasn't tight, but there was no way she could remove it.

"Don't make a sound, or you are dead."

That much Greek she understood.

DANIEL DERRY WAS AWAKENED from sleep once again by the sound of a key in the lock to his small room. He had no idea if it was day or night. There were no windows in his room, but there were two in the hallways.

Outside those windows, it was almost always dark.

Maybe he had been kidnapped by vampires, who only worked at night. He knew that wasn't true; it was far-fetched. But so was the fact that he had been kidnapped. He'd asked the doctor lady several times, "Why? Why me?"

She never answered.

He wore a long-sleeved Death by Rock'n'Roll T-shirt and cargo pants, the outfit he'd had on at the mall. His kidnappers had given him a neat pile of T-shirts, sweatshirts, sweatpants, socks, and briefs, all nondescript. But he feared that if he changed, they'd take his real clothes while he slept, and he couldn't stand that. His real clothes were his one tangible link to his old life. They were proof of his identity. He couldn't lose them.

The door swung open, and the lights turned on. A largish man in jeans and a lab coat was at the door. Another goon stood nearby, in the shadows; Daniel couldn't see which one.

"She needs you," said the man in jeans. "Now. Come on."

Daniel groaned and made a production out of pretending he'd been awakened from a deep sleep.

His older brother, Zeke, had a watch that their dad had given him for his birthday. It told time in 24-hour increments and contained a compass and a stopwatch and all kinds of cool stuff. Daniel had a $40 Swatch with nothing but a dial and two hands. The clock said it was 8:36, but he no longer knew if it was A.M. or P.M. or even what time zone.

It was 8:36 at the Pentagon City Mall in Virginia, USA.

Wherever that was.

He groaned again for effect and sat up, then slowly stood and walked over to the door. Truth was, he almost didn't mind when they came for him. It relieved the terrible monotony of being in the small room alone. They'd given him a bed, a desk, a rocking chair with a standing lamp, and a bookshelf with lots of books in English. But you couldn't read forever.

"You going to be a good boy?" the man in the lab coat asked.

Daniel turned around and put his wrists together. The man snapped on real old-time metal handcuffs, which held Daniel's hands behind his back. Then they went into the hall together, the man in the shadows following them.

It was dead quiet in the halls. Outside the windows were woods and snow.

The door to the laboratory where Daniel had been taken before was slightly ajar. Lab coat guy knocked but opened the door without waiting for an answer.

The woman Daniel assumed was a doctor was there. Her lab coat was longer than the guard's. It hung below her skirt, and although she had it buttoned, the belt didn't encircle her waist, but the ends were tied to themselves in back.

She was thin and pretty. Her hair was pulled back into a ponytail, and she wore lab glasses. She'd been sitting at a desk facing away from the door, but when they entered, she scooted back on her round padded stool and said, "Ah, Daniel.

"You want to go outside?" she asked. Her English was accented, but he couldn't place her native language.

The question was shorthand. It meant, "Will you cooperate and let yourself be tied down to the chair and let me do stuff to you, whereafter I will, in turn, let you go outside into the yard until you get cold enough to want to come in? Or are you going to struggle and make lab coat guy give you a shot to go limp?"

Daniel had discovered that shots really hurt when you were struggling and some big goon punched a needle into your muscle as hard as possible and then pushed the burning stuff into your arm as fast as he could. He'd only tried it once.

"I'd like to go outside," he said.

She nodded appreciatively. As he walked toward the metal chair, he heard an unexpected sound. It was sort of . . . a chortle. Then a little sneeze. It wasn't the doctor, and it sure as heck wasn't lab coat guy. A couple of loud breaths—and then a scream. An earsplitting baby scream.

Lab coat guy looked like someone had shot him. The doctor said, "See to it."

He looked like he'd rather die.

"Is that a baby?" asked Daniel.

"No, it's an elephant," said the guy gruffly. "You, lie down." He unlocked Daniel's handcuffs and pushed Daniel's long sleeves up as far as they went.

Daniel climbed onto the chair, positioning his arms and legs. It was uncomfortable. There were thick leather straps that wrapped around his ankles, thighs, wrists, arms, and chest. Lab coat guy seemed to take an extra long time buckling the straps. The baby, who was in a sort of incubator box across the room, kept up the wail. It was shrill and loud.

"See to it," the doctor said again.

This time when Daniel looked over, there was a little head popped up over the side of the box. It had thick black hair and large round eyes, which were currently scrunched in either pain or anger.

"Feed her and change her," said the doctor.

She had rolled her stool over toward Daniel. She held a needle and syringe with extra vials to fill with his blood. He sighed. His brother, Zeke, had one weakness in this world: He was deathly afraid of needles, made a big deal every time he had to get some kind of shot, and was probably remembered at as many military posts around the world as his dad was. Daniel never made a fuss because after Zeke's theatrics, certainly no one would have noticed his.

And here, certainly, nobody cared.

He'd done this before. His arms were strapped down, so it wasn't like he had a choice. He looked the other way as the doctor probed for a good vein. "Make a fist," she said.

Across the room, the baby had pulled herself up to a standing position. The guard had run out of excuses and was heading over to follow the doctor's instructions. The toddler screamed louder as the man got closer. She wore a little shirt with brightly colored flowers.

You go, girl, Daniel thought.

HER CAPTOR WALKED QUICKLY, forcing Jaime in front of him. He was significantly taller than she; she could tell because her head kept knocking against the bottom of his helmet. They made a quick turn into another alley. As she planned her next move, she heard a heavy door scrape open, and she was thrust through it in front of him. The stench of garbage swirled around her. The door closed behind her and the air became merely musty. She assumed she had been brought in a service entrance.

He held her left hand in a vise grip as she heard the scrape of metal against metal—a caged service elevator was her guess, borne out as she was forced into it and the door clacked closed again.

She bided her time as the cage laboriously climbed four floors, bouncing enough to be disconcerting as it passed each landing. The ropes at her wrists were prickly and tight. She was taken from the cage and heard it descend.

Jaime was taken down a hall with a tile floor and shoved into a room. A heavy door closed behind her. To her surprise, she realized the windows must be open, as she was able to hear children playing outside.

She was thrust roughly onto a simple wooden chair. Her captor wasted no time, questioning her now in English.

"Who are you?"

"Jaime Lynn Richards."

"Where have you come from?"

"I just flew in from Germany."

"Where are you going?"

"I'll be going back to Germany."

"You're American military. What is your rank?"

"I'm a chaplain."

"That's not what I asked."

"Major."

"You were missing for three years. Where were you during this time?"

Before she answered this final question, she succeeded in freeing her wrists, and with one clean action removed her blindfold and stood up, brandishing her chair as a weapon. Before her stood a strapping man, six feet tall, with tousled black hair and a devilish grin.

"For crying out loud," she said to him, "can you just once let me come up in the passenger elevator?"

WITGARD VILLELLA KNEW for a fact that science would save the world. That is, science would save the world if human beings quit acting in an irrational manner and took advantage of the information at their disposal.

Villella was a short man, balding, full of energy, and contentedly misanthropic. Today he sat at his desk, staring at the e-mail that had just come through on his computer.

Great news! Am looking forward to presentation on Tuesday.

Tuesday. That was good news and bad.

Good news because the breakthrough was so close. So close.

Bad news because the breakthrough Allende expected to hear about hadn't actually happened yet. But without new funding, the plug would be pulled. To get Allende to kick in the final underwriting amount, Villella had to lie and say it had. Well, not lie. Fudge the timing. In research, things never went smoothly, yet Villella pulled it off, time and again. Fantastic things. It would happen again.

Tuesday. That was three days from now. Three days to change the history of science, the history of the world.

It would give Witgard great satisfaction to be present when science once again changed the world.

Witgard Villella had grown up in heavily Catholic Spain in a family who worshipped science. Both his German mother and Spanish father were research scientists; Witgard's sister was a brilliant student. The family didn't know what to make of Witgard, who could make neither heads nor tails of scientific theory and saw only gibberish when he looked at the Periodic Table.

Witgard was a poor student and a worse athlete. Once, a well-meaning elementary school teacher gave her class a talk about how everyone was gifted in some area—whether it was the arts or science or sports. Nothing resonated with Witgard. One of his classmates even taunted, "Except Witgard, he's not good at anything!" Over the laughter of his classmates, Witgard heard his teacher say, "Well, perhaps he's good with people. Perhaps he's good at being a friend."

As he hunkered down at his desk, Witgard knew he wasn't good with people, at least not in the social sense. Most of them were too hopelessly stupid for him to like, let alone cultivate as friends. It was a miserable couple of years until Witgard discovered what he *was* good at: *manipulating* people. He was able to insert himself into a situation and get both sides to listen. He had the ability to stop fights and get people to work together—if it was toward a goal that would benefit Witgard. In high school, he started a homework service that employed nearly a third of the class and was paid for by another third of the class. Witgard didn't stop there. He became known for coming up with entrepreneurial ideas and seeing them through.

Even though Witgard was clueless when it came to performing scientific research, he did appreciate the ideas and breakthroughs the rest of his family discussed at dinner. While his family thought he was hopelessly dense, he now began to think scientists were the ones who were stupid. They worked for a pittance, fought for grants, labored in small, windowless laboratories, and signed away the rights to the fruits of their hard work to corporations. He also thought scientists were amoral prigs, always bragging and flaunting and comparing who had published most often and most recently. They weren't above appropriating information and ideas from graduate students and one another.

Witgard also noticed that breakthroughs were coming fast and furious in every field of science and that the most brilliant scientists were often hampered by the incredibly slow and arcane methods of pleading for research funding.

He reserved his greatest scorn for those who ran the think tanks that claimed to delineate public morality and whose members would whip the public into a frenzy of thinking certain lines of research were immoral. By now society should realize what happened when the public was allowed to dictate morality: witches burned at the stake and heretics crushed with stones. Absurd.

The current climate in the scientific community provided a great avenue of opportunity for Witgard. There was a lot of money to be made for companies that were not in the public eye, didn't care about tax breaks, and weren't concerned about the legal boundaries placed on research. He found he was adept at operating within the scientific underground and had become known as one who could provide funding and space for research that was not necessarily legal.

Discoveries and breakthroughs started coming—and Witgard's lifestyle became more comfortable. And now, if this Sunmark woman was correct in her theories, he was the one who would be making the profits from it.

Villella's practiced fingers blazed over the keyboard.

He went to his e-mail program and chose "new message."

Time is of the essence, was all he wrote before he pressed "send."

A WATCHED POT NEVER BOILS, thought the scientist as she stared hopefully at the computer screen. She gave a wry laugh even as she repeated the adage. Of course the act of watching water as it heated would have no effect on the outcome. However, it did tend to affect the watcher.

She felt like she had been staring at this screen forever, but it had only been five minutes. Five minutes at the end of a long day of purifying mitochondrial DNA (mtDNA) from blood samples, resuspending it in sterilized water, and adding a master premix of chemicals for the Dye Terminator Cycle Sequencing. Now she was using a special computer program to analyze the sequence of the mtDNA.

She had blood samples from five subjects. She should be seeing a pattern in their mtDNA, at least if her hypothesis was correct. But the computer had not been able to find a common sequence to them all. And even more puzzling, the program could not match these subjects to any known haplogroup. She had hoped the recent addition of the fifth subject would provide enough data to correlate the results, but so far nothing.

She didn't have time for this! Her backers had given her a "no-kidding" cutoff time for tangible results from her studies, and that time was almost here. *Time is of the essence* was the last admonishment she'd received.

Mitochondria, she thought. *O mighty mitochondria . . . you are the bane of my existence!*

Mitochondria were her specialty. Those were the tiny powerhouses that sat inside human cells and produced most of the energy needed to grow and live. About the size and shape of long, threadlike bacteria, mitochondria were self-sufficient to the point that they even carried their own set of DNA, which was inherited completely from the mother. People related by blood on their mother's side of the family would have similar mtDNA. Scientists had been able to trace entire races of people back to ancient times by common markers in their mtDNA and called these haplogroups.

She had been so sure these subjects had a common ancestry, that they were from a race of very long-lived people whose mtDNA might hold the secret to long life.

She brought her attention back to the computer screen, which was flashing the "analysis complete" message. Perhaps this would be the time. Perhaps the answer was there, flashing, ready to be read.

Britta stabbed the "enter" key and held her breath.

"WHEN DID YOU KNOW it was me?" Yani asked.

"Not till the alley," answered Jaime.

"Pretty good escape. Under two minutes. Assuming you'd decided to let yourself be brought into the building."

"Thanks."

"Ten down?"

"Absolutely."

"Ten down" was code for "let's take ten minutes to catch up on other topics before getting into the business at hand."

Jaime took a step back and looked at Yani. She hadn't seen him for over a year, yet he looked just as she remembered him. His hair was tousled from the helmet, but it was still jet-black and long enough to be noncorporate. His black leather jacket was unzipped, and he hadn't taken off the black motorcycle pants that had served as part of his disguise. Even with the outer garments on, she could tell he was in top physical shape.

Yani was the mysterious guide, called a Sword, who had invited her to Eden three years before. They had unexpectedly worked together on a mission during the first days of the Iraq war, and Yani had proved himself to be honorable and trustworthy. If he hadn't, Jaime would never have accepted the invitation to go. Yet when she'd awakened in Eden—same procedure as her recent return, she'd let herself be drugged for the trip so she did not know the way in or out—and asked for Yani, no one knew of whom she spoke.

It had taken a while for the others to figure out she was talking about the man known as Sword 23. When they finally made the connection, she'd enjoyed the widening of the eyes, the intake of breath. For in that most egalitarian of societies, Sword 23 was accorded something akin to rock-star status.

Throughout history, at any given time there were only 12 members of the rarified group of men who knew the way in and out of the hidden society of Eden. None of the Swords intermingled with the Eden population. When they were not out in the Terris world on assignment, they stayed on the Mountaintop, a compound set apart up on the northern mountains where Operatives were trained. Once their training was complete, Operatives did live normal lives among the populace when they were in Eden. Swords did not.

During her time there, she'd discovered that gardeners (as Eden dwellers called themselves) loved to tell stories of true adventures and accomplishments—hero epics, was how Jaime thought of them—and the Swords were always prime fodder. But Sword 23 was a legend among legends.

Jaime had been disappointed—OK, *very* disappointed—that Yani was no longer to be a large part of her life. But Eden had been so teeming with life and joy that she was soon completely entranced. Meeting her mother again during this lifetime was something Jaime had never expected; it was a huge life shift, one that she made gradually.

All residents of Eden, before they chose a life track, spent a year learning to garden, and Jaime had loved her year. It had helped her come to terms with her new life, her relationship with God, her new outlook. She'd always thought she had a "black thumb," but in fact she'd loved the simple daily routines that helped coax new life from the soil, to produce fruits and flowers where there had been none.

She had been so content with gardening, the contemplative life had been such a welcome change, that she'd thought the simple, spiritual track might be the one she chose. Until the day Sword 23—Yani—had shown up in her garden.

Without thinking, she'd run to embrace him, and he'd welcomed her with open arms. He'd explained he'd come at the behest of Clement. Clement was the head of the Integrators, the track that included those who chose to move back and forth between Eden and the Terris world.

"There's been talk about you up at Mountaintop," Yani said with a smile. "They think you're a prime candidate to be an Integrator, possibly even return to the Terris world. Clement knew we'd worked together. He called me in and asked what I thought of your potential."

"Oh?" she'd asked. "And what did you say?"

"I said I thought you could be of help to a great many people."

Jaime discovered the Integrator track included those trained to be Messengers, Operatives, and Swords. Messengers lived full-time in the Terris world. They picked up and delivered messages to and from the Swords exiting and returning to Eden. Operatives, on the other hand, were stationed in the Terris world and were trained to intervene in situations to which they were assigned. Only the very top Operatives at any given time were hand-chosen to join the elite circle of Swords.

Once Jaime had met Clement and the others at the school, she realized that although times of contemplation were necessary, she was a person of action. It was true that she knew the Terris world; she loved its inhabitants. She wanted to help.

She also sensed that the deep and immediate bond still existed between Yani and herself. They had spent some wonderful weeks at Mountaintop together, although he soon returned to the Terris world on Sword duties.

Jaime had wondered what it would be like, seeing Yani again in a Terris setting.

Now here he was.

The main difference between now and the first time they'd met, in Iraq, was that she recognized the smile lines in the crow's-feet by his eyes.

His dark brown eyes, which could hold you captive simply by force of will, were locked with hers, and again she felt nearly helpless to free herself. He was danger and safety, both at once. He was familiar yet completely unknowable. She'd come to terms with this.

It was so good to see him, and it had been such an exhausting and difficult journey to arrive here at the safe house in Athens, that her impulse was to hug him in joy and gratitude. All right, that wasn't her *real* impulse. At least, not all of it.

But being a Sword required total sacrifice. They were not allowed to have emotional entanglements that might compromise their ability to keep the secret that was entrusted to them. Yani was a Sword. And as much as she hungered to hold him, she held sacred the pledge that he'd made.

Which was why she was beyond shocked when he wrapped his arms around her shoulders and pulled her forcefully to him. Everything since her return had a slight feel of unreality to it, and she had fantasized this moment in her mind so many times that it felt natural to give herself over to it, to him. Yani was unknowable, unattainable, certainly untamable—and yet when his mouth captured hers, it was as if he gave himself, he shared the fire that burned so brightly within him. How many women had longed for him, and now, here he was, real, alive, not the thing of fantasy but substantial, and strong. And he wanted her. She recognized the taste of his mouth and the shape of his body as she molded into it. She lost touch with time and space and allowed her spirit to fly free into a moment when the entire world was their embrace.

When they came up for air, finally, he didn't release her but held her to him. She closed her eyes and again felt she was home, no matter where she was or how dangerous the circumstances. Together they could take on the world.

"I didn't expect to see you so soon," was all he said.

"There were special circumstances," she said. "And if I wanted to keep my military commission, I had to return. Even this much time away was pushing it."

"So you're back? You're still U.S. Army?"

She nodded.

He stepped back and sat down, pulling a chair up beside him for her. A lock of hair had fallen out of the ponytail she'd made for her helmet, and he gently brushed it away from her face. "Your first reentry," he said. "Tell me about it."

"I came back through a family of Iranian goat herders," she said. "Besides the fact that I nearly had my head blown off flagging down an American convoy, everything's gone pretty smoothly. I was sent to the Landstuhl Regional Medical Center in Germany. The way was opened for me to be here on a four-day pass. I know I'll have more inquiries to face when I get back. But first things first."

"You went through Landstuhl? What was the worst of it?"

She grimaced. "To tell the truth, the CT scan and the EEG weren't as bad as I feared. I'm never a fan of gyn exams, but hey . . . and three years' worth of catch-up vaccines, also not the best. But honestly, even though I centered myself pretty well, the worst part was knowing what I needed to do and having to wait to be released to do it. Yeah. The waiting was the worst."

"It always is," he said. "But thankfully you were able to be released on leave before the bulk of your Repat/Reint process. But, I'm sure it's been deferred, not dismissed."

"Thanks for the reminder. But I have been trained in what to expect; you know that."

"I know. But I've gotta say, Jaime." He shook his head and looked concerned. "The thought of you spending three days locked with Special Ops for intensive questioning . . . anyway, if one of them cracks, tell him he has my complete sympathy!"

She rolled her eyes and smacked him with a fist. "Thanks a lot," she said, but it felt good to laugh.

"Well, then, unless there's anything else you need to tell me, perhaps we'd better get to it," he said.

Anything else to tell him. Her whole life had changed three years ago, and it had shifted again, seismically, just now. What do you talk about? Either everything or nothing. And there wasn't time for everything.

"I missed you," she said. She leaned forward and kissed him again. Finally she willed herself to stop. She kept her eyes closed and centered herself. When she looked at him, he was all business, sitting casually.

"You have a pendant for me?" he asked.

She reached around her neck and unclasped the small necklace that hung there. Then she handed it to him. "So what do I do?" she asked.

"Will you deliver it? Do I wait here for the Terris-based Operative who's on this mission?"

He looked at her, puzzled.

"I'm the Terris-based Operative," he said.

"No," she said. "You're the Sword. But you know how to contact the Operative. Do I wait here?"

"They didn't tell you?" He looked confused for a moment, and then it came clear for him. "They didn't tell you. Why would they?" He took her hand. For the first time since she'd met him, it seemed to Jaime that Yani was struggling for the right words.

"I'm the Operative on this. I'm no longer a Sword."

"*What?*"

"It was my choice," he said. "It was a difficult decision, but after much reflection and prayer, it seemed the best way."

Jaime sat, stunned. So. The kiss . . .

She knew that Operatives were allowed to have emotional commitments to others, get married, and have families, even. Those commitments could only be made if the Operative felt he or she could withstand the abduction, even the torture and murder, of loved ones without cracking. Since very few outsiders knew of Eden, or that there existed such people as Operatives of Eden, it was a slim chance, but one that had to be taken seriously. In fact, both Jaime and Yani had family members who had been murdered because of their connection to the place known as Eden.

So he was now an Operative rather than a Sword. He hadn't broken the code when he'd kissed her. This time.

But it was such an honor to be chosen, called to be a Sword! Jaime found that she felt let down that he was no longer a member of that rarified group.

She couldn't even look at him when she whispered, "But why?"

He didn't answer. He took the silver rectangular pendant from her hand and stood up. "Excuse me a minute. I'll be back."

He had taken his handheld reader from his pocket and started into the other room before she realized what he was doing.

"Where are you going?"

"What do you mean? You've delivered the pendant. I need to see what it says. Who I'm working with."

Her mouth was open in astonishment yet again. "I need to see it, too. I know most of what it says, but I have new information. And it's likely there's information I don't have. We need to put our heads together and formulate a course of action."

Now it was his turn to be flummoxed. "Jaime. You're a Messenger. It's an important and dangerous calling." The memory of Yani's murdered sister Adara sprang to their minds as he spoke. "But you know there are only certain things—"

"Yani. I'm not a Messenger. I'm the Eden Operative on this. *I'm* the one you're working with."

They stared at each other.

"You're not the Messenger?" He couldn't help but frame it as a question. "You can't be the Eden Operative. I'm sorry, Jaime, but you know as well as I that you've only had two years of training. Two years! No one is ever given an assignment after two years, even as a Messenger. I was shocked that you could already be a Messenger."

She pushed the pendant into the reader that he held in his palm and hit the "on" switch. She closed his hand around it and pushed him toward the back hall. "Go see for yourself," she said.

PATSY COVINGTON SAT WATCHING the light snow fall through one of the 40-foot windows in the great room of the main lodge. Both of her children were sitting across the room by the huge roaring fire, being entertained by Meghan and a young man who had taken a very sincere interest in the nanny. He was demonstrating his seriousness by helping to entertain Portia and Bartlett. Patsy couldn't help but smile at how perfect Portia looked in her miniature version of her mother's ski outfit. Portia even wore the headband with aplomb. What a darling girl.

Meghan's suitor would make it easier for Patsy to vanish for an unremarked-upon length of time to the "upper lodge" and the advanced slopes.

Truth was, Patsy hated skiing. The only parts she liked were shopping for the cunning outfits and smelling the crackling fires in the lodges. The occasional toddy was fine, too.

Fortunately, of course, she didn't have to ski at the upper lodge. She didn't have to ski anywhere. She would collect her key to the suite at the upper lodge; then she'd fly out, finish the final stage on her latest project, and return to pick up her family and fly back to the States on the same day the last victim breathed his last, so that it would appear they'd been traveling all that day.

She didn't usually enjoy killing people, but these particular subjects had outlived their usefulness, and every day they remained alive presented a danger to Patsy and her children. Granted, the contractor had given Patsy a generous bonus to add the final subject and to extend the final deadline. But enough was enough. In three days, *finito*. They would disappear.

A thirtysomething gentleman with thick black hair and heavy rings on his fingers caught her eye from across the room. She was used to this. Viscount or baron?

He nodded and held up a flute, filled with champagne he'd just poured from a newly opened bottle of Fleur. Viscount, she bet.

Well, might as well make sure there was one more person who remembered her here. She smiled in response, and he picked up the bottle, along with an unused flute, and headed her way.

WHEN HE RETURNED, his demeanor had changed. The real Yani, the Yani she'd come to know in Eden, was again submerged deeply under the veneer of business.

"Should we look at it together?" she asked. "As I said, I have some new information."

He clutched the reader tightly. She noticed his jaw was set in a firm line. He said, not in a pleasant voice, "I want you off this assignment."

"What?"

"As you know, included with the information on the pendant is the name of the Operative who is your backup, should something happen to you. In this case, that Operative is based in Athens, right here—and happens to be much more seasoned than you are."

"I've been assigned to this! And nothing *has* happened to me."

"You were just blindfolded and kidnapped off the street in broad daylight!"

"I knew it was you!"

"It's not personal. You're not ready. You would put yourself, and me, and all those we're trying to save at risk. There's no reason for that. I don't care who you are, Jaime Ingridsdotter!"

She flinched at the sound of her Eden name being used in an accusatory manner. "Listen to what you're saying. You're implying that Clement can be influenced by such considerations? You know as well as I do how impossible that thought is! How can you think he would even consider such a thing?" she demanded. This wasn't at all what she had envisioned it would be like, starting on her first official assignment.

They locked eyes. Her return gaze was as strong as his. She said, "I'm not quitting. And if you force me off, which I know you have the right to do as senior Operative, I will make sure Clement knows exactly what happened. And *you* can explain how you second-guessed his decision."

Yani looked away for the briefest moment.

He sighed. "All right. If you're here, there must be a reason. However, we're going to be clear from the start who is the senior Operative, and whose orders must be obeyed, without hesitation or question. Got it?"

Somehow, in the last five minutes, their relationship had shifted. The fact that it had was gut-wrenching, and she fought to understand what had happened and why. But she was military—and one thing she understood was chain of command. She understood what he was saying to her. He was giving her operating procedure and defining their working relationship. She could accept it or she could get off the assignment.

She centered herself as she'd been taught. She remembered who he was, how many years of experience he had, how he was the best—the very best—at what he did. He'd been an Operative for years before he'd been chosen to become a Sword. He'd earned his position. He'd earned her respect. Perhaps more than anyone else on earth, he'd earned her respect.

Jaime replied, "It's long been a dream of mine to work with you. I understand that you may not feel the same way about me. But I will do everything in my power not to let you down. And yes, I understand and respect your seniority."

Yani replied, "All right. Let's look at the information on the pendant, and you tell me what you know."

They sat together on the small sofa and looked together at the background on the assignment. Jaime had been familiar with most of it, having been briefed before she'd left Eden. It gave specific dates and places of each kidnapping but had been filed before Daniel Derry had been abducted.

Those kidnapped were listed:

Jimi Afzal, 26, son of Ankar and Mary Afzal, from London
Ryan Stevens, 12, adopted son of Rebekah and Troy Stevens,
Warwick, New York
An Bao, 1½, daughter of Mei Ling and Ming Zhou, Henan
Province, China
Inaba Mikelti, 25, daughter of Anya and Paul Mikelti, taken
from an AIDS hospice she ran in Africa

Jaime brought out her notebook to update Yani on the information she'd gotten from Abe Derry the day before. First, she updated the list, adding:

Daniel Derry, 15, son of Abraham and Eirene Derry, taken
from Pentagon City Mall, Virginia

Jaime explained that it was Abe who had put together that the kidnap victims were the children of seven of the gardeners—including himself and Eirene—who had transitioned to the Terris world during the same door opening, twenty-four years earlier.

"It was he who figured out that the only other member of the group who has not had a child kidnapped, as far as we know, was a scientist by the name of Jorgen Edders," Jaime said. "It seems like our first course of action would be to find him. Athens was his last known address."

"Let's see," Yani said, typing the code that denoted his top-level clearance into the handheld reader. It took only a moment for the information to pop up. "Dr. Edders is dead," he said.

"Dead? When? Any children?"

"No, never married, no children. Died August 18, 2004, in the Dolphin Nursing Facility, right here in Athens. He'd been a professor in the Department of Genetics and Biotechnology at the University of Athens for twenty years."

"So, are we to assume that because he is dead, and had no children to be kidnapped, that's a blind alley?"

"No," said Yani thoughtfully. "Someone might go to the trouble to kidnap their own child as a ruse, but it seems unlikely. I can't imagine any of the parents of the victims are involved, although I will put your backup to work on it. But I believe our first line of inquiry should be about Edders and the people with whom he worked."

"Did he have friends or even romances?" Jaime asked. "If he had no children, what became of his personal effects?"

"Those seem like questions worth asking," Yani said. "How about it? Did you ever feel like Jorgen Edders was like an uncle to you?"

As a matter of course, every gardener listed a niece named Mary Gardener and a nephew named Michael Gardener on any papers they filled out, in case there was an emergency and someone from home needed to become involved in their affairs.

"Why, I had a flash of that feeling just moments ago."

"Fine. I'll visit the university where he worked. You head for the nursing home. Let me get directions. We'll go separately, but we'll stay in communication. And let's try to get there while it's still visiting hours."

"Yes, sir," she said. Then, "Do you think there's still a chance any of the kidnap victims are still alive?"

"I have to admit it's easier to dispose of someone than to keep him or her alive for months on end." He saw her stricken look and said, "We have no proof any of them have died. But the sooner we find them, the better their chances."

"As I told you. I have a four-day pass. After that, I'm back in the grip of the military and you can work with whomever you think best. But give me these four days," said Jaime steadily.

"Four days may well be more time than we have," Yani replied.

They stood, and he put a hand on her shoulder. "Jaime. We worked together well before you'd had any training at all. I'm confident that you are now much better equipped to handle whatever we'll encounter during the successful retrieval of those kidnapped."

"Yes, sir," she said. And she tried to tell herself that was enough.

NESTOR STEPPED ONTO the *Gerianne* II, his private yacht, and immediately felt himself relax. Perhaps because he was always in perpetual motion, he felt as much, if not more, at home on the *Gerianne* as he did at any of his stationary residences.

"All is ready?" he asked the captain, not intending to wait for a reply.

The *Gerianne* was classed as a mega-luxury yacht. She had been built in 2003 to the specifications Nestor designed. She was 85 meters long, with 36 staterooms, two dining rooms, a cinema, a full-sized pool, three Jacuzzis, a full gym—and an owner's suite with panoramic windows. He regretted momentarily that he and Gerianne had met the boat at Samos, instead of flying into Rhodes or another island that would give him a longer ride to their destination.

This trip he was indulging his wife, letting her have her way, temporarily, at least.

And his wife was glowing. She was shrouded with the joy of her upcoming meeting. She was the one who knew the yacht's staff by name—all 40 of them—and inquired after their families and their pets. In the early days, she'd been uncomfortable occupying—let alone managing—his penthouses, villas, jets, and yacht. But it was funny what a human being could become accustomed to. Now Geri was quite at home overseeing travel on a mega-yacht that bore her name.

"You're not going to your office, are you, darling?" she asked hopefully.

"No. I'm a man on holiday. Today, I'm yours."

"Let me talk to the chef, and I'll meet you—where? The spa? Our suite?"

What a fine invitation. Her hair swept her shoulders, and her eyes danced as they had so often in her youth. She was shapely and lithe—not one of Wolfe's "social X-rays," thank God. Nestor liked a woman with curves. He was glad he was the facilitator of his wife's good mood and planned to exploit it fully. "See you in the suite."

She turned to walk and talk with Pepe, the steward. Nestor jaunted down the chrome and glass center staircase into his favorite room: the receiving parlor. He loved the elegant modern angularity of it: the high ceilings, the box chairs, the large square panes of glass that partitioned the music room from the waterfall room. Someone had set out a vodka tonic, little ice.

Nestor was home.

He took a seat and looked out the wall of windows to the town of Vathay, which climbed the hills behind the harbor. He knew many people found the Greek islands charming, but he was from a Greek island and all the square whitewashed houses seemed redundant to him. He sometimes felt like he was traveling through a movie with a lazy set designer.

Yet at this moment, he, too, felt the undercurrent of excitement. Nestor pulled out a small card from his wallet. On it was emblazoned one of the great inspirational quotes of all time, one that kept him going, day in and day out.

> *I don't want to achieve immortality through my work. I want to achieve it through not dying.*
>
> —WOODY ALLEN

Let so-called visionaries like Bill Gates and Warren Buffett spend their billions prolonging the suffering of a few peons. Nestor had other plans for his fortune. He was going to change the world . . . truly change the history of the world.

He had been born for this. Science stood on the cusp of medical technology that would make it possible to retool the human body so that someone who had the resources could, in fact, live forever. They were so close. New breakthroughs were coming every day. It was now not unusual to live to be 100. Even without enormous breakthroughs, scientists were guessing that by the mid-twenty-first century, it would be possible to live to 120 or even 150, with the right care at your disposal.

For the last decade, he had been financing a very promising strand of cloning research. Not cloning as in making vacuous twins of yourself but cloning to grow extra, perfect body parts that would fit flawlessly into your own body system as the old ones began to wear out. No organ rejection, no mismatches, since the new organ would in fact be your own organ. But as promising as this research was, it was clear now that cloning probably would not be feasible as an ongoing, renewable source of parts in his lifetime.

Nestor was CEO of an international society called the Immortalists, a group of scientists, researchers, philosophers, and money men who knew that earthly immortality was not only possible, it was a given. It was solely a matter of time. And Nestor firmly believed that the time-table was dependent on available funds. That was where he came in.

He had the available funds, and he sure as hell wasn't going to spend them to help peons stupid enough to catch AIDS or to be uneducated and caught in the midst of some remote civil war. The planet was overpopulated as it was. He thought of their deaths as self-correcting.

He was going to use his funds to trace the line in the sand dividing the time that the worthy elite—the princes—of the world died and the time they did not.

Nestor knew that Geri had hesitations about some of the research he funded, some of the avenues of experimentation they followed. That was, frankly, one reason he'd chosen her as a partner. He didn't have time to wrestle with moral and religious qualms. So he had hired Geri—well, married Geri—to do it for him. He had been raised Greek Orthodox and figured he still believed most of that crap; he just didn't have time to mess with it or figure it out. So he left it to her.

Unfortunately, Geri wasn't Greek Orthodox, she was some kind of Southern something from Texas, but he figured that maybe her religiosity balanced out his lack of time for the same thing. They'd get to heaven as a package, right? Not that there was such a place, but as a businessman, he knew there were always advantages to hedging his bets. Or was it the Mormons who believed in the package deal thing? Whatever.

He was letting her follow her conscience. This was more than fine with him, as it currently meant having a well-mixed drink on his vessel of choice, with a romp in the bedroom promised.

"Darling." Gerianne had come up behind him and was massaging his shoulders. She picked up the remote that sat on the small table beside his drink and pushed a button. A swell of jazz poured from the speakers that surrounded them.

"Let's dance," Geri purred into his ear.

He smiled and stretched and stood into her embrace.

JAIME STOOD IN THE HALLWAY of the ground floor of
the Dolphin Nursing Care Facility in central Athens. It was a long-
term-care facility associated with the University Hospital. She was
impressed at how it managed to seem well run and antiseptic, yet at the
same time the rooms were cheerful and well differentiated. She had to
wait only 15 minutes before the head administrator of the facility welcomed her into his office.

Dr. Andropolous, his name was, and he remembered Jorgen Edders
well. Brilliant man. Had been a department head at the university.
They had been honored to care for him during the last months of his
life. Luckily for Jaime, she understood conversational modern Greek,
even though she was reticent to speak it. However, Dr. Andropolous
assumed since she was American that she'd prefer English, which he
spoke with little accent.

Once he was convinced that Jaime was indeed authorized—Mary
Gardener was listed as Jorgen Edders's niece—to see the records, Dr.
Andropolous shared with her the medical records and death certificate
of Dr. Edders. He had died of a fast-growing brain tumor. His colleagues
at the University Hospital had taken all measures possible to save his
life but had finally been unsuccessful.

Jaime was given the names of the doctors who had treated him.
Dr. Andropolous even walked her through the halls and up a staircase
to the nursing station outside the room that had been Jorgen Edders's.

As they walked, Jaime looked at the medical and legal documentation surrounding Edders's last days. She rifled through them and finally found what she was looking for: the signed paper denoting his power of attorney. It had been given over to someone named Britta Sunmark.

The head nurse on the second floor remembered Dr. Edders and rattled on in Greek for a while about what a fine gentleman he was, how quickly the tumor's growth had clouded his faculties, and was continuing on in that direction when Jaime asked if she remembered Britta Sunmark, the woman who had power of attorney to make decisions about Edders and see to the disposition of his property.

"Oh yes," said the rather zaftig nurse. "Sunmark was a young woman who had been his research assistant. She was a constant presence as Dr. Edders was failing. Very faithful."

Jaime set the file down on the blue counter at the well-lit nurses' station and copied down the research assistant's phone numbers from the power-of-attorney papers.

"I don't know that they'll work," said the nurse. "It seems to me we tried to contact the young woman, perhaps six months after Edders's death, and those phone numbers had been disconnected with no forwarding number."

"That's so," said Dr. Andropolous, in English. "As I recall, she had left her post at the university as well. We never did locate her, did we?"

The nurse shook her head. "Never did," she repeated, also in English.

Red flags immediately sprung up in Jaime's mind, and she underlined the name "Britta Sunmark" in her notes next to the old phone numbers.

Dr. Andropolous excused himself to continue his daily duties, and Jaime listened with attention as the nurse described the peaceful death of Dr. Edders; then good-byes were said all around.

As Jaime returned to the center hall of the first floor, a young nurse's aide hesitantly came up behind her. "Perhaps I may help," she said in English. "My name is Isis, and I have been working here when your uncle died."

Jaime gave the girl a warm smile. "Thank you for finding me," she said. "It is nice to meet you."

"If you cannot find the woman Sunmark," said the girl, in what occurred to Jaime was nearly a whisper, "you may be able to find her fiancé."

"She had a fiancé?" asked Jaime.

"Yes. He was here very much," said the girl. "His name was Constantine. I have for him a cell phone number." She handed Jaime a folded piece of paper with a series of numbers written in blue ink.

"Thank you, Isis," said Jaime. "How did you know Constantine's phone number?" she asked.

The girl blushed deeply. "He was a friendly man," was all she said.

"Well, thank you again," said Jaime.

"Good luck," said the thin aide, and she disappeared quickly back up the staircase.

DANIEL DERRY LAY with his ankles crossed and his hands behind his pillow on his bed, running over the details of his kidnapping as he had daily for the last two weeks.

He had been at the mall that Sunday with his friends. The Sunday before Valentine's Day. He hadn't admitted it even to his small posse, but he had been shopping. During a fifteen-minute stint when he had professed to be using the restroom, he had slipped over to Kay Jewelers and impatiently waited his turn, knowing exactly which gold bracelet he wanted, knowing exactly how he wanted it inscribed.

It was the first Valentine's Day that he had a girlfriend, and he had used an unwise amount of his savings to purchase the bracelet. His friends all thought he and Janel were just friends; Janel was almost one of the guys, after all. But she wasn't one of the guys. She was a girl. She was Daniel's girl.

He tried to envision the look on her face if he'd given her the gift. Would she have been pleased? He had been planning to ask her to the junior prom. Would she have said yes? What would her parents have thought?

They seemed to like him. Her parents were military, too. That was good because even if they were bigoted enough to care that his mom was white, the fact his dad was a general did carry weight with military people.

Oh, who cared about her parents? Daniel missed her. His girl. He had a girl. She had loved to hug him and kiss him. Oh, man, could she kiss. He ached for her arms around him, the feel of her breasts beneath her shirt.

She never called him Did. She called him Daniel.

And no one would ever know to pick up the bracelet. It was engraved. It was paid for. It was sitting in an envelope in a drawer in a jewelry store in the Pentagon City Mall.

Did Janel know he'd been kidnapped?

How had she found out? Who had told her?

He tried to envision the scene at the Derry house when he hadn't come home. Did they know that crazy lady with the kid had duped him into the parking garage? Did they know he'd been drugged? Or did they think he was one of countless runaway teenagers?

That was the only thought that made him panic: What if they thought he couldn't measure up to Zeke, so he'd run away?

But they had to know. He'd been on his way back to his friends; he'd seen them in the food court, had waved that he was coming back—and then the lady came running in, all upset.

Certainly his family knew he'd been kidnapped. And if they did—for once in his life, the tumult at home would be about him.

That was usually where his litany of memories would end, because he couldn't stand to picture his mother upset.

His brother and sister, well, OK. A little bit.

Daniel sat up as he heard footfalls outside his room. He glanced at his watch. It wasn't the time of day that the guards usually came. This must be something different. He didn't want to think about what.

He sat up and scrunched himself back, pushing his pillow into the wall.

The door swung open. There were two guards, including Mr. Lab Coat Guy. It was what they had with them that Daniel found unsettling, to say the least.

But he couldn't find the words to ask the question.

He sat, staring, and waited.

YANI HAD CALLED JAIME as she'd returned to her Vespa from the care facility. She was wearing the new helmet he'd issued her, sleek and white, which had a communications device inside. "I'm not far from you," he said. "Come through the Zografou Gate by the Medical Center, and go straight until the road dead-ends by the mathematics building. Make a right. I'll find you there."

It hadn't taken her long to do so. Since it was Saturday, she wasn't surprised to find most students by the dormitory and the ball fields, leaving the departmental buildings nearly deserted. She was surprised, however, to find Yani in jeans and a forest green polo shirt, a lightweight navy windbreaker on top, sitting on a bench, sipping a can of soda. She parked her bike several yards away and walked over to him. The sun had come out; she guessed it to be in the mid-sixties Fahrenheit. Not bad for February.

"Find anything?" she asked, removing her helmet and sitting beside him.

"The only thing I found in the departmental files was that Edders was indeed the department chair until six months before his death. His tumor progressed very quickly. At some point, all his research files were removed by his research assistant, a woman named—"

"Britta Sunmark," finished Jaime. "She also held Edders's power of attorney."

"Hmm. Interesting. Because Ms. Sunmark is also missing. All I could find out in the time I had was that she had switched departments, from the Department of Cell Biology and Biophysics to the Department of Genetics and Biotechnology, specifically to work with Edders three years ago."

"When you say 'missing,' do you mean there's a chance she was also abducted?" Jaime asked.

"No. She left suddenly, though it seems under her own volition. It wasn't suspicious enough that her colleagues called the authorities, but it was quick enough that she left them all fairly annoyed."

"Any hints as to where she might have ended up?"

"Well, since today is Saturday and the offices are officially closed, I was able to look around in the office which had been Sunmark's, which yielded nothing, and the office which is now the office of the director. This was in the back of a very long file drawer."

Yani tossed a Xeroxed copy of a grant application into Jaime's lap. She squinted down at it in the winter sunlight. It was filled out in a small, controlled script by one Britta Sunmark. It was for a grant from a corporation called FIA—Future Imagined and Achieved. The grant was filled out in English, although the corporation's address was in Greece.

"Look at page seven," directed Yani. He had his arms spread wide across the back of the bench, and he sat relaxed as she thumbed through. On page 7, the blanks were suddenly left unfilled. *I must speak to you in person to convey the enormous importance of this work,* was all it said.

"OK, she's got my attention," Jaime said.

Yani took the pages and slid them into his satchel. "Now all we've got to do is find Ms. Sunmark to find out to which 'work' she alluded. Did you have any luck with contact information?"

Jaime shook her head. "No. They said they tried to contact her several months ago, but none of her numbers were current. However . . . as I was leaving, a young nurses' aide suggested I might be able to contact her through her fiancé, a guy named Constantine. His number." She handed it over to Yani. "Do you want me to call?"

He sat a moment, contemplating, then said, "Yes, but we don't want to let him know someone's looking for him. Let's find out where he is. That might get us close to her."

"How do we discover where he is without letting him know someone's looking for him?"

"All cell phones these days also serve as GPSs. Which is how the cops can find you if you can leave your cell on in the backseat of a car if you're being kidnapped. What I need you to do is to make a call from a University of Athens number and keep him on the line long enough for me to get a read on his location. How's your conversational Greek?"

"What should I say?"

"What's an innocuous reason to call from the university? We don't want him to think Britta's colleagues are either angry or hunting her down."

"That's simple," she said. "Alumni organization."

"That would work. There's one lone receptionist in the building today. You go in and think of some way to have her let you use the phone, and I'll distract her long enough that she can't hear what you're saying. I'll have my handheld on, and will give you a signal when I've found him. Do whatever you need to keep him on the line till then."

"Got it," she said. She'd put on her flustered-American persona and headed inside.

"I'm so sorry," Jaime said in a flustered voice to the pretty girl with the nose ring. "I'm . . . American. My . . . cell . . . phone . . . doesn't . . . work." She spoke each word slowly and shook her useless phone. "I'm supposed to meet a friend. Can I use your phone?" This last was accompanied by hand gestures pointing to the phone at the front desk of the Facility of Biology.

The girl shook her head and gave a slight shrug: *Sorry*.

"Please," Jaime wheedled, sounding slightly spacey and very desperate. "I'll do anything. I'm a half an hour late, and I got lost, and I don't know what to do. I don't know where to go. It's an emergency! Please. Anything. I'll give you five euros. . . ." She started digging in her purse.

The girl, who had seemed rather bemused by the whole performance, finally spoke in English. "Oh, all right. Keep your money. But I'm not supposed to let anyone use the phone. Be quick."

"Oh, thank you. Thank you! I really appreciate it!" Jaime dug through her purse for the small piece of paper with Constantine's phone number as the girl handed her the receiver from the other side of the desk. As she did, Yani strolled through the front door.

"Hello, Nikki," he said in fluent Greek. "Professor Beis told me you'd be here. Could I have a word with you, please?"

The girl looked at him, rose nervously, and followed him across the entrance hall.

Constantine answered on the fourth ring and had done everything in his power to rid himself of the irksome clerk from the UoA, but he'd had the manners not to hang up on her until Yani gave her the high sign, at which point she'd said in Greek, "So the address we have here for Ms. Sunmark is no longer good. OK, thank you." She hung up.

She waved a cheery "thank you!" to the nose ring girl and headed out of the building and back around the corner to her bike. She put on her helmet and started the bike, traveling slowly, waiting to hear from Yani.

"Good work." His voice rang suddenly inside her helmet, and she nearly crashed into a waste can. "My hunch was confirmed. Ms. Sunmark's fiancé is currently on the island of Patmos—as is the headquarters of FIA, to whom she applied for a research grant. Her actions, and the proximity of the island, make me think we should head on over and take a look."

"Patmos? Isn't that the island where the Apostle John was supposed to have had the vision that became the Book of Revelation?"

"Can't put anything past you," he said, and she wanted to smack him. Which felt good. She smiled to herself. "Meet me back at the safe house, and let's get going," he said. And she headed out.

NO CORRELATION!

No common factor in mtDNA of the five subjects.

The scientist had run the analysis again, with the same results. Staring at the computer screen wouldn't help.

Don't panic, she told herself. *Think. What factors would lead to these results?* Either the hypothesis is in error, the test procedures are faulty, or the subject pool was tainted. She didn't even consider the first choice; too much depended on that being correct. And her methods were beyond reproach. So suppose, just for a moment, that there was something wrong with the subject pool.

She opened her computer files and stared at the five folders representing her test subjects. "One of these things is not like the others. . . . ," She began to sing to herself, remembering the song from an American children's show. What would happen if she reran comparisons, each time leaving out one subject? What if one specimen was in the pool by mistake? That could possibly be the error. It might take a while but could be worth it.

She knew she was taking a risk. If she tried it and it didn't work, she'd be out of time. Yet she could think of nothing else to try, no other variable to account for.

"OK," she said, and sighed. "Let's see who was kidnapped by mistake."

GERI STEPPED OUT of the car in front of her hotel and breathed deeply of the air of Patmos. She had been pleasantly surprised that the trip from the harbor at Skala had taken only five minutes. She knew, in the back of her mind, that the entire island was only eight miles long, but it was all so mystical to her that she hadn't settled into reality yet.

The island was open for tourist trade from mid-April through October, and it was only because colleagues of Nestor's knew the Stergiou family, who owned the Petra Hotel, that he and Geri had been welcomed so warmly and given a large suite overlooking the Aegean during off-season.

At first Geri had been disappointed that Nestor had sent her to check in while he stayed on board the yacht and did some work from his office. Yet at the same time this felt right. This was her trip; they'd come here of her volition. Finally, there was something she was bringing to the table. She'd long been aware of, and even had participated in, Nestor's meetings with the Immortalists, although she'd felt very hesitant about it. But what if this was both what the Immortalists were looking for and what God had intended? Still, she had common sense, and she wanted to check the whole thing out and get the lay of the land before she brought it to Nestor's attention. It was fitting she begin this quest on her own.

A handsome youth had taken her bags to her suite, a Stergiou relative, she assumed. She'd followed him inside, through the beige and browns of the lobby, which was decorated with mostly religious paintings and sculptures and with arches dotted with candles. It felt tranquil and spiritual and . . . right. As they reached her rooms, the young man said, "Someone is waiting to meet with you. He is outside on the restaurant terrace."

Geri's pulse quickened. Why did she feel like a young girl on her first date? It was a strange feeling, and a lovely one. She looked around the room quickly, appreciating the earth tones of beige, brown, and gold—and the door that led to a private terrace overlooking the Aegean, the incredible, sapphire Aegean. She glanced in the mirror in the marble bathroom and was content that she looked as she had 20 minutes earlier on the yacht. She asked the young man just to set down her bags. She could unpack later. She followed him back through the quiet walkways of the hotel.

He pointed her through open doors to the back patio. She looked out, past a wall made of local stone, to a shorter, thin wall that separated the terrace from the calm sea. And there, standing with his back to her, was a man in a blue monk's robe. She knew it was *him*.

How could a Greek Orthodox monk so enthrall a Southern Baptist girl?

She clutched the Bible that she'd picked up from her carry-bag.

As if he knew she was there, he turned around.

He was sturdy. Handsome, definitely, but not uncomfortably so for a monk. His dark hair was not covered. The most noticeable thing was his dark beard, which had grown long enough to reach the front of his robe. Underneath, his jaw was square. He looked kind and down-to-earth. Then he saw her, looked directly into her eyes, and opened his arms in an expansive gesture.

"Welcome to Patmos," he said. "I don't yet know why, but I know it is God's will that you are here."

And she exhaled, delighted that somehow he knew it, too.

"SHE'S YOURS," said Lab Coat Guy, and he plunked the toddler down onto the floor of Daniel's cell-room. "You take care of her, or I throw her out in the snow." He dropped a plastic bag of diapers, with just a couple left at the bottom, onto the floor, as well as two filled baby bottles.

"That's not much," was Daniel's first comment.

"You won't need much," grunted the man.

That was the end of the conversation. The door banged shut and was double-locked from the outside.

"Wait," Daniel said. "What's her name?"

But it was too late to be heard.

The toddler sat where she'd been planted, looking every bit as stunned by this development as Daniel.

He got up and went over to where she sat, staring up at him. She was still wearing the flowered shirt, with little red pants. They weren't very thick; in fact, they looked like pajamas. Her hair was jet-black, and her eyes were large and intelligent. She looked Chinese or maybe Korean? He wasn't very conversant with racial differences. She was Asian; he could tell that, anyway.

He pointed to himself. "Daniel," he said.

She stared.

"Daniel," he repeated. He pointed at her.

"Nayal," she said, pointing to herself.

"Nayal?" he asked.

She pointed at herself and said again, "Nayal."

He was excited that she'd told him her name, until she pointed at him and also said, "Nayal." Daniel.

He sighed and tried another direction. "Daniel," he said, pointing at himself. "Baby," he said, pointing at her.

"Bai," she said. Then she shrugged and pulled herself up to look around the room.

He got up to follow her. He had never really been around babies before and only knew that you couldn't let them swallow quarters. Not that he had any.

She wanted to get up on the bed. She tried a couple of times, but the mattress was too high for her to swing her chubby little thigh up. She lifted her arms straight up and just stood, waiting. Daniel looked at her for a moment before realizing she wanted him to lift her up. So he did.

As he did, he felt a small bump under her shirt at the elbow and lifted up her sleeve. She also had a small wad of cotton held in place by a Band-Aid. So the vampires wanted her, too. Why? Was the blood in her little body somehow similar to the blood in his?

She was looking at him expectantly. He pointed to her bandage. "Ow," he said.

"Ow," she said. Then she stood up.

He glanced back over to where the guard had dropped two diapers and two bottles. What had he said? "You won't need much"? What did that mean? Were they going to be sent home? Or . . . something else?

The little girl held her hand out, and when he extended his own, she grasped two fingers in an iron grip and began to bounce on the bed.

Daniel sighed. This was a new development. A new development indeed.

"TELL ME SOMETHING of your journey, how you came to be here," said Brother Timothy as they walked the narrow streets of Patmos. Geri was caught off guard, delighted by his quiet interest, which felt very genuine—but everything about this island was enchanting. The evening sky was tinged with a curious combination of orange and pink. She wore a knee-length black sweater jacket over a linen pantsuit, as she'd been told she would need to dress modestly for the monks. That was fine with her. Dressing modestly was her natural choice. She'd had to work hard to learn how to fit in at Nestor's cocktail soirees over the years.

She'd expected Brother Timothy to launch into whatever incredible news was known as "the Patmos Project," but she could tell he was a quiet man, a contemplative man, and he wanted first to talk about that which was most important in life, the spiritual path that had brought them both to this place, to this moment.

She loved that it was winter season; the streets were quiet, if not completely deserted. The sea that had formed and informed the island was choppy and restless and the wind was chilly, but both gave her the feeling of privilege—that she was at a special place at a special time.

She found it easy to talk to Brother Timothy. Geri's least favorite thing about being Mrs. Allende was that she had to be provocative in her dress and circumspect in her conversation. Now that the requirements were flipped, she felt free, truly able to be herself.

She talked of growing up in a small Texas town, about saving all the money she'd made working at the Dunkin' Donuts. How, after college graduation, her wanderlust had taken her to Europe with a backpack. When she ran out of money, she'd come back through New York City and stayed in the apartment of two college classmates who were going on vacation and needed a dog sitter.

How every morning she'd treated herself to an inexpensive breakfast at the diner on the corner, had gotten to know the waiters and recognized her fellow customers. How the last week she was dog sitting, one man who always ate breakfast at the corner booth by the plate glass window had asked if she would join him at his table. She'd enjoyed his company and had accepted his invitation to dinner.

His name was Nestor Allende. She'd even imposed on her returned friends and stayed with them for a couple of weeks so she could continue to see Nestor. They'd had such a good time—until the first time he'd invited her back to his apartment.

Geri had been unnerved, not because his behavior had been forward but because his apartment was a penthouse overlooking Central Park that took up the whole floor of the building. It had servants' quarters and servants—a maid, a chef, a driver. Geri had panicked.

The next day, she'd fled back to Texas.

Brother Timothy laughed softly at that, appreciating how over-whelmed she'd been by Nestor's world.

But it hadn't taken Nestor long to find her. He had worked hard to allay her fears and had very effectively played on her wish to see the world. He had also spoken fervently of his spiritual journey and his desire to have an authentically spiritual wife. He talked of his calling to change the world and his need to have a partner to help him.

Nestor Allende was a hard man to resist.

They'd been married in the mega-church her parents attended near their home in Texas. It had been a huge, splashy wedding, even by Texas standards. Then, for all Nestor's promises, they were usually traveling or in some foreign country on Sundays. Geri went several years without attending church at all.

Until both of her parents died in the same year. She had sent money so that her sister had been able to afford the best care for them, but

Geri was crushed that she hadn't been able to be around very often. She hadn't been there when either of them had passed.

Nestor made large contributions in both their names to the American Cancer Society, but Geri put her foot down. She wanted a home base and a home church and a *home*. It was one thing to see the world; it was something else to never take off her traveling shoes.

Nestor had agreed and had even given her a list of his holdings and the locations in which he could be persuaded to build a headquarters for Allende International. She'd chosen Phoenix, Arizona. True to his word, that city became the new headquarters for his business interests.

Nestor still traveled almost constantly, but now Geri had a mansion to call home. Soon she had a church home as well. It was another mega-church, but this one was great because the pastor, Roy Raeburn, and his wife, Reese, took such a personal interest in the members of their congregation.

In Geri, at any rate.

Geri paused, for the first time realizing how winded she was, walking up the steep cobblestone cutbacks that formed the Patmos streets leading up toward the imposing building that was the monastery on the hill.

"Are we going to the Monastery of St. John today? Now?" she asked as she paused to get her breath. She noticed that the tall monk next to her was not winded in the least. But then, he must be used to the climb.

He smiled. "No. In the morning. But I did want you to see the island, to see the view, to feel the power."

She turned and looked up toward the tiers of square white houses behind which the fortress sat, daring time to challenge it. She heard no car motors, no radios blasting music, nothing to give her a clue that this was 2006, not 1006 or even 6. That was part of what made Patmos timeless.

"There is somewhere else I want you to see, however. If you're up to continuing our walk."

Geri stole a look at her watch. It was only 6:30! And she was not meeting Nestor for dinner until 8:00 P.M. "I'm fine," she said.

"So, tell me about *your* spiritual journey," she said to the monk. They began to walk once again, this time downward on the other side of the climb to the monastery.

"From early childhood, I knew I was different," he said, and then he laughed out loud. "Every time I say that, I feel like I'm about to say I'm gay," he said. "But I was *different* different. Not many nine-year-olds feel the call of God on their life."

Geri looked at him, remembering herself at nine, and felt once again at home.

THIS IS A GOOD DAY, thought Eric Carlson as he shut down the power to his amateur radio rig. His frail five-foot, three-inch frame seemed to grow and strengthen as he swaggered boldly over to a large world map spread over one entire wall of his bedroom. He jammed a green-colored pushpin on a tiny island in the South Pacific and stood back to proudly survey his handiwork.

Ever since he had heard about a remote American military installation on Johnston Island and the ham radio operator assigned there, Eric had been trying to make contact. Now, finally, he would receive one of the cherished "QSL" cards that would serve as proof of his radio conversation with that operator.

Yes, this was a good day. No, it was a great day! For tonight this 13-year-old would have his weekly radio appointment with his father, Dr. David Carlson, professor of electrical engineering at Oklahoma State University. He had introduced Eric to amateur radio and had helped him prepare for the required tests to obtain a license. His dual American and Swedish citizenship had qualified Eric for a license in either country, and he had chosen to apply for a license in the United States.

Eric had tested while visiting his father in Seattle, Washington, two years earlier and had surprised everyone by achieving the highest possible level, "Extra." Now, it was Eric's sole means of communication with his estranged parent. Mom would not be pleased, but she would never know!

The only thing that could make the day better would be if it were warm enough for Eric to explore outside.

Eric had seen very little of the estate where he now lived. Five months ago he had been bundled onto a small yacht for a short ride crossing the Lilla Värtan strait from Stockholm. But he was kept below in the cabin and could hardly see the landscape. Following a short walk from the dock along a path lined with birches on fire with fall colors, he had reached an elegant two-story home, surrounded by a stone wall. His new home. Soon after his arrival, temperatures had dropped, snow had fallen, and the home had become, for all practical purposes, his prison.

Extreme cold could set off migraine headaches for Eric, and during February in Sweden the winds could be bitter. But maybe before supper, it would be warm enough. He hadn't had a migraine in a week. Yes, perhaps today he could explore. It got dark so early that he couldn't go far, but the idea alone gave him a ray of hope.

A little hope each day was what kept Eric going. Hope for a new radio contact, hope for just a little excitement, hope for a pain-free day.

The headaches that wracked his body with unbearable pain were the result of a rare disease whose name he couldn't even pronounce. Understanding the microscopic cause behind this disease was well beyond his intellect. But this much Eric knew: The disease would significantly shorten his life span, the headaches would only get worse, and he might possibly rant and rave like a lunatic before all was said and done.

It was enough to depress even the wisest and most stoic individual. But Eric had not succumbed to the temptation for self-pity. His blue eyes sparkled with mirth, and his attitude toward life was more like that of an explorer than an invalid. Each day had potential, and he refused to become a prisoner to his health or his future.

Eric pulled back heavy window curtains. The dark was fast encroaching, but the outlines of the snow-covered birch trees near his window were not bending in brutal wind. Yes, perhaps, if he dressed warmly, he might slip out for a few minutes of exploring and make this the best of all possible days.

NESTOR SAT IN HIS FAVORITE CHAIR in the waterfall room of the *Gerianne* and gazed absentmindedly through the picture windows at the lights climbing the slopes of Patmos. He shook his vodka tonic and watched the ice cubes swirl as peripatetically as his thoughts.

In his mind, he played with the inevitable: What would life look like if humans lived 150 or 200 years? What would it look like to live forever? Would those who didn't invest wisely have to work for 200 years instead of 45? Would the planet become vastly overpopulated, or would they consign the great unwashed masses to certain third-world countries, almost like Indian reservations? Would the first-world countries, along with the clear skies, clean water, and sweeping vistas, be kept intact for the Immortalists?

Would you only keep your friends and loved ones who could afford the physical upkeep and lose the others to mortal death?

Would there be tragic accidents, human error perhaps, that would still cause the untimely loss of loved ones?

The joke was, sometimes Nestor himself had no interest in living forever. Sometimes he was just plain tired.

And yet there were other times, when the wine was perfectly aged, the women exciting, the deal closed. Those were what he called his Zorba days, and he thought fondly of his father and mother.

Nestor's father had taught him to grab life by the tail and hold on. For years Nestor had thought his mother had only played a small part in the molding of his character and his life philosophy; as a matter of fact, he thought she'd been holding back both his father and himself.

His mother, Athanasia, was a large, handsome woman, whose house was always full of life and love. Nestor knew whenever he came home he'd be greeted by friends, relatives, animals, and the smell of delicious home cooking. His mother was very devout and had a keen sense of justice. She often called on Chiron to "mold our son's character," which meant punishing Nestor for his wrongdoings. His father never questioned Athanasia's decrees, always meted out punishment when asked. Nestor was always whipped in the kitchen, in front of his mother, so she could be sure that the price had been paid. Afterward, his father would take the boy out "for a talking-to." When he was young, this meant his father took him out for gelato. When Nestor reached his teens, it meant wine and womanizing. One part of Nestor hated his father for cheating on his wife, but at the same time he admired Chiron for his way with, and enjoyment of, the ladies. Also, it was clear that the ladies loved Nestor. He was consequently spared the awkward "getting to know girls" stage that all the other teenage boys faced. For him, women were never something to be pursued; they were selected from the pool at hand.

But one day when Nestor was only 15, his father climbed a small ladder in the kitchen to get a bowl for his wife and keeled over from a massive heart attack, leaving Nestor to care for his mother and 3-year-old sister, Anna.

Nestor left school and began running the business. He had worked often for his father as a fisherman and boatbuilder. Nestor moved up and up, soon turning a fleet of boats into a shipyard. He was very proud of himself, and his family was doing very, very well, with the guiding help and advice of his uncle, who was the company's financial advisor.

Then, only two years after Nestor's father died, his little sister became ill with meningitis. Despite the best medical attention, she died. His mother, who seemed able to handle her husband's death, now went off the deep end. She became depressed and shut herself away, not listening to any of Nestor's pleadings to travel the world with him. She became reclusive and depressed, finally letting herself be committed to a psychiatric center. One of the last times she spoke was when Nestor came to plead with her to join him and enjoy his new wealth as a shipping magnate, to move into his new villa.

When she refused, he said, "What would it take? What would it take to make you want to live in this world again?"

"Stop death," was her only answer.

Athanasia became a hollow shell of a woman, never speaking, hardly eating. Nestor decided she had "checked out" and quit going to see her, in order to save himself.

Nestor lived the high life, enjoying wine, women, and song, though he soon found it was monotonous and not nearly as enjoyable without his mother's rigid morality to be acting out against. So when he found Geri, a woman with a sense of adventure, a belief in heaven and hell, and a willingness to punish her husband for his indiscretions, his life took on a new zest. Once again it was fun to "get away with" things.

Meanwhile, Nestor found a group of people working toward earthly immortality, found them to be scientifically very close to meeting their goal, and began funding them. What good was being rich if rich people's children and husbands died just like everyone else's?

He took to funding the most promising projects. Unfortunately, those who wanted to move ahead quickly often had to work outside the bounds of traditional science. Sometimes, as with this project that had finally met with success, he had to find creative ways to fund them. It wasn't that he was Teflon—or, these days, Calphalon—it was that he couldn't afford for his name or businesses to be linked at all. He didn't want to know what they had to do to produce results. He simply wanted them to make it happen.

Nestor sighed deeply and motioned for his drink to be replaced once again.

He seldom thought about these disturbing things; it was this time of day. When he was alone as day turned to dusk, the melancholy would overtake him.

He didn't even know if his mother was dead or alive.

But he did know he'd be alive—and perhaps forever.

AND THERE IT WAS. The scientist, smiling for the first time in days, stared at the new computer correlation. Subject Number 2 . . . the boy from New York.

Britta paused, frowning for a moment before hitting "save" and making a second copy of the results on her external hard drive.

She had purposefully avoided recalling the histories of the subjects, the background, home, personality, that made each a unique individual. These were reminders that they had families and lives and were missing all of that. It was much easier for Britta if she could focus on the label on a test tube or the number in a mathematical series. She needed to forget the faces of these very real, very human subjects of her experiment.

She turned quickly back to her computer screen, trying to refocus her thoughts. It had been the second variation, dropping that one subject and rerunning the correlation on the four remaining. The results had been amazing! She had never seen genetic markers in four different subjects match so closely.

Well, of course they didn't match everywhere. There were many areas of the genome having to do with physical attributes that she was sure would show a high variance. But the ones she studied, those markers she had tagged as responsible for the health and function of the mitochondria, were so close, they looked as though they were from the same person. These were the sections that played a major role in longevity, and Britta was certain she now had the genetic pattern that was representative of a very long-lived race of people.

It was incredible. This was the breakthrough they'd been seeking! Surely now Witgard would continue the funding and would extend the time she had with the subjects. He had to understand the small blood samples taken for genetic mapping wouldn't be enough. She now needed to replicate massive amounts of this DNA and test insertion of the new strands into other foreign mitochondria. Working with blood from the original sources was easily superior to trying to create new DNA from scratch.

Of course, this was merely putting off the inevitable. Britta had been told she had the subjects for three more days. FIA had never told her the plans for disposing of them, and she had not asked. She didn't want to know.

But in her heart, she knew. There was no way they could let these people live. It was too dangerous. It broke her heart to look in their eyes and see their fear, the despair. So she didn't look. She treated them like inanimate objects, hoping she could fool herself into believing they had no feelings. But that hadn't worked.

So maybe, just maybe, she could convince Witgard to give her a little more time. Maybe, with this breakthrough, she could give them more time to live.

Britta rolled her chair over to a second computer she used for administrative functions. She called up her e-mail program and composed a message to the address she had used so many times, hoping Witgard was monitoring his e-mail and would quickly respond to her message. She hit "send" and stood up to remove her lab coat. It had been a long day, and there was nothing more she could do. Time to go home.

FEBRUARY 25, 2006, 7:11 P.M.

SEVEN THOUSAND FEET ABOVE THE ISLAND OF ANDROS,

HEADING SOUTH

JAIME SAT IN THE co-pilot's seat of the Gulfstream 150 watching the lights flicker on in homes on the Aegean island below. After tracking Constantine to Patmos, they'd returned briefly to the safe house, where Yani had made a phone call on the scrambled line, picked up a few new electronic toys, and headed out. It felt good to have a direction, to be moving, to take steps to find the missing kidnap victims.

This time Yani thought it was safe for him and Jaime to travel together, and his motorbike was certainly larger than her Vespa. "We're heading for the Athens Airport," he said. "Want to drive?" And he'd thrown her the keys.

How could she say no? They wore their helmets with radio devices, so he could guide her through the busy streets and out of town. He sat close behind, his arms wrapped around her, which she could not forget for one minute, even in the midst of rush-hour traffic.

At the airport, the Gulfstream was waiting for them. She knew that there were boats, cars, and airplanes scattered about the globe, property of companies and organizations that were more than happy to let Eden Operatives use them when necessary. Yani filed his flight plan and came jauntily across the tarmac, his black bomber jacket and black shades below his curling black hair, all of which made him look hopelessly cool. A young Greek man was in the hangar, had the plane gassed up, took them aboard, and made certain they were ready to go. He shook hands with Yani enthusiastically and wished them both Godspeed.

"So you're a pilot?" Jaime said when the Greek gentleman had deplaned.

"You would hope," said Yani. "Here, help me with the preflight checklist."

"Why?"

"You'll want to get your pilot's license. It'll come in handy. Consider this your first lesson."

"Given this plane, you must be instrument-rated."

"Technically, I'm licensed as an Airline Transport Pilot, which means I'm also certified as an instructor. Lucky you."

He told her they were flying to Rhodes, where a yacht would be waiting to take them the rest of the way to the smaller island of Patmos.

The flight to Rhodes wouldn't be that long, and when they reached their assigned altitude, she could still make out lights below as they flew over an island in the midst of the pitch-black sea. "Hold course and altitude," he said. "Your plane."

She took the control yoke, acknowledging, "My plane," and he put his arms behind his head as if he didn't have a care in the world.

She wasn't nervous at all; in fact, she'd always enjoyed flying. She would certainly never forget the first time she'd gone up in a private plane. It was shortly after her family's Presbyterian church in Springfield, Missouri, had gotten a new pastor. The Reverend Anderson, who had been at the church since Jaime was a toddler, had retired and moved his family somewhere warmer. Mrs. Anderson had been a willowy, proper woman whose house was filled with fine china and who advocated the constant use of coasters. She had two willowy daughters who had both "come out" at the local country club and with whom Jaime had never felt she had much in common.

But six months after Pastor Kent had arrived, he'd invited 16-year-old Jaime to go up in his Beechcraft. Jaime's older sister Susan and her boyfriend had dropped Jaime off at the Kents' on their way out somewhere that clear late-April morning.

The difference between the Kents' house and the Andersons' was like night and day. First off, Jaime was greeted at the door by two mutts, one obviously part mastiff and the other part Chihuahua.

"Come in!" called a female voice from inside, and Jaime entered to find Mrs. Kent pulling on cowboy boots and getting ready to head in to her law office. The house wasn't exactly a mess, but it looked comfy and well-lived-in. There were no coasters to be seen.

"Oh, hi, Jaime," said Mrs. Kent. "I hear Ash's taking you up this morning. Good luck!"

"Yeah, nice knowing you!" said their 11-year-old daughter, Lexi, happily, as she appeared from the kitchen door holding a half-eaten egg sandwich.

"OK, kitchen's closing!" came Pastor Kent's voice. "This short-order cook is outta here!" And he appeared in the doorway just behind his daughter.

"Lexi, your ride's here!" called the older brother's voice from down the hall. He obviously had a front bedroom and a view of the driveway.

"Yikes!" said Lexi, and she grabbed her jacket and ran for the door. Her "love you!" ran into the same farewell of her parents.

Jaime and Pastor Kent were in the car next ("call me Asher," he said). Remembering that morning, Jaime knew that since all the abuse scandals, a pastor would never be allowed to take a teenage girl flying without chaperones, but that was then, when things seemed innocent, and most times, such as this one, actually were.

They rolled up to his Beechcraft where it was tied down at the Springfield airport. He parked on the grass and began instructing her on how to undo the tie-down cords.

"I still don't know why we're here," Jaime finally blurted when he opened the passenger door and they prepared for takeoff.

"We're here because when I mentioned that I owned my own plane at youth group last week, it was the first time I saw any light in your eyes since I've known you," he said simply.

Then he was on the radio to the tower, and they were taking off into the lazy blue of the sky, and somehow she did feel the slight warmth of her long-extinguished pilot light whooshing to life.

They flew over farms and streams and old cemeteries. They flew over horse farms and fields. "So why is that?" Asher finally asked. "What's happened to the light behind your eyes?"

Jaime stared at him again. He'd been at their church for six months. Had he not heard she was a poor little orphan girl, whose parents had died tragically yet heroically bringing medical care to refugee camps in Pakistan? Everybody knew that. It was her identity, everywhere.

"My parents are dead," she said.

"Yeah," he answered. "So are mine. Do you suppose they raised you to be brittle and shatter when tragedy happened? Or did they raise you to be strong and vibrant and alive, to help the world after they're gone? From what I've heard, they seem like the kind of folks who would have wanted to leave a positive legacy, not a trail of broken kids."

All of Jaime's rage boiled to the surface. It was obvious he'd planned this, even thought out things to say. "What's next? You're going to tell me that God needed another brilliant doctor for all the refugees in heaven, so he took my dad? And he needed a beautiful flower, so he cut my mom down in the bloom of health? Or that I must be able to handle it or God wouldn't have let it happen? Well, maybe I can't. Maybe I can't fucking handle it!"

Asher shot a look over at her. Instead of chiding her for her anger, her attitude, or her language, he said, "Who's been feeding you that bullshit?"

"Everybody," she said, tears pouring down her cheeks. "Basically, everybody." And to her own horror, she began to sob.

"Jaime," Asher said, "do you remember in Matthew, when Jesus' friend Lazarus dies? When Jesus arrives, he doesn't say to Lazarus' sisters, 'God needed the most handsome ficus tree, so he shattered your lives to take yours,' or, 'You'll see him again one day,' or even, 'Give me a minute; I can fix this.' No. What Jesus did, in the face of Mary and Martha's grief, and of his own, was . . . he cried. Jesus wept. And that's exactly what he's doing with you, right now."

Well, that was some sort of small help. That her pastor wasn't calling her an idiot for still grieving after a year and a half.

"Here's something I've heard, usually from Christian parents who have lost a child, but I bet it might be true for a child who has lost her parents, as well. You are given a rare and precious gift, which is this: You never again fear your own death. While most of the rest of us live day to day fearing our own death. Or at least struggling to 'store up our treasure in heaven' instead of loving the things of this world. But I'd guess your treasure is already there. It's no longer an issue for you. Do you fear your own death, Jaime?"

"No." She shook her head. "I wish I could die, now!"

"That would stop the pain," he said. "But it would also stop the beauty." As if to underline his statement, he made a swooping turn with the plane and headed over a winding river below.

"See, here's the thing," he said. "If you come to a time that you choose to let go of your pain, God will turn it inside out. Inside-out pain becomes empathy, and it becomes the greatest gift in the world for you to give to others."

"And you know this . . ."

"Because, as I said, both my parents are dead. My dad died of cancer, and my mom was killed in a convenience store robbery in Los Angeles. She had run in for a cup of coffee while getting gas. I can't think of anything that is more the height of senseless evil than that.

"What I'm saying, Jaime, is that your pain is shattering, and deep, and real. But if you can trust that God mourns with you in this, instead of being the cause of it, the transformation can begin. It's not something you do. It's something you hand over."

She was quiet. She was thinking.

"Here. Take the controls," he said. "I'll show you how."

Together they'd flown for another twenty minutes. It wasn't exactly busy airspace, and he let Jaime fly over her house and her school and her favorite park. And then they flew over the cemetery where her parents' ashes were interred.

"Look, Mom and Dad!" she said. "I'm flying!"

Asher grinned, too. And he said, "So, I also hear you're the only one in youth group who's not going to Glendale's Junior-Senior Prom."

Deflation.

"No."

"Why?"

"Just not."

"Don't have a date?"

"Don't want a date." She had liked this guy, begun to even think that pastors might be human, and now this.

"'Cause boys are idiots?" he asked. "Because, frankly, at your age, we mostly are."

"Because I had a boyfriend in Pakistan and that's why I got sent home from the refugee camp two weeks before my parents died!" she hissed. Man, she was speaking her mind today. "My boyfriend was Muslim, and my dad said it could cause an incident, but I refused to stop seeing him, and my father got mad and sent me home!"

"Whoa," said Asher. "How do we even begin to start unpacking that one?"

"Oh, I've already done it," said Jaime. "The last time I saw my parents, we had a fight. If I had backed down, or hadn't ever met this guy, I would have stayed with them. Likely my mom would have stayed in the camp with me instead of going on the trip with my dad, and she'd be alive. Or I would have gone along and died with them. And then I'd be a hero, too, and the school would have had an assembly and hired grief counselors, to help everyone who was freaked out that I died. Wow. I missed my chance."

Asher surprised her again. "You know, you have great wisdom for being sixteen. I think you have a great future ahead of you. That you'll help lots of people."

Hadn't he just heard what she said?

"So, let's get this. You're never going to date again because your dating either killed your parents or left you alive by mistake."

"Something like that," she mumbled.

"Well, teenage dating is certainly associated with strong emotions," he said, "but I don't think either one of us is going to sign off on it having the power to start monsoons or cause mud slides. Nope, sorry, you're going to have to get past that one. You personally can claim neither the credit nor the blame for your parents' death. You know that, right? In your head, at least, if not yet in your heart."

She was quiet for a minute. This was one of her favorite torture devices. Was she willing to give it up?

"Yeah, I guess so," she admitted, barely audibly.

"Good," Asher said. "Then supposing there was a guy, kind of cute, kind of fun, no strings attached, who would like to take you to the prom. Would you go?"

"What?"

"Just supposing."

"Who is it?"

"My son Luke."

Luke didn't have a date for the prom? Football player, drama guy, *senior* Luke? That seemed impossible.

Wait, was this a pity date his dad was forcing Luke on? How humiliating.

"Luke left a girlfriend back at his old school when we moved here. He's been very faithful to her. Really liked her. She dumped him a couple months ago, and he's having a hard time getting past it."

"And he would ask me as a favor to you."

"No, he would ask you because he thinks you're cute." Asher slid a glance sideways at her. "Not that you heard it from me."

So Jaime had gone to the prom with Luke, and he'd become a good friend. Well, a good friend who was a really good kisser. As much as anything, their relationship helped redefine Jaime to the other kids at school, and even helped redefine her to herself. She started spending as much time at the Kents' as at her own house, which her grandmother and siblings seemed relieved to let her do. And when Luke went away to college in the fall, she kept coming to the Kents', even without him there.

She and Luke had eventually gone their separate ways, but she'd always be grateful to him and to Asher, who had been a proud participant in Jaime's own ordination to the ministry.

Back in the Gulfstream, which was much larger than Asher's old Beechcraft, Jaime shot a glance at Yani. Maybe she'd remembered Luke for a reason. He had taught her that you can stay friends, be grateful to another person, even, without having to remain romantically involved.

But right now she and Yani didn't need to be friends, they needed to be colleagues, and lives depended on that. *Get past it,* she told herself. And yeah, it was fun to be up in a plane again. She would definitely get her license when this was over. Absolutely.

THE SUN HAD SET while Geri and Brother Timothy visited the Cave of the Apocalypse, where, according to tradition, John had been given the vision that became the Book of Revelation. Now the air had a biting chill. Geri pulled her sweater coat more tightly around her and watched the colors of the paper lanterns that caught the breeze over the outdoor café in the central square of Chora near the foot of the monastery.

Brother Timothy had said they'd order tea, but when the waiter asked if they preferred red or white wine, their eyes had met over the menu, they'd shared a flicker of a smile, and Brother Timothy had responded, "Red."

"Would you like to order dinner to go with the wine?" he asked her. "If so, I suggest the lamb casserole."

Geri shook her head. "I'm dining with Nestor on the yacht before I bring him to our hotel. He's finishing up some business—and our chef is both fantastic and underused."

"Very well."

The waiter had returned with their drinks. "Ah, Mykos, could you bring us a light sampling of hors d'oeuvres?" asked Brother Timothy. The waiter smiled and headed off with the order.

Geri raised her glass. The monk smiled and touched his to hers. "So you're allowed to eat outside the monastery?" she asked.

"I'm only a seminarian," he said. "I came here two years ago to help Father Chrysostomos catalogue the books and other antiquities in the monastery libraries, and, well, I'm afraid I became so involved that I haven't yet made it back to school. But that's all right—sometimes your calling in life isn't quite what you expect."

"So please," said Geri. "What is this Patmos Project all about? What can you tell me?"

"Let's go back a little bit," he answered. "What do you know about Patmos and the monastery?"

Geri hesitated. She looked down across the layers upon layers of twinkling lights as the whitewashed houses on the slope to the sea were illuminated against the gathering dark. She had done research on the monastery, and on Patmos, before they came, but she was afraid Brother Timothy was seeking a specific answer she might or might not have.

"Could you tell me what you consider relevant?" she asked.

He smiled gently. "Spoken like someone who is used to conversing with those who are both intelligent and slightly full of themselves." She blushed.

"As you know, Patmos—indeed, all these Dodecanese islands—have been inhabited for well over three thousand years. The Aegean Sea is surrounded by countries with thousands of years of written history. Whatever happened in the earliest days, the island of Patmos itself was not deemed important by the Romans when they conquered it more than two thousand years ago. In fact, they used it as a place to send prisoners—the most famous of which, according to tradition, was the Apostle John, the man whom many believe was Jesus' best friend.

"After Jesus' resurrection and his ascension to heaven, his disciples were scattered by persecution. In many ways, this helped spread the good news, the message of love. As you know, many of these once-fearful men were greatly empowered to repeat the words of Jesus. Many were killed for doing so.

"Tradition has it that the final time John was arrested he was one of the few apostles who had survived to old age. Since he wouldn't shut up, Roman Emperor Titus Flavius Domitianus exiled him here, to this forgotten chip of land. He was meant to live out his final days in silence and obscurity."

"Didn't quite happen that way." Geri smiled.

"No," Brother Timothy agreed. "It certainly didn't. According to tradition, John converted the other inhabitants of the island to Christianity, and then had the vision which would become the final book of the Christian Scriptures, the Book of Revelation.

"Since that time, Patmos became a holy island, the destination of many pilgrimages. When the Roman Empire was divided two hundred years later, the Byzantine Empire recognized Christianity. A fantastic basilica was built here to honor John and his vision. How I would have loved to see that basilica!"

Brother Timothy sat for a moment, his eyes far away, envisioning the grand and holy building of which he spoke. "But during the sixth to the ninth centuries, the island was often raided and the Grand Basilica of St. John was destroyed.

"However, there were those who felt called to rebuild. One of those was a monk named Arsenios Skinouris. In 1085, he was visiting the newly founded monastery on Kos, and there he shared his vision with the Reverend Father Christodoulos. Christodoulos immediately understood the importance of building the Monastery of St. John here on Patmos.

"Within fifteen years, the current Byzantine emperor had given control of Patmos to Christodoulos, and he and Skinouris began the monastery here where we sit."

Geri couldn't help but steal a glance up at the towering structure, black against the sky, that rose behind her. "I do know that by the end of the twelfth century the monastery was famous. The island was a monastic state. The monks even had trading vessels. The monastery has stood since then, although control of the island has changed hands. The island was even taken by Germany during the Second World War, wasn't it? Then it was autonomous until 1948, when all of the Dodecanese Islands chose to unite with Greece."

"You are quite right," the seminarian said. "Very good!" He poured himself another glass of wine from the decanter that had been left on their table. He took a sip and closed his eyes. "Here's where it gets interesting."

Geri leaned forward, her forearms on the small table. Brother Timothy crossed himself, an action that appeared as natural as breathing. But his next question wasn't quite what she expected.

"Tell me what your church—what Pastor Roy Raeburn—believes the Book of Revelation talks about."

"Why—just what it says," she said, almost in a whisper. "That time is so short. We're living in the end times! There are wars and rumors of war. Israel is a sovereign state. Earthquakes, famine, the euro—it's all happening! Reverend Roy believes that those of us who are true believers will be taken up, raptured, at any second! Then the final war here on earth will begin."

He had touched a chord with her. Rather than excitement, though, her face was clouded with concern.

"This frightens you?"

"I'm just . . . I'm just afraid that Nestor may not . . . that he may be left behind to suffer through the Tribulation. I've tried . . . I've tried to talk to him, to convince him not to support some of the things he supports, but . . . he doesn't listen. And I do love him. Honestly, I do!"

Brother Timothy did not respond. Instead, he drained his goblet and poured yet another glass of wine. Geri's own hand was trembling when she reached for the decanter, but he poured for her, his own hands steady, resting on hers, the strength in his hand calming hers.

"Geri," he said, "suppose I told you that you don't need to worry. Suppose I told you that you and your husband were safe. In fact, could be untouchable."

"What?" She looked confused.

"Suppose I told you that Reverend Raeburn's interpretation of Revelation is well-meaning but incorrect?"

Now she looked completely nonplussed. "I don't understand. You mean you're post-Trib instead of pre-Trib?"

Brother Timothy chuckled gently. "There's the genius. You keep people arguing about the merits of apples over oranges—and you can pretty well keep the entire grape vineyard for yourself."

"Brother Timothy, please. I don't understand. What vineyard are you talking about? Where is this vineyard?"

"This vineyard is the most important secret that John encrypted in his book of prophecy. But it's as plain as day if you know what you're looking for—and where to look. It's a vineyard that is only meters from where you now sit."

She grasped his hands. "Please don't speak in riddles. I need to understand what you're talking about!"

He leaned in closer to her. "I don't mean to speak in riddles. I know it's time you must return to your husband. But you're staying here, on Patmos, tonight, are you not?"

"Yes, of course, at the hotel where you met me."

"Then I'll meet you there in the morning. And please, don't worry. What I'm about to share with you is not some strange theological hiccup; it's something tangible and real, something you can see and touch. It's a message of great joy."

"You can't tell me—even a little?"

"The time is close. The mysteries of which John wrote—they are tangible, and they are here. They hold the answers you seek—and the answers your husband seeks as well."

"How early can you come tomorrow morning?"

"I must attend Orthros—in English, the service called Matins—but that is before sunup. When will you be up?"

"I'll be up and on the terrace by seven o'clock. Can you be there then?"

"Yes. Until seven o'clock, then. Let me walk you back to Skala. The roads are steep and can be treacherous after dark."

"Thank you," Geri whispered. She didn't know what tomorrow would bring, but she did know she trusted Brother Timothy. It was as if she were being rocked away by the tone he used when he spoke of John and of the secret at the heart of Patmos.

She left a large bill for Mykos the waiter. And she took the monk's offered arm as they walked together down toward the harbor.

THE COOL CLOTH did nothing to ease the throbbing in Eric's head. He felt as if a series of explosions were detonating behind his eyes. The darkness in the room did not help, either. With each burst of pain came a wave of nausea threatening to make him vomit. This migraine was one of his "doozies," and he had not seen it coming.

He had been so excited at the thought of venturing outside. Eric had convinced his nurse, a twentysomething bodybuilder type on loan from a Stockholm nursing facility, that he was up to an outdoor excursion. The nurse had even agreed it might be good for Eric and was preparing to accompany him outside when the first symptom appeared. He quickly got the boy to his bed and administered his Imitrex, but it was too late. The disappointment at once again being held prisoner to his health was almost worse than the actual pain in his head. Almost.

Adding insult to injury, his mother was standing by his bedside patting his arm with a pained expression and saying, "There, there," as if she were comforting a child. Well, he wasn't a child! And what he really needed right now was quiet, to focus.

In his quest for relief from frequent headaches, Eric had done research on methods for coping with pain. He had searched medical sites on the Internet and ordered books and audiotapes. He had tried a number of dietary variations, relaxation techniques, and mental exercises to manage his headaches. None helped.

Then one day a friend of his father's offered an alternative. Eric's father had begun taking him to a Lutheran church in Stockholm when he was a child. The pastor had come to visit Eric when he first became ill and begun to teach Eric some of the basics of meditative prayer. Eric was a quick study. He had a very mature sense of himself, his surroundings, and his future. That was what impressed the pastor most about his young charge, his acceptance that his stay on earth would probably be quite short, and faith that there was something much better waiting out there for him.

Ever since Eric's father had left for the States, the pastor had not been allowed back to see Eric. But that did not prevent him from practicing his meditation.

"Little me. Big God." He smiled to himself as he felt himself take a long, slow deep breath and let it back out again. The traditional mantra for meditative prayer was usually a single word like "love" or "hope," but Eric had chosen a phrase from a card given him by his pastor. "Little me. Big God."

Eric's breathing, which had been ragged during previous waves of pain, was now calm and steady. He no longer felt the throbbing pain in his head. Instead, he had a sense of another place, a beautiful place where his mind and body could find relief. He sensed love and care and warmth. Most of all, he sensed peace.

"This must be what death is like," he mused. He did not fear death. Instead, he saw it as an adventure, one that would bring him to a place of healing. His beautiful place.

"Little me. Big God." As his heart slowed and his muscles relaxed, the migraine medicine was able to make its way to the source of pain and do its work. Mercifully, Eric fell asleep.

JAIME LAY, feeling the constant surging of the waves beneath the boat, watching Yani sleep. The cabin was dark, with just a smattering of light filtering in from the hallway and none at all from the darkness of the sea that surrounded them.

Yani had piloted the plane from Athens to Rhodes, where they'd been picked up at the airport by two men, Aeolus and Costas, both of whom Yani obviously knew well. Costas would fly the plane to the island of Samos, the island that boasted the closest airport to the much smaller Patmos. Aeolus, meanwhile, drove them to the harbor and welcomed them aboard the yacht *Kairos,* which would carry them the five-hour trip by sea from Rhodes to Patmos. The *Kairos* would then dock in the harbor at Patmos, ready to take them the hour trip to Samos, and the airplane, by sea.

The yacht was 18 meters long, and she looked built for speed. Jaime and Yani boarded and went below. At the bottom of the short flight of stairs was a circular table near the galley. The lines were sleek and modern, the boat looked brand-new and welcoming.

Aeolus went straight forward to start the engines. At least Yani wasn't piloting the yacht also. Instead, Yani led Jaime into the small hall off of which opened three cabin doors. He opened the door to the master suite and motioned her through. He put down his duffel bag.

"This is the equivalent of a safe house," he said simply. He closed the door to the hallway and the room turned a murky black until her eyes began to adjust.

She watched him take off his windbreaker and shoes and sit on the bed. Then he looked up, as if surprised to see her still standing by the door. "You do know—"

"Protocol for a safe house, yes," she said irritably. "During an active operation, the Operatives stay together for safety."

"That, yes," he said, and he exhaled. "Mostly, what it means, Jaime, is this is your chance to sleep. And you need to sleep. We're in the midst of an urgent operation. We don't know when the next opportunity will come."

As he spoke, Yani had dropped onto the thick white duster on top of the bed, closed his eyes, and gone to sleep.

Just like that.

One thing Jaime knew about herself: Nothing woke her up like being told she needed to sleep. It hurt no one but herself, of course, she knew that, but she'd gone through God knows how many deployments more sleep-deprived than she needed to be.

And she sure as hell wasn't going to fall asleep here.

Finally, she took off her shoes and stretched out on the bed, willing her muscles to relax. Even with all that had happened over the last few days, and with all the complexities of what lay ahead, one thought emerged and kept swirling through her mind on an endless loop: *Did I blow it?*

When Yani thought she was a Messenger, he had welcomed her warmly. When he discovered she was an Operative, everything had changed. He had shut down completely, on both a personal and a professional level. He'd said he wanted her off the mission. Her inexperience—and the resultant incompetence—was a danger. To herself, to Yani, to those they were trying to save.

Dear God. She'd worked so hard. She'd made so many difficult decisions, taken so many risks just to get here, only to be rejected completely by the one person whose opinion meant the world to her.

And yet, when he thought she was only a Messenger, he'd welcomed her. He'd held her. He'd possessed her.

Had she blown it?

Yani wasn't the chauvinist type. He would be the last one to try to keep a woman "in her place," in a position subservient to his. So what happened?

He'd given up the greatest honor she'd ever known existed. He'd given up being a Sword. Was this somehow like the O. Henry story where the man and woman had each given up what they held most dear, only to discover that was what the other had counted on?

She had to get a grip. She was a professional, and she believed completely in the successful resolution of the mission which had been entrusted to her.

If only Yani hadn't held her. Kissed her. Claimed her.

He'd made it clear that to him, now, those minutes had never been. So be it.

As she listened to the steady chug of the motors of the boat, it occurred to her that now when she thought of Yani, she didn't usually think of him in terms of Paul, or what Paul would think, or how Paul would act. For years after her husband had been killed by a terrorist bomb on the Pedestrian Mall in Israel, she had measured all men, and her feeling for them, by the standard of Paul.

Now she wondered why she had to be attracted to men who could very happily live without her, or any woman. Was it their drive, their sense of purpose, that attracted her? Or was she just a masochistic idiot, who only fell for the men who had blinders on? Whichever, it took a lot to get her to let her guard down and fall in love. But when she did, she fell hard.

For idiots who apparently could turn their feelings on and off and drift off to sleep next to her on a bed without a second thought.

Lord, center me; quiet my mind. Center me; quiet my mind.

Jaime tossed as restlessly as the winter sea below. She thought she had been called to be an Operative. It seemed Clement, the wisest man she knew, had confirmed this. But Clement would also have known that Yani had given up being a Sword. And Clement had paired them on this mission.

Lord, center me; quiet my mind. Center me; quiet my mind.

Her mentor, Renata, had instructed her well about her first reentry. "Suddenly the world will seem to you a screaming muddle," she'd said. "You'll want to plant your feet and yell, 'All of you, slow down; be quiet! You must stop the foolishness before another child dies of hunger, before another man is unjustly tortured, before another woman is raped. You must stop!'

"But you can't stop and yell, and if you did, it would make no difference.

"There will be time enough to live your life as an agent of change. No, during your first reentry, you must narrow your focus. Concentrate only on the task at hand. Take it to completion."

The task at hand. The kidnapping of five people, two females, three males, all the children of former Eden dwellers. Who could want them, and why? And how come they were taken from the families that had emerged with Jorgen Edders?

It seemed Britta Sunmark was their best lead. But with only three days remaining of Jaime's four-day pass, there wasn't time to follow leads willy-nilly. If time was no object, Ms. Sunmark would certainly be a person of interest, to be found and interviewed. Hopefully she would be found within the next 24 hours and would either yield more information or be counted a dead end.

Dear God, it was hard lying here next to Yani. Jaime had spent countless hours trying to figure out who he was, and she felt no closer to the answer than she ever had been. But she knew what he was and what he stood for. And she knew he exuded a magnetism she had seldom encountered. As if he were a magnet and she were nothing but one out of a million iron filings, irresistibly drawn.

He'd treated her as an incompetent.

That fact alone helped her find her footing. Clement would not have sent her if she were. He would not.

Her focus needed to be entirely on the abductees. Her focus now was Daniel Derry. Did, whom she'd known since he was a lanky 11-year-old.

Did had always had a sense of humor, a feeling of moldability that neither his brother nor his sister had. They were each so accomplished, so polished, so sure of themselves. Daniel, by contrast, had been a bit awkward, a bit unsure, and entirely approachable. The others you admired. Daniel she identified with. She loved that kid.

She would find him. She would bring him home.

She stretched out again and began a guided meditation, meant specifically to relax her muscles. Even if she didn't sleep, she could rest.

She held the picture of awkward, completely lovable Daniel Derry in her mind. And she prayed herself to sleep.

SUNDAY

"JAIME, WAKE UP." Yani's voice was gentle.

"Jaime," he said again, shaking her shoulder, and she sat upright, getting her balance, pulling herself to consciousness.

She looked at him through the filtered dark and thought, *Don't be caught off guard by his tone. He only calls you Jaime because he knows Paul called you Richards. You told him that. For him, your first name is not a term of endearment; it's a term of differentiation.*

She noticed that the door to the hall was open; there were small running lights along the corridor. She looked at Yani. He had his windbreaker and shoes on.

"What time is it?" she asked. "Are we there?"

"Yes, we're at Patmos. It's about 4:45 in the morning."

She must have fallen asleep, after all. Jaime found her shoes, pulled them on, and retied them.

He was using a small flashlight the size of the fingernail on his thumb. "We're not putting on lights," he said, and she nodded.

"How do we get ashore?" she asked.

"There's a dinghy. Aeolus will take us. I've already been ashore," he said. "I've gone through whatever files are at the office building owned by Future Imagined and Achieved—FIA. I did find one mention of Britta Sunmark. It was on an empty manila file folder. Nothing in it. Not even a Xerox copy of her grant application. No trace of her relationship with them, or the project she's working on. Not in files, on Rolodexes, or on the computers."

"You were already there?" Jaime asked. "Why didn't you wake me?"

"I'm waking you now," he said. "The only thing I did find, on one of the back Rolodexes, was an address for our friend Constantine."

She looked down at the small scrap of paper he held with a street address and number.

"It's here on Patmos. Go see if you can find him before he leaves the house for the day."

"All right," she said, trying not to let her annoyance show that he'd already started the mission without consulting her. "Where are you going?"

"Back to FIA. I didn't have time to check all the backups on the computers, to see if the files had existed and been wiped or if the key information is kept off-site.

"It's dark enough that we can go in together on the skiff," he said. "But after that—"

"I know, I know. We won't be seen together at all."

"Especially here," Yani said, standing. "It's a small island."

THIS TIME, they woke him from a sound sleep. For a wonderful moment he had no idea where he was.

And then Daniel was awake, the two guards silhouetted against the open door to his room.

He tried to swing his legs around to sit up, but there was a weight on them.

He cleared his vision and looked down.

It was that baby.

"Come on!" The guard seemed unusually gruff. For some reason, Daniel became afraid. He tried to move the toddler, but she was sleeping and made a noise that made it clear that she was obviously objecting to the idea of being awakened.

"Bring her, too," said Lab Coat Guy.

"Easier to leave her," said the other guy.

"No, it wouldn't be safe." Daniel spoke without thinking. "I mean, this place isn't baby-proof. She could get in all sorts of trouble."

"Doc says bring her," Lab Coat Guy said, ignoring Daniel.

The second guard grimaced and reached down to grab her, but Daniel was quicker. He scooped her up and held her to his chest. She woke up, confused and cranky, looked at him as if ready to howl her objections. Then she saw the two men standing behind her, and she grabbed on to the material of Daniel's shirt with both hands and clung to him.

He struggled to his feet, trying to find his balance with the extra weight.

Lab Coat Guy grabbed Daniel's arm and jerked it forward. He started walking in front of them.

Maybe it was being awakened from a deep sleep that had scared him. Maybe these guys were acting like they always did . . . or maybe his time was almost up. He held the little girl closer. She smelled moist, not like she had a dirty diaper or anything, just kind of baby-sleepish.

He knew the short walk around the corner and down the hall to the lab by heart. The only point of interest, besides passing the locked, windowless door to the yard, was that he walked through the galley kitchen. He made a point of seeing what food items the guards had around that they weren't sharing. But this time something surprising happened as he preceded the guards through the kitchen and passed the locked outside door.

The door directly in front of him that led to the laboratory opened, and another burly guard came out. He was herding somebody also. This guy had short black hair and looked like he was old enough to be out of college.

The guards glared at each other as if this was a terrible faux pas. Daniel came to his senses quick enough to say, "I'm Daniel," as he passed.

"Jimi," said the other prisoner.

Lab Coat Guy shoved Daniel in the middle of his back hard enough that he stumbled and nearly fell. "Shuddup!" Lab Coat Guy commanded.

He opened the door to the lab and pushed Daniel and the baby through, then slammed it shut again.

The doctor lady was there. She looked stressed. "The boy first," was all she said.

Daniel took it as a hopeful sign that they hadn't killed Jimi and he'd just come from here.

Lab Coat Guy shoved Daniel toward the chair. "Can I go outside?" Daniel asked.

"What? It's too cold," said the doctor.

"You always let me," he said. "I have my coat. You give me your word."

"It's dark and cold," she repeated.

"You give your word," he said, standing, looking at that awful chair. "Please. It's all I have."

Now she looked like she was upset. "All right," she said.

The goon grabbed the baby away and shoved Daniel down. He caught himself on the arm of the chair and stood for a moment, trying not to cry. There was something so . . . *What does it matter?* about her response.

He carefully climbed onto the chair and positioned his arms and legs. For the first time, just the fact that Lab Coat Guy was tying him down made him feel so helpless, even claustrophobic. They could do anything to him, anything at all, and no one would ever know.

He looked over at the baby. She was squirming like crazy. It was all the guard could do to keep ahold of her. She saw Daniel look over, and thrust her arms toward him. "Nayal," she said.

But he couldn't help her. He couldn't even help himself.

The doctor came over, as usual, with the blood-drawing needle on a tray. She set it down on the larger tray connected to the torture chair. There were so many vials. What if he didn't have that much blood left? She reached across and looked at his right arm and its multiple puncture marks.

Then she picked up his left. It was also peppered with needle tracks. The grimace still hadn't left her face. She picked up the short rubber tie and wrapped it around his upper arm. Then she started thumping his arm, looking for any remaining possible vein.

Daniel looked away as she inserted the needle. For the first time, though, she couldn't find a vein. She didn't say anything. She thumped again. He started to cry.

She didn't bother to tell him everything would be OK.

He went somewhere else in his mind, tried to think about Jimi, who he was, what that meant. The doctor had found a vein, and she was taking blood and blood and blood. It was going on forever. It was never going to stop.

Daniel was beginning to feel sick, not only weak but nauseous. Just crappy. And his arm was burning. It hurt so much. Just when he thought it would never end, that the rest of his life would be pain and burning, she stopped. He kept his eyes closed. He couldn't move.

Someone undid his bonds, but he couldn't move. He felt like he was floating, but he was so heavy he couldn't move. Heavy floating.

"Get up!" yelled Lab Coat Guy.

Daniel didn't care.

The goon circled the chair and pushed at Daniel from the other side. Finally the two of them together had gotten him up, and Lab Coat Guy had tried to walk him across the room. It only worked for a few feet. Daniel passed out and slid to the floor.

When he came to a few minutes later, he was still in a heap on the tile. He heard the little girl screaming and crying, taking big gulps of air, then choking on her own tears. He wanted so desperately to hurt someone, to take her and go. But he could barely sit up.

She cried for a long time. And then she stopped.

The doctor lady came over to him then. She helped him sit up against a wall, and she gave him orange juice to drink. "Any better?" she asked.

He looked away. She nodded to the goons and they came and each grabbed an arm and made him stand up. Then one of them held him while the other one went over to the chair and undid the restraint that held the form of the baby. She was limp.

He walked over, and Lab Coat Guy started pushing Daniel toward the door.

"Give her to me," Daniel said, fiercely. The goon seemed only too happy to comply. He accepted the small bundle and pulled her to him with his right arm.

Then Daniel turned around to the doctor.

"You said I could go out," he demanded. "You gave your word."

The doctor said, "I think you'd better lie down for a while, then have some lunch. Then you can go out. I promise."

He still felt like crap. But he cradled the little girl—at least she was still breathing. And this time, he looked with interest at the other closed doors as he was taken back to his cell.

JAIME SAT IN THE DARKNESS, watching as Britta Sunmark's fiancé, Constantine, awoke in his small whitewashed house on Lefkon Bay and began turning on lights. First the bedroom light had gone on, then the bathroom light. The bedroom shades were drawn, so Jaime couldn't tell if he was there alone.

He apparently had showered and dressed, because when he appeared in the kitchen, his black hair and beard were wet and he was wearing jeans and a gray Henley. He turned on lights under the kitchen cabinets. She was surprised to see he had a professional-quality beverage machine, which made one cup of coffee, tea, or cappuccino at a time. She envied him for the time it took him to choose his beverage, pop the container into the machine, and turn it on.

Apparently he was alone. At least he didn't make a hot beverage for anyone else, and no one joined him as he moved through the living room to go out onto the small terrace overlooking the ocean. He held his mug in both hands and looked out over the dark Aegean while he sipped his morning drink.

In a moment he went back inside, got a pastry from the kitchen, and sat down on the living room sofa and had breakfast while reading what appeared to be a paperback novel.

Jaime sat comfortably, hidden from view by a stone wall across the street. She had already put a locator device on his scooter, so she wouldn't have to follow him too closely. She tried not to get antsy. It was all she could do not to go ring the doorbell and ask where Britta Sunmark was. There would be time for that. Just not yet.

At about 6:35, he got up, returned his plate to the kitchen sink, and disappeared back into the bedroom. When he reemerged ten minutes later, Jaime's eyebrows raised in surprise. He'd changed clothes.

He now wore a blue *anteri*—a monk's inner robe. It was of Greek Orthodox style, rather full in the waist, which he tightened with a cord. He didn't have the *skoufos,* the flat brimless hat, or the *exorassa,* the outer cassock. This implied he was either a seminarian or a novice and hadn't yet been tonsured and accepted as a full-fledged monk.

She shook her head. This made no sense. How could Britta Sunmark's fiancé be a monk? And why would a monk live by himself on Lefkon Bay? She didn't know what Constantine looked like—perhaps she'd been watching the wrong house!

But before she could start looking for house numbers to correct her error, the monk came outside, flung a messenger-style bag across his back, hiked up his cassock, and took off on his scooter.

Jaime took a moment to make certain she had him as a moving dot on her display screen. Then, after he disappeared around a bend in the road, she went over to his house. Her lock jimmy worked like magic. She easily let herself in through the terrace door. Whoever he was, he apparently wasn't overly concerned about either being robbed or having his stuff rifled through.

He had a small version of the typical Patmos house—rectangular, whitewashed, rooms divided from each other by arched doorways.

The first thing she found, on a kitchen counter, was a small stack of mail. It was addressed to Constantine Sozon. OK. This was the place. She glanced at her handheld screen, watching him drive farther and farther away. She didn't want to spend much time here when he could possibly be headed straight for Ms. Sunmark.

Jaime glanced around walls and tabletops for photos, saw none, went quickly into the bedroom—where he had made the bed—and pulled open the single drawer in the wooden bedside table.

Inside she found what she had been looking for. It was a photo of the man who had just left, with an unidentified woman. They were sitting, smiling in a café, leaning in toward each other. The woman had white-blond hair and looked as though she could possibly be a Scandinavian person named Britta. She was half a head shorter than he, or so it seemed, though they were both seated. Of course, it could be Constantine's sister or his cleaning woman. Or, if he was as friendly as the nurse's aide had implied back in Athens, it could be any female person between here and there. There was no way to prove it was Britta Sunmark. But it was the only photo Jaime could find. So she quickly scanned it into her handheld and replaced the original. Then she let herself out. There was no way to relock the terrace door, so she'd just have to hope he wouldn't notice.

She crossed the street and walked ten meters off the road to where she'd hidden her own scooter. Constantine was still traveling, heading south, just now passing Chora.

Fortunately, there weren't many roads on the island. It was still dark as she took off following the direction he'd taken.

OK, friendly monk with a fiancée, she thought, *show me what you're up to.*

THE SKY WAS WEARING the silver veil that signaled the coming dawn. Geri sat at a round marble-top table settled next to the terrace wall overlooking Grikos Bay. Nestor was still awakening slowly in their suite, but she had been up for hours. First she had slipped out onto their private terrace, just over the bay, holding her Bible. It had been too dark to read, but she had been happy to hug the book to herself and sit quietly at the small table, listening to the lap of the water.

This was where history had happened. There was something holy, right here on this island, and now she was a part of it. She envied John being here when the island was modest. It seemed so funny to her that when God spoke quietly to a holy person it was human nature to build a huge edifice atop the spot. What if they'd said, "This is where John had his vision. We're leaving the island pristine and serene so that others may come, humbly seeking their own experience"?

Instead, it seemed humans continued to worship other humans' experiences rather than making themselves available to have one of their own.

When the clock had crept past six, Geri had showered, dressed, quietly left her room, and come through the hotel out onto the restaurant terrace. There was a beautiful long open-air bar made of local stone. On the far end, the same stone continued as a horizontal rock wall with rock pillars on either end, which formed a sort of picture frame, with curtains open to profuse vegetation. Straight ahead was Grikos Bay, Tragonisi Island not far offshore.

She'd found the light switch that illuminated the bar and the rock walls. Then she'd sat with her journal in the winter morning air. A little before seven, a young woman from the hotel had found her there and brought out a pot of coffee and some pastries.

And then, at seven precisely, Brother Timothy strode through the door. Geri loved his confidence and exuberance. She loved that he strode.

He saw her at once and took the second chair at her table. She'd gotten a second coffee cup, and he gratefully accepted the steaming beverage that she'd poured for him.

"So tell me," she said.

He leaned and put his large hands over hers. He looked at her intently.

"I will tell you," he said, "about the wonderful thing I found as I worked, going through and classifying so many ancient artifacts, texts, letters, and scrolls in the monastery library.

"We talked yesterday about John's vision, what it meant, and the stupendous original monastery and basilica that was built here on Patmos—and which was destroyed.

"But what happened thereafter, and what John's vision truly meant, was passed on, like most history lessons, by men with an agenda. Men who will only reveal what they want you to see, and will slyly conceal the rest. Men who profit from these secrets, at the expense of people like you and me whom they keep in the dark.

"I don't believe these secrets were meant to be kept by an elite few. The world deserves to know what I have recently discovered."

Brother Timothy paused. He pulled a handkerchief from his pocket, wiped his brow, which was sweating, even in the chilly air.

Geri smiled at him, encouraging him to continue.

"A year ago I came to the Monastery of St. John to study some of the documents contained in their library. These documents were original letters written by the hand of Arsenios Skinouris, the monk who sought out the Reverend Father Christodoulos in 1085 to request assistance in rebuilding the Monastery of St. John here on Patmos. As you may recall, it was Christodoulos who was successful in getting the emperor to agree to the building of the new monastery. In fact, the emperor gave control of the island to Father Christodoulos.

"You can imagine how excited I was to find original letters written by Skinouris himself! Most of his letters talked about plans for the monastery, and even contained drawings and schematics for the interconnecting courtyards, chapels, and stairways.

"One of these letters, however, contained a theological treatise about the fall of Babylon and the dawning of a new heaven and new earth. He closed the letter with *Blessed are those who wash their robes, so that they will have the right to drink from the river of life and may enter the city by the gates.* I found the language and word usage familiar, and that night went to the passage in my Greek New Testament that closely matched the close of that letter. It was in the Revelation of John, chapter twenty-two, verse fourteen. Do you remember? It says: *Blessed are those who wash their robes, that they may have the right to the tree of life and may enter the city by the gates.*

"Of course, a monk from this monastery would naturally pattern his writing after his Patron Father, Saint John of Patmos! It should have occurred to me. There was nothing surprising in that at all. But I was intrigued by the slight change in the text, and wondered what might have caused Skinouris to alter it. Hoping for some clues, I began to search for other letters written by Skinouris. In doing so, I found scores of schematics in his hand, for the various levels of the monastery, and nothing more. However . . .

"While searching, I discovered a tin filled with documents saved when the Grand Basilica was burned to the ground by the Turks in the sixth century. These documents were notes and letters of the senior cleric at the basilica when the Turks captured the island.

"Now, here is where it really starts to get interesting. When these documents were placed side by side with the letters from the monk Skinouris, even my untrained eye could tell they seemed to be written by the same, distinctive hand. But this was impossible! How could they have been written by the same person some five hundred years apart? Surely someone had placed this tin of letters here as a prank, hoping some unsuspecting fool like myself would fall for the joke.

"But my curiosity got the best of me, and I am afraid I did something rather devious at this point. (May God forgive me!) I 'borrowed' a few of the notes from the tin, and one of the letters from Skinouris, sealed them in a Ziploc bag, and took them to the mainland without telling anyone or asking permission. There I found an expert in handwriting analysis. He assured me these must have been written by the same hand. My next step was lab analysis of the paper and ink from the notes and letters. The results? The notes from the tin were fourteen hundred years old, give or take a few decades. The Skinouris letter was nine hundred years old. The only logical conclusion was that the cleric of the sixth century and the monk of the eleventh century were one and the same!

"After finding a safe place to store the letters, I returned to Patmos. I had to discover the secret of this man who had lived some five hundred years, or more. *Can you even think such a thing is possible?*"

Geri was staring at him, her mind taking in what he was saying but reserving judgment. Of course she could think of such a thing. She heard Nestor and his scientists talk about it all the time.

"I began to study the schematics. Why was he so intimately involved in the plans for the monastery? Skinouros had sketched out stairways and courtyards with hidden doors and hallways that seemed to lead nowhere. Many of the sketches had special markings with no legend. An x here, a check mark there, but no description or explanation. He also drew many sketches of a laundry area deep in the basement underneath the chapel. Why would he be so focused on the place where robes and linens would be washed?

"I had to wonder. The story goes that the current monastery was designed to be labyrinthine, passageways and tunnels going nowhere, false passages, things like that—to fool the pirates and marauders. But . . . what if there was a plan behind all of it? What if some passages were fake—but others were not? What if something was being purposely concealed?

"Then it hit me. Return to the text of the monk's treatise. *Blessed are those who wash their robes, so that they will have the right to drink from the river of life.*

"The river of life, eternal life, fountain of youth, call it what you will, this man had discovered it. And who could this man be but the one to whom the angel first brought a vision of a new heaven and new earth?

The man to whom this same angel revealed the hidden location of the river of life, from which he drank, and lived for centuries as a guardian of its secret location. Saint John the Apostle!

"Geri, I know this sounds crazy, believe me. But does it really sound any more incredible than the other things written in John's vision? Just hear me out.

"Looking at all the maps that the holy man had drawn, it occurred to me that the river of life must be flowing deep beneath the bowels of the monastery chapel, and his schematics must reveal the key that will unlock the secrets hidden below.

"I now know this to be true. Parts of the vision which John had were not of some distant heavenly landscape at all—they were right in front of him, here on Patmos, as he wrote!"

The monk sat up and finally took a deep breath. "I'm not expecting you just to believe all this on my say-so. I've found it, Geri," he said in an urgent whisper. "As have those called before me. It's there. It's real. I can take you to it. You can dip your hands in the flowing stream. The river of life."

He sat for a moment, now in the full winter sun. He bent down to the knapsack he carried. And he carefully removed a gallon-sized Ziploc bag. He undid the seal and took out two documents. Both looked old. The types of paper were very different.

He put them down, side by side on the marble table.

Geri looked at the words written in Greek. The handwriting, as Brother Timothy had said, was very distinct.

And it was obviously the same.

"Oh, dear Lord," Geri breathed.

"Indeed," said Brother Timothy. He put his hand over hers once more. "Geri, as I said, I believe there's a reason you're here. And I don't want you to take my word for any of this. I want to show you. I want you to see it with your own eyes."

EVEN THOUGH IT WAS EARLY on a Sunday morning and none of his office staff was in, Witgard Villella let himself into the small square building that served as official headquarters of FIA in Skala. He often felt he slunk in on Sundays, because most of the year-round residents of the small island were Greek Orthodox and working on Sunday was not on the approved list.

He wondered what they'd think if they understood what FIA did. Or at least, what business they were in. He sometimes felt as though he was running the only scientific research foundation that supplied him with continual cliffhangers. Yet another fizzle or a Nobel Prize? Stay tuned until Tuesday. . . .

Witgard's college degree was in business, not science, though he felt he now understood enough about processes such as cloning and recombinant DNA to make informed decisions about which projects to fund.

The Sunmark project had made perfect sense. If she could isolate the strands of DNA that did not succumb to the typical, inbred breakdowns due to aging, so many diseases could be stopped in their tracks. If those strands could indeed be recombined with other mitochondrial strands, then anyone who could afford it could be assured a long, healthy life.

It was stunning to Witgard that science had come to the point where this could even be a possibility. And if it worked, he would hold the golden key to the information and the procedure. All who wanted to reach the blessed state, where the light switch that told their cells to start breaking down would not be flipped, would have to go through FIA. Which meant Witgard himself could not only live forever, he could do it in fine style.

He would no longer have to depend on convincing people like Nestor Allende to write another check. Witgard would have the ultimate salable commodity: eternal life.

There was the unfortunate wrinkle in Sunmark's research: The subjects were not willing participants. For the rest of his life, he would have to worry about whether there was any way, any at all, to link the kidnappings either to one another or to Sunmark and therefore to FIA.

There shouldn't be. After tomorrow, when everyone was taken care of, he would breathe much more easily.

As for now, once again, he would continue to clear out his hard drive. There was absolutely nothing in the FIA office that would link him directly either to Sunmark or to the hired kidnapper. He did need to be able to reach Sunmark by e-mail, but out of the hundreds of addresses in his computer, how would anyone know that "Rdvrdm4" was her? The letters were purposely random and the messages completely wiped after each transmission.

Nestor Allende, also, could never find out about the messier parts of the research. Although who knew what Allende would consider acceptable to be the financier of a world-altering breakthrough? Certainly countless thousands of people died each day for much less important reasons, many for no reason at all. The lives of these five would have served a much higher purpose than they otherwise would have.

They should be proud. They should be grateful, even.

Ah, well.

He booted up his computer to see if he had any news from Sunmark or any of his other grantees.

Enough with the cliffhangers, already.

He was ready to move into marketing.

"EXCUSE ME, do you mind if I take some sugar?"

"Sorry?" Geri sat by herself at the marble table, her mind miles away. She looked up to find a blond woman pointing at the rectangular ceramic bowl that held packets of sugar and sweetener.

"They brought me some tea but no sugar. Do you mind?"

"Oh. No, of course not." She held up the container.

"Thank you. Say, are you American also?"

"Yes," said Geri. "Are you?"

The woman nodded. "It's unusual to find other guests here during the off-season."

"I know," said Geri. "I'm here on business."

"I guess I sort of am, too," said the woman. "I'm clergy, so I would at least consider it a busman's holiday, if not completely work." She had sat down again, at her own table back against the large rock wall adjacent to the bar. There was no one else on the terrace.

"You're clergy?" Geri said, blinking. She'd been so lost in her thoughts it was taking her a while to land again back on planet Earth.

"Presbyterian minister." The woman smiled warmly. "Can I ask you a question? Don't mean to pry, but that monk with whom you were just talking, is his name Constantine, by any chance?"

"What? No. Timothy. Brother Timothy."

"I thought I must be mistaken. He looks very much like someone else. You know that feeling?"

Geri nodded yes. "So you've been to seminary?"

The woman smiled in a friendly kind of way. "Yes indeed."

"It's just—I'm wondering—I'm confused, actually. . . ."

"I can certainly understand this island could bring up interesting questions."

Geri looked again at the woman. She was thin but not skinny and had shoulder-length blond hair. She was 30, maybe? You could be a minister at 30, surely. Geri wasn't sure what her own pastor, Reverend Raeburn, thought of women pastors, but the woman seemed intelligent, open, and nonjudgmental.

Maybe it was safe to talk to her . . . hypothetically. Nestor certainly had no basis for theological opinions on all these issues.

Geri hesitated only another moment. "My name is Gerianne Allende. Would you mind if I came over?" she asked.

"Certainly not," said the American minister. "I'm Lynn. Shall we see if we can get another hot pot of coffee or tea?"

"Sure," Geri answered. Then she said, "Do you mind if I ask you a personal question?" She slid onto the wooden chair across the table.

"You can ask, certainly," replied the woman. "I'll do my best to answer."

"HAVE YOU EVER THOUGHT about how you are going to die?"

OK, this was one question Jaime hadn't expected. But the woman seemed serious about it and intense in her questioning. Jaime took a breath.

Jaime had heard the monk say he would be back, and by watching her handheld, she'd seen that he had headed straight for the monastery in Chora, as he'd said he would. So she had some time to talk with Geri, in hopes of finding out more about what was going on. "Well, I don't spend too much time thinking about how, because there's really no way to know. I have faced death several times. Some have been in terribly frightening circumstances, but despite the circumstances, each time I've felt confident that God was with me, to see me safely home." She looked at Geri empathetically. "Is there a reason you ask?"

"Here's the thing," Geri said. "For as long as I've known him, my husband has been preoccupied with death. Not with death, exactly—with *not* dying. Were you aware, for example, that only two centuries ago a human being's life expectancy was only half of what it is now?"

Jaime shook her head.

"But now we not only understand how you get sick—unseen entities such as germs and viruses—but we are decrypting the codes inside our DNA, the codes that make us susceptible to cancer or heart disease, or just plain aging. Soon—very soon—we'll have figured so much of it out.

People might be sitting here in a hundred years, chuckling and saying, 'Can you believe that only a hundred years ago we thought living to one hundred was unusual?'"

The attractive dark-haired woman paused, and Jaime studied her more carefully. She seemed vivacious and intelligent. Now, however, Jaime couldn't tell if she was excited or troubled. It seemed some of each.

"How about you?" Jaime asked gently. "How do you feel about facing your own mortality?"

"That's just it," Geri said. "I never have really faced it. Because, you see, I don't believe I'm going to die."

"Oh? How so?"

"Well, you don't, either, do you? I mean, you're a Christian, right? A Christian minister?"

"How would that keep me from dying?"

"We're going to be raptured," Geri said, in a breathless whisper. "Back in Phoenix, where we live, our church has a giant Apocalypse Clock. We're, like, ten seconds from midnight. It could happen any moment. We'll be 'caught up in the clouds' with Jesus. Reverend Raeburn preaches about it almost every Sunday. Jesus will come and take the believers with him, and those left on earth will face seven years of Tribulation, at war with the Antichrist. And it's all happening, just as John said it would, in Revelation. There are 'wars and rumors of war.' There are earthquakes and famines. Believers are being persecuted. The euros. The giant tsunamis. It's all happening, right here, right now."

"And because you're going to be raptured, you don't really have to worry about dying."

"Yes. Although, of course, my husband doesn't understand. I've tried to broach it, tactfully. . . ."

"There are very few tactful ways to broach not being among the elect."

"I know." She looked crestfallen. "But I do love him. And I know he's a good person. He even says he's a Christian."

"Is there something specific that is bringing this all up for you just now?" Jaime asked.

"I've been talking to this monk . . . well, you know—Brother Timothy, the man who was just here. My pastor, Roy Raeburn, put me together with him, I'm fairly certain. But Brother Timothy says there's a different interpretation of the Book of Revelation. Much different than the interpretation Pastor Raeburn preaches every Sunday."

Jaime took a sip of her tea and grimaced. She'd forgotten she'd put sugar in it, since that was the only ruse she'd been able to think of to open a conversation with Constantine's friend. "It's cold," she said, and dumped the small amount remaining back into the foliage, hoping the plants didn't mind as much as she did. "Would you pour?" she asked Geri, since the pot was sitting on her side of the table. Her new acquaintance reached across to pour her another steaming cup. Jaime hoped Geri didn't notice that her condiment preference had changed.

"So you've never worried about dying, because you know you'll be raptured."

"Yes," the woman admitted. "Although, the threat of being raptured, well, I shouldn't really call it a threat, should I? Anyway, knowing you'll be raptured at any time can make you nervous. And, worst of all, knowing of all the people you love who will be damned if you haven't managed to convince them. I mean, if they haven't accepted . . . oh, you know."

Jaime stirred her tea, although it was sugarless this time.

"Geri," she said gently. "It might actually comfort you to know that Reverend Raeburn's interpretation—the idea of a rapture, of all the Christians magically being whisked off the Earth, then seven years of Tribulation, then another sorting—that is actually *not* traditional Christian theology. Although it's been popularized, especially lately, by novels and movies, and sermons, it's not accepted by either Catholics or mainline Protestants as the correct reading of the prophecy in Revelation."

Geri looked at her as if she'd been shot. Jaime realized Geri had probably been expecting her to agree heartily with Roy Raeburn, bless his heart, and denounce the unmet Brother Timothy without even knowing his proposition.

"Rapture theology was started only about one hundred and fifty years ago in Scotland, by a preacher named John Nelson Darby. His new theology was that Jesus would return twice—the first time to 'beam up' all the Christians, and the second time to destroy the world after 'picking up' the folks who finally got it right and fought the Antichrist. But that scenario isn't in Revelation; in fact, you've got to pick and choose verses through the rest of the Bible to cobble it together.

"And, despite what you may hear and see in today's media, most mainline Christian denominations still don't go along with it."

Geri sat staring at her. Finally she said, "You're making this up, right?"

Jaime smiled. "Where God's love, and basic Christian theology, is concerned, I try my best not to make stuff up."

"Does Pastor Raeburn know about this?"

"I'm sure he does—that is, he ought to. It's not a secret. The notion of a 'beam-up' rapture gained foothold because a commentator who agreed with Darby named Cyrus Scofield published a popular study Bible with notes in the margins linking all those disparate verses, and treating dispensationalist theology as if it were accepted by the Church. Many folks thought if they read it in Scofield, it must be right. But why are you asking about all this now? What is your friend Brother . . ."

"Timothy."

"What does your friend Brother Timothy believe about John's vision?" She hoped she didn't sound too eager to get to what was going on with the unusual monk.

"He has a different interpretation also."

"Does he live here on Patmos? Brother Timothy?"

"What? Oh yes, he works in the library at the Monastery of St. John in Chora."

"Is he one of the monks there?"

Geri still seemed distracted, but she said, "No, he's a seminarian. But he's very involved in helping catalogue things in the library, as I said. It has interrupted his studies. I'm sorry, I don't mean to be rude, but I need to talk to my husband before Brother Timothy returns to take me to the monastery."

"Of course," said Jaime.

"It's been nice meeting you." And with that, Geri disappeared without revealing anything about Brother Timothy or what he'd been talking to her about.

Shortly thereafter, Jaime picked up her things and ducked back into the hotel also. She had rented a smaller room than Geri's, but it would make a good home base and would keep Jaime near the center of the action. She didn't feel the need to go under "deep cover," but there was no reason to broadcast her presence, either. That was why she'd identified herself to Geri by her middle name, Lynn.

Once back in her room, she dropped onto one of the brown carved chairs and turned on her handheld, scrolling to the correct screen. There she could plainly see Constantine's—OK, Brother Timothy's—scooter parked at the monastery in Chora. She could see Yani in Skala. And the more sophisticated listening/locator device she had planted on Geri was apparently working, too. It pulsed gently very nearby, likely in her room here in the hotel.

Jaime couldn't help but smile for a moment. For although the stakes were high and the clock ticking, it was worth taking just a moment to enjoy being the one who had the good toys.

DANIEL SAT HUDDLED against the wall by his bed feeling crappy. Any air of adventure this situation might have had was gone. The guard had brought him breakfast, and he'd forced himself to eat the toast and drink the orange juice. He still felt sick, and weak.

Worse, the baby had been unconscious for a couple of hours after they'd returned. Daniel had fallen asleep, it just seemed the best way to deal with the overwhelming horror of it all, but even after he'd awakened, he hadn't been able to wake the baby. They had brought her a bottle when they'd brought his breakfast, but she was still unconscious, her breathing shallow.

He'd held her and rocked her in the rocking chair for a long time, trying not to think about what the morning's activities meant.

But he knew.

He knew that the doctor lady wouldn't take that much blood unless the supply wasn't going to continue to be available. She'd been stocking up.

She'd taken so much blood it had made him sick, and it had nearly killed the baby.

After he'd rocked the little girl for 20 minutes or so, she'd finally opened her eyes and looked at him. She'd looked so confused. He'd picked up the bottle that sat on the floor by the rocking chair and held the nipple by her mouth. It was when she finally started drinking that all the fear he'd been squeezing down got out, and he'd started crying.

He'd thought she was going to die, right there in his arms. It wasn't loud crying, only tears running down his face, but he knew Zeke wouldn't have cried at all. It didn't matter anymore. What Zeke thought or did, didn't matter anymore.

Daniel had to face the likelihood that he'd never see Zeke again. He was on his own.

Well, sort of.

He had seen that guy in the hall. Every time Daniel had been taken to the lab, he'd passed all those closed doors. He'd never stopped to think who was behind them. But there was at least one! One more prisoner, like him. One guy who looked older and capable and maybe able to help them get away. What did he say his name was?

Jim? Jimi?

Time was getting really, really short. Daniel had to find a way to reach out to Jimi. They couldn't just passively await their fate.

Daniel had to do something.

He *would* do something.

NESTOR LOVED IT WHEN Geri wanted something. Partly because he enjoyed being the provider. Partly, too, because he enjoyed having the power to grant or deny her petitions. Partly because she was so cute when she begged. And partly because she was so predictable.

Today she wore black slacks, a white open-collared shirt, and a blue designer sweater. It fit well and looked attractive, yet would be suitably modest to be worn up to the monastery, where she'd said she was going today.

He was going back to the yacht to work. He pulled on a blazer. Nestor had hated dressing up as a kid, hated wearing suits of any kind, but now he felt uncomfortable, even on casual days such as this, without some kind of jacket.

His wife was sitting on the sofa in the living room of their suite, consternated, not knowing quite how to be the one with the potentially unbelievable line of conversation. "So, supposing I did agree with you that somehow . . . possibly . . . potentially . . . there was a way to live, if not forever, for several hundred years . . . in our current bodies?" she asked.

Nestor looked at her, one eyebrow raised.

"But if it wasn't in the way you expected?"

"Changes that are large, and important, seldom do happen exactly as expected," he replied. "That part wouldn't be important. But, darling, keep in mind that while I wouldn't mind if it were unexpected, it must be real. It must be able to be proved scientifically."

"Why must everything be scientific?" Geri burst out. "Can't it just be real? Isn't that enough?"

"Then don't be upset. If it's real, it can certainly be proved."

"Sometimes you have to go with faith," Geri said.

"I have nothing against faith," agreed Nestor, checking his watch. "Unless it entails someone asking for money—specifically my money. Or unless it entails risking my health—or yours."

This didn't calm her. His usually implacable wife was still clutching and unclutching her hands and running her hand over the top of her head and scratching the hair energetically in back.

"Well, whatever has brought you here, whatever you're checking into, you're a very smart woman. I don't believe anyone will be able to hoodwink you. They haven't as yet." He chuckled. "Now, I believe my car's out front. As you know, I have some important work that needs to be done this morning in my office on the yacht. Whenever you're done with . . . whatever it is you're doing, give me a call. We can do a bit of exploring here on the island, or else have a pleasant dinner on board, or even island-hop."

Geri stood and Nestor put both hands on her shoulders and kissed her eyelids. "Have a productive day, my faith-full one," he said. And he headed out toward the front drive.

JIMI AFZAL SAT ON HIS plain metal bed, knees pulled up to his chest, leaning his back and head against the cold wall. Cupped in his hand was the business card he pulled out of his pocket once a day. That was all he allowed himself . . . once . . . otherwise the frustration was unbearable.

On the front of the card, in raised gold foil, was the name *Ian H. Rachmann,* followed by *Executive Editor, Golden Rachmann Publishing.* On the back was scribbled in Jimi's own hand: *Mon., Dec. 5, 9* A.M. This card was his lifeline, because it was the only connection Jimi had with the life he'd known before this unending boredom, the unending darkness and frustration.

As each day passed, and he pulled out the card once again, Jimi felt a little more hopeless. How long had he been here? He had been so intent on keeping track of the days when he was first kidnapped but eventually grew weary of that, especially after Christmas Day. That had been horrible, realizing what day it was, wanting something, anything, to brighten his favorite holiday. But no. The endless routine, the food, the tests, the attitude of the guards . . . nothing had changed. It had been a day just like any other in this horrible purgatory. And each day since had been pretty much the same.

Jimi carefully placed the card back into his pocket and lifted his feet, stretching out fully on the bed. Supposing he never got back? Supposing he was going to die here?

His parents had always been very emphatic with him about being grateful for each day, living each day fully, as if it was your last. But he'd been a driven kid. He wanted to dream, to plan, but also to *do*. He wanted to be a full editor at Golden Rachmann within three years, work toward his own imprint either there or somewhere else, and have his own publishing company by 35. With all the changes in the publishing world, the ease of electronic printing and e-books, it was a whole new world. Completely possible.

He wanted to publish books that contained ideas, that started conversations, made the world a better place. He wanted to make a difference.

If he died now, had he? Had his life made a difference at all?

He had planned to be married in his mid-thirties. He didn't want to have to worry about supporting a family until then. But because of that, he hadn't ever had a serious romantic relationship. That would be one loss, one thing he'd do differently.

Who would miss him? His parents. His friends. He did have good friends.

And yet who besides them would mourn what the world might have become, had he been allowed to live?

As he stared up at the ceiling, he tried to occupy his mind by working through the content of the first series of books he planned to write. Would the professor still be willing to work with him? Would Mr. Rachmann still hear his pitch?

This kind of distraction usually worked for him, but today he found it harder to concentrate. The incessant knocking of the hot-water pipes overhead was really irritating. There must be a lot of air in the system, because it seemed worse than usual. Or, maybe this was some kind of new experiment, messing with him mentally . . . him and the other lab rats they seemed to be holding here.

The more he tried to ignore it, the more he couldn't help but focus on the knocking. Soon he realized this was not simple air in the pipes; it had a pattern. Air bubbles are random; they don't have patterns. He stared at the pipes above his head and realized they traveled through the wall into the next room, probably running the length of the building. As he paid even closer attention to the knocks, he started to pick out a pattern. The first set was all very fast knocks, each set having one more knock than the previous. One knock . . . two . . . three . . . up to ten. Then the knocks were slower, once again one, two, three, up to ten.

Then it changed to a combination of one slow knock followed by the quick ones. First one quick, two, three, up to six. There was a long pause; then the entire series started all over again.

Could this be the kid with the baby he had met in the hall? Some sort of code? Jimi added them up, realizing there were twenty-six variations. The alphabet, most likely. He didn't know Morse code, but he didn't think this matched with that. Probably something the kid made up. It was not easy to follow, especially when the fast knocks reached eight or more, but it just might work.

Two more repetitions through the series and there was a long pause. The next series did not follow the original pattern. Four quick knocks, pause, one quick knock, pause, four long knocks . . . Jimi was losing track now; he needed to write this down—what would four long knocks be, the fourteenth letter of the alphabet?—while he was trying to figure this one out, more letters were passing by.

Slow down! he thought. If he had the code thing right, the first two letters were *d* and *a*. And the third would be . . . *n*. Dan. The kid with the baby, he said his name was Daniel. That was it! But how should he respond, and with what? He grabbed the spoon that had been left with his breakfast and stood on his bed to reach the pipe. The next time the knocking paused, he started tapping.

Ten quick taps. Pause. Nine quick taps. Pause. Three long taps. Pause. Nine quick taps. He waited a bit, then repeated the series.

He stopped and waited. Soon the response came, very slowly. *H-i* pause J-i-m-i.

Jimi sat back down on his bed. His world had now become larger, and a ray of hope brightened the day.

JAIME SAT BACK on the terrace, watching the full sun now over Grikos Bay. For someone like her, who had grown up in Missouri— landlocked—it was amazing to realize that some people had the sea to gaze on every day of their lives. She wondered what that would be like, how it would inform your relationship to the world.

The young woman tending the hotel desk on this off-season day felt it was unacceptable to have Jaime sitting there eating nothing, so she'd delivered a plate of fruit and goat cheese. Jaime had never realized that work as an Operative could offer so many opportunities for food. She very much enjoyed watching the local fishermen go about their morning business. What she was really doing was waiting for Geri.

Geri had told her that she was to meet Brother Timothy at the monastery at 10:30 A.M. When Jaime had mentioned she was planning to explore Chora today as well, the two women had made a plan to walk up together.

Jaime knew from surreptitiously watching her handheld that Geri was still in her hotel room while Constantine/Brother Timothy was already up at the monastery.

This all continued to be frustrating. Could it be that the elusive Britta Sunmark was right here on Patmos? Jaime and Yani knew Britta had applied for a research grant from FIA, which was based right here. Yani had found an emptied file with her name on it in their offices. Ms. Sunmark had been working with Jorgen Edders for several years before his death, had power of attorney for him, and had disappeared soon after his death, and after writing the request for the research grant.

The nurse's aide had said Ms. Sunmark had a fiancé named Constantine, and FIA had a name and address for Constantine, right here at a place where his mail was delivered.

But what it all led back to was those five kidnapped kids—two of them in their twenties but really kids just the same. Could Jorgen have somehow compromised their identity to Britta? Yani had said that Operatives had interviewed the parents of each of the victims, and all seemed perplexed and saddened by the compromising of their group. It seemed extremely unlikely that any of the parents from that group had given away the identities of the others. However, if Edders had died of a brain tumor, it could be that he had not been fully cognizant of what he was saying at all times—due either to his physical condition or to the drugs he'd been given to combat the pain.

Could the kids be here on Patmos?

She hoped Yani would be able to find more information on the hard drives of the computers in the FIA offices. He was trained to find ghost information that users thought they had erased from their computers. There had to be something more substantial to tell what Ms. Sunmark was up to and where she was.

Jaime wondered if Yani had given her the "babysitting" assignment while he'd taken on the avenue of exploration most likely to be fruitful. Of course he had. Sure, he'd given the speech about having confidence in her back at the safe house in Athens, but he had to say those things or they wouldn't have been able to work together.

He'd shown his true operating procedure this morning on the boat: He went and did, then came back and reported to her, giving her instructions. For the easier jobs.

She looked at her handheld and was able to see him in Skala. What was he up to?

It helped that all gardeners who had entered the Terris world had permanent tracking devices. If she'd had the proper security clearance and "need to know," she could have found any one of thousands of people throughout the world.

As it was, she had Yani. Lucky her.

She knew she also turned up as a flashing dot on Yani's screen. He knew where she was, sitting here on this terrace in Grikos. In fact, the only time Yani had lied to her was about a tracking device. Well, it hadn't been a lie at the time. When he had gotten her to agree to let him insert a locator device shortly after they'd met in Iraq, he promised it was harmless and would become benign in a few days. Then, knowing she would be invited to Eden—and knowing the insertion was painful and not something you'd want to repeat—he'd made a snap decision to insert a permanent device instead so she wouldn't have to undergo the procedure again.

Was it thoughtful on his part or just another example of his arrogance?

She'd also discovered, to her chagrin, that his success in this process had served to enhance his legend at Mountaintop. Usually an insertion required a half-day stay in a sterile surgical suite. He had managed to convince her—by using a deadly headlock, thank you very much—and complete the procedure in ten minutes in a dusty desert environment.

What a guy. Although dropping her pants for Yani was not exactly what she wanted to be known for.

But they *had* worked together well three years ago, when she'd found out through a baptism of fire that she was his "backup" on a difficult assignment in Iraq during the opening phases of Operation Iraqi Freedom. Nothing like having to negotiate travel through a country at war.

Helping him had gotten her kidnapped and nearly killed. It had gotten Yani's sister Adara murdered. It had changed Jaime's life, in many ways, not all of them bad.

As she pondered this, the cell phone in her pocket vibrated. It was another of her "toys"—it looked and operated like a normal cell phone, but it was, in fact, an enhanced satellite communications system, complete with filter and security fill, so that conversations could not be picked up by other interested parties.

"What are you eating?" Yani's voice was casual. He was speaking in his American accent.

"Some figs. They're tasty. Want me to save you some?"

"No, thanks, I was able to catch a bite here on my own."

"Are you back inside?"

"Just got in. There's been company, but this guy—his name is Villella—finally vacated the premises. Were you able to find the address?"

"Yes, it's way out overlooking Lefkos Bay. It was the correct current address, mail delivered for Constantine. However—get this: He left dressed as a monk named Brother Timothy. He met with a woman at the Petra Hotel on Grikos Bay. They had an intense conversation, and he's meeting her at the monastery to show her something."

"That's odd."

"Extremely. The woman, Geri, and I are planning to walk up to Chora together. I'll follow him once we get there. What surprises me is that it's a small island and the monks at the Monastery of St. John are no fools. If it's really Constantine, he has to be playing the dual identity pretty close to the chest."

"Do you think it is him?"

"I suppose the real Constantine could be off on his honeymoon with Ms. Sunmark and his cousin the monk is house-sitting. But somehow I doubt it. I only hope this is getting us closer to Britta and to the kidnap victims."

"There's enough evidence that Sunmark and Constantine are linked that I think we should pursue it to the next level. There has to be some way to discover her location, through either FIA or her fiancé. Let me take one more look here in headquarters, and you figure out just what Brother Timothy is up to. Then let's reassess. It's very odd that a research company would have no files on any of its projects at its headquarters. There's nothing. The office security isn't even very tight. My guess is there's a separate facility and that it's nearby. Otherwise, there would be no point in maintaining an office here."

"Got it." As they spoke, Jaime glanced at her handheld. "They're moving."

The dot on the screen told her that Geri had left her room and was heading toward the terrace where Jaime sat.

"OK, here she comes," she said. "Let's see just what's happening up in Chora."

"Be safe." The phone went dead.

You, too.

Jaime looked across the island, at the huge fortresslike monastery rising before her. It was going to be an interesting day.

"WE'RE GOING TO NEED to be quick."

Geri sat with Brother Timothy in a courtyard between the monastery's kitchen and the refectory, where the monks would all eat within the hour.

"There are two local workers in there now finishing up, as Brother Stasis, the cook, is at mass," the monk continued softly. "I know this is strange, but when those two workers come down, bringing food or water into the refectory, you and I are going to go in through the kitchen, to the steps in the back of the room." He took her hand. "I don't like to sneak around, Geri, but there's no way to explain to the workers why a seminarian would be bringing an American Protestant woman down to the lower level. It's best for no one to ask."

She nodded her understanding.

Geri had wanted to lose herself in the timeless feeling of the monastery: the chanting of the monks, the bittersweet aroma of the incense, the archways, walkways, and courtyards all made from local Patmos stone. Together with the five old iron bells that hung above— two above, three below—the arches and architecture had the power to make time disappear.

Instead, after arriving at the top, main entrance to the monastery, Geri had followed Brother Timothy quickly down a covered walkway, past the main chapel and the museum, and up several stairs into this open-air courtyard.

It wasn't long until a couple of men dressed in black pants and white shirts did indeed exit the kitchen, one carrying a half-dozen long loaves of bread, the other carrying two heavy pitchers of water. Both men nodded cheerfully at Brother Timothy and continued across the courtyard and disappeared into the refectory.

"Come." Brother Timothy stood and strode across the courtyard and up the few steps to the kitchen. Geri followed quickly. She had barely a moment to look around the large stone room, which was filled with scents of cooking. Tall pots sat on professional-caliber stove burners, and chopping blocks still sat covered with onions, carrots, and celery.

Geri found herself responding to the whole atmosphere. She imagined herself in a nun's habit, quietly cutting and chopping, making soup humbly, for the rest of her days.

But Brother Timothy had not stopped. She hurried after him across the stone floor. In the back of the room, a rectangular opening in the floor revealed a stone staircase descending against the back wall. A wrought-iron banister led down. Brother Timothy had already disappeared below. Geri thought she heard the voices of the two men coming back as she hurried down behind him.

He stopped at the foot of the staircase. There was an electric light switch on the wall, but he didn't flip it. Enough light filtered down from the kitchen that once her eyes adjusted, Geri could see well enough.

Against one wall stood two large, modern professional washing machines and two large dryers. Against the opposite wall ran a long stone trough. A small, steady stream of water ran into it from above.

"The laundry," she said softly.

The monk nodded. "The thousand-year-old laundry," he whispered in return. "This is the room Arsenios Skinouris so labored over in the plans. The water there comes from a natural spring. It's always flowing, always moving."

Geri looked at it and dipped her hand into it. "It's cold," she said with a shiver.

"'Blessed are those who wash their robes, so that they will have the right to drink from the river of life and may enter the city by the gates.'"

He headed across the darkened room, toward a wooden door, its top rounded into an arch. She followed him across. He stopped in front of it. She found she could hardly make out his face in the shadows.

"I do not know why you have been called to be here," he said. "It may be you have either wisdom or some sort of resources, either spiritual or material, that is needed at this time. I don't know. You will see if the Lord speaks to you. All I know is that I am to bring you here."

With that, he opened the ancient door. Outside the door, in iron brackets on the wall, were two torches, the kind Geri had seen in paintings from the Middle Ages. He lifted one out of its holder. The base was nearly a yard long. She didn't know what was on top, but it leapt to flame with the touch of a lighter that he'd produced from beneath his cassock.

"Come," he said.

She stepped into the dark tunnel, and he closed the door firmly behind them.

WHOA! THIS IS SO COOL, thought Eric as he wandered down the path through the deep woods. He wished he'd been able to explore it weeks before.

An hour earlier, he'd dug through his dresser, layering long underwear, a T-shirt, and two sweaters underneath his ski bib overalls. Over the top went a hooded parka and Moon Boots. The finishing touch was the thickest pair of gloves he could find. The resulting effect was that he moved more like a robot than a teenage boy but felt warm and toasty as he walked on this crisp, clear morning.

Eric gave himself an hour to explore the estate. Any more and he risked being found out. So he was trying to make the most of his time and move out smartly in spite of his extra clothes. He had already discovered a path that led to the waterfront where an empty dock looked forbidding in the icy water. From there the path disappeared into the woods, winding away from the shore through groves of birch mixed with thick clumps of evergreen.

Each birch grove was bright and cheery as the sun shone down through bare tree branches. The occasional stand of evergreen, however, provided a contrast of shadows and scented air. The path, while not straight, was well-worn and easy to follow. Eric had no concern about losing his way as he explored this new world.

The time passed quickly, and just as his hour was almost up and he was ready to turn back, Eric unexpectedly came to a dead end against a high chain-link gate. He couldn't see through the gate, for thick green canvas covered the fencing. To the right and left, evenly spaced spruce bushes stood like sentries in front of tall chain-link fencing.

What's a fence like this doing in the middle of my island? he thought. Noting the tightly wound razor wire along the top of the 12-foot-high enclosure, he was stymied about what would require that sort of security.

Since he could not see through the gate, he tried to push between two of the bushes. It was hard work, as the thick branches scratched at his face, but he managed to push enough aside to reach the fence, where he discovered there was no canvas covering. As he leaned forward to peek into the enclosure, Eric was shocked to find himself face-to-face with a young man who was, he guessed, only a few years older than himself.

"*Vad heter du?*" Eric asked the teenager.

The young man behind the fence seemed every bit as shocked as Eric.

"I'm sorry, I don't understand what you said," replied the young man in English.

Eric easily switched to English. "I said, who are you? What's your name?"

The boy wore a parka and a dark ski hat. The coat was unzipped, and underneath he saw a T-shirt emblazoned with the words "Rock'n'Roll." He had dark skin and intelligent eyes. He seemed to be American, at least to speak with an American accent. He looked back over his shoulder as if afraid someone might see him talking to the fence. "I'm Daniel. Daniel Derry. Who are you?"

"Eric Carlson. What are you doing inside this fence? Is it some sort of reform school or something?"

"No, I've been kidnapped. We've been kidnapped. I think there are five of us. We're prisoners here." Daniel turned slightly sideways, and Eric could see that he was holding a little kid, bundled tightly against the cold.

What was he talking about? How could they have been kidnapped? "No way!"

"Yes, way. And, look, I've got to sit with my back against the fence and talk without looking at you. If the guards see me talking with you, it could be dangerous for both of us."

"Wow," said Eric as he pulled his head back slightly so that it could not be seen. Was this guy just messing with him? Sometimes older kids did that, making up stories to see who would fall for them. Eric was never fooled by these stories, but this one was almost too crazy to make up!

As Daniel slid to the ground, he put the toddler down on the snowy ground. She just sat, with a plunk. He crossed his arms on top of his knees and put his head down, as if resting. "Where are we?" His voice was muffled under his arms.

"Tranholmen Island."

"Where is that? I didn't recognize the language you were speaking."

"You mean you don't even know what country you're in?"

"I was kidnapped in Virginia, United States, knocked out, and woke up here a couple of weeks ago."

"Virginia? Wow. Now you're in Sweden, on an island in the Lilla Värtan, not far north of Stockholm. The estate where I live is about two hundred meters back that way through the woods, but we just moved here a few months ago, and I didn't even know this compound existed until now. Are you being held for ransom?"

"I don't think so. They are doing some weird medical experiments. There haven't been any pictures or phone calls or stuff you expect with a ransom demand. And there are three or four others also being held, but they don't let us talk to each other. The thing that really worries me is the guards don't cover their faces at all, like they're not worried about us I.D.'ing them. That tells me one thing . . . when the experiment is done, so are we." His voice fell. "And I think that time's come."

"*Seriously?*" Eric stared at the huddled figure sitting against the fence. The toddler leaned against him, hugging his leg. She looked up at him with large dark eyes. Could this be true? Could these children be captives?

Eric's quiet, controlled life was suddenly spinning. He had to break this down and think rationally—but there didn't seem to be any rational way to think about this.

The fact was he liked Daniel. Thought he could have even been a friend, and friends had been few and far between in Eric's short span of years. He was not about to lose that possibility before it ever had a chance to develop. "I'll try to help. I'm not exactly strong, I don't have any weapons or anything like that, but there has to be something I can do."

"Eric," Daniel said. "You don't need to be strong. You just need to be our person on the outside. Did you ever see that old movie *The Great Escape* about a bunch of POWs making a break for it? Getting outside is only half the battle. Knowing where you are and how to find your way out of enemy territory is the other half. You're the one who knows how to get us away from this place."

"I can find out," Eric said softly.

"That would be great. But you'll need to be fast—and you'll need to be careful. If they catch you, you might get locked up with us, or hurt or something. So don't tell anyone about this. I have a plan that will get us into this yard, but we'll need to get through the fence and, after that, find the quickest way to the mainland and the police. Do you think you can help me with that?"

"I'm on it. I have some ideas already."

"I think I can be back out in this yard around four P.M. Can we meet then?"

"I'll be here." Eric leaned farther back into the bushes as the door from the building opened and a burly man in some sort of lab coat stepped out, motioning for Daniel to come in. "Don't give up," whispered Eric. "I've got your back."

He watched Daniel's shoulders straighten as he picked up the little baby and headed for the open door and the return to his cell.

THEY PADDED QUIETLY down the old stone passage. It was dry and cool. Every now and then they passed another bracket on the dark stone wall, but none of them contained torches. They came to one sharp turn and then another. It seemed they were walking in the dark for a very long time. When another tunnel branched off to the right, Geri started to turn down it, but Brother Timothy put his hand on her arm and guided her straight ahead, to what looked like a dead end. As they got closer, the torchlight revealed the outline of a door in the rock. Geri remembered that the whole monastery had been built to be purposely labyrinthine.

The monk produced a large old-fashioned iron key and inserted it into a lock she hadn't noticed, even when looking at the door.

It swung open. He stepped inside the room and flipped on a light switch. Seeing her surprise, he laughed. "This room is just below the museum. Fortunately, they ran electricity down. I still don't have a computer hookup, as in the upstairs library, but the light is very handy."

He stepped back, allowing her to enter. She gave a small gasp of delight.

Before her was an ancient library. A large wooden table groaned under stacks of papers and manuscripts; old dark wood shelves lined the walls. On one wall, the manuscripts were boxed and neatly labeled. On the wall across, they still burst forth from piles, wooden boxes, and metal chests.

"You can see how Brother Stefanos, the librarian, needs help," said Brother Timothy. "It will take decades to sort through everything that is here."

Geri nodded wordlessly.

"Come over. There are some things I want you to see. But first, if you don't mind—" He pulled a couple of disposable gloves from a large box and took two for himself. "We don't want to get any oils on the parchments," he said.

She put them on and stepped over in front of where he stood.

On the polished wooden table sat a small stack of long parchments. Geri saw they were floor plans of the monastery. "These are some of the papers that Arsenios Skinouris drafted for Father Christodoulos, many centuries ago."

Geri looked at them as Brother Timothy brought each to the top of the stack before her. In fact, they showed the current layout of the monastery: refectory, kitchen, church, chapel, walkways, and court-yards. On the second level were the monks' cells and offices and the large public library.

Then he brought out the sketch of the tunnels they were now in. Instead of small notations, labels, and measurements, in the laundry room was a verse in the same handwriting as the rest of the notations. The words were in Greek, but Brother Timothy translated as she read:

Blessed are those who wash their robes, so that they will have the right to drink from the river of life and may enter the city by the gates.

"I had to ask myself, why does he keep writing that? What did he mean? Was it only an allusion to keeping your soul pure? But if so, why write it on the plans for the laundry?"

Geri shook her head.

"I wanted you to see this. I wanted you to feel the original parch-ment, to hold it in your hands. Now come."

They went back out of the library, locking it again behind them. Then, to her surprise, Brother Timothy retraced their steps back along the inky blackness of the stone hallways until they stood in the laundry once again. She noticed that he hadn't doused the torch, even though the daylight filtered down from above.

He put his fingers to his mouth, requesting her quiet.

Then he went to the long stone trough along the far wall, where the spring water still ran. Together they stood. His head was slightly hung, as if in prayer.

Then he stooped, dipped his cupped hands into the water of the trough, and brought them up. He stood tall and raised his hands above Geri and then let the cold droplets pour onto her head. A new baptism.

"Amen," he said.

"Amen," she answered.

He put his foot onto what seemed to be some sort of ancient stone built into the wall at the end of the trough.

It wasn't a stone at all. It was a lever. And as he stepped on it, the closest end of the long trough slid sideways in a groove. And there, between the ancient laundry and the wall, was a dark hole.

"I'll go first," whispered Brother Timothy, and he put his foot down into the hole and kept stepping down, until he disappeared below into the dark.

DANIEL SHRUGGED OFF his parka awkwardly, trying to keep a strong grip on the baby as he removed his outdoor clothing. Lab Coat Guy stood by, arm held out and snapping his fingers as he impatiently waited for the young man to hand him the coat.

A second guard, sitting in the lab kitchenette with his feet propped up on the table, smirked as he observed his co-worker's frustration.

Spying an open pack of Trident Splash gum on the counter, Daniel asked politely, "May I please have a piece of gum?"

"Forget it!" said Lab Coat Guy with a nasty snarl. "You're more trouble than you're worth already. You were lucky the doc agreed to let you go outside. Get moving!" And in his typical fashion he gave the boy a shove down the hall. Daniel, who had now come to expect this behavior, managed to keep his balance so as not to drop the toddler.

"Here, kid," said the other guard, who seemed in an unusually upbeat mood. He grabbed the pack of gum off the counter and flung it in Daniel's direction. The boy reached up with his free hand, snagged the package expertly, and quickly stuffed it into his pocket before anyone decided to take it back.

"Oh, come on!" whined Lab Coat Guy. "That was *my* gum."

"Give the kid a break," said the other man. "You have a lot more where that came from."

Daniel continued to move slowly toward his cell, not wanting to be caught in the middle of the argument. Lab Coat Guy stomped up behind him, opened the door, and pushed him in, flicking the bolt lock shut from the outside.

Daniel set the baby on the bed and immediately pulled out the gum to examine the pack. Four pieces, what a score! He'd hoped for one, maybe two at the most. But this was perfect.

Sensing his excitement, the little girl clapped and giggled, "Nayal! Nayal!"

Daniel smiled and grabbed the baby up into his arms as he danced around the room. Then he stopped, holding the baby up so they were face-to-face, and whispered to her conspiratorially.

"Now, my little partner in crime, we're ready to put together the final pieces of this escape. So let's get to it!"

He set the baby back down on the bed and picked up the fork from the table. Then, stepping up and straddling his young charge on the bed, he reached up to begin tapping out a new message on the hot-water pipe.

The infant reached out and grabbed a handful of Daniel's pant cuff, contentedly leaning her head against his leg as he tapped out a new message to his fellow captives.

JAIME SAT IN THE empty courtyard between the refectory and the kitchen, surreptitiously listening to Geri and Brother Timothy and following Geri's position on her handheld. She needed to know just who this Constantine/Brother Timothy was and what he was up to. He'd seemed harmless enough when she and Geri had arrived at the lower entrance to the monastery, and Geri had introduced the two of them. But this all seemed like a wild-goose chase—one that had little to do with finding Britta Sunmark. Unless she was somehow here on Patmos, perhaps even near the monastery?

How much responsibility did Jaime have for Geri, the woman she'd just met? It didn't seem that she was in extreme physical danger, and Geri had willingly gotten herself involved in whatever this was.

A chilly breeze blew, and Jaime heard the chanting that signaled the end of the Sunday service in the main chapel.

She had to decide. Once service was out, there was no way she could follow Geri.

"Where are you? I can't see you, it's so dark," Geri's voice said in her ear.

"One more foot down, and you can grasp the railing," Brother Timothy replied.

Oh, drat, thought Jaime.

As the two kitchen helpers brought another load of butter, olive oil, and condiments past her through the courtyard, she heard the opening of the church doors down around the corner.

She made her decision, slipped quickly up the steps into the ancient, now-industrial kitchen, walked straight to the back, and ducked down the open staircase to the darkened laundry below. She sighed again to herself as she flattened herself out of sight against the cold stone wall and attempted to catch her breath.

THIS TIME, when the knocking started, Jimi was ready. He dove for his table and grabbed the pencil and paper he had been using to play word games. Trying to keep track of all the letters was hard, but he had developed a shorthand to help catch most of the message. He would simply write 5 when he heard five short knocks. Underline the number and it indicated long knocks. So, 13 was one long knock followed by three short. Then he would look back using a little cheat sheet he'd devised and see that 13 was the code for *m*. This way he seemed to catch enough of the letters to get the gist.

This was the third message today. As Jimi scribbled his code notes, the knocking paused. Then another set started, but this time it was not as strong, in a different rhythm, as if coming from another source. As if . . . someone else was knocking?

Jimi tried to read his hurried scribbles. "Name . . . Inaba?" What kind of name was that? He didn't even know if it was a man's name or a woman's.

He tried to keep up with the distant conversation, which now went back and forth between Daniel and this Inaba person. Jimi sighed as he looked back to see the holes in his message. Whenever they would repeat a phrase, he would try to fill in the missing letters. Finally, the conversation was beginning to take shape.

Escape . . . tonight . . . baby . . . medical . . . Daniel was saying. What? Was the baby ill? Was that why the sudden push for escape tonight? Or was that just part of the plan?

Jimi himself had sensed a change in the attitude of the guards. They seemed more relaxed, upbeat, acting like his old officemates did on Friday afternoons. The demeanor meant "the job's almost done." And that lady scientist, she had turned really cold. It was as if she couldn't bear to look at him. This was not good. He couldn't agree more with the kid's assessment: It was time to get out, NOW.

But how would they escape their rooms? The rooms where they were held weren't traditional jail cells with key locks and high security. But his door had a bolt lock with a knob on the hall side of the door. It was enough to keep him captive, because there was no way from his side to unlock it.

Could the kid have figured something out?

Jimi climbed on his bed and started tapping his own message. *What can I do?*

The answer came back. *Don't sleep. Be ready.*

WITGARD VILLELLA noticed that his keys were jangling as he let himself back into his office. There was no place he could be today that calmed him. He thought he was past being nervous. About anything. But the cost of this current project—not the material expense but the risk of bringing in the subjects and keeping them—was astronomical. He was not in the business of brokering kidnapping.

Mostly, he was not in the business of getting caught having done so. It would ruin everything.

How had he let himself be talked into this?

How had he gone from being a funder of promising research to wanting human beings dead—quickly?

His foot drummed the floor quickly under his desk. Was that a noise in the back office? No, of course not. He was being hyper-sensitive.

Witgard decided he could risk one call on his cell. Who was tracing his cell? Nobody. He was raising his blood pressure for no reason. No reason at all.

The rings sounded tinny. Finally a female voice picked up.

"I just wanted to make sure Mother was coming. We miss her and we're so glad she can come a day early," he said.

"Mother's on the way. Don't call again," came the gruff reply. And the call went dead.

He sat, again drumming his pencil, not even aware that the beat he was unconsciously playing was from a song by the Black Eyed Peas—or that Yani sat in a small office behind him, humming the melody under his breath.

ONCE IN NEW YORK, Geri had attended a star show at the planetarium. Through use of projectors on a domed ceiling, it had transported the attendees off of planet Earth, out through the solar system, the universe, and the galaxy. While all the patrons had been overcome by awe at the unending vastness of space, Geri had found herself inexplicably terrified. As Earth disappeared into a phalanx of heavenly bodies, Geri lost her moorings and felt lost and untethered, adrift in an endless sea of stars. Nothing familiar, no touchstones, absolutely no way to orient herself or point the way home. If the planetarium doors hadn't been secured shut, she would have bolted.

She felt that same detachment as she followed Brother Timothy through the dark maze of hallways carved from the rock underneath the monastery. If Timothy disappeared, she would be alone, shut into total darkness, no clue as to how to go backward or ahead. She was adrift. She would be engulfed by the never-ending darkness, lost forever in the labyrinthine bowels of the earth.

She was again terrified.

She understood now the extreme act of will that faith required. If she did not trust in Brother Timothy, she would be lost. If she did not trust in God, she would be lost in a sea of vast expanse—both outer space and inner space. She understood now that the greatest expanse of infinity existed within her own mind.

She made a sound, and the monk turned back to her, lifting his brightly burning torch ever higher so she could see her sure footing. His robed arm grasped hers near the elbow.

"This is where it becomes clear," he said, and she knew immediately what he meant.

Either you believed, or you did not.

You were guided by an inner compass, or you were lost.

"Come," he said, and they moved together into the darkness ahead.

THE SUNDAY BELLS TOLLED triumphantly overhead as Jaime pressed herself against the rock wall of the lower level. After a moment, her pupils adjusted and the light filtering in from the opening above the staircase allowed her to get her bearings.

As Geri and the monk had discussed, she was indeed in the laundry. Industrial-sized machines stood against one wall, and a long wooden table sat in the middle of the stone floor, with wire baskets underneath for sorting the laundry.

Against the wall running perpendicular from the back stairs was the laundry trough with the old pipe and constantly running stream.

There was only one door in the laundry, and it seemed Geri and Brother Timothy had reentered this room before they vanished again. From their discussion and the loudness of the water, it seemed the two of them had been standing near that trough when Jaime had heard a scraping sound and they had exited the room.

Jaime instinctually put her hands under the water to feel the icy flow. Were there stairs somehow under or behind the trough? And, if so, how were they accessed?

She traced the top of the stone trough with her hands but felt nothing. Then she got down on her hands and knees and did the same around the bottom of the trough. This time she found the wooden pedal. She couldn't move it with her hand, but when she stood up and added her body weight to pressure from her feet, it obligingly swung away from the wall.

Below her was pitch-black.

She took a moment to go back to the door to the hallway and open it. There were iron brackets on the wall, but apparently Constantine/Timothy had taken the only torch.

Across the room, she heard the stone trough beginning to roll back into place. Without further thought she ran toward it, put a foot down to find where the ladder rung was, and swung down onto it as quickly as she could.

The heavy stone nearly scraped her head before she ducked out of the way.

Then it was shut, and she was suspended on the rung of an ancient wooden ladder in the pitch-dark.

And she again waited to catch her breath.

PATSY COVINGTON WIPED a drop of hot chocolate from Bartlett's lip and smiled at the boy. "Mommy's going to the upper lodge, but only for one night. I'll see you tomorrow," she said.

The boy was playing with a small metal airplane that Meghan's new beau had given him and hardly noticed what Patsy said. Portia heard her, though, and snapped to attention. "Back tomorrow, promise, Mommy?"

"Of course, baby."

"Don't get hurt on the big mountain!"

"I'll be careful," she said.

"Love you, Mommy," Portia said sincerely, her small hands enveloping Patsy's larger one.

"Love you, too."

"Can we go swimming?" Portia said, turning to Meghan. The resort had an Olympic-sized indoor pool.

"Finish your lunch, darling," said Meghan, smiling at her.

Patsy turned from the table, her overnight bag slung jauntily over one shoulder.

She headed for the small luxury bus to the upper lodge, where she would check in, leave some toiletries, and muss the bed before leaving in a rental car that sat waiting for her. She would meet a private plane in Germany and fly to Sweden, where the final stages of the project would be completed. With the luck that came from careful planning, she'd be back to check out from the upper lodge in the morning and rejoin her children for lunch at the Main Lodge before heading back for the States.

Patsy was just as glad that Witgard was moving the schedule up a day. As much as he'd paid, she still wanted to get the job done, the evidence disposed of, and the book closed.

Patsy loved closure. She settled back into the wide, comfortable seat for the short ride. And she wondered if the five kidnappees—and three guards—had any idea that they were breathing the air of their final day on earth.

JAIME LISTENED TO the sporadic conversation between Geri and Brother Timothy as they continued their journey through the labyrinth under the monastery. It was being picked up by her handheld and broadcast to a wireless earpiece. Jaime had it tethered to one of her belt loops on a cord long enough that she could use the handheld itself as a flashlight; the beam it emitted, although powerful, was very small and focused and illuminated only one step at a time.

There were no wall brackets now, no torches placed on the walls in centuries gone by. It was nerve-racking, this walk through the earth in the dark. A few minutes before, she had come to what seemed a dead end, and only through sheer determination had she been able to backtrack to find the continuation of the passage. The door itself was flush with the rock wall and had no handle, so it opened only at a touch at the right point.

Could it possibly be that the kidnapped kids were here somewhere? You could effectively lose someone here for a very long time.

Now she came to what looked to be another dead end. The wall in front of her was rocky but without an opening. The small beam of light went up and down the abrupt end of the passageway without finding anything. Now what?

It was chilly. Jaime took a step backward and shone the beam on the wall to the right. Nothing.

Another step back. Nothing.

One more. And there, again, was the smallest hairline crack. She ran her fingers up and down, standing on tiptoe to find the correct outline. She pushed firmly where the doorknob could be expected. Nothing. She shone the light again, up and down. She found only one small carving, of a heart, on the far side of the door.

A heart. Hmm. Playing her gut impulse, she shoved the center of the door—where the "heart" of the door would be, or opposite the "heart" of the person who stood at the door—and it pushed open. She put one foot forward and saw that the door was going to close behind her.

With an intake of breath, she stepped back.

Why should it bother her that it would close behind her? Certainly she wasn't planning to come back this same way—at least, not alone.

She muttered something unpleasant about the pirates and brigands who were allegedly responsible for the mazelike pathways of the monastery, and the need that the builders had felt to leave false passages that went nowhere. With that, she had a sharp intake of breath. What if this door was one of those passages? What if it led nowhere and the door was irrevocably closed behind you? No one would find you, ever—or, at least, not for a very, very long time.

She didn't want to become another one of the lost.

She paused a moment to collect her nerve. Maybe she was just spooking herself.

She went back to the ending of the passageway and slowly came back, looking on the left side. There was nothing. She made her way back to the door on the right side, and there was nothing opposite it on the left.

All right then.

But something persuaded her to take one more step backward, then two. And there, on the left side, was the dim outline of another door.

Here there was a Λ, an *alpha*. The beginning. She expelled a long breath and pushed on this one—again, at heart level.

It, too, swung open.

"God help me," she breathed.

She walked through.

The door slammed shut behind her. She turned back and pushed, hard. Nothing.

She continued forward, the only way she could go.

GERI WAS EXHAUSTED. Just plain tired. How long were they going to keep walking? It seemed like they'd walked for miles, but their progress had been halting and slow, so they might not have traveled as far as it seemed they had.

As if reading her thoughts, Brother Timothy turned around and smiled at her in the torchlight. "Take courage," he said.

"Could we just stand for a minute?" she asked.

He nodded. "But not for long. We're almost there."

As they stood silently, hands intertwined, she noticed two things: the sound of rushing water and a faint breeze. They must truly be almost there.

"Let's go," she said, and there was renewed vigor in her tone.

The monk turned in the passageway and led her forward. The path ended its slope a couple of minutes later. Geri was surprised at how much easier it felt to walk on level ground.

The sound of the water became louder and louder and her step brisker. She saw a rectangle of light at the end of a passage, and it was all she could do to keep herself from running toward it.

When they got there, she found it was a hard right angle, and as she turned into the final passage, she cried out with delight. "Is that . . . ?"

"Yes," was Timothy's simple answer.

Geri clapped her hands like a young girl and ran forward toward the final opening. The tunnel ended abruptly and she suddenly stood, mouth agape, hands pressed together over her heart. Before her was a large cavern—a huge cavern. She dropped her head back and looked up—and up—and could hardly see the top. It was flooded with light, although she could not immediately locate the source; whether it was sunlight filtering in through cracks in the rock or human-made illumination, it didn't matter. For right in front of her, running briskly through the floor of the cave, was a river. A beautiful, clear river.

It spilled in a glorious waterfall from the side of the cave where she stood.

"Is this it?" she whispered.

"Indeed it is," replied the monk, also in a hushed tone. "The river of life, spoken of by John. It was a river he knew well."

She ran forward and knelt by its side.

"Careful," the monk said, coming to put a hand on her shoulder.

"Of course." She backed away.

"I mean, think carefully before you commit yourself to these waters. I cannot guarantee that if you drink from it, you will live forever, but I do guarantee that should you do so, your life will be forever changed."

She looked up at him now, studied his youthful face and black beard. "Have you drunk from it?"

"Yes," he said. "And it has changed me in many ways. I feel as though I've become guardian of its power. Perhaps you have been brought here to help me."

Geri turned away from him, and stared, transfixed, at the quickly running water. Above the falls was a magnificent carving in the rock. The lamb, on a throne, a cross behind his back, with a banner flying from the cross.

Then the angel showed me the river of the water of life, as clear as crystal, flowing from the throne of God and of the Lamb.

"So this is truly it."

After a moment, she realized Brother Timothy was standing behind her. She looked up at him and he offered her a small carved wooden cup. "It is made from an olive tree in Jerusalem," he said. "It seemed fitting."

She thought she would jump at the chance when the moment came, but she was suddenly afraid of the power the water represented. "Will you drink with me?" she asked.

"If you wish."

She nodded. He knelt down beside her. The breeze now blew through her hair. She took off the scarf that held it in place. His lips moved as if in prayer, and then he leaned down and dipped a cup into the stream. He brought it up, very full, smiled, and poured more than half of it into the first cup, which he extended to her.

Geri accepted it.

"*In nomine Patris, et Filii, et Spiritus Sancti,*" he said. He crossed himself and drank the water from his cup.

It might have been the first time in Geri's life that she'd crossed herself. But it seemed natural and right, so she did it. Then she put the wooden cup to her lips and drank the water from the river. Every drop.

"Amen," said Brother Timothy.

"Amen," echoed Geri.

The meaning of it all overwhelmed her. She was having trouble deciding which path to let her thoughts go down. The light in the cave began to seem much brighter. She lay down, prostrate, and let her conscious mind go.

JAIME CLEARLY HEARD the sound of running water over her earpiece and Geri and Brother Timothy talking about the river of life and drinking from it. The fact that there was a river explained why all the paths were leading down. This one was smooth but sloped precipitously, and it was all Jaime could do to keep from setting ahead at a jog.

Finally she succumbed, her penlight aimed at the ground, and let herself slip ahead more quickly. She was nearly running when she saw that up ahead the path flattened out. It was a relief. She nearly tumbled out onto the even surface and subconsciously realized it would take her three or four steps to stop her momentum.

She'd barely had time to make this realization when her third step on the walk didn't hit a walk at all. She stumbled and realized there was no longer any floor in front of her. There was nothing.

She gave a small cry, knew her balance was lost, and tried to fling herself backward onto solid ground.

Jaime sat down hard, both her legs free-falling, realized she had no balance on the ledge at all, rolled backward, flinging her feet up, praying there was something, anything, there to hold them.

The problem was, there was nothing to grab hold of. There was a very narrow shelf, but she couldn't get her balance on it. Hot tears burned her eyes. She didn't want to tumble into an abyss. She didn't want to die—at least, not this way!

"*Please, God!*" she cried.

Somehow, she managed to flip onto her stomach, with both hands on the ground. The shelf wasn't wide enough to hold all of her, but she managed to get enough of her weight onto the wedge of earth that she stopped falling.

Jaime lay for a minute, afraid to move. Finally, she pushed herself back and lay on her side. She made herself lie absolutely still until she was sure that she was no longer falling. She breathed, feeling the firm earth beneath her hands. Her breathing was ragged, and her heart revved like a motorcycle.

She had to be more careful.

It occurred to her that she no longer heard anything from either Geri or Brother Timothy. She cautiously reached one hand up to her ear. The earpiece was gone.

Rats.

Was this it, then? Had she fallen for it, taken the "pirate path," let the door to the world close behind her? Was she relegated to stay in this purgatory until she eventually died from thirst? It didn't seem like a very pleasant way to go. Maybe it would have been better to hurtle off into the darkness and have done with it.

She measured the width of the shelf in her mind. If she was canny and careful, it seemed possible that she could creep back to where the passage led back up. She remembered very well that she'd tried the door after it had closed behind her, and knew it wouldn't budge. But, if she could get back there, at least she could sit without threat of falling into the chasm before her.

But what was the best way to get there?

"Lord, help me; quiet my mind. Give me wisdom," she breathed.

She didn't dare sit up or even get onto her hands and knees. Instead, she laboriously pulled herself forward, an inch at a time.

It took her five endless minutes to reach the path she'd come down, at which point she felt secure enough to get up onto her hands and knees. As she continued to crawl forward, her hand hit something—which she found to be her earpiece. Thank God. Moving up into the pathway a foot or so, she took the handheld that she'd been clutching and checked that the tether was still strong. This was now her last link to humanity.

She wondered if she could complete a call from in here. To whom? Yani, of course. And tell him what? *Come, chase down many dark passages, take whatever doors I try to describe that I took, and come be stuck with me?*

Or, more likely, *Go, get my backup, and use that person to find the kidnapped kids, like you should have in the first place. When you've successfully completed the mission in the way you wanted to all along, come find me. I'll wait here.*

She would almost rather thirst to death.

Yani was treating her as incompetent, or so it felt. As if to prove him right, here she sat, stuck, between heaven and earth.

She tried to find a signal, to know if she even could get a call out. It looked iffy.

Jaime knew she needed to center herself, to start thinking clearly, to think outside the box. Or the passageway.

She shone the light beam forward into the depth. She couldn't see anything at all. No bottom, no sides.

Rats.

She took a moment to bemoan the fact that she was trying to stop swearing. Because if ever a time was made for swearing, this was probably a lot like how it would feel.

On the plus side, she did seem to have plenty of oxygen. And while it was chilly, she was wearing a jacket and was not uncomfortable.

She put the earpiece back into her ear but heard nothing. What was going on down there?

She sat in the pitch-black of the cave that had no beginning and no end and did her best to think.

FEBRUARY 26, 2006, 12:26 P.M.
BENEATH THE MONASTERY OF ST. JOHN
CHORA, PATMOS

GERI WAS STARTLED by the sound of the trumpet. It was vibrant and clear, and the tone was so rich that she felt it pulsate through her whole body.

Where did the sound come from?

She looked up and was amazed to find that she was outside and above her was the most incredible clear sky, a blue that was close to sapphire but shimmering. She felt a wind, and when she looked down to make certain she had her balance, she gasped. She was not standing on earth at all. She was high up in the clouds—clouds that billowed and churned. They were a bright, pure white, but they must have been reflecting the sun, because they were laced with gold. She reached out to touch them and found them soft.

It was then the voice spoke.

"Geri," it said. It was not loud, but it was otherworldly and full of authority.

She gasped. Before she had time to figure out what to do, the angelic voice continued.

"Grace and peace to you from him who is, and who was, and who is to come! From him who loves us and made us to be a kingdom, and priests to serve his God and Father—to him be glory and power forever and ever! Amen."

The trumpet began again, mixed in with the sweet sound of bells, and the clouds began furling and unfurling around her feet.

Geri trembled and felt a hand on her shoulder. She turned around, expecting to find some manner of heavenly host, but instead she found a man, dressed simply in a robe with a plain rope belt, standing behind her. He was clean-shaven and had silvering hair. When he spoke, his voice was comforting and sure.

"Grace to you, and peace, Geri. I am John, your brother and companion in the suffering and kingdom and patient endurance that are ours in Jesus. I was sent here to Patmos because I dared to teach the world of God. Many years ago, on the Lord's Day, I was in the Spirit, and I, too, heard a voice like a trumpet."

Geri couldn't help herself. She grasped his arm as he stood slightly behind her, and held on to him for support. His smile was kind. With his free hand, he directed her attention to the sky before them.

"See what you also have been chosen to see," he said. At this, there was a great swell of music and a swirling of light and color, and Geri had to hide her eyes, the light shone so brightly. And there in the distance was a large chair—a throne—and a circle of colors.

John rested a hand on her left shoulder, as if to say, *It has all led to this.*

As he continued, the throne disappeared and a large cloud descended in front of them. "Then I saw a new heaven and a new earth. I saw the Holy City, the New Jerusalem, coming down out of heaven from God, prepared as a bride beautifully dressed for her husband."

As she saw this before her, a shimmering city in the clouds, the first voice, the angel's voice, said, "Now the dwelling of God is with men, and he will live with them. They will be his people, and God himself will be with them and be their God. He will wipe every tear from their eyes. There will be no more death or mourning or crying or pain, for the old order of things has passed away. He who was seated on the throne said, 'I am making everything new!'"

No more death. The words resonated in Geri. *No more death.*

John, who still stood a step behind her, now pointed down, and she saw the cave, the very cave where she and Brother Timothy had sat by the river only minutes before.

John said, "Then the angel showed me the river of the water of life, as clear as crystal, flowing from the throne of God and of the Lamb.

No longer will the curse of death reign over humankind. Blessed are those who wash their robes, so that they will have the right to drink from the river of life and may enter the city by the gates!"

Geri sat down—right there, on the cloud above the cave—and she began to cry.

John knelt beside her. "I have waited for you," he said. "For you and Brother Timothy, who will keep the secret of the river of life and bring the worthy here. You have been given the gifts and the means. When the time is right, you shall bring the worthy, that they shall not die, and God's kingdom shall be established here on earth."

She looked up at John, through her tears, and she nodded.

"Close your eyes," he said.

She did so willingly. "The Spirit and the Bride say, 'Come!' Let him who hears say, 'Come!' Whoever is thirsty, let him come, and whoever wishes, let him take the free gift of the water of life."

The wind blew, and briefly there was a pungent smell.

"Amen, come Lord Jesus," said John.

Geri couldn't stand it anymore. She fainted dead away.

"HOLY SHIT," was all Jaime could think to say, even to herself.

Angels? Trumpets? The Apostle John? Whatever was happening, she had to get down there.

It was unacceptable to be stuck here. Simply unacceptable.

She stood up, grabbed her handheld from where it was still tethered to her belt loop, and stood up. She turned on the penlight again.

Jaime remembered Brother Timothy saying something to Geri as they walked, something about having courage and almost reaching a railing.

Supposing Jaime hadn't taken a wrong turn? What if Brother Timothy and Geri had come this way? If you'd need to have courage in any part of your descent, this would be it.

Supposing Brother Timothy and Geri had made their way across this tiny shelf? Why would there be a shelf here at all, if this was just an abyss and nothing more?

Take courage, Jaime said to herself. She put her back to the wall and flattened herself as much as she possibly could. Then she started moving sideways. Her heels and half the ball of each foot were firmly on the ledge; her toes were over air. She shone the light stream just ahead of where she was walking. The ledge went on as far as the beam shone.

She began shuffling sideways.

She paused once and allowed herself to look back to where the path up disappeared behind her. Then she continued on.

Why would someone go to such trouble to build a shelf if it didn't go anywhere? she asked herself.

Finally, she saw it. The railing of which Brother Timothy had spoken.

It took another couple of minutes of the sideways shuffle to reach it. But when she did, she found it was made of metal, which surprised her, and that it was solidly fastened into the ground.

Then it turned a corner, the shelf disappeared, and she was once again on a downward-sloping path.

Jaime allowed herself to exhale mightily and to start carefully down the path, never going faster or farther than her light would illuminate.

THIS IS UNBELIEVABLE! Britta read and reread the data she had produced earlier that day. The odds of four very different subjects having such similar, almost twinlike, sections of their DNA, were astronomical.

The next step would be to compare these sequences against the database she had built from years of DNA research. Every octogenarian (or older) she encountered, she had asked permission to draw a blood sample. Then, after mapping their mitochondrial DNA, she placed the results into her database. She had hoped she might find, in that database, the clues to a long life.

If Dr. Edders were here, he would be so excited. She paused. *Or would he?*

The scientist remembered back to their many hours of friendly arguments about research ethics. She had thought some of the scenarios he presented were ludicrous, but now she wondered if he hadn't been trying to tell her something.

"Just suppose . . ." He had caught her attention one day while they sat in the lab, drinking the sick excuse for coffee that one of the graduate students had thrown together.

"Just suppose we were to isolate some very strong mitochondrial DNA patterns, patterns that enabled their hosts to live two, maybe three times longer than the average human."

Britta laughed, because she knew he was exaggerating to make his point.

"And then suppose further, we had perfected this technique of yours to insert the DNA strand into another host and successfully encouraged it to replicate."

Britta waited for the punch line. There was always a punch line with Jorgen Edders.

"Who gets this new DNA? The rich? The powerful? Or maybe those who score high on an IQ test and so merit extra time in this world to use their extraordinary gifts?"

Britta knew he was baiting her, but she still found herself taking this a little bit personally.

"For starters, those who could benefit medically from this discovery? Those whose lives have actually been shortened due to their own DNA pattern."

"Yes, very appropriate. But I ask you, who finally decides who is worthy? At some point, a wealthy corporation will buy the technology, because you and I know that research requires money. And the scientist is not the one who ultimately will decide who gets to enjoy the fruits of their—our—labors."

It was the way it had always been and would always be. The tension between pure science, for the joy of discovery, and the need for corporate funding.

"So are you saying that something like this should not be pursued because the wrong people may benefit?"

"No, not at all. I just want to be comfortable that the human race is ready to handle such a gift if we hand it to them."

Britta had thought her mentor was speaking hypothetically. But maybe he'd known more about what they might discover than he had let on.

And now here she was, facing the very situation he mentioned. She had sold out to a corporation, which would ultimately use her research in whatever way they chose. And which, at this moment, was deciding the future of her research.

Well, she wouldn't let it lie only in their hands. She couldn't. She did not trust that they would make her results available to the scientific community at large.

Britta placed a CD in her computer and started copying all of the relevant data on her project.

THE SOUND OF rushing water got louder and louder. Jaime was fairly sure she was nearing Brother Timothy's "river of life."

As the passageway made a final turn, Jaime noticed something completely out of context. The stone wall beside her had a doorknob.

Hunh, she thought. And she opened it, just a little, and looked through.

The light was blinding.

She stepped back into the darkness, closed her eyes, then opened the door again, looking at the ground until her eyes adjusted.

The ground had a tile floor.

When she could, she looked up and found herself in a passageway. Straight ahead, perhaps thirty feet on, was another closed wooden door. The passage seemed to make a right turn there also.

Fortunately, the passage was empty. The walls themselves were still made of stone, but fluorescent tubing lit the hall from above.

Hunh, thought Jaime again.

She stepped into the passageway and closed the door quietly behind her. She again flattened herself against the inside wall, and continued down the hall.

Jaime came to the end of the wall and stood, wondering if she should risk opening the wooden door. Before she did, she peered around to look down the adjacent passage.

It was a short hall and also currently unoccupied. But what caught Jaime's attention was that in the midst of the passage, on the same wall as the door, was a huge picture window. It was perhaps 10 feet long and 6 feet tall. Beyond it, even from her corner angle, she could see movement.

She couldn't help herself. She snuck out into the hallway and stood before the window.

It was tinted and thick, which led her to believe it was one-way glass—that she could see out, but no one on the other side could see in.

And what was on the other side was a pounding waterfall.

A huge one. She was behind it, looking through the cascading flow. It took her a moment of squinting to get to the point where she could decipher what was in the glowing light on the other side of the free-falling water.

It was an enormous cave. She couldn't see the roof, but the interior stretched on and on. There was a pool at the bottom of the waterfall, and from it ran the river of which Brother Timothy must have spoken. The expanse alone was awe-inspiring, as was the brilliant light—especially after coming from such a length of pitch-black as she just had.

But wait—how was there such light in a cavern? It made no sense.

Jaime looked to her right down the hallway and saw another doorway. It, too, was arched, and the door itself was made of wood. The hinges were black iron.

It was now or never.

She walked quietly down the hallway and stood at the door, her ear pressed against it. The noise of the waterfall was suddenly much louder, and she realized the plate glass in the window must be soundproofed as well as one-way.

She heard nothing besides the rushing water.

Jaime pushed down on the old-fashioned door lock and pulled the door back toward her, opening it an inch, just enough to look out.

The roar of the water was now overpowering. The walkway outside the door was a light-sand-colored earth, packed firm. There was, however, a wall approximately three feet high that ran along the edge of the walkway. It was made of the same porous material as the rest of the cave. From below, it likely blended in with the wall behind, and an observer would probably not notice that it shielded a small walkway.

At the end of the walkway was what appeared to be a natural opening in the cave wall.

Jaime got down on her hands and knees to crawl along the passage. At one point she peered over, half-expecting to see Geri or Brother Timothy somewhere on the flat bank of the river of life. And yet . . . the dramatic scene Jaime had most recently overheard through her earpiece had not included running water.

How odd.

Jaime reached the opening in the cave wall and stood tall. She was in an alcove, a natural smaller cave within the cave. She used the mirror function of her handheld to look around the corner.

No people.

But the interior of this cave had been turned into high-tech office space.

Electric lights illuminated the space, which was done in white tile. Before her, there were two doors. One was heavy metal, and the other was a heavy metal with a keypad lock beside it.

Much to Jaime's surprise, this second door currently sat cracked open.

What to do?

Chances were, there were people inside. Locked doors didn't usually sit open unless someone was either beyond them or nearby.

And yet . . . Jaime certainly hadn't killed herself getting here *not* to find out what was going on.

Jaime crept ahead, her senses on high alert. She heard nothing besides the waterfall behind her. She got to the open door and listened—again, nothing. She flattened herself against the wall between the two doors and peered into the open room.

It seemed to be uninhabited. Jaime slipped inside.

Against the wall to her immediate left was a console of some kind. It had a flat computer screen, a keyboard, and lots of interesting buttons and levers. Certainly worth exploring. Back behind it was a small snack area—a small white rectangular table, a small refrigerator, a water cooler, a microwave.

And along the entire wall to her right were filing cabinets. Good old-fashioned metal three-drawer filing cabinets.

They weren't locked.

That meant either the material they contained wasn't very important, or their owners were fairly certain no one unauthorized would be standing where she stood, perusing the contents.

But peruse them she did, senses still on alert. The file cabinet farthest back actually had a label that read: *Current Projects*.

No kidding.

She pulled the long drawer open. The files were alphabetical.

Jaime thumbed quickly toward the back. And there, honest-to-God, was a fat file marked: *Britta Sunmark*.

Jaime took it out and rifled through quickly. Ms. Sunmark's whole proposal was there, filled out in English. Jaime didn't take time to read it, instead scanning what seemed to be the pertinent pages quickly into her handheld. She did see the name "Jorgen Edders" several times.

She also saw that the project had been named the Edders Sequence Protocol.

The most current information that she sought didn't seem to be in the Sunmark file. Jaime instead turned to the file drawer next to it, also marked: *Current Projects*, this one containing files A–M.

And there, so very helpfully, was one marked: *The Edders Sequence Protocol*.

This one had budget figures and architectural drawings and dates. It also had an address on an island in Sweden. Jaime scanned in the pages as quickly as she could turn them.

She was still looking through the folder when she heard someone coming. She barely had time to bang the file drawer shut and sit down at the snack table when the door opened.

And framed in the doorway was Constantine/Brother Timothy.

It had been hammered into her—first line of defense: *talk*.

"Hello," she said. "Oh, Brother Timothy, I have never been gladder to see anyone in my life!"

The monk moved quickly past his surprise at seeing her there to a look of concern for her obvious distress.

"I'm sorry, I was trying to catch up with Geri, but I got lost, so lost—"

As she had stood up, he put a compassionate hand on her shoulder, moved past her, and beckoned her to sit back down. "Let me get you a drink. You must be so tired!" said the monk. "Tell me what happened!"

She watched him move back toward the water cooler.

Which was why she had her back to the door and didn't see the second person, who came up silently behind her. In fact, she didn't know he was there at all until he put the porous white mask over her mouth and nose, and held it in place while she breathed in two shallow breaths and collapsed onto the white tile of the floor.

WHY DID THINGS always happen this way?

The best possible news and the worst possible news always at the same time. Hand in hand. Twins.

Witgard had allowed himself a time of exultation over Dr. Sunmark's victory. He had allowed himself a quiet triumph to know that the Good Mother was on her way and the damning evidence would soon vanish. Everything was going right! Everything was happening just as he'd hoped!

Then, the phone call from the damn monk. And nothing was right anymore.

"What do you mean, there's an intruder?" Witgard screamed into the phone.

"It's a woman, a priest of some sort that Geri Allende knows. She said she followed Geri down into the cave by mistake." The monk knew that was impossible. Bogus. "What do I do?"

"Where is she now?"

"She's here. She's passed out. Phil used one of the masks, so she won't be out long. But I have to be with Geri when she wakes up. What do I do?"

He sounded not panicked, exactly, but whiny. Like this wasn't in his script.

It sure as hell wasn't, thought Witgard.

"I'm coming," he said. He had to find out who this intruder was, what she knew, and how to deal with the situation. It was something he'd have to handle himself.

"What do I do?" Constantine asked again.

"I said I'm coming."

"But I have to leave, and Phil doesn't want to have to handle this, even with the guard downstairs. Everything's working out, isn't it?" It sounded like Brother Timothy was reassuring himself. "Even this phase of Britta's project wraps in two days, I know. Just tell me how to handle this."

"Britta's project wraps tomorrow," said Witgard, and immediately chided himself for giving out more information than the man needed. "The guard doesn't need to be in on this. You and Phil handle it. Shoot her with some Versed, and put her in the Cave. I'll be there long before she comes to her senses."

"The Versed? But I've never used it. That's not my job."

"How much of an idiot are you?" snapped Witgard. "The successful outcome of this project hangs on your ability to follow simple instructions. I'm on my way."

Witgard was so agitated, it never occurred to him that someone might be following him as he left FIA headquarters . . . which he never again would assume was deserted on Sundays.

"DAMN, DAMN, damn, damn," Constantine muttered under his breath. His hands were shaking as he dialed the codes needed to make an international call from his cell phone.

"What?" said the feminine voice on the other end.

"Britta, it's me. I just talked to Witgard."

"I know, I know." She sounded harried. "He's not giving me any more time, even though I've found the strand I was looking for."

"It's worse than that. He's moved it up a day."

"No!"

"Witgard said so, just now. Didn't give me specifics, but it sounded like he meant it. Thought you'd want to know."

"Are you all right?" she asked.

Constantine was amazed that she took the time to be concerned about him, given the fact that her whole life's work was hanging in the balance.

"I guess. There's an intruder in the cave. I've got to see to her. But I thought you'd want to know."

"I did. Why, after all this time, he couldn't just—"

"I know. I know."

Constantine considered asking Britta for instructions on how to inject the Versed, but he already felt like the fact she was a scientist put her three levels above him. "Gotta go. See you soon, my love, I promise," he said, trying for some kind of positive ending to the conversation.

There was a pause, and when Britta spoke, it was in a gentler voice. "Hey."

"Yes?"

"Thanks."

He almost smiled as he hung up.

Phil was still there, still in his Apostle John garb. "Do you know where the Versed is?" Constantine asked, although it was always a third man, Alec, who administered it, and the script that required it was one they rarely used.

"Fridge."

"Can you get it ready while I see to her?" Constantine asked. "Do you know how to give the shot?"

"I've seen Alec do it, but . . ." Phil shrugged. "I can fill the hypodermic, though, sure."

The woman seemed out, didn't respond when Constantine took off her sweater and pushed up the sleeve of her shirt.

Phil handed him the needle. Constantine offered him the chance to do it one more time, but he shook his head.

No point standing on ceremony. Constantine had to get moving. He only had another 20 minutes for certain before the window of time when Geri might come to. He jabbed the needle into her upper arm and pressed the plunger down until all the liquid was administered.

Then he withdrew it, put it on the ground, and took the Band-Aid Phil handed him.

"Only thing," said Phil, cleaning up after him, not looking Constantine in the eye. "Only thing is, I think it's supposed to be given intravenously."

"So you're a lotta help all of a sudden!" said the man in the seminarian's robe angrily. "You couldn't have mentioned this before I gave it to her?" He looked carefully at the woman, even pried open an eyelid. "She seems out. I'll help you carry her in, but you need to set her up. I'm gone."

"Yeah, OK," said the man dressed as John, and between them they easily picked Jaime up and carried her into the next room.

WHEN SHE AWOKE, it took Geri a full minute to come to her senses. Her mind was full of images so brilliant and so real that everything else seemed gray in comparison. She wasn't groggy, and she didn't have a headache. She was simply opening her eyes somewhere completely different from where she'd last been, which was odd and disorienting.

It slowly occurred to her—her surroundings didn't just seem gray; they were gray. She was in a cave—a small one, about seven feet by six feet. All there was in this cave was the soft mat on which she lay, a couple of hand-woven blankets, a small wooden chair, and a carafe of water.

Sitting on the ground next to her was Brother Timothy. She saw him and smiled.

The monk poured a small stream of water from the carafe onto a piece of fabric he had and laid it gently on her forehead.

"Are you all right?" he asked. "You passed out at the river, and seemed to be having an . . . experience . . . of some kind."

"Yes," said Geri. "I did."

"Here. Sit up a little. Take a sip of water."

Geri's throat and lips were dry, almost parched. She sat up on one elbow and accepted the small stoneware cup gratefully, drank it down, and asked for a refill.

Then she lay down again and closed her eyes. "What is this place?" she asked.

"It's a hermitage. A small living space for monks called to spend time alone with God."

They sat companionably for a few more minutes. "Do you want to tell me what happened?" Brother Timothy asked. "Please don't feel compelled. Only if it's right."

"I had a vision," she said quietly. "I believe God spoke to me." Geri opened her eyes and looked at the monk. "Has that ever happened to you?"

He spoke as softly as she. "I believe so."

"If this is John's river of life, the one around which God's future will be fulfilled, the one that will wipe mourning and death away forever . . . what is it you need me to do?" Geri asked. She hadn't moved.

Brother Timothy sat silent until she sat up again and looked at him. "I don't know," he said simply. "What did God ask of you?"

"He said I have been given resources," she said, "and I suppose that is true. If this is the river of life, what do we do? What must be done?"

"I hardly know where to begin. If these are the waters, available to all . . . well, they must be made much more accessible. As you know, God's spirit does not choose only the fittest and strongest. In fact, often the opposite. But provisions must also be made for the monks of the monastery . . . they are called here for a purpose. The people of Patmos must also be provided for. They must be ready, and their island must be ready . . . if it is to become the spiritual center of a new beginning, a new beginning for the people of the earth."

"And how much would all of this cost?"

"I don't know. There would need to be an airport here, and pilgrimage hostels, and security . . . it would cost quite a bit even to begin to make a plan! It would involve engineers and holy people working together. God help me, I wouldn't know how to start."

"I'm supposing a financial foundation would be helpful for all of this," said Geri simply.

"Well, yes, but . . ."

"But nothing. That's the easy part."

Geri was sitting up now, rubbing her arms to warm them up in the damp air of the cave.

True, her husband was very particular about the proven scientific merit of projects he funded. He would find her tale of caves and heavenly cities and talks with angels and long-dead apostles preposterous at best. And yet.

There was always more than one way to skin a cat.

They were supposed to be on holiday. But Nestor was spending all day working on his yacht . . . well, technically, it was her yacht. The *Gerianne* wasn't only named for her; it was actually purchased in her name for tax reasons she didn't quite comprehend. But she wasn't interested in the yacht today; it only served as a backdrop.

"Where are we, Brother Timothy? Can you help me get to the harbor at Skala? I need to speak to my husband."

"That is one thing I can accomplish, and quite easily, too. Do you feel well enough to ride on the back of a scooter?"

Geri stood confidently, the promise of a glorious future dancing circles around her. She'd already decided she didn't want her name splashed over anything. She wanted to be a silent participant, a humble benefactor. After all, God had brought the money to her, for such a time as this.

She took Brother Timothy's hand and stood up, ready to go out and get it.

JAIME'S FIRST COHERENT thought was that she needed to get a supply of T-shirts that read: *You Knock Me Out,* to hand out to the brotherhood of people who seemed intent on rendering her unconscious. It was becoming a popular sport. A white supremacist she could understand. But a monk? That was a new one.

She kept her eyes closed while she collected her wits. She didn't have a headache, which was both unexpected and appreciated. Her right upper arm still ached from where the alleged monk had shoved the hypodermic needle into her.

Whatever mask the unseen man had put over her face had only served to make her disoriented. She didn't think she'd ever fully lost consciousness, although she'd known she was too woozy to make an effective escape attempt. So she'd faked unconsciousness to see what information she might glean or when she might be lucid enough to make a run for it.

She'd heard the call Brother Timothy had made to Britta Sunmark. It now seemed completely likely that he was the same man the young woman at the care facility had identified as Constantine, Britta's fiancé.

For what good that did Jaime.

And whatever the Versed was supposed to do, she was fairly certain that getting an intramuscular dose of an amount meant to be delivered intravenously had spared her the worst effects.

The Versed, combined with whatever inhalant was on the mask, had made her woozy for a while; she didn't know how long. She didn't really recall being moved or ending up where she was now.

Jaime decided it was time to try to discover just where she was and what she could do about it. What was her guess? Another part of the cave. A cell, perhaps.

She opened her eyes, and her jaw dropped.

She was lying in the clouds.

They were pillowy, luxurious clouds, a distant light outlining them in gold. She reached out to touch them, and they were just as she'd dreamed clouds would be when she was a girl—softer than cotton, lighter than air, yet substantial enough to hold her up.

She sat and looked upward. The sky was that rare summer blue. She couldn't see the sun itself, but its beams were all around her. It was fantastic.

Jaime laughed, in spite of herself. She fell down onto her stomach and watched the clouds part and billow, adjusting to her form. From there, she looked down. She could see the Aegean Sea, far below. She could pick out the island of Patmos, the harbor at Skala, populated with what seemed to be toy boats, and she could see the huge dark monastery on its majestic mountaintop.

Wow.

Then the music started. The same trumpet tones that had greeted Geri and a choir of voices that could only be described as angelic.

Then she heard it. A voice, full of authority, began, "Grace and peace to you from him who is, and who was, and who is to come!"

And Jaime was being propelled forward, closer and closer to a glimmering, bejeweled city that was descending from the higher clouds.

"Wow," she said.

And she knew exactly where she was.

SHE CAME UPON them post-coital, although barely.

Nestor and the woman were in bed in guest cabin one. Geri did appreciate that about her husband—he always brought his mistresses somewhere outside Geri's own life trajectory, so that she wouldn't have bad memories of them, in her own bed, say.

And with this one, since she ran the yacht's spa and workout facilities, he could have done her in the spa—but that would have ruined that part of the ship for Geri.

So cabin one was a pretty good choice.

The woman went the haughty route—"he loves me, not you; if you gave him what he needed," blah, blah, blah, "right, Nestor, darling?"

"Shut up," Nestor said to her gruffly. "Get dressed and get out."

The young woman's jaw dropped. She was either late twenties or early thirties, hardbody, of course, and thought she was pretty smart.

"But Nestor—"

"I said shut up," he said, not breaking eye contact with his wife. "I'm telling you to go, put your clothes on, and get to your quarters."

The mistress read the situation, and quickly. "You can't fire me," she snarled. "If you fire me, I'll charge sexual harassment so fast, it'll be splashed over every paper in the world."

"No one said you were fired," Nestor said. "Just get the hell out."

It took only minutes for the young woman to vanish into the bathroom, pull on a skirt and top, and grab the rest of her things.

Geri knew she would never be seen on the yacht again after today. She'd be transferred and paid on the condition that she kept quiet. Along with so many others.

"You," Geri said to Nestor. "Our quarters. Now. I'll meet you there in five minutes."

Geri turned and left the cabin.

Her business meeting with her husband had just begun.

BRITTA SUNMARK stared into the fire as she sipped a hot cup of herb tea, trying to regain her focus after the troubling call from Constantine.

She knew this day would come—they couldn't keep prisoners forever, and yet. . . . Didn't Villella understand what was at stake, how much more difficult and complex the continued progress would be if she did not have access to the actual subjects?

Only last night Britta had spent an hour watching helplessly as her son, Eric, writhed in pain, waiting for his migraine headache medicine to take effect. Finally, mercifully, he had fallen asleep.

Now, bare feet propped on a hand-carved wooden coffee table, she looked through the flames and remembered a similar scene, but with another young man, strapped into a hospital bed, straining against his bonds and screaming.

"Britta, you must protect me!" His head quivered against the straps but could not move. "The men with the drugs, I know they're coming. They'll take me away and do horrible things to me! Please, Britta, unstrap me; hide me!"

In his moments of lucidity, the young man understood that the drugs he feared were the only thing to ease his pain. But at 22 years of age, the battered shell of a man resembled little of what had been Britta's vibrant, loving brother, and his reality did not coincide with hers. All young Britta could do was watch, powerlessly, and pray for a miracle—or his death. And then, when praying didn't help, she stopped.

No one should have to suffer like that. Even though she'd only been a teenager at the time, she knew there had to be a way to stop the suffering—and if no one else would bother to figure it out, she would. She would do whatever it took to find the cure.

Britta had little idea what future events she would set in motion with that pledge. Her brother had died from his disorder, which was called MELAS, short for Mitochondrial Encephalopathy, Lactic Acidosis, and Stroke-like episodes. MELAS results from problems in the gene structure of the mitochondria, and so she had dedicated her education, her life, to research on mitochondrial DNA.

But the cruel hand of fate had not finished with Britta. Genetic structure of the mitochondria is passed from a mother to her children, and Britta's son, Eric, had inherited the disease from her. She had devoted her entire career to developing a cure for MELAS and now was racing against time to heal her son. She could not lose him the same way she had lost her brother. She would not.

The fire was now reduced to embers, giving off a fine red glow but little warmth. She replayed her teenage words once again: "I will do whatever it takes to find a cure." Britta wondered if her younger self would have found kidnapping an acceptable means to her goal.

Damn the consequences, Britta didn't care! Here she was, on the verge of a breakthrough that would, in public circles, have meant a Nobel Prize. The genetic Band-Aid she was creating to splice into a patient's mitochondrial DNA not only would heal MELAS, which was her goal, but could potentially extend a person's life well beyond today's norms— which she knew full well was the goal of Witgard and his foundation.

Over the last year, she admitted she had moments when she had doubted the rantings of her mentor, Jorgen Edders. As he lay dying, he had revealed in one of his weaker moments that there existed a hidden race of humans whose DNA patterns were so strong they lived inordinately long lives. Now, finally, she had found that to be true, had isolated the strands. If she continued to work with it, it would provide the perfect genetic Band-Aid. This Band-Aid would provide the closest thing to immortality humanity had ever attained.

Britta had known all along that the source of her funding and the method in which the subjects were attained were such that her results could not be made public, at least not in the near future, and certainly not under her name. Britta would receive no accolades, publish no papers. But her career, her accomplishments, meant nothing if Eric suffered the same fate as her brother.

Enough reflecting, time to head back to the lab. She had taken as much blood as she dared. She would have to use the mysterious sequences locked therein to re-create the mitochondrial strand synthetically. The scientist stood and closed the glass fireplace doors, then padded barefoot into the kitchen to rinse out her mug.

She had never met the assassin who had kidnapped these children, and she certainly did not ever want to. How would she know when the person arrived? Should she just get Eric and barricade him with her inside the estate today?

But Witgard had said she had only until Tuesday to make her presentation. And, for now, her subjects were still close at hand.

Britta slipped on her boots, grabbed a heavy coat, and headed out into the cold Scandinavian air.

COME ON! *There's gotta be something here that can cut through chain link,* the boy thought.

Eric was digging through a tool room at the back of a large wooden garage detached from the estate house. The garage, which was big enough to hold four large vehicles, currently housed two snowmobiles, a 40-foot motorboat on a trailer, and a snowblower. In the back was a workbench with Peg-Board hanging above, multiple toolboxes and storage bins stacked beneath, and a large vise clamped on one end.

The garage was not heated, and the cold was beginning to seep through his protective clothing. He stomped his feet on the concrete floor and started looking back through drawers and boxes he had already tried.

He found multiple sets of pruning shears, screwdrivers, hammers, saws, and even an ice pick. But nothing like the bolt cutters he had hoped to find. Eric picked up a hacksaw, considered it for a moment, but couldn't picture how he might angle it to cut the fence, so he flung it down in frustration.

He had to find something. That boy, Daniel, needed him. It was not very often that someone needed him. In fact, it seemed he spent most of his life needing others. But this was his opportunity to help, and he wanted to do his part.

There had been one other time when Eric had the opportunity to help others. It was during the aftermath of a hurricane in Honduras.

All normal communications out of that country had been down, and amateur radio operators around the world were helping send emergency messages to families. He had picked up a few of those messages and passed them on. He would never meet the people he helped, but deep down inside he knew he had made a difference.

This was what he wanted to do now. Eric Carlson needed to make a difference, for Daniel, for that baby, for himself.

He pulled out every toolbox he could find, looked at every implement hanging on the Peg-Board. Nothing. No bolt cutters. Not even a heavy pair of wire cutters.

"Master Eric." He jumped as a voice came from behind. "You shouldn't be out here in the cold." He turned to see his nurse looming in the doorway, all six feet of him. He didn't look the least bit cold, in spite of the fact that he was dressed only in T-shirt and jeans.

How did he always show up like that, out of the blue? It was creepy.

Think fast. "I need some tools for my radio. Have to do some work on the wiring. Thought I could find something out here."

"After your headache last night I think you should be resting. You can work on the radio some other day."

The man reached out to guide Eric toward the door.

"Wait, here's something I might be able to use." He had spied a small set of wire cutters on the workbench. Not very heavy, but they were his only option at the moment. He grabbed them and stuck them in his waistband as the nurse ushered him toward the door.

They crossed a snow-covered path between garage and house and entered the mudroom on the first floor of the estate. Eric removed his coat and gloves, hanging them on pegs, and then stripped off his snow pants. All the while his mind was racing, wondering how he would sneak out later without the nurse seeing him.

How could he distract the nurse? It would have to be something good . . . something to keep him occupied, keep him from checking in to see how his young charge was doing.

Eric trudged up the stairs to his bedroom.

"You're probably right," he called back over his shoulder to the nurse standing at the bottom of the staircase. "I do need some rest. I will do just a little tinkering on my radio, then I plan to take a long nap this afternoon."

The nurse nodded in satisfaction. "I'll be in the family room watching TV if you need anything," he said as he turned and headed down the hall.

Eric smiled to himself as he closed his bedroom door, clutching the wire cutters to his side.

"GERI, I'M SORRY," Nestor Allende said again. He knew it sounded hollow. He said it every time.

The president and CEO of Allende International lay on the bed of the master quarters of his yacht, waiting for his wife to speak. His hands and feet were each tied with strong silk scarves to the nearest bedpost. He was lying naked on his stomach, three pillows stacked beneath his pelvis.

Geri had quit giving the "I'm very disappointed in you" speech long ago. Now she always got right to the terms of his punishment and subsequent forgiveness.

"I will not sleep with you again until you've been tested for STDs," she said.

"All right," he said.

"You must accept your punishment and make restitution," she said.

"All right," he said, his voice meek.

She walked to the bed stand and put down a small tray where he could see it. On it were a wooden hairbrush—oh, this was serious—and, even worse, much worse, a glass of ice water that also contained a peeled and whittled piece of ginger root.

His heart raced. *Awww, no . . .*

"Geri," he pleaded, "I love you. I'm sorry! How much do you want? Just tell me how much!"

His wife sighed. "I want you to understand that this isn't a game, Nestor. I want you to stop this, for real."

"I will. I will! Any amount, just name it!"

"We'll get to that. And whatever amount it is, I want it wired to me, into my account, today," was all she said.

Her voice was full of authority and firm decision. And Nestor steeled himself for a very unpleasant half hour to come.

SHE WAS IN A state-of-the-art virtual reality room. That was the most plausible—in fact, the only—explanation. Jaime sat up in the clouds and wished for a brief moment that she had time to experience and enjoy it.

That moment passed, and she snapped back to the fact she had a very limited amount of time to make her exit. First thing, she had to get out of the equipment she was undoubtedly wearing.

Jaime looked at her hands and saw . . . her hands. OK. She knew she was almost certainly wearing a very high-tech pair of gloves. But since she couldn't see them, it was going to be a trick to get them off. Or, as Yani would say, a challenge.

She used one hand to feel the other but met with only frustration. Not only could she not see the gloves; she couldn't feel them. She tried pulling them off but couldn't. They were almost certainly fastened on somehow.

Assuming they were there.

Oy.

She pulled at the invisible gloves again, and again met with no success.

Maybe she'd need to go for the headgear first, so she could see what she was actually dealing with. Jaime wondered if it was a helmet or just glasses of some sort.

She was doing her best to keep her train of thought, knowing that she was still slightly woozy—and there was a whole Technicolor drama being played out all around her. In fact, she was now below a throne from which light shone so brightly she had to squint.

Jaime put her hand to her head and pulled at the place where glasses would be. This time, she could feel some kind of elastic pinching at her head. She tried grasping the glasses and pulling straight up.

It worked.

She sat, clouds no longer around her, holding a pair of very expensive high-tech goggles. Out-of-focus colors, images, and sounds continued around her—and she even felt a wind blowing when something was happening at the throne—but she concentrated on removing the gloves. They were thick, with a metal wire conductor running down each hand. Upon closer inspection, Jaime saw they were latched on with a sort of industrial-strength Velcro at the wrist.

It took longer to remove the first one, since her other hand was still gloved. Once it was free, the other one came off easily.

Her thoughts were becoming clear.

Jaime reached into her back pocket. To her great relief, her handheld was still there, still tethered to her belt.

That meant she still had all the information she'd scanned in the file room.

It meant she knew where Britta Sunmark was.

It meant she was at least one step closer to getting to the kidnap victims.

But it was no good if she couldn't get out.

Jaime flipped on the phone function. For the first time, she got no signal. It made sense. She was in a cave inside a larger cave surrounded by powerful electronics. She doubted anything short of the actual angel Gabriel could get a message through.

She had to get out, to get the information to Yani.

Free of her electronic tethers, she looked around.

The most recent virtual reality technology with which she was familiar was a setup called, appropriately enough, the Cave. Whatever she was in was a seriously upgraded version. For one thing, the floor panels were raised and served as a fourth wall projecting the images.

She looked around to determine the location of the door. She couldn't see it at first. Even the corners were fully projected. Impressive.

She could still tell that the throne, where the subject's attention would be focused, was at the front of the box and assumed the door was at the back. She dropped to her knees on the ground and began to crawl back. It didn't seem anyone was watching her closely on a monitor or she'd be busted already. But she didn't want to go walking around without the gear inside the box in case someone glanced at the monitor she'd seen in the other room. She stopped crawling a yard from the back wall and studied it. From there, it was easy to find the outline of the door. She noted with interest the metal plate that identified the manufacturer: *Allende International.*

Jaime supposed she was still in the cave below the monastery. It was her supposition that the console in the file room ran the programs in the virtual reality Cave, and it was likely the Cave itself was set up behind the second closed door. If that was correct, she should exit into the same alcove from which she'd accessed the file room.

She remembered Brother Timothy saying, "I have to leave." It seemed as if they had drugged her and dumped her in the virtual reality room to await someone else.

Was anyone else left there as a guard?

Once Jaime was out, what to do?

There had to be another exit from the big cave. No one could bring in plate glass windows and complicated electronics or heavy file cabinets the way she'd come down.

How to find it?

If she could get back to that large one-way picture window, it would serve as a vantage point from which to see the whole cave.

Bottom line: She had to get the information out to Yani, now.

Jaime said a short prayer and pushed on the door.

WITGARD WAS NOT at all in the mood to climb the winding road to Chora. He couldn't believe there was an intruder in the cave. Constantine said she claimed to be a friend of Geri Allende's, but how could that be? Getting to the cave was not a romp in the park.

Witgard purposely kept himself suspended between nonchalance and panic. If she wasn't some kind of cop, what did he care? It's not like there were competing labs breathing down his neck. FIA was flying so far under the radar at this point that no one could see them as any kind of threat.

Who the hell could she be?

And what was he to do with her?

Witgard assumed that when he got there she'd still be doped, so it might be possible to get some truthful information from her. Then what? All he had to do was keep her out of the way until Tuesday, no matter who she was.

Constantine had told him that there were two monks' cells hollowed out on the circuitous path between the monastery laundry and the cave. There must be some way to keep her there for a few days. No one would be able to hear her scream; that was certain. Did those cells have doors with bolts? It was possible. If not, they could keep her bound and the door barred.

When he got there, Constantine would be gone, but Phil should remain, as should Anton, the burly armed guard.

Witgard preferred the streets of Chora with only the local population. It was so much more laid-back, so much more of a family affair. All the locals knew one another. Several nodded to him as he continued his way up. He wished it were low tide, when he could have either walked in the hidden lower door or taken the boat on the river into the cavern. Now the lower door was water and the river poured into the sea from the cave, with no headroom above.

Still, he needed to arrive before the woman came to her senses. That left only one remaining choice.

He had timed his arrival at the monastery to coincide with the monks' after-meal reflection. They would each be in their cells with the Holy Scriptures.

It was as expected. As he reached the top of the climb to the monastery, one young man, a local hired as kitchen help, hurried past him, probably late for Sunday meal with his own family.

Thus there was no one in the walkway to see him move the large, flat stone from the opening of the ancient cistern. No one to see him flip the small spring that rolled the concave bottom of the cistern open, letting the small amount of holy water drop down to the wooden floor of the glorified dumbwaiter below.

Witgard lowered himself in, crossed himself as usual with the sway of the small box, and flipped the cistern closed again.

Then he began the long, long descent in the dark.

JAIME HAD GUESSED correctly. The door from the virtual reality room opened directly into the alcove. The door to the file room was now firmly shut and, she assumed, locked. She quickly got her bearings. To her left was the passageway that led back to the room behind the waterfall. To her right was another passageway. She figured it must be the one that led down into the cave.

Which way to go? She'd have to go left to retrace her steps, though she was hoping to find another way out. She decided to head for the window behind the falls to scope things out. Jaime headed left. The rush of the waterfall provided the aural backdrop to the open cavern, and the light spray of mist filtered back as she again ducked down behind the short wall on the walkway. She positioned herself as unobtrusively as possible and looked up over the wall.

At first she saw no one. The cave was as massive as she recalled, and the river that ran through it was perhaps 12 feet wide. She didn't see any kind of bridge across it. As she watched, two men appeared below her, their heads close together as they talked, so they could hear each other over the sound of the rushing water. One of the men was slight and mid-height. The other was large and burly, his head once shaven but now bristly. He wore a shoulder holster, which contained a weapon.

She watched for another couple of minutes, but no one else appeared.

Jaime's confidence was building. She had actually attained her goal—gotten in, found the information they were after, and freed herself.

Now she needed to find the exit. It had to be close by. No one could bring in all this equipment unless there was a direct portal.

She couldn't see anything from her raised perch. She'd have to go down.

She crept backward and hurried across the alcove, past the office and virtual reality room. As she suspected, that short hall led to a staircase cut through the cavern wall.

It was now or never.

Jaime descended the stone steps. She paused at the bottom and listened for voices or footfalls but heard nothing. She ducked down and looked around the corner. Both men were standing on the flat riverbank far enough from the waterfall that they could continue their discussion. Their backs were to Jaime.

This allowed her a few minutes to peruse the interior of the cave for any possible mode of egress. Nothing. She did, however, spot what seemed to be an interior door on the opposite side of the cavern that echoed the one in which she stood.

Then something interesting happened. Both men looked up across the river. Whatever they saw or heard caused an instantaneous response. They jogged toward the waterfall and disappeared behind it, momentarily reappearing on the other side of the river. Aha.

They stood by an interior cavern wall and looked up. Jaime's gaze followed theirs. Only by focusing her attention on that one part of the cavern wall did she notice two dark brown vertical pieces of metal that blended well with the porous brown/black of the cave. Together they looked like tracks coming down from the roof of the cave. As she watched, a rectangular segment of the roof of the cave came lose from its surroundings and began a slow descent along the tracks.

It was a large rectangular wooden box on a pulley, a cross between an elevator and an old-fashioned dumbwaiter. The box had a door across the bottom half, but the top half was open. Inside stood a short man in a business suit.

The two men on the ground stood awaiting his arrival.

This must be the man with whom Brother Timothy/Constantine had the telephone conversation. He opened the wooden door while the contraption was still a foot off the ground and hurriedly stepped off. The three men conferred, and the slighter one pointed back up toward where the file room and the cave were. The new man nodded his head. They began walking back across the cave to where Jaime stood.

She didn't have much time to make her decision. That dumbwaiter might be the only direct way out. She needed to get there and get out before they noticed she was gone from the virtual reality room.

And, since the men were now heading toward the walkway behind the waterfall, her best shot was up and over.

Jaime hoped the door back past the picture window was the one that led to the opening on the other side of the cave.

She bolted back up the stairs, through the alcove, and crawled quickly along the open walkway. When she got to the door that opened to the area behind the falls, she hoped the men were looking anywhere but up. If she'd been fast enough, they could still be behind the waterfall themselves. She opened the door and slipped through. The sudden silence was breathtaking, and she rushed past the window behind the falls, to the closed door just beyond it. She pulled it open and was once again greeted by the sound of the falls—and, as she'd hoped, a staircase down.

She extended her arms and ran one palm against either side of the staircase walls to balance her as she fled downward. Once the men opened the virtual reality room, she was caught. There was no other way out, so she needed to be in the dumbwaiter and up top before they figured out where she'd gone.

At the bottom of the stairs, she stopped and peered around the corner. The men had crossed the river behind the falls and emerged on the other side.

Should she wait for them to be entirely out of view? That might not give her much of a head start. She would need time to figure out how to run the contraption. And from the length of the trip to get down here, it seemed like the shaft must be very long. If they stopped her in the midst of her ascent, she was a goner.

The men's focus was on getting to the steps and heading for the virtual reality room.

Jaime took the chance. She darted out and made a beeline straight for the box. A glance over her shoulder when she got there told her she'd made it undetected. The door was on a metal hinge, and she pulled it back, got in, and shut the bolt from the inside.

Then she slid down onto the wooden floor and looked up to try to figure out what to do. The mechanism seemed straightforward. There was a large metal switch that went up and down. It was currently down.

Should she wait? Or should she start it and get the heck out of there? The most dangerous part would be the forty feet or so it needed to go up within the confines of the cave, where it could plainly be seen by anyone.

It took both hands to push the lever up. There was a jolt to the wooden cage, and it started grinding up along its track. If this was an amusement park, she'd demand to see the inspection certificate before going any farther. She didn't have that luxury.

The machinery of the dumbwaiter was fairly loud. Only the rushing of the water masked its progress. For such an old contraption, it climbed quickly.

Jaime was huddled against the back corner of the floor looking up at the fast-approaching cave roof when the entire box shook violently. Something had fallen onto the top of the box. Something heavy.

Within moments, a pair of legs appeared over the side and swung forward, to catch the side of the wooden car.

But as they did, there was yelling from below, and gunshots. Blood spurted from the person climbing into the dumbwaiter.

The person who'd been shot lost his grip and tumbled off, making the long drop to the cave floor below.

But she saw his face and his expression of pain and surprise as he fell past.

Oh, shit.

It was Yani.

NO, NO, NO, NO. This couldn't be happening.

Jaime stood up and looked over the side of the dumbwaiter.

She was three-quarters of the way up the exposed track along the cave wall, which meant Yani had fallen maybe 25 feet. He was lying on the ground, but he was moving. He'd been trained how to land after a fall, but she didn't know how seriously he was wounded from the gunfire.

Jaime grabbed the lever with both hands and stopped the progress of the wooden box. It swung for a moment. Then she coaxed the lever the rest of the way down.

It began its creaking descent.

She knew the men were coming. She didn't have time for a safe landing. She might have a minute while they focused on her counterpart before noticing her, but she couldn't count on it. She opened the wooden door, swung her legs down, and jumped.

Jaime rolled when she landed, her feet still absorbing the waves of pain. She saw the men moving, a blur across the opposite side of the cave, as she knelt by Yani.

His breath was raspy; the left side of his shirt was soaked with blood.

"Were you hurt in the fall? Can you walk?" she said, but even as she spoke, she realized there was nowhere to walk *to*.

He nodded. "Let's get out of here."

Yani put his arm around her shoulder as the men disappeared behind the waterfall. As he struggled to stand, his breathing instantly became more labored, and he leaned heavily against her.

Shit.

Jaime had exactly three seconds to formulate a plan. That was how long until the guy with the gun came out from behind the waterfall.

Yani needed medical care right away. And if these goons captured them and got them upstairs, there was no way she was ever going to get Yani back down into the cave—or back up to the monastery.

They had only one chance.

Jaime absorbed the weight of his body, and as the first man came charging out on their side of the river, she half-walked, half-dragged Yani the few feet to the rushing current of the river of life and pulled him in with her as she fell.

THE WATER WAS FREEZING. It felt like a million little icicles piercing her clothing. Jaime bobbed back to the surface, still grasping Yani around the shoulder. The current was carrying them quickly through the cave—but toward what? The so-called river of life ran into the cave wall opposite the waterfall, but there was no headroom between the water and the cave. None. And she had no way of knowing where the river spilled out or if it ran under a water-hollowed passage with no air and no headroom for miles.

But behind her the men were shouting and running, and twice the air was punctured by the retort of the guard's pistol. Not that she could get herself and Yani out of the river at this point anyway. The water was moving too fast, and taking them with it. They were within a couple of yards of the cave wall.

Was Yani even conscious?

"We're going to have to go under," she said.

"I know," he answered.

She stayed up until the very last second, then grasped a lungful of air and ducked underwater, never letting go of her partner. He did his best to duck with her, and she pulled him downward with all her might.

And then they were under, and the world was black and frigid.

There was no variation. There was no slight filtering of light. There was no world other than the water and the rock wall above.

Her lungs began to burn.

Was this how her mortal life was going to end?

It could be worse. The water was so cold that if there was nowhere to come up for air, they would lose consciousness quickly. Already she couldn't feel her fingers or toes.

The burning spread, filling her chest. She was going to have to gasp soon, even if it meant taking in water, rather than air. The beginning of the end.

Lord, be with me, she prayed. *Be with us.*

Jaime had closed her eyes as she prayed, and she opened them to find silver specks glistening in the water around her. She began by wondering what the specs were—but then stopped abruptly. If she could see specks—if she could see *anything*—they must be nearing light. They must be nearing air.

She used her last reserve of energy to kick hard, to swim forward. She had to make it. She kicked and kicked again and realized that Yani was mimicking her, adding his final strength to hers.

And then the light got brighter, and she fought with everything inside her to make it forward and up into air.

Jaime burst out into the February afternoon, panting, drawing in air as fast as her lungs would process it. Yani was also gasping, but it didn't seem he was getting the oxygen he needed. She looked around wildly to try to orient herself.

They'd fought their way to the surface as soon as the river spilled out into the Aegean. The coast of Patmos was to her left—and, farther on, to her right.

The current of the river was pushing them out to sea, but she fought it, pulling them back toward the rocky stretch of land. Yani did his best to help, but it was clear he was in terrible pain and unable to catch his breath. Something was seriously wrong.

"Jaime, I . . . can't . . . breathe," he said, as if she hadn't noticed. "And . . . so cold."

"Yani, we're there. We're almost to land. See? It's right there. We can make it."

Her kicks still had some power to them; his were at least making him a neutral weight against the tide.

And then, thank God, they got out of the flow of the river and were picked up by the tide. It pushed them in waves back toward the shore.

When they got close enough in that Jaime could reach the bottom, she began dragging Yani, hopping up when she could to let the pull of the waves push them forward, while standing her ground as the current receded.

It seemed like years, but finally she got them both to shore. She left Yani lying on a rocky outcropping and climbed steadily up and around the curve of the bay to see if she could discover where they were.

When she rounded the curb, she nearly wept with relief.

For just above her was the terrace of a hotel room.

Farther up was a now-empty restaurant, with a sandy-colored rock wall overlooking the sea.

It was the Petra. The terrace restaurant was where she'd spoken to Geri only that morning. And the suite was the one Geri had pointed out as hers, the most expensive suite in the hotel, the one with a balcony hanging out over the sea.

Now all Jaime had to do was get Yani around the corner and up an outcropping of rocks. Then she could see about saving his life.

JAIME RETURNED TO the rocky shore to find Yani unconscious. The wind, which might have felt pleasant were she wearing a sweater and sitting in the sun, was blasting through her soaked clothes. She was cold to the bone and risked going into shock.

She didn't know if Yani was unconscious due to shock from the icy sea, from blood loss, or in response to an internal wound. He was still gasping for breath, his chest heaving.

What to do first?

Get him inside, obviously. Then what? Fight his hypothermia first, then her own? Then proceed to get medical help?

He could die of his wound before she got him warm. Or he could die from hypothermia while she treated his wound.

But they would certainly both die if she didn't get them inside and at least ensure that she'd remain conscious herself.

Jaime knelt down next to him and ran a hand from his cold forehead over his thick black hair, slightly curling because of their swim. "Yani," she said urgently, "can you hear me?" He roused slightly, the faintest acknowledgment.

"I know you're cold. I know you can't breathe. But there's a hotel just around the corner here. I can't carry you. Can you help me make it? If we can get there, there's an unoccupied room, just waiting for us. If we can get there, I've got you; you'll be fine."

He opened his eyes and looked at her.

"Please. Do this for me. I'll help you. Can you walk? Just a few steps." In spite of the circumstances, Jaime smiled to herself. Now she was using *the tone*—that voice of liquid reassurance that felt to her like condescension whenever Yani used it on her.

I'll try. It was more a mouthing than an utterance.

He was able to sit up, and she helped him to his feet with great difficulty. She stayed on his right side, away from the gunshot wound, and helped him—all six feet of him—to his feet.

She could tell it took all his energy to stay upright, and she ached for him.

Step-by-step, foot-by-foot, they progressed over the rocks. Several times he stumbled, but they didn't have time for her to let him go down, so she caught him, always caught him, and pushed ahead.

"Look!" she said when they reached the bend. "Look. See that terrace? That's where we're going. We can make it. We're only a few feet."

The terrace itself hung out over the water, and it was much easier to wade the last few feet than it was to clamber over the rocks. But then, another problem: how to get over the terrace wall?

She didn't know what internal injuries he had. She didn't know which way she could successfully move him and which way moving him could finish him off. She did know there was no way she could ever hoist him up herself. He had to weigh two hundred pounds, which was way more than she could lift.

"Jaime," he said.

"What?" She was almost in tears but didn't want to let him see it.

"Get a chair."

Of course. She climbed as high as she could on the ground, put her hands to the top of the terrace wall, and flung herself over. She let herself lie there for a few seconds, only because her body was trembling so hard from the cold, she was afraid she couldn't get her balance.

Geri had obviously been on her terrace that morning, because her Bible was still on the small table next to a coffee cup and a half-drunk glass of orange juice. The doors behind were unlocked.

Jaime opened them and hurried into the suite's sitting area. There she grabbed a brown wooden chair with a carved back, brought it out, and practically threw it down over the terrace wall. Then she jumped down and planted it as firmly as possible. She climbed up onto it and made a stirrup of her hands to help Yani up. He did his best to hoist his arms, torso, and legs up onto the terrace. The guttural sound from his chest was spooking her, but she pretended not to notice.

He climbed onto the chair himself—she helped push him up and over at the end—and then he lay down on his back on the wall.

He passed out cold.

During her two years of specialized agent training, Jaime had done intensive emergency medical studies. Now her mission was a given: triage, prioritize, stabilize, get to help.

Jaime knew she had two great advantages. First, she had a small medical kit in her bag, which was in her room right in this hotel. Second, through her handheld she had immediate live access to a physician.

The situation was complicated by the fact that Jaime was so cold. She couldn't stop shaking. And if she passed out, she would be of no help to anyone.

First . . . what first?

First she had to get Yani out of those cold, wet clothes and into some warmth. She knew there was no way she could possibly get him back to her room. The hotel wasn't laid out in traditional fashion, with doors opening off a hallway. Each room was an apartment on its own, separated by walkways and steps in the side of the hill. Even if she could drag him, unconscious, up all those stairs and across the entrance driveway, they'd undoubtedly attract a lot of unwanted attention.

No. She'd have to warm him here and then go to her room, get the kit, start the core reading on Yani, and during the time it took to work, she would take a shower and warm herself.

Jaime grabbed Yani under both his arms and dragged him into the room. It was no use asking him for assistance anymore; he was out.

Jaime bent down and used the strength of her legs to put her arms under his. She barely made it inside. She was running out of energy herself. There were two low white couches in the sitting room, forming an L against the walls and around the corner, but they weren't wide enough to be helpful. Inside the door, there was a beige rug.

Thank God. She laid him carefully on the rug, then was able to more easily drag the rug, with him on it, through the open arched doorway into the bedroom. She felt only momentarily guilty as she perused the buffed sand-colored walls and completely white bedclothes. Not that blood exactly matched any color sheets, but this wasn't going to be pretty. She threw back the blanket. It was another production to get his torso up and onto the low queen-sized bed.

She swung Yani's legs up onto the mattress. From there it was easy to sit on the bed herself and try to get the dripping, frigid clothing off his body.

The easiest part was unzipping and pulling off his windbreaker. It was stuck to his side where the bullet had pierced him, but she pulled it away. For once, thankfully, he was wearing a buttoned shirt, and she unbuttoned and removed it from his uninjured side, then carefully peeled it from the bloody wound on his front and slowly removed it from his back.

There was an exit wound.

Again, thank God.

She laid Yani down and quickly went down to remove his shoes and socks. His black jeans were harder, because they were so wet and fit so closely. But she unbuttoned and unzipped them and carefully pulled one leg off, then the other. The skin on his legs was so cold! She gently rolled him toward her, pulled back the blanket and top sheet a little farther on the bed, and rolled him back onto the dry inner sheet.

Then she peeled off his navy blue briefs.

She shouldn't look, she shouldn't care, she had no time to care, and yet—he was gorgeous. The proportions of his naked body were so . . . right, and the potential of the rest of him was apparent even pulled from freezing water. Michelangelo could have done worse if he'd needed a model on which to base his sculpture.

Yani . . . Yani . . . *Yani, damn you! Why didn't you trust that I had it handled?*

She intentionally retreated to righteous anger. She wrapped the sheets and blankets around him as tightly as possible and made a mad dash for her own room.

JAIME'S ROOM was up an outdoor flight of stairs, across the hotel drive, and up another flight. It was a single room plus a bath. All Jaime took time to do was scoop up her overnight bag, which held a change of clothes, and grab the small supply bag she'd stashed separately behind the floor mirror.

Then she turned and ran back toward the Petra Suite. Of course the Allendes would have the finest in the hotel. And thankfully, Geri was away.

She'd left the door to their suite unlocked. Jaime hurried inside and threw the bolt behind her. She rushed to the bed to make sure Yani was still breathing and found his gasps had gotten much worse. She touched his forehead, which was still icy cold.

Dear God.

She pulled out her handheld, pressed the button to open it, and said a short prayer of gratitude that among other things, it was waterproof.

Jaime was still shivering herself, and as she tried to handle the device her fingers prickled as if hundreds of pins were jutting into them. She was also grateful for the voice recognition technology!

"Operative wounded," she said, and her words were instantly translated into text. "Gunshot wound to side. Breathing extremely labored. Also danger of going into hypothermic shock from escape through February seas. Please respond."

She pressed "send" and a small red light indicated the message had gone out.

Jaime darted into the bathroom to start the shower water toward warm; then she sat down on the foot of the bed next to Yani and opened her supply kit, taking out the smaller medical case.

There were circles of blood on the sheets over Yani's wounds, but at least the ice-cold water had slowed his heart and helped stop the bleeding. There was a rasping in his labored breathing now.

As she opened the medical case, her handheld beeped a response. *Is patient bleeding copiously?* it asked.

"No," she replied.

Where is entrance/exit wound?

"Entrance wound, mid left back, slightly higher exit through lower left chest."

Core reading will give me the info I need and will attend to the hypothermia, came the response. *Do you have access to device?*

"I'm on it," she answered.

The core reader was a device that, through a combination of heat sensitivity, magnetic imaging, and pulsing, could read a subject's temperature, heart rate, and blood pressure, and could also image body organs and find current defects. If she was ever caught with it, it would stymie the current Terris-based medical community. The information it gathered could be transmitted instantly through Jaime's handheld to the medical personnel on the other end. It made a long-distance diagnosis possible. The imaging waves emitted also had the side effect of sending pulses of heat through the patient's body, temporarily raising his or her core temperature by several degrees.

That alone might save Yani's life.

She dug the ends of the sheets out from where she'd tucked them together underneath him and unwrapped them, carefully turning him on his uninjured side. She stuffed pillows in front of him so he wouldn't fall onto his stomach, which might further hamper breathing.

The core reader was disguised inside what looked like a large, fat laundry marker. Jaime bet it would write on a shirt if she tried it. She unlocked it with the code and took out the device, relieved when she turned it on and the electronic output panel sprung to life, the codes and numbers flashing ready.

The reading was taken rectally. Such poetic justice after Yani's now-famous insertion of her locator device. Wouldn't you know he'd be unconscious. She prepped the device, accomplished the insertion, watched just long enough to see the numbers begin to change. The process would take four minutes.

Then she ran for the shower, peeling off her own soggy clothing as she went.

Jaime was still shivering as she emerged, but at least her skin was losing its blue hue. She didn't have time for shampoo, so her hair wasn't completely free of that lovely briny fish smell, but oh, well. She toweled off and pulled on dry clothing from her bag. Best of all were the thick socks she'd packed. Her feet still hurt, but the socks helped enough that she knew she'd be OK.

No matter how cheerful her interior banter, fear gripped her like a vise in the instant before she opened the bathroom door. Every time she left Yani's sight she was terrified he'd be dead when she returned—which was, unfortunately, a rational fear. She was terrified that the bullet had punctured a lung and he'd be gone before she could get him help.

But the moment she pulled the door open, she heard the loud, rasping, sucking sound that came from him attempting to breathe.

He was still alive.

Not only that, his skin had a much healthier coppery tone. The crusty white/blue had not suited him at all. She expelled her own breath, breath she hadn't even realized she'd been holding.

As she approached the bed, she made another surprising discovery—he was awake. His eyes were open and even able to follow her progress.

"Don't die," was what she wanted to say.

"Don't roll over," was what came out instead.

"I'm . . . being . . . good," he answered, each word hard-won.

"Don't try to talk!" she said. This was torture.

She sat down beside him within 15 seconds of when the reader beeped. She withdrew it and plugged the small wire into her handheld.

"Jaime," Yani said.

She looked up and his eyes met hers.

Without meaning to, she blurted, "Just tell me why! Why did you come to the cave? I had it handled! I got the information. I know where Britta Sunmark is! I was on my way out! Why didn't you trust me?"

A single tear escaped her eye, and she repeated, *"Why didn't you trust me?"*

"It's . . . not . . . didn't . . . trust . . . you. Can't . . . trust . . . myself . . . when . . . you're . . . in . . . danger. . . . It's . . . bad. Wrong . . . I . . . know. Not . . . you."

With great effort, he reached his hand up and touched her face.

Her handheld flashed that she had a response.

"We'll discuss this later, OK? Let's get you fixed and out of here."

She was staring at the words on the handheld. It wasn't good news.

AS I SUSPECTED, *it's a pneumothorax,* it read. *That means the bullet has punctured the pleural space around the lung. The pleural space is like a big vacuum that surrounds the lungs. When it's punctured, the vacuum seal is broken and the lung cannot inflate or deflate to allow breathing to occur. And apparently, after puncturing the pleural space, the bullet has grazed the lung itself.*

The doctor's text continued, *This is good news, bad news, and good news. Good news is that it did not severely puncture the lung. It grazed the lung. There's a small tear. The bad news is, without intervention, he's going to suffocate, and soon. The good news: We've got someone on the scene to make a stabilizing repair. You.*

"Tell me what to do," Jaime responded.

The reply on her handheld was instantaneous.

From your medical kit, you'll need rubbing alcohol, gauze, four-inch square bandages, adhesive tape, the scalpel. From elsewhere, you'll need a bowl of water; tap water is fine. Also some kind of tube, anything, a couple of straws will do. And if for any reason there's not a scalpel in your kit, find something pointed, about that size. A ballpoint pen. Anything like that. Find those things and switch to your earpiece. Call me back using the following security code: 17999746, and I'll talk you through it.

Jaime left the list visible in the communication box and started with her medical kit. She found the required gauze, tape, bandages, alcohol, adhesive tape, and the small scalpel. Then she stood and scanned the suite for a bowl, any bowl. She found one with oranges in it, dumped the oranges onto the floor, and raced back into the bathroom to wash the bowl and fill it with tap water. She put the bowl on the floor by the bed and began looking for a tube of any kind.

Any kind.

Nothing.

She hurried back out onto the terrace, looked at the remains of Geri's early-morning snack, and was thrilled to find a bent straw still in the orange juice glass. Jaime grabbed it, ran it into the bathroom, cleaned it out with running water, then ran some rubbing alcohol through it. It would have to do.

Jaime rifled through the outer supply bag and found her earpiece, which had an attached microphone. With shaking fingers, she dialed the code the doctor had given her. She knew this time she was shaking in response to the phrase: *He's going to suffocate, and soon.*

Yani seemed barely conscious. His chest was rising and falling now, it seemed, with monumental effort. He was pulling in air through his mouth as quickly and deeply as he could, but it was not helping.

"OK," she said when the connection was made. "Operative here, as requested. Are you the physician?"

"I'm Anna," responded the doctor.

"Jaime," she said, relieved that it was a secure line and they could therefore talk freely rather than just text.

"Jaime, do you have the items requested?"

"Affirmative."

"You're using your earpiece, and you can hear me clearly?"

"Affirmative again."

"All right. This is what's going to happen. First, you're going to securely bandage the entrance and exit wounds. But within moments of doing that, you're going to have to insert a chest tube, because stopping up those holes will stop his breathing completely. You can't hesitate. You'll have to be ready to go right to it. Do you understand?" asked Anna.

"Yes," replied Jaime. "You'll tell me where?"

"I'll tell you everything. It's like I'm there, only using your hands. All right. Here we go. Let's do the exit wound first."

Anna's directions were clear, and the procedure was simple. Yani was still on his right side. Jaime cleansed the wound in his chest, gauzed it, and put on a tight bandage.

When she was done, suddenly his breathing became frantic.

"I've made it harder for him to breathe," Jaime told Anna.

"Then you've done it right. Now you're going to have to put him on his stomach and raise his right arm up over his head. You can put a pillow or two under his head and shoulders. Then, clean and bind the entrance wound the same way."

That also was accomplished quickly.

This time, when the bandage was in place, something changed. Yani's head was on one of the pillows, his face turned toward the wall, and he was sucking in air, trying to take in oxygen. It wasn't working.

"Take the alcohol." Anna's voice was firm and calm. "On the side of his back opposite the bullet wound, is his arm raised above his head? . . . Good.

"Now. There's a line that runs straight down from his armpit. Put your hand, fingers on top, at his armpit. Then move down about two inches. The palm of your hand should be in a line directly below the armpit. Are you there?"

"Yes," Jaime said, "yes!"

"Feel for the ribs. If you open your thumb away from your hand to make a V, your thumb should be resting on his third rib. Can you feel it, Jaime? Can you feel the rib under your thumb?"

"Yes," Jaime said. She used her other hand to count down his rib cage. It was almost certainly the third rib.

"With the other hand, quickly swab that area with alcohol. Fast! You're going to go in right above that rib. Above the rib. Is your thumb on the top of the rib?"

"Yes!"

"You have no questions about where your thumb is supposed to be? It's there?"

"Yes. Yes!" Yani was gurgling, suffocating before her eyes.

"Great. Then take the scalpel and plunge it in, angled up, right where your thumb is. Push it in to the second ring on the handle and stop."

"Plunge in the scalpel?"

"Yes. *Now.* You haven't time to think. To the second ring. No farther."

Jaime held the razor-sharp tip of the scalpel right over where her thumb was.

Dear God. And oh, shit.

She plunged. His body bucked, but only slightly.

"*Now what?*" she demanded into the mouthpiece.

"Take out the scalpel and replace it with the straw."

"The straw?"

"Yes. And put the end of the straw that isn't in the patient into the bowl of water."

Jaime withdrew the scalpel and inserted the straw into the hole, threading it down until it was as deep as the scalpel had been.

Then she got the bowl of water from the floor, put it on the bed next to Yani, and let the other end of the straw hang over into it.

Immediately, bubbles appeared and floated to the top of the water.

"Are there bubbles?" Anna asked.

"Yes."

"OK. You're going to tape that straw in place. Then, congratulations. You've just done your first chest tube."

Jaime felt her arm muscles go limp. She stumbled back into the chair she'd positioned by the bed earlier. Yani's chest began to rise and fall rhythmically. His color began to return before her eyes.

"Now what?"

"This is a patch. You've got to get him to a doctor."

"Do I have to find someone local, or can I bring him in?"

"Technically, he could spend the rest of his life like this, but I wouldn't recommend it. Yes, you can bring him in, providing you can keep him intubated."

Just as Jaime was trying to figure out how to act on this information, she heard a new sound.

The key in the lock of the hotel room door.

PATSY COVINGTON SAT in her rented Volvo on the A13 near Vaduz in the midst of a monumental traffic snarl, listening to her daughter's Hilary Duff CD. While many tourists couldn't fathom the aplomb with which both the Swiss and the Germans embraced a traffic jam, which they called a *Stau,* it was very much in sync with Patsy's own feelings even when she was en route to a job.

Well, she wouldn't even say *en route to a job*; for her the job started the moment she left her family and ended the moment she returned and released the nanny for the day. Everything in between was work. And once she started work, she went into what others might call a Zen state. Nothing bothered her. Even difficulties such as an accident on the Autobahn. She was a pro. She knew to build in extra time for unexpected occurrences. In her line of work, the unexpected *was* expected. Only a novice wouldn't plan for it.

Patsy would never fly out of an airport that was near where she was staying. Instead she was driving to neighboring Germany, where she would cross the border with one of her many forged passports. She was well on the way when traffic came to a standstill. In her experience, Germans usually took a *Stau* as an excuse for a party, but it was cold enough today that they'd stayed in their cars.

She hummed to herself and again played the scene in her head of what tonight's executions would look like . . . one by one she'd have the guards bring the kidnap victims to the boathouse on the dock by the compound. Once inside, they'd be shot once, execution-style, in the head, their bodies dumped through the trapdoor designed for just this purpose. The bodies would rest in a netted area, underwater, under the dock, the bones finally being carried away once the fish and the tides had reduced them to small enough pieces to slide through the netting.

When the fifth victim had been disposed of, Patsy would dispose of the guards. The first would also be shot execution-style, the second and third in either the heart or the back of the head, depending on the speed of their reflexes.

She would sleep so much better once this was accomplished and she was back home.

She was even planning to take a couple of months off.

It had been a complicated job, and she had been well paid for it. Enough so that she could take some time to take the kids to the Smithsonian and other places of cultural interest. They were going to grow up to be enlightened citizens of the world.

She turned up the volume on the CD player and smiled.

THE KEY JANGLED again in the lock, this time with greater force. The door opened but was stopped by the inside bar Jaime had thrown.

The doctor asked through the earpiece, "Where are you headed?"

"Samos. By boat. It'll take an hour," Jaime said quietly.

"I'll have someone waiting."

Jaime disconnected and removed the earpiece, pocketing it quickly.

"Hello?" The voice came from the front door. "Housekeeping? This is my room."

It was Geri Allende.

Jaime moved into the sitting room. "Geri? It's Lynn, the woman you met this morning. Are you alone?"

"What? Lynn? Why are you in my room?"

Jaime could see her through the opening in the door. "It's a long story. Are you alone?"

"What? Yes. Let me in."

Jaime opened the door, took Geri's hand, and pulled her inside. "Thank God you're all right!" Jaime said. "Come in, quickly. You're in danger!"

"What are you talking about?"

Jaime took Geri quickly past the door to the bedroom and sat her down on the beige sectional sofa that ran along the sitting room wall.

"Geri. We don't know each other very well, and all this is happening very quickly. You're being used as a pawn in a very dangerous game."

"What are you talking about? I still don't understand why you're in here. Are you a thief?" Geri stood, ready to go into the bedroom to inventory her things.

"No. Not at all, although I can understand how you could get that impression." Jaime's grasp on Geri's arm pulled her back. "Listen, Geri, I know this sounds crazy, but the son of a dear friend of mine has been kidnapped. I have been helping the authorities track down the kidnappers. It turns out there were others taken by the same people, for the same purpose. And there's new information that the captives are going to be murdered, and soon."

Geri stared at her, clutching her purse to her chest. "What does this have to do with me?"

"This morning I followed a man named Constantine, who has ties to the kidnappers. But the surprising thing was, when he left his house, he was dressed as a monk—well, as a seminarian—and he came here, to meet with you."

"*Brother Timothy?* No, you're mistaken."

Jaime held up her hands in a "hear me out" gesture. "After you disappeared with him through the monastery laundry—"

Geri opened her mouth but didn't interrupt.

"I was concerned enough about who he was and what he was involved with that I followed you."

"Wait—you're not a minister?"

Jaime almost smiled at the non sequitur. "Yes. I am an ordained Presbyterian minister."

"Did you make it down to the cave?" Geri's eyes lit up. "You saw the river?"

"Yes. It's a fantastically beautiful place."

This time it was Geri who grasped Jaime's hands. "I'm glad you saw it! When I was there . . . the things I saw . . ."

"Geri, it was a fantastic cave, and a fantastic experience. Someone has spared no expense. But . . . there's no easy way to say this . . . you were drugged."

"What? No, no, I wasn't. How could I have been?"

"There must have been something in the 'water of life' that Constantine gave you—"

"But he drank the same water!"

"From the same cup?"

"No, he poured it into a different cup, but—"

"There must have been something in your cup. I'm telling you, Geri, you were drugged and taken into a virtual reality room, a very advanced one."

"Why are you saying this? You don't know the vision I had! You don't know the Word I got from God!"

Jaime had a rush of anger for what these people had done to Geri. It wasn't as physically life-threatening as being kidnapped, certainly, but they were using her, manipulating her in the most heinous way.

"Yeah," Jaime answered softly, "Actually, I do know the 'Word' you got. You see, they found me and caught me. Your 'Brother Timothy' shot me up with Versed and the man dressed as the Apostle John helped him drag me into the virtual reality Cave. I saw it all—the clouds, the throne—heard the trumpets . . ." She sighed. "As I said, someone spared no expense."

"But why? Why would someone go to this trouble? What is it they want?" A look of incredulity crossed Geri's face. "My husband's money. That's it, isn't it? I got him to give me sixteen million dollars. Today, just now. Wired into my account. I was going to give it to Brother Timothy."

"The only thing that doesn't make sense," Jaime took a deep breath, "is that the virtual reality Cave was manufactured by Allende International."

"How dare they! How dare they buy something from my husband's company to use against him!"

"Geri . . . I could be wrong, and I certainly don't want to imply anything about your husband. But my guess is that he is investing in the research which is made possible by the kidnapping of these people, including the son of my friend. However, the whole kidnapping thing is quite unsavory and so he doesn't want any direct links—"

"*Money laundering?* You're saying my husband is using me for money laundering?"

"Geri, I don't know. At this point, I don't have enough evidence to accuse anyone of anything. What I do know is that a man named Witgard Villella was on the way over to get information from me when I escaped. That Brother Timothy does go by the name Constantine, and he is involved with the scientist we think has the kidnap victims. We also know these people are very dangerous, Geri."

"How do you know that?"

"Because when my partner came to the cave to try to save me, they shot him and they tried to shoot me."

"What? They shot someone? With a gun?"

"Yes. It was only by the grace of God we escaped. I pulled him into the river of life, which took us out of the cave. Fortunately, it spat us out right here, practically below this hotel. My partner was dying, so I had to get him out of the water and to relative safety. Yours was the closest room; he couldn't have made it any farther. That's why I barged in like this."

"Your partner?"

"Who's working with me to try to save the kidnap victims."

"Did he die?" Geri was understandably aghast.

"No. I had to intubate him, and now I have to get him to help. And then I've got to go save those kids, before it's too late."

"Where is he? Your partner?"

"In your bedroom. Like I said, I couldn't get him any farther."

Geri stared at her, hard, for a couple of seconds, as if to try to read what was behind her eyes.

Then Geri stood up and marched toward the arch that served as the bedroom door.

ERIC SHUFFLED QUICKLY down the icy path. He knew he was running late and was worried he would miss his rendezvous with Daniel. When Eric finally reached the fenced enclosure, his boots slipped on the path and he almost crashed into the fir trees along the fence. But as he pulled aside the branches, he was relieved to see the back of his friend against the chain link.

"I was afraid you weren't coming," said Daniel, obviously tense from the wait. He had the little child sitting on his knees and was playing peekaboo with her.

"Sorry. I had to slip by my nurse. He thinks I'm taking a nap."

"Your nurse? You have a nurse?" Daniel started to turn around to look at the boy behind him but caught himself.

"Yeah, I know it sounds weird, but I get sick easily."

"That sucks. And I bet it makes you real popular with your brothers and sisters!"

Eric shook his head. "Don't have any. I'm an only child."

"You don't know how lucky you are."

"You can't mean that." All his life he had wished for a brother or sister, and here was someone who would gladly give up what he had.

"You can have mine. You don't know what it's like, living in the shadow of Zeke the Great, who does everything right, honor roll, sports star, soooo popular. . . ."

Eric smiled. "I'd deal with it."

"Although right now, I wouldn't mind if Zeke walked through that gate. I would give anything to see even him."

Daniel's voice was full, and Eric suspected he was close to tears, which was not cool with another guy around. So he quickly changed the subject.

"So, is everything going OK for tonight?"

Daniel grabbed some snow and started packing it into a snowball. The baby was fascinated and tried to poke it with her fingers.

"I think I have everything I need. Did you find something to cut the fence?"

"I found some small wire cutters. They aren't very heavy, but I think they'll work."

"How far will we have to go once we get outside the fence?"

"We'll have to go most of the length of the island, which is about a kilometer, then across an ice bridge to the mainland. There is a little town right there. But it'll be dark, and the path is icy. It may take a while."

"Oh, man. Then I need to ask you another favor. Can you dig up some coats? I have this parka, but the baby only has this thin jacket." They both looked at her. She was wearing a polar fleece jacket that was clearly made for someone much older. On her it brushed the ground like a kimono. "I don't know if the others have anything at all."

"What sizes?"

Daniel grinned. "Why? You going to a mall? Seriously, we'll take anything you can find. Don't let anyone know what you're doing. Besides the baby, there's a slim guy who is taller than me, and two or three other people."

"I'll bring whatever I can find. What time?"

"My plan is to break out of here at 1 A.M."

"I'll be here," said Eric with such conviction that Daniel stood and turned to look him directly in the face. Daniel could see the intensity and commitment in his new friend and felt moved.

"You could be risking your life, doing this. I mean, seriously."

Eric gave Daniel a small salute. "See you tonight."

Eric turned and headed back for the path.

Thing is, you've gotta have a life before you can risk it, he thought. *And I think I'm finally getting a life.*

GERI GASPED when she saw Yani lying on her bed, his side bandaged and the straw protruding from his back. "Dear God," she said, "you weren't kidding."

The sheets were wound around the lower half of his body, but even half-dead, the strength was obvious in his arms and shoulders, as was the curl in his black hair.

Jaime put her arm around Geri's shoulder. "No. I wasn't kidding."

"So everything you're telling me, about the virtual reality room, the drugs, the kidnapping, it's all true."

"I'm sorry, but—yeah. And the thing is they're planning to kill all the kidnapped children very soon. There's a baby, and two young kids—my friend's son is fifteen. Can you imagine? We've got to find them before they're murdered."

She could tell Geri was overwhelmed.

"But who would murder children? Nestor would never, ever, in a million years, be involved with something like this! He would never have anyone shot. Never!"

"I'm assuming he doesn't know about any of this. In fact, he's obviously going to great lengths to distance himself. But right now, I've got to get my partner to a yacht in Skala Harbor. I'm sorry to have barged into your room like this. But once I can figure out how to transport him, without this Villella person finding us, we'll be gone."

"This is all . . . just incredible! If what you're saying is true . . . it can't be . . . but you were there; you were in the cave. . . ."

"I was. Honestly. I saw it all, the river of life, the vision, the clouds. The clouds had golden edges. And I came down behind you under the monastery. There was a whole long ledge that was only like eight inches wide! I nearly went hurtling off it into space. But what you didn't see was the one-way glass window behind the waterfall and the control room up the staircase in the side of the cave. Geri, they shot my partner. Look at him—he nearly died! Have you ever had to put a straw into someone?"

But Geri was in her own world. "I was so close. I was ready to change my shoes and find Brother Timothy and give him a check for sixteen million. I mean, within minutes!"

Jaime put a hand on Geri's shoulder. "I'm sorry about that. Truly, it's a terrible abuse of trust. But I need to ask you for a favor. I have to get my partner to our boat, and when I do, I need you to somehow explain to the proprietors what happened to their bed."

Geri looked at her. "You're serious? That's your favor? There's no explanation needed; I just pay for new bedding. But how are you getting him to the harbor? Calling an ambulance?"

"No, I can't risk being seen by anyone involved with this whole scheme. I'm going to call our captain and have him bring the dinghy. We're going to have to carry my partner down, best we can."

"Let me help you. I have a man on our yacht; he's my own employee. I trust him completely. He never tells anything. I use him to ferry me when I don't want Nestor to know I'm coming. And he's very large. He could carry your friend."

Without waiting for a response, she pulled out a beeper at her waist and clicked in a text message. It vibrated in return. "He just dropped me; he's still in the motorboat. He can be back in five minutes," she said. "Please. It's the least I can do in response for your risking your life to follow me down."

Jaime hesitated only briefly. She had been trained at one of the few places that stressed the importance of making "willful decisions to trust," especially when it would be to the benefit of the person offering assistance.

"OK," she said. "Thank you. Let me call my captain and tell him to be ready."

Jaime also chose to type her text to Aeolus back on the *Kairos,* telling him to look out for them and be ready to set sail for Samos, where they would find both their plane and a doctor waiting.

Then Jaime went out onto the terrace, where she found Geri already on the lookout. Given the overwhelming nature of what was going on, and the ramifications it would have on Geri's personal life, Jaime was surprised by Geri's next question.

"So, if you are really a pastor . . . ," Geri began, her eyes on the rocky islands across the way, "so if life isn't about waiting moment by moment for a rapture . . . what is our purpose? What does God want us to do?"

Jaime turned and looked at Geri, tried to bring her mind back around to what she was saying. All Jaime wanted to do was get Yani back on the *Kairos* and go get those kids.

"Wow. You don't ask the easy questions, do you?" she asked, still watching for the boat.

"If there's no rapture, if we're not going to be lifted out of here, what's the point? What do we do?" Geri asked again.

Jaime tried to be patient. She knew Geri's whole picture of the world, of her husband, was unraveling. But how to answer in less than an hour or two?

"Are you familiar with Jesus' Sermon on the Mount?"

"Of course."

"That's what I always come back to when setting my own priorities. It's Jesus' statement, all in one place, of what the Kingdom of God looks like. And he was very clear that God's Kingdom starts here and now, not just when he returns to renew the earth and live among us in the New Jerusalem. Feed the poor, comfort those in grief, work for justice, take our stewardship of the planet seriously." Jaime wanted to honor the seriousness of Geri's question, but at the same time she was willing the boat to show up, around the corner. *And, oh yeah, stop kidnapping people. . . .*

Geri's long black hair was free, and it danced in the afternoon breeze. She looked at her hands, as if trying to frame her next question correctly. "My husband is a good man. He has devoted his life to achieving immortality—or near immortality—for the very wealthy who can afford to use science to keep themselves fit and healthy, perhaps for hundreds of years. Somehow this doesn't sound right to me, although I can't exactly say why. I know we live much longer now than people used to live, and that's a good thing. . . . I don't know."

Patience, give me patience . . . and something coherent to say, Jaime prayed. She ducked back inside to check on Yani, who appeared to remain stable, at least.

Then she returned, and both women stood together on the terrace of the hotel on Patmos, their eyes scanning the sea before them. It was clear Geri was still awaiting an answer.

"Look at the Aegean; it holds such power and mystery. And the sky and the clouds, and everything we saw re-created so exquisitely in the virtual reality room. But in a way, this is also only virtual reality. There is another, much grander reality awaiting us when we see God 'face-to-face.' Can you even imagine it?

"Trying to cling to these bodies—well, it's sort of like being in prison, getting a pardon from the governor, but refusing to leave the jail. Why would you refuse freedom? Why refuse to become the full person you were created to be? To me, it makes no sense."

Geri added, "It's not about wanting to live forever in these bodies, at least not for me. And I think part of what bothers me about the people who are trying to do that is the whole division between rich and poor, who gets to live forever and who's dying even from malnutrition and genocide right now because those of us who have the money and power to change things are looking after ourselves instead. How am I going to explain that, when I see God 'face-to-face'?" Just saying the words seemed to lift a weight off Geri's shoulders.

"These are important things to consider," said Jaime.

Geri said, "Will you pray for me? I mean, to make the right decisions? I guess I suddenly have sixteen million dollars to spend."

Even as she spoke, a small motorboat appeared from behind the rocks to the right, the very rocks that Jaime and Yani had tried so hard to swim past to get to the hotel.

The man at the helm was muscular and tall, and Jaime thought they had a good chance between them of getting Yani down to the boat, even while he was intubated.

Jaime smiled. "You got it. And you pray for me, too," she said to Geri. "And for the kids."

PATSY COVINGTON WAS a great believer in visualization. On every job she used it successfully. During kidnappings, she visualized the victim unconscious in the car long before he or she was actually there. But the victims always did end up occupying the space Patsy had already claimed for them.

With removals, she pictured the victims already parted from their bodies and the bodies disposed of. As far as she was concerned, the eight people she was offing tonight were already dead. She felt as relaxed as if they were gone and dumped, unable to identify her or cause trouble for anyone, ever again.

In some ways, then, her Cessna Grand Caravan was like a time machine, she thought, as she and the pilot hurtled down the runway in those few rattling moments before takeoff. It was as if the plane was a time machine to the past, where the future in which she was already living would be created.

She enjoyed that idea so much that she pictured herself piercing the space-time continuum as the Cessna left the ground, heading for Barkarby Airport, northwest of Stockholm.

JAIME KNEW THEY WERE in a race against time to save the lives of the kidnapped Eden children. In a way, it was a miracle of its own that Yani was alive and walking across the tarmac next to her. It was hard to believe that three hours ago he had almost died, and now here he was walking on his own to the plane. The doctor whom Anna had arranged to have meet them at Samos had explained that while a pneumothorax was indeed very dangerous, when it was fixed quickly and correctly, a patient could be up and around quite soon. But now that Yani *was* alive, Jaime gave herself a moment to mourn the time it had taken the doctor to repair his pneumothorax. She hoped the extra time spent would not keep them from successfully completing their mission. She hoped to God Daniel Derry was still alive.

Jaime let Yani precede her up the steps of the Gulfstream 150. At least he wouldn't be flying this time and insisting she pay attention. In fact, the doctor only let Yani go with the assurance he'd spend the three-and-a-half-hour flight to Stockholm resting. "Then don't go scaling any walls, at least for a day or two," the doctor who'd been awaiting them on Samos had warned. Jaime wasn't sure where they were going, but she would put money on the fact that there were walls that needed scaling.

"We're ready for takeoff, sir," said Costas, the pilot who'd met them in Rhodes and brought their plane to Samos. Since Yani was injured, Costas would fly them to Stockholm. Aeolus, who had captained their yacht, was co-pilot. "As soon as you're settled, give the signal."

Aoelus helped Yani into the cabin. Yes, OK, it ticked Jaime off that everyone connected with their mission, everyone connected with Eden, treated Yani like he was a celebrity or visiting hero. Not that they disrespected her, but they all called him "sir," not out of protocol but from the obvious respect they had for him. How can you blame someone for displaying respect? The doctor didn't call Yani "sir," but certainly seemed more jocular than he needed to be when warning him about scaling things.

"You ready?" Aeolus asked Jaime, who had boarded behind them and fastened her belt across the wide brown leather seat.

"Yes, thanks," she said. At least they'd remembered to bring her along.

Aeolus turned and reentered the cockpit. The checklist already complete, the plane turned and headed for the runway.

Jaime turned on her handheld and again flipped to the names of those missing. She was reading the information on Inaba, the young woman kidnapped from the African hospice where she'd been working, when the wheels left the runway and the plane headed up.

"Jaime."

She reluctantly turned around. Yani was lying on a berth that pulled down into a bed from the cabin wall. His head and shoulders were propped up on a backrest, and two seat belts crossed his body under the blankets, one above and one below his bandaged wounds.

They hadn't had any time alone since Geri had shown up at the hotel room, which was just as well. Given the opportunity, Jaime would have had trouble not smacking him silly.

He was waiting for her to meet his eyes. Yani, the wounded hero— and her along for the ride.

"Come sit by me."

Oh, wow, lucky her. She didn't move.

"Are you angry?"

"Am I angry? If you'd trusted me, you wouldn't have nearly died and we could have taken off two hours ago."

"Close the cockpit door."

The door to the cockpit had been open for takeoff. The plane was now beginning to level off, and Jaime felt safe enough to unbuckle and comply with his request.

Then she went back and sat, not by him, but in one of the large leather chairs that faced backward from the cockpit, where she could at least see him as they talked.

"So tell me, what were you doing, falling onto the dumbwaiter just as I was getting the hell out?"

"Villella got a call saying they'd caught you. I followed him to the monastery. I couldn't exactly ride down with him in the makeshift elevator car, but I could use the rope to rappel down. I was almost there, ready to make my final descent into the cave, when the car started coming back up. Once it reached the roof of the cave, I would have no way out, no way to get down to you. I had to jump for it, onto the car, and then on down into the cave. Unfortunately, that caught the attention of Mr. Villella and his friends."

"I had the information. I was on the way out. I had it handled."

"Jaime, you've learned my secret," Yani said seriously. "Something even Aeolus and Costas might not know. In fact, if you weren't my partner, I'd have to kill you."

Jaime looked at him, aghast. The truth was, she knew he could kill her, and easily. He'd had her in a death grip soon after they'd first met. You don't tend to forget that kind of thing. "Yeah?" she said, trying to sound casual. "Whatever this secret is, does Clement know?"

Yani smiled. "Oh yeah. Clement's well aware."

"What secret do I know, then?"

He sighed. "You might find this hard to believe, but . . . I'm not perfect. Obviously. In fact, I'm human in a way that endangered both our lives. I screwed up, big-time. Thank God you were there to pull me out." At least he looked sincere. "You deserve to be mad at me. In fact, you should be, at least for ten minutes or so. That's really all the time we can spare. But the fact is, my imperfection bought you a chance to earn your stripes. Which you did, by the way, with flying colors."

"So you no longer want me off the assignment?"

"Jaime, I never thought you couldn't do it. What I told you in the hotel room back on Patmos was true. It was myself I didn't trust, never you. I didn't trust myself to act in a coolheaded way, were you ever in danger. And I think I proved to both of us that those fears were well-founded."

She was staring at the pattern of swirls on the gray-blue carpet.

"Now the question is, can you forgive me, and move past the anger? We're no better off if you become the one with issues. We've got to work professionally, both of us clearheaded and issue-free. I'm apologizing, and releasing the issues on my side. Can you do the same?"

Oh, drat. She needed her righteous anger to keep her balanced.

"I'll see what I can do," she said. "But first let me really enjoy these ten minutes."

"Fair enough," he said. He opened his arms and again beckoned her over. This time she went and sat next to him on the pulled-down berth. He took her hand. "Jaime," he whispered, "thank you."

She felt the anger draining from her muscles, the tension flowing out her fingertips. Darn him anyway.

"Rest here a minute," he said. "You deserve it."

"Is there room?" she asked. "There can't be. You're injured." In response, he slid toward the wall, leaving enough room for Jaime to lie down on her side, her back toward him. He draped one arm casually over her shoulder.

"Is there anything else you want to say?" he asked. "Whatever it is, get it off your chest. I can take it."

"Speaking of chests, don't you *ever* make me intubate you again, do you understand me?"

"I'll do my best to avoid it. But I've got to say, kudos to you. You saved my life."

"Yeah, well, this once." She exhaled deeply, letting the rest of the tension drain away.

"So you took all my clothes off?" His voice had a much lighter tone.

"Yep. Saw you totally naked. Took a core reading, in fact, in case you don't remember that part. But don't worry; it's not how I get my jollies," she said, echoing his line to her in a similar situation. Then, perversely, "Oh, wait, I lie. Actually, it is."

"That's fair," he said, the smile still in his voice. "'Cause when I said it, I lied, too."

How did he win, every time? But this time Jaime was smiling herself, as she shared the warmth of Yani's berth, and she let herself surrender to an hour's sleep.

"WZ5JNT, DE, AA7ZU." Eric smoothly flipped his thumb and forefinger against the paddles of the electronic key, tapping out his father's amateur radio call sign, followed by his own. He had been listening to the radio all evening, but the frequencies had been dead, no activity, until about 15 minutes before. Then suddenly they had opened up. When he began to hear call signs from the midwestern United States, he decided to try to reach his father.

Over and over Eric tapped out the Morse code message, hoping his father would hear his radio call. Then he would pause a few seconds to see if there was an answer. This was not their normal meeting night, but he really needed to talk to his dad.

Earlier that afternoon, Eric had returned to the estate and managed to slip back into his room just before the nurse came to check on him. After receiving a clean bill of health for looking so rested, he had begun to dig through hall closets in search of coats.

Now he sat, with a trash bag full of coats hidden under his bed, waiting to slip out for his 1:00 A.M. rendezvous. This was starting to seem real, not like a game at all. Eric was nervous and very worried. He needed to talk to someone. Someone he could trust.

It wasn't that Eric did not trust his mother, but she was so very protective, she would flip if she knew what he was up to. And she might not even believe him. He couldn't afford to have anything stop him right now; this was too important.

He had considered talking to the nurse—he seemed to be a pretty good guy—but Eric just didn't know him well enough to trust him.

But Eric's father had always been supportive. He didn't talk down to Eric but listened to his ideas, and supported even his most challenging projects. This project was a little bigger than anything he had undertaken before, and he needed help.

"CQ OK. CQ OK." Having no luck reaching his father, Eric decided to see if he could reach anyone in Oklahoma who might give him a call.

He tapped out the "CQ" again, and this time there was an answer. It wasn't from his father, but Eric recognized the call sign of a friend in the Stillwater, Oklahoma, Amateur Radio Club.

Eric responded, asking the man if he would call his dad and ask him to meet on this radio frequency. The other man signed off, and Eric sat and fidgeted while he waited.

After ten nerve-racking minutes, he heard a faint signal. He grabbed his headphones, hoping he could block out other noises and focus on the code.

"AA7ZU, DE WZ5JNT, AA7ZU DE WZ5JNT BK." [To AA7ZU from WZ5JNT, *break*.]

"WZ5JNT, DE AA7ZU. HW COPY DAD? BK." [To WZ5JNT from AA7ZU. *How do you read me, Dad? Break*.]

"GD CPY ERIC. UR RST 548. HW R U? BK." [*I read you fine. Your signal is pretty strong. How are you? Break*.]

"DAD NEED HLP. MET TEEN FROM DC. NAME IS DANIEL DERRY. RPT DANIEL DERRY. SAYS HE WAS KIDNAPPED. MAYBE 5 OTHERS. I BELIEVE HIM. BK."

"QTH? BK." [*Location? Break*.]

"HR ON LILLISTRA. IN FENCED COMPOUND. BK."

"HAVE U TOLD UR MOM? WZ5JNT BK."

"N. AA7ZU BK." [*No. Break*.]

"Y? BK." [*Why? Break*.]

"DONT THNK SHE WUD BELIEVE. ALSO VY WORRIED. DANIEL SAID MED EXPERIMENTS. BK."

"AS." [*Stand by*.]

Five excruciatingly long minutes passed as Eric waited for another message from his father. Did he believe him? Would he call Mom and alert her to Eric's activities? Finally he heard the message continue.

"AA7ZU DE WZ5JNT. ERIC, DESCRIBE DANIEL."

"ABT 15 YR, LITTLE TALLER THAN ME, SLIM, BLACK. ROCKNROLL TSHRT. BK."

"WEB ARTICLE. 13 FEB 06. BOY DISAPPEARS IN ALEXANDRIA VA. NAME DANIEL DERRY. FITS YOUR DESCRIPTION. BK."

"U BELIEVE ME THEN. BK."

"NEVER DOUBTED U. BE VRY CAREFUL. SAY NOTHING TO MOM. I WLL CALL POLICE."

Suddenly Eric realized his mother was standing there, tapping on his shoulder. With his headphones on, he had not heard her enter the room.

"Eric, it's late," she said with concern. "You really need to shut off your radio and go to bed."

"But Mom, I'm in the middle of a contact!" As he spoke to her, he continued to work the electronic key. "GOTTA GO. CUL." [*See you later.*]

"No arguments. Get ready for bed now."

As he removed his headphones he heard the last of his father's call.

"88. SK." [*I love you. End of transmission.*]

Under his mother's watchful eye, the young boy flipped all the switches on his radio and neatly placed the key and headphones in their storage spaces. He purposefully avoided meeting her gaze, not wanting to take any chance that her mother's intuition would sense that something was up.

Britta walked up and wrapped her arms around her son from behind, leaning her chin on top of his head.

"I know you want to make as many contacts as possible, filling up that silly map of yours with hundreds of pins . . . but there will be other days."

She hugged him tightly to her. "I promise, there will be many more days."

ABE DERRY sat in the study of his two-story brick residence in the general officer housing area of Fort Belvoir. Piled before him on a massive desk were the files he had requested from the office, hoping to find a distraction in his work. But they sat untouched as he stared out his second-story window at the light snowfall visible in the twilight sky.

He had returned from Germany the previous afternoon to find his wife secluded in her studio, taking solace in working with her hands. Eirene had discovered that sculpting was an excellent way to focus her thoughts and emotions, and her meditative artistry had helped to calm her while she waited for news of her missing son.

That evening, as they lay in bed together, Abe had held her tight and told her all he had learned from his meeting with Jaime. Could they find hope in her words? Did the fact that there were other gardeners from Eden whose children had been abducted provide comfort or make the situation seem even more horrible?

They had agreed that hope was not something to be found in the facts. Hope did not hinge upon little scraps of information they could sweep up and cling to. Hope sprung from the certainty that life is good, the world is ultimately good, and we are in good hands. So here he sat, seeking signs of hope in the evening snowfall.

The phone rang. Abe let it go for three rings before picking up, as the FBI agents, sitting downstairs preparing to monitor the call, had requested.

"Hello," he said with the cautious tone he had adopted over the past two weeks.

"Is this Abraham Derry?" The voice on the other end of the line was unfamiliar, male, but there was no sound of electronic muffling, which could have been used to disguise a voice. *Probably not the kidnapper,* Abe thought.

"Yes, who's calling?" He found it hard to remain calm through these calls. There had been many false leads over the last few weeks.

"My name is David Carlson. I live in Oklahoma, and think I may possibly have information about the location of your son."

Abe's heart stopped beating. Was this another crackpot? There seemed to be many people who wanted so desperately to be noticed that they made up the craziest things to get attention.

"Go on. . . ."

"My ex-wife lives with my son in Sweden. Let's just say she and I don't get along very well, and I haven't seen my son, Eric, for a year. But he and I maintain contact by radio. Today he told me he had stumbled upon a fenced compound and saw a young teen inside the fence, who seems to match your son's description. The teen said his name was Daniel Derry, and when I looked it up on the Internet, I found the article about your son's kidnapping."

"How did he describe the boy?"

"Eric said about fifteen years old, slim, black, and wearing a parka and a T-shirt that said something about rock and roll."

Abe resisted the temptation to jump out of his chair. The T-shirt his son was wearing had not been in the news. But Sweden?

"Where exactly is this compound?" Abe could hardly contain himself.

"Eric told me they had moved to an estate on an island north of Stockholm. He called it Tranholmen Island."

"Do you know anything else about the location or the situation?" Abe found it natural to kick into "commander" mode, drawing all pertinent information from the briefer and preparing to give orders and make things happen.

"Not much, I'm sorry. I can't say I've been invited to visit! But I get the impression it is a very small island. I looked it up on MapQuest and found it in a waterway called the Lilla Värtan Strait, just off the shore from a town called Danderyd."

"Anything else you can tell me?" He heard the man hesitate, as if there was something he wished to say and just couldn't.

"No," he said finally. "I tried calling the local police here, and they were very wary about acting on information from an eleven-year-old boy. They said they would 'pass on the tip' but didn't sound too enthused. But look, Mr. Derry—"

"Abe, please, it's Abe."

"Abe. I know my son. He does not make up things like this. So I got your number myself off the Internet. I thought if I could talk with you directly, maybe you would want to pass on the information to the FBI."

"Consider it done," said Abe with a slight smile, for he knew they were recording every word of this conversation. "And would you mind leaving me your phone and address? They'll undoubtedly want to contact you for follow-up questions."

"Certainly." And as the man rattled off his contact info, Abe sat marveling at two very important bits of information. One, his son was alive. Two, in Sweden?

"David," he said as they were closing. "Many people would not want to get involved. They never would have called. Thank you for your efforts."

"I hope it helps. Good-bye." And he hung up.

"Yes. Hope. That is what this is all about," Abe said to himself as he pushed back from his desk, preparing to go downstairs and discuss the implications of this new information with the FBI.

"HERE WE GO, GIRL; are you ready?" said Daniel Derry to his little friend as he noted the time on his wristwatch. Daniel had spent the last half an hour wondering if he could really do this. But he remembered what his dad always asked when he had to make a choice: What's the downside?

The downside of trying to escape was that they risked being caught and killed. Admittedly, a potentially bad downside.

On the other hand, the downside of not trying to escape was that they'd definitely be killed. That certainly put the first downside in perspective.

Daniel pulled the pack of gum out of his pocket and one by one unwrapped each of the four pieces, sticking them ceremoniously into his mouth. As he stuffed in the final one, he found it a bit tough to chew but worked hard to make sure the glob in his mouth was wet and squishy.

The toddler was watching all of this with curiosity and reached up toward Daniel's mouth to try to get some of the gum from him.

"Nope. Sorry. This is working gum."

As he continued to chew, he pulled the toddler onto his lap and rubbed one hand across the baby's forehead. He tried to push hard enough to make the skin turn pink without hurting the little girl. She squirmed and batted at his hand, not so much out of pain but because he was holding her very tightly and she wanted to be up and moving around.

Just as she started to really fuss he stood up and carried her to the door. He began to pound, hard, and to yell.

"Somebody come. Please! I think the baby is sick." He continued to make as much racket as he could until, finally, one of the goons opened the door.

The man was half-dressed, shirttail hanging out, no socks, and he needed a shave. He looked as if he had been lounging in his room before going to bed.

"What is it?" he growled testily.

With the baby in his arms, Daniel stepped right into the doorway. "I think this kid is sick. She got really hot, and has some sort of rash on her forehead. She needs to see a doctor or something."

The baby was still squirming and seemed very unhappy.

"We don't have a medical doctor here, kid, and we're not gonna send for one."

"Please, there has to be something, someone who could help? What if it is something really bad . . . or contagious?"

The goon took a step back from the two captives, suddenly aware that he might be standing too close to a sick child. He thought for a moment, then, never taking his eyes off Daniel, stepped to the door of the next cell and opened it.

"Hey, lady. You're some sort of nurse, right?"

"Yes, I am a nurse," came a calm, musical voice from inside the cell.

"Well, come out here and check out this baby. See if you can do anything for it."

A lithe young woman, the one who said her name was Inaba, emerged from the next cell. She had beautiful dark brown skin and wore a brightly colored dress of orange, brown, green, and yellow. The dress flared at the bottom, and she had matching pants. But the outfit must have been made for warmer weather—it looked possibly African?—because someone had given her a green short zipper jacket to wear over the top half. Daniel did not move from where he stood in the doorway to his cell but let her come to him as the goon watched them closely.

The young woman reached toward the baby and felt her forehead. "Oh, you poor little thing. You're so warm! I'd better have a look at you."

As Daniel handed the baby to her, she stood directly between him and the guard, who did not see Daniel slip the wad of gum out of his mouth and stuff it into the hole for the bolt lock.

He nodded to the woman, who stepped back, saying, "I'll take her and see what I can do."

Without one glance at the guard, she walked calmly back to her cell with the infant. The guard closed the door behind her, then turned to Daniel.

"OK, kid. Enough excitement for one night. Back inside. Go to sleep."

As the door closed behind him, Daniel held his breath, hoping the man did not notice the lack of a telltale click of the bolt lock falling into place. When it was apparent the man would not return, Daniel sat back on his bed and stared at his watch as he waited to begin phase two of the escape plan.

MONDAY

IT WAS WHEN THEY got to the other side of the ice bridge that led from the town of Danderyd that the "what-ifs" started for Jaime. What if the captives were being held at another, more remote, location? What if Britta was not involved with them at all, she was doing research of a completely different kind? What if the kids had already been murdered? What if there were guards with guns?

On the other hand, Jaime had heard Constantine talk to Britta and warn her that she was to lose her subjects a day earlier than expected. Certainly that was the link that tied it all together? As for the dangers ahead, Jaime had been well trained, and she was with one of the most experienced Operatives in the entire world. She prayed again for wisdom, justice, and a positive outcome.

"It looks like there's a large estate this way," Yani said, holding the satellite photo of the island and pointing at the large building near the center of the island on the southern shore. They had studied the satellite image on the plane, gotten readouts that told them the island was not owned by a single corporate entity such as Villella's; it was divided into various plots. "We're looking for something large enough to hide five people."

A small road in front of them ran about 20 meters and forked. Yani gestured to the right-hand fork. Jaime nodded.

It was cold, windy, and dark, so they moved silently toward their destination. Yani had followed the doctor's orders and rested for the whole flight, and now he seemed up and ready to rock and roll. Jaime suspected he'd collapse tomorrow or whenever the mission was successfully completed. But for now, he was Yani in mission mode, the Yani she knew best.

They came to a place where the road forked again. Yani stopped. His handheld was flashing. "Perfect," he said, "perfect. Someone is using Constantine's phone to call someone on this island. Bring us home, Brother Timothy, bring us home." Jaime was grateful they'd taken the time to find the information from Constantine's phone back at the University of Athens. Yani touched the earpiece in his ear to activate it and waited as the connection was made to someone on Tranholmen.

The global positioning function of the phone lit up in flashing red on Yani's island map.

"We've got her," he said victoriously. "We've got her."

Together they agreed that the road that made a hard left off their current path was a quicker route, and they hurriedly turned down it. Yani continued to listen to the conversation. Both Operatives wore black coats and all-terrain boots, which had inserts that used tiny pinpoints of light to illuminate the path just before them. The island was pitch-black, which Jaime found comforting.

Tranholmen Island was not large; it was 1.2 kilometers from end to end. The conversation between Constantine and Britta ended, but the lighted location of the scientist kept flashing, a beacon on Yani's handheld.

"He was checking in to make sure she was all right," Yani reported, "which leads me to believe we've come to the right place, the center of the action."

Both Operatives were athletic, and Yani had recovered enough that he could keep up as Jaime moved quickly down the path, which joined up with another, and another.

"I think there's a more direct route," Yani breathed, "but it's perhaps good to come upon the site from the side."

No sooner had he said that than a house appeared before them, light shining from most windows—at least from those they could see above the 10-foot-high stone walls.

Jaime smiled and shook her head. "I could've told you," she said.

Yani smiled, too, his last of the night. "OK. Primary directive: Find the captives. This place is certainly big enough that they could be well hidden inside."

"I take it this is where we split up," Jaime said.

"Yeah," said Yani. "You still comfortable being seen?"

That meant if they ran into someone such as Britta, Jaime would reveal herself in an attempt to get information. Yani would remain invisible. Both of them had listening devices sewn into their jeans, which were made to look like the other silver studs sewn into the seams.

"Yep," Jaime replied. "Let's get going. Should we at least check the front gate, to make sure it's not standing wide open?"

"Even if it is, I'd advise against strolling through."

"I agree."

Yani put his back against the wall and cupped his palms. Jaime stepped into them and up onto his shoulders. From there, she was able to hoist herself to the top of the wall.

"Godspeed," was all Yani said. Then he was gone.

She stayed still and prone on the top of the wall, surveying the inner yard. There were several tall trees and, in past them, a large, square manor house. Even though it was very late, many rooms had the lights blazing. Something was indeed happening here tonight.

She swung her legs, let herself down as far as possible, and dropped the rest of the way.

It looked as if the house was made from the same stone as was the wall. Jaime decided to scope the perimeter of the house to see if there were any clues as to where five captives might be hidden.

Around the back of the house were two doors at an angle to the ground, which she assumed used to be the coal chute into the basement. The basement seemed like it might be a feasible prison, certainly. The wooden doors were held together by a padlock. She got out her lock pick and had the padlock off in under a minute.

As she opened the first door, she heard footfalls crunching on the snow and looked up in time to see the shape of one large hulk of a man round the corner.

She quickly shut the trapdoor and moved into the black shadows of the house. But it seemed he'd heard something. He moved toward the coal chute doors and actually stood there, studying the padlock, which was now on the ground, for a minute before he opened the door. It was as he pulled it open that he looked up and saw her.

He stood a long moment, surprised, and then he said, "Who teaches the errant father?"

"Excuse me?" she said, which was apparently the wrong answer. The hulking man pulled a Luger, black in his hand against the black of the night.

As he came closer, Jaime saw that his hair was thick and blond. His neck was thick also, and she would lay money on the size of the biceps under the heavy parka.

She pretended to be frightened, pulling in on herself, but as he got closer, she suddenly came to life and kicked the weapon from his hand. He roared and lunged at her, grabbing her foot, pulling her to the ground. Then he kicked her hard, as she again scrambled to her feet. She had been trained in hand-to-hand combat and in unarming an opponent. But he was thinking differently, as if he was distracted.

She decided to make a run for it while he tried to find his gun in the snow. But he lunged and managed to grab her by her jacket. Thinking fast, she managed to slip out of it and stood, shivering in the dark night. Just as quickly, he grabbed her, saying, "I don't know who you are, but I don't have time for you."

He spun around on his heel while she was still planning her next move, took three steps forward, and dropped her over the side of another rock wall. This one was waist-height and circular. And as she fell straight down into air that got ever colder, she realized it was a well.

ERIC WAS TEMPTED to laugh at the image he must have presented as he shuffled down the wooded path toward the research complex, carrying his trash bag of coats.

I look like a Swedish tompte, he thought, picturing the little gnome-like man who filled in for Santa. It was a moonless night, and the boy carried a small flashlight in his free hand to illuminate his path. His breath was clearly visible and Eric could feel the chill through his gloves.

When he had slipped out of his room, Eric had seen no sign of his nurse. Eric had noticed, though, that his mother was still working in her office, and really hoped she wouldn't stop by to check on him before she went to bed.

In the dark, the path seemed much longer than it had that afternoon. Everything looked so different, even eerie, as trees loomed on the outer edge of the flashlight glow. He began to wonder if he had taken a wrong turn somehow and tried to calculate how long it had been since the last turn he had made.

Suddenly the light shone on a clump of fir trees directly across his path. This was it, the stand of trees shielding the chain-link fence! He dropped his burden and shone the light across them to find the largest opening between the trees. He found one spot that seemed a bit larger than the others, pushed between the branches, and dropped to his knees.

Quickly the boy had the wire cutters out and began to work on the bottom-most link of the fence. Eric squeezed the handles together as hard as he could but could not snap the link in two. With both hands he tried to press even harder. Still nothing.

Next he tried clamping the tool down on the wire, then rotating it back and forth in a sawing motion. This began to leave an indent in the link—a small one, but it was a start.

For five minutes Eric rotated the cutters back and forth, squeezing hard with his fists clamped down on the handles. Finally, the link snapped. He sat back, shook his tired, sore hands, and looked at his watch.

He knew that if it took that long to cut every link, he wouldn't be ready when they came out!

His arms were shaking from the effort to cut the first link, but he leaned back in and started to cut on the next one, putting the whole force of his upper body into his work.

JAIME HAD BEEN expecting to hit water, so she was surprised when she landed on a hard surface instead. He'd dropped her in feet first and she'd managed to land correctly, but her feet still throbbed, and she had really scraped her left arm in her attempt to right herself. Oddly, the Teutonic icon who had so casually tossed her down had also tossed her coat down after her. She had the feeling he was parking her somewhere out of the way until the night's events transpired, and then they'd haul her up for questioning of a not-friendly nature.

She pulled her parka on gratefully and put her gloveless hand on the hard surface below. The well couldn't be that deep. Beneath her hand was solid ice, several inches thick. At least it had broken her fall and was now holding her up.

Looking up, she couldn't see the sky. There must be a small roof built over the well. The rounded stones from which it was built were small, and she wasn't going to bet she could successfully climb out. There was a rope with a bucket up above, but the bucket had been pulled out of the well. It was probably sitting on the ground beside the well. In any case, the sturdy rope was well out of reach. She sat down and sighed, took out her handheld, and called Yani.

It took only a couple of minutes before his head appeared over the top of the well.

"Hi," he said.

"Shhh," she said. "Is Dolph around?"

"Don't see anybody." Yani was looking over the rear of the well, farthest from the house, from where he would have the most expansive view of the yard.

"So?" she said. "Can you help me outta here?"

"Oh. Didn't know if you needed help. Didn't want to presume."

"Well?"

"Well?" he said.

"Well, what?"

"Do you need help? I wouldn't want to rush in, if you have it handled."

"I would appreciate some help," she said.

"How do you ask nicely?"

Oooh, she could smack him. "Please. Please help me out."

"You're sure?"

"Pretty please," she said. He would pay for this later. She'd make sure.

Yani checked the rope for strength; he cut the bucket off and threw the rope down. Once she had it, it was a couple-minute climb up the rocky side.

"I've heard falling down a well can traumatize a person for life. Hope you can muddle through," he said casually.

I'll muddle you, she wanted to say, but as they both looked toward the house, they both saw it at the same time—a petite woman, short blond hair, turned on a light in a large downstairs room. It was the kitchen.

"Think that's Britta?" Jaime asked.

"Let's find out," Yani replied.

And again, he was gone.

PATSY COVINGTON WALKED onto Tranholmen Island like she was striding onto the main set of a movie about her latest job. Commanding the stage. All eyes on her. All energy radiating from her, drawing other, weaker humans in her wake.

She would be so glad to have this job finished. But this was the thrilling part. Actually getting to kill people, for money. People who needed to be gone.

The drama of it was so much fun. The emotion was so high. Most people had to go to amusement parks or horror films to manufacture the thrills. But she lived it. She saw the terror, heard them beg, smelled the gunpowder and the blood, tasted the victory, felt the adrenaline surge. You think chocolate gives you an endorphin surge, sweetheart? Try killing people who would rather not be dead.

Patsy was on foot, her sleek Volvo waiting near a pub just across the bridge. She knew exactly where she was going and that it would take her exactly sixteen minutes to get there.

Sixteen minutes to get there, half an hour to do her work (as the compound was purposely built close to the dock), sixteen minutes to walk back, and voilà! She would be back in Switzerland for the breakfast buffet.

She hummed to herself as she marched swiftly into the dark, providing her own sound track for the drama that was her life.

JAIME FINGERED THE LOCK PICK in her hands and looked at the back door. There were three steps up to a small outdoor alcove with a single bulb burning above. Estate house in the middle of nowhere, chances were good it would be alarmed. And the last thing she wanted was for Dolph to show up again and decide he wouldn't throw her down the well; he'd kill her and be done with it.

If an alarm did go off, she'd hide out of sight and, as quickly as possible, enter either by a door that had been opened or by breaking a window in a room that had been left unattended.

There wasn't time for hand-wringing. She climbed the steps, used the lock pick, then stood a moment, waiting for the alarm, ready to jump down, out of sight.

Nothing. She opened the door a couple of inches. Still nothing. She walked into the back hall and closed the door behind her. The hall lights were not on, but light from rooms in the front of the house allowed her to see.

The paneled door to her left must be the kitchen they had seen from outside. She opened it and stepped in.

It was a large, old-fashioned kitchen, the kind servants used to bustle around in, with a large fireplace at one end and a long worktable running down the middle.

The door swung shut, and the woman who had been the sole occupant of the kitchen turned around. Jaime had never seen terror like the terror in her eyes.

"How did you get in?" she asked. Her white-blond hair was shaped around her face, and she was dressed in brown slacks and a brown-weave sweater.

No point in being coy. Jaime held up the lock pick.

"Why are you here, in the house?" the woman cried. "The research is going well! Allende still needs me, certainly!"

"Are you Britta?" Jaime asked.

"*Yes.*" This, too, was anguished.

"I'm a friend of Jorgen Edders."

"Is it done? Have you fin—you're what?"

"A friend of Jorgen Edders."

"Then you're not . . . *her?*"

"It seems clear whoever *she* is, I'm not who you were expecting."

Britta crumpled against the center table, a cry escaping from the very center of her being. "This is not what I meant to have happen at all!"

"Look, I don't know what Dr. Edders told you, exactly—"

"I wish he hadn't! All I ever wanted was to save my son. What mother wouldn't want that? The rest—living forever—that's craziness. Who would want that? This world is nothing but pain and betrayal—why would you stick around? Why?"

"I'm sure you had the best of motives."

"When the brain tumor got worse, Dr. Edders began to talk . . . he always talked to me, of course; I was his assistant; we hit it off . . . but he began saying incredible things, about people with a strain of mitochondrial DNA that didn't break down as early as most, and could be useful in the design of a recombinant strain—"

Jaime stalked over to Britta. "Listen. We can discuss it later. Right now, I'm here because my dear friend's fifteen-year-old son is about to be murdered. Where are they? Where are the kids?"

"Your friend's son? Fifteen? Which one—?"

"Daniel. So please, tell me where they are. You don't even have to come."

"I can't." She slid down to the floor, against one leg of the long center table. "I can't, or they'll kill me. I know they will."

"I thought you just said that dying sounded good!"

Britta glared at her. "I have a son. I can't leave my son."

"Tell me where they are. No one will ever know how I found out. You can stay here with your son. Please. You seem like the kind of person who doesn't want the deaths of five kids on her conscience."

Britta put her head down on her knees and knotted her fists. When she looked up, she whispered, "OK. But you can't tell anyone I told you."

No sooner had she spoken those words than the hall door burst open once again, and the body-builder type Jaime had labelled Dolph stood there, this time not confused at all but in a rage.

"Your freakin' kid is gone!" he bellowed at Britta.

"What? No!" she screamed, and scrambled to her feet.

"What is he up to? Did you put him up to this?" The large man strode to Britta and grabbed her arm.

"What are you talking about? How can he be gone? You and I both know he can't be outside in this kind of weather! And you're his nurse, dammit, get your hands off me!"

Somehow, this had snapped Britta back to herself. She pulled free from the large man and looked at Jaime. "Come on," she said. "I'll take you there."

"How stupid are you, lady?" roared the nurse, pulling out a pistol. "You're not going anywhere! And wherever your damn kid is, you'd better get him back here, or I'm not responsible for what happens!"

"You work for Villella," Britta said. "I should have known."

"I somehow don't see a Nobel in your future," he said, and pointed the gun between her eyes.

JIMI STARTED as he heard the lock to his door flick open. He had dozed off on his bunk, losing track of time. He looked up to see the boy, Daniel, peeking around the door and quietly motioning him to come out into the hall.

So he did it! Somehow the kid had figured a way to get his door open.

The teen held his finger up to his lips and whispered, "I don't think they leave a guard awake at night, but we'd better be careful just in case."

There was a convex mirror up in the corner of the ceiling at the end of the hall. It was used by the guards to watch for movement down this hall, but in the same manner, it also allowed someone in this hall to look back in the other direction. Jimi could see there was no action near the guard room and sleeping quarters.

Daniel slipped quickly across the hall to the door opposite Jimi's, flicked open the lock, and disappeared into the room.

"What . . . ?" Jimi heard the muffled surprise of its occupant.

"Shhhh!" Jimi heard a quiet interchange, then Daniel reappeared, followed by a boy a few years younger than himself. The three first escapees huddled in the hall like a football team planning their next play.

"I'm Ryan," whispered the new addition to the group, wide-eyed and excited at this great upturn in his circumstances.

"Jimi."

"Daniel," whispered the teen, completing the circle. "Now here's the trick. The last door down there is in full view of the guard station.

But when they first brought me in, it was the middle of the night, and it looked like the guard had been sleeping by the desk. Let's hope he's doing that now."

"We'd better lock these cell doors behind us," whispered Jimi. "That way, if the guards make a quick check later tonight, they might not realize we're gone."

Daniel nodded agreement, and Jimi and Ryan started locking doors. Daniel peeked carefully around the corner to check for any sign of guards, then quickly moved to the last, unopened cell. He unlocked the door and slipped inside.

A few moments later the teen emerged with the toddler in his arms, followed by the most exotically beautiful woman Jimi had ever seen.

Wow. That must be Inaba.

Daniel quietly closed the last cell door and locked it, joining the rest of the group who huddled out of view of the guard station.

"So far so good," he whispered. "Now, I'm assuming you need some sort of password or key to get out through the main exit, so we're heading for the exercise yard. We need to slip past the guard room and the sleeping quarters. I think we'd better crawl one at a time, in case one of the men is awake."

At the teen's mention of the exercise yard, Jimi tried to puzzle why they would escape into a locked yard. He started to speak up, then thought better of it. Daniel seemed to have a plan. There must be a reason for heading that way.

"I'll go first," Jimi offered, and Daniel nodded. Jimi dropped to his knees and peeked around the corner. Holding up his hand with crossed fingers for all to see, he disappeared down the hall. Looking up in the convex mirror in the corner, Daniel could watch as Jimi crawled safely past the guard station and sleep room, then stood and motioned for the next person to try. Daniel sent Ryan around the corner, followed a few moments later by Inaba. Finally, with the toddler held firmly in one arm, Daniel crawled around the corner and down the hall to join the rest of the crew.

They were now standing in the kitchenette and waiting area outside the lab. On the side wall was the door to the exercise yard, with one of those quick-release "panic" bars often used on exit doors.

Jimi knew they should waste no time loitering here, near the guards' sleeping quarters, but he had this sudden fear that some sort of alarm system would trigger when they opened the door. He held his breath as Daniel stepped over to push the bar, and was relieved to be met with silence as it swung open and they passed through into the yard.

As they quietly closed the door, cutting off any light from inside the building, the group could see a small flashlight moving outside the fence on the opposite side of the enclosure. Daniel hurried over, and the rest followed quickly. There they found a young boy, with a panicked look on his face, frantically trying to cut the fence. He was using a very small pair of wire cutters and had only managed to sever four links in the fence. Jimi could see it was in no way big enough for them to crawl through.

"My hands, they are so tired . . . I can't . . ." The disappointment in his voice was clear.

"That's OK; we can take it from here." Jimi stepped up and motioned for him to pass the cutters through the fence. The boy did so, then held the flashlight on the fence as Daniel and Jimi, together, squeezed the cutters over the thick wire. They both grimaced, but there was a resounding snap. They moved to another, then another, quickly cutting three more links. Then, with the boy outside pulling and them pushing, they bent back the fence enough to start crawling through.

First went Ryan, then Inaba, who waited for Daniel to hand the toddler through to her arms. Then Daniel, followed finally by Jimi. He was free.

ERIC CARLSON STOOD about 25 meters down the snowy path from the fenced compound, waiting as each person crawled out from the cedars and made his or her way to the small glow that was his flashlight. As the last one approached, he couldn't help but marvel at the motley nature of this little band of escapees. What common factor would have made them victims of kidnapping? Or was it just random chance . . . bad luck to be in the wrong place at the wrong time?

On the surface, there was no commonality. Daniel had that gangly, growing look of a young man in his teens. He had fairly dark skin, but some of his facial features, nose, forehead, lips, looked more European than African. In stark contrast, the little toddler who was clinging to his leg looked like she was of Asian descent.

Another, younger boy, maybe 12 or 13, stood next to Daniel. He was sturdy and blond, with his straight hair in a longish cut. He could be Scandinavian also, but from his speech, Eric pegged him as American, probably from the Northeast.

And then there was the biggest surprise . . . that beautiful, petite, brown-skinned woman who had emerged from the trees. Her clothing was light and colorful, and her voice had a slight British lilt to it. She had large eyes that calmly took in her surroundings. How could she be so calm?

Finally there was a man, tall, copper skin, maybe in his twenties, who had the look and air of a businessman. His accent was definitely British.

"Everyone, this is Eric," said Daniel, pointing to the Swede. "We'll hold other introductions for later, but for now, he has some coats for us, but we better hurry."

Eric opened a large plastic bag at his feet and began handing out the coats it held.

"I'm sorry, mister," said the young boy to the businessman when the rest of the coats were distributed. "I couldn't find any men's winter coats. I hope this ski jacket of my mother's will fit."

It was bitter cold out, and even though the man was stomping his feet in an attempt to keep warm, he seemed hesitant to don the lime green parka the boy was holding out. Then the need for warmth overcame the man's pride, and he took the parka. He stuffed his arms into the sleeves, and his wrists came well out the ends. The man smiled and shrugged, mouthing, *Thanks,* to Eric.

"What now?" said the man, turning to Daniel. In spite of his obvious elder status in the group, he seemed to defer to the teen as the key architect of this escape.

"We're on a small island," he said, adjusting the weight of the toddler he held in his arms. She had been wrapped in a small child's jacket and was laying her head on his shoulder as the warmth began to make her drowsy.

"Eric is going to show us a path to the bridge that will take us to the mainland and, hopefully, to the police."

At that moment, in the direction of the compound, they heard the back door open and the shouting of the guards.

"C'mon, we better get going," said Eric, who turned and headed quickly down the path. No one needed any encouragement to follow.

"THEY'RE GONE."

Patsy Covington stood fuming over the guard who was sleeping on a cot by the desk in the watch room.

"What?" he said drowsily as he sat up and tried to shake the sleep out of his eyes. "That's impossible."

"You idiot, of course it's possible!" She was down in his face now, and he didn't like that. "I have just checked on the prisoners. Every cell was locked, and every cell was empty. Go wake up your worthless buddies. Now."

Patsy stalked out into the hallway while the hapless guard scrambled to put on his shirt and boots.

How did they do it? she wondered. This was by no means a maximum-security prison, but the locks were sound, the walls were solid. Was it an inside job? Had one of the guards helped them get away?

She heard mumbles and shouts come from the sleeping quarters as the other two sleeping men were roused. Soon the three came stumbling back out into the hall, boots only partially laced, shirts unbuttoned.

Patsy was disgusted. These men had come with good references. They were supposed to be professionals.

"Listen to me very carefully." In a calm but deadly tone, Patsy now addressed the three guards. "You will find where and how the prisoners escaped, and return to me with that information. Your lives depend upon it. You have five minutes."

The men looked at one another for a moment, then scattered in three separate directions. One went back to the hall with the cells, another moved toward the front entry, and the third headed for the lab and the exercise yard.

After about three minutes, the first man returned.

"Well?"

"It looks like one of them jammed some gum in the door so it couldn't lock."

At this point Patsy didn't care how they'd gotten the gum. She knew that one way or another it was due to the incompetence of these men.

The second man returned from the front gate.

"Nothing," he said, breathless. "The door has not been messed with, no tracks. I don't think they went that way."

Both men turned, expectantly, toward the direction of the yard, hoping their comrade would have something more to offer. They resisted the temptation to look at their watches, wondering if she was really serious about the five-minute rule.

"I found it!" the third man yelled, bursting through the door from the exercise yard. "I found where they got out. There is a section of fence cut and bent. It looks like they headed down the path."

"Where does the path lead?"

"I think it heads across the island, past the estate."

"Well," she said with a half smile. "That will be all for now."

"Don't you want us to help find them?"

"No, I'll take it from here. You can go back to sleep, all three of you. Might as well . . . no prisoners to watch."

The three men shrugged and headed back toward their sleeping quarters. They did not see the look of steel in the woman's eyes, or notice that as they moved toward their beds, she followed them, with gun drawn.

"YOU'RE NOT AUTHORIZED to hurt her, are you?" Jaime asked, moving quickly around the table.

"Who the hell *are* you?" Dolph spat.

"It's my guess that Mr. Villella still has urgent need of Ms. Sunmark, isn't that right?"

"Yes, but I'm sure as hell allowed to shoot you," he said, pointing his gun at Jaime instead of Britta. "Both of you, stand together. And tell me where your brat is," he commanded the scientist.

"Why? Is *she* here?" Britta asked, admirably not changing facial expressions when a stranger walked in the open kitchen door while Dolph was facing the other way.

"Yes, the Good Mother is here. If you and Eric had just stayed put, everything would be fine—" And those were the nurse's last words before Yani grabbed the back of his neck and rendered him unconscious.

"I'll take care of him," Yani said. "You go."

"The compound is this way," Britta said, running down to the front door and grabbing her wool coat on the way out the door.

IT WASN'T EASY to follow the path with only one small flashlight to guide the band of escapees. They dared not run, because it was slippery and they couldn't see the footing very well. But they pushed it as fast as they dared, afraid that it was just a matter of time before their escape route was discovered.

Daniel was walking with Jimi, who had taken the sleeping toddler to spell his aching arms.

"How did you do it?" Jimi asked. "How did you get past the door lock?"

Daniel smiled at the memory of his recent accomplishment.

"With Inaba's help," he nodded toward the woman on the path ahead of them, "I plugged the lock hole with gum. I had hoped the guards wouldn't notice and I would be able to just push the door open after they went to sleep. But when I checked the door, the lock had gone partway into the hole and it wouldn't just push open. So I had to use the table knife from dinner to pry it open the rest of the way."

Daniel held his arms out to take the toddler back, and they passed off the sleeping child, whom he draped over his shoulder. He then noticed that Eric had come to a stop and dropped to one knee. Daniel moved quickly to his friend's side.

"No," the boy was saying, holding his head. "No, not now. . . . Please, not now!"

He had a funny look in his eyes, and his breathing was ragged. Daniel leaned over his friend and put a hand on his shoulder.

"What's wrong? You don't look good."

"I think I'm starting to get a migraine. A bad one," whispered Eric, almost crying. "You're going to have to take them the rest of the way." He said this with such disappointment, it made Daniel's heart ache.

Inaba slipped up beside them and went to one knee so she could be at eye level with the young man.

"Tell me your symptoms." Her voice was calm, reassuring. She had the air of someone who would not be flustered in the face of medical problems.

"Right now I see flashes before my eyes, and some tunnel vision."

"Then you shouldn't be in this cold and under such exertions. Do you have medicine? How far is it to your home?"

"There is a shot of something they usually give me. I live on Lillistra Estate, about 200 meters back that way." He pointed back down the path the way they had come.

"Then we should take you to—"

"No!" said the boy emphatically. "They'll be looking for you. You've got to head for the bridge."

"The rest can go; I'll stay with you," she said.

"No," said Daniel, once again taking charge of the situation. "I'll stay with him. The rest of the group may need you before this is all over. Eric is my friend, and friends stick together. I'll get him back to the estate and catch up with you."

Daniel handed the infant to Inaba, who reluctantly took the child. The baby stirred slightly with the exchange, then fell back to sleep.

Jimi stepped forward. "Where do we go?"

Eric, one hand to his head as if he was having trouble concentrating, pointed down the path. "It's not much further. Just keep straight on this path. It'll take you to the bridge, which is a wooden pontoon thing frozen right into the water. Cross it and you will be in Danderyd."

Jimi stepped over to Daniel, taking his hand in a firm grip. He started to say something but seemed at a loss for words.

"Hurry," was all he could manage.

"Take my flashlight," said Eric, holding it toward Jimi. "We can find our way without it."

And the little band, now smaller by two, continued on down the path.

"SO WHO WAS THAT?" asked Britta about Yani's surprise appearance as she jumped onto one of the snowmobiles in the garage of the estate.

The unseen, answered Jaime to herself, climbing onto the other. "Another friend of Jorgen Edders," she said aloud.

"Good timing," said Britta.

"Listening device," said Jaime.

Both engines gunned to life, and Britta flew forward first, heading out the open front gate. It was a three-minute ride to a walled compound. A heavy chain-link fence surrounded a parking lot—for snowmobiles, Jaime guessed, as cars weren't permitted on the island—in front of a low building. Britta had a key card out to push into the standing lock device, but the tall door was standing open.

She roared to a stop and jumped off the snowmobile, Jaime pulling up beside her.

Britta used the card to open the heavy metal door to the building. She ran and pulled open a door down a hall, but it was empty. "The girl is gone," she said. "Dear God."

She was shaking like a leaf, but she checked all the holding cells in which the kids had been kept. All the cells were empty.

Then, trembling even harder, she opened the door to the guards' bedroom. All three guards were dead inside, one by the doorway with a clean shot to the back of the skull, one shot in the chest and sprawled across a bed, the other shot in the back, seemingly while making a run for it. Britta screamed, then covered her own mouth with her hand to stifle the sound. Obviously, the assassin was here. It was happening.

"Which way?" Britta asked wildly.

Outside in the hall, Jaime noticed that the door to an outside compound had not clicked shut all the way. She pushed it open and looked outside, allowing herself to use the high-beam flashlight feature of her handheld.

"Look at this," Jaime said. When the researcher joined her, she pointed the beam of light to where the fence was cut and bent back.

"I know where they must have gone. The snowmobiles will be our best chance to catch up." And Britta raced back to climb onto hers to lead the way.

"WE SHOULD BE THERE by now!" said Eric in frustration.

The two boys had left the path, hoping to take a shortcut to the estate. But after twice stopping for Eric to throw up, they had lost all sense of direction. Now, for the third time, Daniel stood by as Eric retched into the snow.

"I'm sorry," said the young boy as he knelt, waiting to see if he would continue to vomit. "But I can't help it. When my head hurts this bad it makes me sick to my stomach."

He was so embarrassed that his friend had to witness this, this total weakness. Why couldn't he be like other boys? Why couldn't he be strong and athletic? Now, because of him, they were lost in the woods.

"I'm sorry," he said again for the umpteenth time. "It's all my fault. You should be on your way to the bridge."

"Stop it!" said Daniel angrily, not wanting his friend to keep beating himself up. "Just stop it. Without you, we never would have made it past the fence. You saved our lives."

Sensing that Eric had finished vomiting for the time being, Daniel reached down and pulled him up, placing the boy's arm over his shoulder. As he supported Eric around the waist, they staggered through the dark woods like a couple of drunken sailors.

They both raised their heads as they heard a mechanical whirring in the distance.

"Snowmobiles," said Eric. "Hey, do you really think they were going to kill you?" he asked as they stumbled around logs and bushes in the dark.

"For sure!" Daniel's breathing was becoming labored as he bore the weight of two persons. "These were some bad people, and they weren't going to want us alive to identify them later. The only one who seemed to have a heart was the lady scientist, but she was too focused on all those blood tests to care."

"Lady scientist?"

No, I won't believe it. I can't believe it.

"Yeah, some blond-haired lady, always wearing this white lab coat."

The tears started running down Eric's face now. He couldn't stop them.

Daniel noticed his friend's distress and said, "Is the headache that bad?"

"Uh, yeah . . . it's that bad."

As he said this, they stepped through the trees and found themselves back on a path. But which path? Where did it lead?

"You know, Eric, if we stick to the path, we could move faster."

"You're right. But where are we?"

"I was about to ask you that. Now think. You're a smart guy. How can we find your place?"

"Think," said Eric. His eyes glazed over as he tried to work past his own personal distress and his throbbing head and find a way out of their predicament.

"Daniel, lay me down on the path," he said suddenly.

"What?"

"Just do it!"

"You really are weird!" laughed Daniel as he helped his friend stretch out on the flat surface. "If you start making snow angels, I'm outta here!"

That made Eric chuckle for a moment, which he followed with, "Just shut up for a sec."

Little me. Big God. He closed his eyes and focused on the mantra, blocking out the snow, the pain, the sounds from the distance.

"Little me. Big God," he whispered quietly, over and over.

Daniel watched in awe as his friend's entire body seemed to relax right before his eyes. After a short while, Eric stopped chanting and slowly opened his eyes. Looking up into the sky, he did not move from his position on the ground. He simply raised one arm and pointed straight up at the few stars visible through the trees.

"Aha!" said the boy triumphantly. "The Big Dipper! I can't see the North Star, but I know exactly where it is."

He reached his arm out toward Daniel, who helped him up off the ground.

"And since I now know that way is north . . . ," he pointed back into the woods, the way they had come, "then I also know we need to go this way to find my place." And he steered his friend down the path.

"Whatever that was you just did, you've *got* to teach it to me!" said Daniel.

"It's a deal," said Eric, smiling to himself, noting that he no longer felt sick to his stomach.

The two boys had only taken a few steps toward their destination when they heard a voice from behind them.

"Yes, I'm impressed, too. However, I don't believe either of you is supposed to be outside, am I right?"

A middle-aged woman whom Eric had never seen before was standing on the path. The tone of her voice and look on her face was that of a school principal having caught two students skipping school. That image quickly faded, however, when Eric noted the large handgun she pointed directly at them.

"I know you!" said Daniel in disbelief. "You're the lady from the mall . . . with the car problems."

"What a smart kid. Too bad it killed you." She was smiling when she rested the butt of her pistol in the palm of her free hand and calmly fired off a round in his direction.

Eric watched in horror as the bullet struck his friend in the chest and he crumpled into the snow.

"Daniel!" he cried, reaching down to help his friend, who now lay limp and unmoving on the ground.

"One step and you join your friend," said the woman. And Eric straightened back up to see she now had her weapon trained on him.

He faced her with an angry defiance, anger that she could so callously hurt his friend, anger at his mother for being part of all this, anger at his stupid disease for robbing him of the strength he needed right now to fight back.

"Who are you?" she asked, seeming only slightly curious about his answer.

"Eric Carlson," he barked, fighting the impulse to cry. The last thing in the world he wanted was to give her the satisfaction of seeing him cry.

The woman's eyebrows raised in surprise as she connected the dots between this boy, the island, and the escaped captives. Eric saw a moment of indecision as she seemed to consider the implications of her next action. Then as quickly as it had appeared, the hesitation vanished.

"Well, no matter," was her offhand reply to no one in particular, and she took aim directly at Eric's head.

So this is it. The end.

He closed his eyes and muttered under his breath, "Little me. Big God."

THE LIGHT FROM the little flashlight bobbed up and down as Ryan walked along the path. Jimi had put him in front because his sharp, youthful eyes would be their best guides on this dark trail. Then Jimi and Inaba each took turns carrying the sleeping toddler.

Jimi noticed that the forest was beginning to thin out a bit. He could see more sky and stars and hoped that meant they would soon reach the end of the path. The baby seemed cozy and warm wrapped in her jacket, and Ryan had that immunity to cold common in most young boys, but Inaba was shivering. In spite of her parka, her lack of acclimatization to this bitter cold was apparent. They needed to reach safety, and warmth, soon.

Finally the woods disappeared, and the small band of runaways found themselves standing on a dead quiet shore. In the clear, starry night they could barely make out the dark outline of the mainland about 200 meters across the icy water. Between them and their ultimate goal was a long wooden bridge with planks frozen into the ice and a thin railing on each side. The planks looked sturdy enough, but they were certain to be slick.

"Cool!" exclaimed Ryan, who immediately moved to cross the bridge.

"Wait," said Jimi, placing his hand on the young boy's arm to slow him down.

Jimi turned to look back the way they had come. He could hear echoes of what sounded like an engine behind them, but it did not seem to be moving in their direction. What was happening back there on the island? Had they really made such a clean escape, or were they walking into a trap of some sort?

But that really wasn't what made Jimi hesitate. He kept hoping Daniel would catch up with them. But there was no sign of him.

He's a smart kid, Jimi thought. He wouldn't need their help to get across the bridge. And besides, if they reached help, they could send someone back for him.

Seeing the dilemma in his eyes, Inaba placed her hand lightly on his arm. "His fate is no longer in our hands," she said quietly.

He bowed his head, nodded, and then turned back to the bridge. He motioned for Ryan to go first, and the young boy moved out onto the walkway. He seemed to have no trouble keeping his footing, and so Jimi encouraged Inaba to follow. For the first time that evening, she seemed unnerved. She looked wary of the bridge and its ability to hold her.

"It'll be OK," said Jimi, with a reassuring smile. He reached out to take the baby from her and leave both her hands free to hold the railing, which she did, very tightly. Then he brought up the rear, stepping carefully to keep his own balance with the added weight of the infant.

The little band was about midway across when, at the far end of the bridge, a dark black SUV roared up and came to a halt. Three adults dressed in dark blue coveralls with matching jackets quickly exited the auto. Two of them were carrying rifles.

Were these allies of their captors? Was this why no one had followed them from the island? They were trapped, sitting ducks in the middle of the water, with nowhere to hide.

They halted, hesitating. Inaba and Ryan turned to Jimi for guidance. Keep going forward or turn back? But before he could decide, one of the team on the shore turned to retrieve something from the SUV. On his back, in large white letters, they could read POLIS.

Jimi sighed in relief. "It's OK." He motioned to Ryan to continue across the bridge. "They're good guys."

Ryan turned and almost ran the rest of the distance, leaving the two adults and their infant charge to continue without a light. He reached the officers and immediately started chattering at a million miles a minute, punctuating his discourse with hand motions pointing back toward the island.

The officers looked bewildered for a moment; then one of them, a woman, stepped forward and put her hands on the boy's shoulders. "Slow down, please; my English is not that good."

As she calmed him down and attempted to make what she could of his excited story, the other two officers moved out onto the bridge with their powerful flashlights and guided Jimi, Inaba, and the baby to safety.

Once they safely reached the shore, the officers quickly bundled the group into the warm SUV and began talking to one another in a language Jimi did not understand. The female officer then got behind the wheel of the auto and made a call on her radio.

When she completed the call, she turned back to Jimi and Inaba, who were huddled in the backseat with the sleeping baby stretched across their laps. The officer's eyebrows arched at the sight of his very feminine lime green parka.

Jimi followed her gaze, rolled his eyes, and said, "It's a long story."

"I'm sure it is." She smiled sympathetically. "You can tell me the whole thing when we get back to the station, where we can better care for you."

"There are two more boys," said Jimi quickly. "They may still be in danger."

"We've called for backup," she responded. "But my partners aren't waiting. They are heading to the island now to see what they can do."

The woman settled back into her seat, buckled her seat belt, and revved the engine. As they pulled away, Jimi turned back to see two blue-clad police officers moving swiftly across the bridge toward the island.

Hurry, was all he could think.

IT WAS DARK AND COLD, and the ride on the snowmobile over the icy ground was anything but smooth. Jaime strained to see ahead as she and Britta searched the dark for the missing captives, but little beyond the immediate area was illuminated by the snowmobile headlights.

Somewhere ahead of them came the muffled crack of a pistol. Jaime saw Britta tense and knew that she herself had jumped at the sound. Their vehicles were now at full speed, Jaime and Britta charging through the forest side by side. Jaime could hardly hear herself think over the racket they made.

After another 30 meters of travel, they rounded a bend and Jaime could barely make out forms on the path. As they closed in, she saw two people standing about 10 meters apart. She did not recognize the thin boy, but she could guess who the woman was who was raising a pistol and taking aim at him.

I don't think so, said Jaime to herself. She revved her vehicle to maximum power and directed it straight at the woman with the gun, standing up from the seat and leaning forward, as if willing the snowmobile to move faster.

The woman in the path was so focused on her prey that she was, at first, oblivious to the attack from the rear. When she did finally turn to see the vehicle bearing down on her, it was too late to jump out of the way. She turned to run, but it caught her from behind with a glancing blow, sending her face-forward into the snow.

As the vehicle made impact with the woman, Jaime lost control of the snowmobile and it careened into a tree, sending her flying.

She landed on her back, all wind forced from her lungs. She willed herself to catch her breath, then turned over and crawled onto her knees, then up onto her feet.

Over the top of the mangled snowmobile, she could see the assassin scrambling in the snow for something. With a rush, Jaime recalled that the woman had a pistol, and it had probably flown out of her hand during the crash.

She ran and flung herself onto the woman's legs, tackling her from behind, just as she was reaching for the gun, which Jaime recognized as a Ruger SP101. Jaime crawled over her and tried to secure the weapon herself, but just as she had one hand on it, the other woman pushed forward and tried to rip the pistol from her grasp.

They rolled back and forth in the snow, each trying to claim sole possession of the gun. The assassin was also athletic and well trained, and while Jaime wasn't able to claim the weapon, she was finally able to send it flying away from them, back into the snow. Now, if she could just grab the woman in such a way as to incapacitate her.

"You tried to kill my son!"

Jaime and the Good Mother both stopped and looked up, surprised.

Britta stood next to them, the Ruger in both hands, pointing directly at the assassin.

The gun quivered in Britta's hands.

Please let her be a good shot, was all Jaime could think.

"Oh, for God's sake," said the other woman. "Let me show you how it's done."

And the assassin broke free from Jaime and lurched again for the gun.

"It's all about my son!" screamed Britta, and Jaime saw her close her eyes as she pumped three bullets into the chest of the Good Mother.

The assassin went limp in the snow.

Jaime lurched forward and surveyed the situation. One woman lay dead in the snow. Another sat next to her, head bowed, weapon in her hand.

So the assassin was dead. But had they gotten there in time?

In the other direction, Jaime could see the young brown-haired boy kneeling in the snow by something—no, someone—stretched out on the ground.

As she approached the boy, she saw. Her worst nightmare.

It was Daniel, lying in the snow. Even in the darkness she could see how pale he was. The teen's eyes were open, barely. The smaller boy was sitting beside him, speaking with him.

Jaime spoke in a voice as calm and reassuring as she could possibly muster. "Daniel, it's me: Jaime Richards. Your dad sent me to find you."

She unzipped his jacket and pulled it back to get a look at the damage, causing Daniel to cry out. "I'm sorry," she said.

She found a clean entry wound in front, then reached around his back, and her hand came away very bloody. The exit wound was large, and beneath him in the snow she could see that he had already lost an incredible amount of blood.

Jaime quickly glanced over at the wreck of the snowmobile but realized that even if it had been operable, he was in no shape to be jostled over the rough ground. Even if she had a car, she guessed they couldn't have reached a hospital in time to stop the bleeding. Her gaze then fell upon the other boy, Daniel's friend, and she knew from his puffy, red eyes that he recognized the gravity of the situation.

As Jaime searched for something to say, Britta approached from behind and put her hand on her son's shoulder. He shrugged her off angrily and refused to look at her. She did not seem surprised or upset by this, but with both hands on one arm, gently pulled him to his feet and drew him away to speak with him. It was obvious that he did not want to leave Daniel's side, but he locked eyes with Jaime, who nodded that it would be OK. His friend was not alone.

Jaime turned to give Daniel her full attention.

"Am I gonna die?" he said softly, sounding much younger than his 15 years.

Jaime hesitated for a moment, tempted to play down the seriousness of the situation. She'd been trained to be with soldiers who were dying on the battlefield or in the hospital, and she knew she needed to give him permission to ready himself during his last minutes in this life.

"We'll get help as fast as we can, but you're hurt pretty bad. It could be that you're going to die, yes." She grabbed the boy's hand closest to her and held it in both of hers. "But I'm here with you, no matter what."

Dear God. This was hard enough when it was a young soldier, a stranger, but this was Daniel, the boy she'd promised Abe Derry she'd bring home.

She'd promised.

Jaime wanted to call on the Voice to help soothe Daniel, to calm him, but she was not calm herself. Yet she knew that if ever in her life she needed to be emotionally strong, it was at this moment. Right now, it wasn't about Abe and it wasn't about her. She was here to help Daniel. God had placed her in this time and this moment to help him, and she had better not blow it.

"I'm scared. Where will I go when I die?"

"Daniel, I won't pretend to have all the answers. I don't know exactly what the afterlife is like, although it must be wonderful. Jesus said he himself was going to prepare a place for us, and he said that in his Father's house were many mansions. I can't wait. I wouldn't miss it for the world."

She was fighting back the tears but knew it was a losing battle.

"Will I see my family again?"

Jaime ran a hand across his forehead, pushing the hair back out of his eyes. "This I know, deep in my heart, where nobody can shake it. Nothing, not even death, can separate you from God's love, or from your family's love."

"But I want to tell my dad, I'm sorry, I've screwed up and disappointed him so many times."

This brought a slight smile. "Disappointed? Daniel, wonderful Daniel, you have no clue the depth of the love your father has for you, how important you are to him. He told me that from the moment you were born, he knew you were the one who was like him, the one in whom he saw himself so clearly. He said that's why he gave you the middle name of Isaac, Abraham's beloved son.

"Besides, we're *all* screwups! That's not the point. Your father loves you. And if you multiply that a gazillion times, you might just know how much God loves you, too. That is why I know that death is a beginning, not an end, and whatever is waiting for you is very, very good."

"Jaime," he whispered. It was obviously getting hard for him to talk. "It's dumb, but . . . there's a bracelet . . . Kay Jewelers . . . mall . . . for Janel."

"Janel. She'll get it. I promise."

Daniel smiled, in response to her, but in response to something else also, something unseen except to him. It was the calmest, most peaceful smile Jaime had ever seen on the young teen's face. His eyes were getting heavier, and his grip on her hand was loosening.

"My mom. Love her. And Zeke, and Sarah."

"They know. But I'll make sure and tell them again. Daniel," Jaime said quietly. "You are now heading out on a grand adventure, so I ask, is there anything you'd like to hear right now to help you along the way?"

"I always liked that shepherd thing they taught us in Sunday school."

"Me, too." It truly was one of her favorite Bible passages. "'The Lord is my shepherd, I shall not want. . . .'" At first she could see his lips moving with the words as she recited them out loud. But soon she felt him stop shivering and become still.

"'Surely goodness and mercy shall follow me all the days of my life. And I will dwell in the house of the Lord, forever.'"

Her tears flowed freely, and she made no attempt to stop them. Britta's son returned to stand beside her. He saw that his friend was gone and bowed his head as Jaime began to pray.

"COME, WE'RE READY for takeoff," Aeolus said to Jaime, taking her hand and leading her from the black Volvo toward the open door of the familiar Gulfstream. Stockholm's smaller Bromma Airport opened at 5:30 A.M., and it was clear Aeolus had every intention of being one of the first planes out.

The last hours had been horrible. There was no other word that came close to describing them. The Swedish police had arrived not long after Daniel died, apparently alerted by a call from the FBI at the Derrys' home, and quickly taken charge.

Costas, who'd driven both Jaime and Yani from the airport, had suddenly shown up at Jaime's side, and no one in authority had questioned him as he'd taken Jaime quickly from the scene. Apparently her dismissal had been cleared at a higher level.

Even though she couldn't possibly do it, there was absolutely no way she could make the call, Jaime would never forgive herself if Abe and Eirene heard about their son's death from anyone but her. Her fingers trembled so badly that she had trouble hitting the small numbers on Costas's cell phone and had to start again three times. Finally, the call went through. Forget death notification protocol. Forget any protocol. When Jaime heard Abe's voice on the other end, she started to cry. "Sir, it's Jaime," she said.

"He didn't make it, did he?" was the father's response.

Jaime held herself together until the end of the call. Then she made Costas stop the Volvo, so she could get out and vomit in the snow at the side of the road.

Now, as she climbed the silver steps to the aircraft, she wondered again about Yani. She hadn't seen him since he had gotten the large nurse, Dolph, out of their way in the kitchen. She knew on this assignment Yani was the unseen, but how could he just vanish? Had something happened to him as well?

The curtains on the plane's windows were all drawn, and the moment Jaime put her second foot onto the interior floor of the aircraft, Costas pulled the door shut behind her. "Buckle in, please."

Jaime fell into the closest seat and numbly pulled the buckle together. She hardly noticed as the jet taxied and took off. It was still dark outside. It seemed like it had been dark forever and it would be dark forevermore.

Her exhaustion was complete. But she would never try to sleep. She knew she couldn't.

The assassin, whoever she was, was dead. As were the guards at the compound and one of the captives. The police had given them the news that the other kidnapped kids had made it safely across the bridge and off the island. Only Daniel had died.

How could that be?

"He stayed with me," Britta's son kept saying. "He stayed with me."

It was clear her son was having some sort of episode or seizure, and they'd let Britta take him back into the house out of the cold. But she did so with an armed guard. It seemed she wasn't going anywhere in the near future.

"Jaime. I'm sorry about Daniel."

The voice was so quiet that Jaime wasn't sure at first that it was actually Yani. She turned around and saw him in one of the backseats, facing the rear.

"Come here," he said gently.

She stood up, closed the cockpit door, and walked back to where he awaited her. "I can't believe it ended like this," she said, the taste of bile still in her throat.

"I know." He ran his hand through her hair. "I'm sorry."

"Where *were* you?" she demanded. "If you'd been there, there might have been a different outcome! If we'd had someone there, Daniel might not have died!"

"Hey." He put two fingers under her chin. "We did have someone there. You."

"No, don't put it on me. I can't stand it if it's all my fault," she said. And she asked again, "Where were you?"

"I was completing the primary mission," he said. "We were successful, Jaime. I know it doesn't feel like it to you just now, but the primary mission was a success, and we saved four out of five captives in our secondary mission."

He tapped the seat next to him, and she sat down. "Are you serious?" she asked. "That's like saying the shuttle blew up, but at least the seats were comfortable."

He held something out to her. It was small and circular. She opened her palm, and he dropped it on her hand.

It was a ring, a silver band encircled by four panels of lapis lazuli.

"What is this?" she asked.

"It's a first mission ring. All Operatives get them upon successful completion of their first mission."

"You keep calling it successful. Are you crazy? I've never felt more of a failure in my life. Or is it because you weren't the one who had to call the person she respects most in this world and tell him she watched his son die? Whatever. I don't want the damn ring."

"It's yours, to do with as you like."

She wished she could open the window in a grand gesture and throw the ring down into the sea.

"In case you're curious, Greek authorities have arrested Witgard Villella, Constantine, and their accomplices," Yani said.

Jaime looked over at him. She had never really seen him looking tired before, but he looked tired now. It wasn't surprising, given his recent injury.

"You have courage and compassion, intelligence and stamina," he said. "The one thing you don't have yet, which comes only with time, is perspective."

"I will never have a perspective in which watching Daniel Derry die is counted success."

"Do you have any doubt where Daniel is now?" Yani asked.

She took a deep breath. "I have confidence," she said. "But do you have any doubt that his parents and siblings will be in hell for the next couple of years?" she asked.

"They're gardeners," he said. "They have perspective."

"They don't have a *son*!" she hissed. He could be so infuriating. He could seem so callous.

"Wait a minute. I thought saving the captives was our primary objective," she said, suddenly realizing what he'd said.

"Secondary," Yani said. "And very important."

"So what was our primary objective?"

"Finding and either capturing or destroying the research. It was done."

"So that's why you couldn't be with me to save Daniel? You were looking for *research*?"

"Yes. That's right."

"And why didn't I know about this? Was I not your partner?" Her voice was rising, but she didn't care. She was sick of him leaving her out of the loop.

"Jaime. As I said, you have courage and compassion. But it was a Level Two objective, and you only have Level One clearance. I couldn't tell you."

"And even now I can't know? What was in the research that was such a secret? And why would people from Eden keep secrets from each other to begin with?"

"All things are revealed in time," Yani replied.

"So I nearly die, several times, and the best you can do is spout fortune-cookie sayings at me?" To say Jaime's look was incredulous was an understatement.

"Well with completion of this mission, with the receiving of the ring, you have actually achieved Level Two status. So how about I spout Bible verses? Or, better yet, why don't you?"

"What are you talking about?"

"Your favorite book. Genesis. According to the story, why does God put a Sword to guard the entrance to Eden?"

"What? I don't know. So no one else will eat from the tree of the knowledge of good and evil and become like God?"

"No. Good try, though, typical answer. But if you read carefully, it's quite explicit: *"The man has now become like one of us, knowing good and evil. He must not be allowed to reach out his hand and take also from the tree of life and eat, and live forever." So the Lord God banished him from the Garden of Eden to work the ground from which he had been taken. He drove out the man and he placed at the east side of the Garden of Eden cherubim and a flaming Sword flashing back and forth to guard the way to the tree of life."*

"And we're discussing this because . . . ?"

"Supposing there was a place where the water was pure, where there were no carcinogens in the air. People ate a diet of fresh fruits and vegetables, and fish with no mercury. Supposing these people enjoyed physical activity and knew how to live without stress. And supposing that, after thousands of years, their DNA adapted to that environment. That's what happens in any species. Suppose it became a physical trait that allowed these people to live longer, healthier lives. Nothing miraculous, just life, and physics, the way God intended."

Jaime was staring at him, simply staring. It was something at which she was becoming quite good. "So you're saying there really is a 'tree of life.' That there's something in Eden dwellers' DNA that allows them to live forever."

"Not forever," Yani replied. "Of course not. But longer and healthier. There are markers in the DNA that have become identifiable—and Britta Sunmark had found them. Jorgen Edders never would have talked of it in his right mind, but apparently as his tumor progressed, he wasn't always aware of where he was or to whom he was speaking. Even so, there are very few people in the world who could have understood what he was talking about, let alone understood the implications of isolating and recombining these markers. Unfortunately, Britta Sunmark was one of them."

Jaime sat, pondering what he'd said. "Of course, it's very wrong to go around kidnapping people for any reason. And killing them is very bad indeed. But what if she'd gone about it another way? What would be so wrong with Terris scientists finding this marker? Couldn't it help a lot of people?"

"There are parts to your question. To answer the first part: Scientists in Eden are working to recombine the DNA in ways that can be brought out to the Terris world and introduced without raising eyebrows. Because, you see, there's no way for Terris scientists to find the marker without finding the specific group of people who carry it. It would become a larger version of what Patsy Covington, the kidnapper, was sent on: a worldwide witch hunt for gardeners, or those descended from Eden dwellers on their mother's side. Britta was right, it's passed along through the mitochondrial DNA, through the mother."

"Dear God. So this whole thing, this 'primary objective,' was about covering our asses. It was about people from Eden keeping secrets from the Terris world—secrets that could save thousands of lives or heal hundreds of diseases."

"The time will be right, Jaime. It isn't yet."

"Why was this kept a secret even from me? I've been to Eden. Why did no one mention it?"

"There's a sequence in which information is disseminated. It's no big secret keeping. It's mostly to keep new arrivals from freaking out under information overload."

"So Eden dwellers live longer and healthier—"

"Especially in Eden," he inserted. "Once they choose to live in the Terris world, with its stresses and pollution, somehow the marker remains intact in the DNA, but the life span is shortened."

"So, please tell me, in English, the upshot of what you're saying."

"Your relatives in Eden were looking pretty good," he said. "Considering their ages."

It started to sink in. The relatives she'd met, many of them from previous generations, yes, they'd seemed old . . . but not nearly as old as they must have actually been.

"Could you give me a for-instance on this?"

"Kristof Remen. The gentleman you met three years ago. How old did you guess him to be?"

"He was pretty spry, but I guessed around eighty."

"One hundred and thirty-nine."

"That can't be true."

"You know he'd been a Sword and retired. You can't begin to train as an Operative until you're thirty; you can't be commissioned until you're thirty-five. You must be an Operative for thirty years before you're even considered to be a Sword. And then the usual term as a Sword is thirty years—not because you're getting physically too old but because of the high stress levels. Kristof had done all those things, and had lived in retirement, both inside and outside Eden, for many years."

"And this is what we were so afraid of the folks in the Terris world finding out. That our DNA is stronger, but we won't share."

"We *will* share, Jaime, but in ways that will seem like logical next steps to outside researchers."

She closed her eyes. "Why is talking to you often as difficult as dealing with the bad guys? This is a lot to take in."

Tired as she was, it didn't take long for the next question to hit her.

"So, Operative at thirty-five, Sword at sixty-five—usually for a thirty-year term, if you don't quit. How old are you, anyway?"

"I was waiting for you to ask. I'm eighty-nine."

Eighty-nine! She thought again of his body, so sculpted and perfect, and young. Well, apparently not young.

"And you weren't going to tell me? You were going to let me fall in love with you, go crazy with wanting you, and not mention we have an age difference?"

"The first time you asked, I told you," he said quietly. "And you know what? You're not the only one who's risked something. I gave up being a Sword. Which meant a lot to me."

Jaime knew that in his understated way he was really saying *which meant everything to me.*

"I never asked you to give it up! I never would have asked you to give it up!" she said fiercely. *Dear God, is everything that has gone horribly wrong my fault?*

"I know. That's why I made the decision on my own. And no matter what happens between us, it was the right decision. It was worth the risk to me, what might have been."

What might have been. Past tense. So he knew. Somehow he knew she couldn't continue.

Any of it.

"None of this is what I thought it was," she finally said. "I'm sorry. I can't do this. I can't be an Operative for a group of people who lie—OK, OK—who withhold information. Who think death is an acceptable price for success. I can't do it."

They both sat silent. Finally she asked, "I don't suppose you can alter the flight plan to land in Germany and let me off."

He shook his head. "You had a four-day pass. You spent it in Athens, on a nice holiday."

More lies. "So when I go back to my continued debriefing, how do I explain that I left in high spirits and I return shaken and depressed?"

"The son of your dear friend died."

In my arms. He died in my arms.

"You're really quitting?" Yani asked. "You don't want to take time to think?"

"No. There's not a flicker of doubt in my mind. Not a flicker. I'm going back to a life of peace and quiet in the Army. I'm spending time with my Terris-based family. Or even with the goat herders. I really liked them."

Now that the decision was made, she felt peace. She was no longer in a flinging mood. She handed him back the ring.

"Thanks anyway. See you around."

Yani shook his head. "No, actually, you won't."

It was one of those times they were talking so plainly and succinctly about the truth, about important things, that it felt natural for Jaime to add, "Since we won't see each other anymore . . . I did love you. And I'm grateful for that. I thought I might never fall in love again."

Jaime thought he might say something in response. But neither of them spoke again until they landed in Greece. And then he was gone.

EPILOGUE

"'. . . FOR THE LAMB at the center of the throne will be their shepherd, and he will guide them to springs of the water of life, and God will wipe away every tear from their eyes.'"

Jaime closed her Bible and slowly surveyed the setting where she and a small group of family and friends had assembled to celebrate the life of Daniel Derry. They were gathered in a memorial park built on an island to honor Teddy Roosevelt. Since the twenty-sixth president was known as a conservationist and outdoorsman, the site was appropriately woodsy and could not be reached by motor traffic.

After Daniel had discovered this island while biking down the Mount Vernon Trail, he had made it a point to eat his lunch there whenever his weekend cycling excursions brought him that way. At the center of the island was a clearing where a hiker or biker would find a statue of Roosevelt, as well as a large, cauldron-shaped fountain.

It was by that fountain that the group had gathered, on this brisk March afternoon, with the temperature reaching into the fifties and sun filtering down through the trees. Daniel's mother, Eirene, had brought a tabletop easel with a photo of him taken during a session for their family's last Christmas card. The photographer had caught both Daniel's shy smile and the depth and sparkle behind his eyes.

Jaime's eyes were dry. She had cried enough over the last week that she was certain there was nothing left. But there were still many tears being shed by the group. The Derry family was just beginning to surface from the shock of their loss.

But the Derrys were also surprised and touched by the guests who were gathered with them for this service. While they had kept it small, only family and close friends, several new friends had asked to be included. When Jaime had given people the chance to say something about Daniel or to share a memory, the first to step forward was Jimi Afzal, who stood by Inaba Mikelti.

"Daniel was a leader, a great leader," Jimi said. "It was he who organized our escape. If it hadn't been for him, none of us would be standing here now." With a wave, Jimi included Ryan Stevens, who stood huddled with his family, as well as Inaba, who smiled and shifted An Bao on her hip.

Jimi and Inaba had spent the last week working with the Chinese consulate, seeking permission for Inaba to bring An Bao back to her family in China. At first it had seemed hopeless, but when Abe Derry called a friend at the State Department, suddenly doors were opened. Inaba's visa had been approved and a flight was arranged for the next day.

Eric Carlson stood with his father, whose arm was draped casually yet protectively over his son's shoulder. His mother had been taken into custody by the Swedish police, and David Carlson had flown immediately to Stockholm to bring his son back to the States.

Eric had looked frightened to step forward, but Jaime could tell he wanted to, and she nodded her encouragement.

"Daniel was my friend," he said, a quaver in his voice. "We were all running away, and I began to have one of my migraines, and he stayed with me. If he hadn't, I know I would have fainted in the woods—we were off the path—and no one would have found me for a long time. I might have frozen to death. But . . . if he hadn't stayed with me, she wouldn't . . . he wouldn't . . ." Eric did begin to cry then, and his dad had hugged him tight.

Daniel's mother, Eirene, had smiled at Eric and said, "Thank you, Eric, for being his friend. We are grateful to you, for being with him, and for being here today."

Then a young girl had stepped forward. She was tall and slim and dark-skinned, with large eyes and long hair. She was at that awkward age when girls start developing, but there was nothing awkward about her. She was a lovely girl, and Jaime could tell she'd be a lovely woman. She was wearing the bracelet Daniel had bought her for Valentine's Day.

"Daniel was so great," Janel said, through much emotion. "I will always love him."

The group of teenagers who were Daniel's friends looked frankly surprised by this, and Jaime could see that Daniel's brother, Zeke, and sister, Sarah, were caught off guard, and impressed, by that one.

It was then Daniel's brother, Zeke, stepped forward. "Did—I mean, Daniel—I know he was my little brother, and all, but Daniel was the guy I always wanted to be," he said. And then he stepped back to his father's side.

Little An Bao was getting restless and shifted enough that Inaba let her get down on the ground in front of her. The toddler looked around shyly; then a look of surprise crossed her face. She walked forward to the easel with the photo and grabbed it. "Nayal!" she said, and looked around, showing it to the others. "Nayal." She hugged the picture to herself.

Inaba hurried toward the girl, trying to return the picture to the easel, but the little girl hugged it to her chest fiercely. Daniel's mother stooped down in front of An Bao.

"Daniel," Eirene said softly, pointing to the picture.

"Nayal." An Bao nodded.

Eirene softly closed An Bao's hands around the photo and nodded to the girl that she could have it. Relieved, the child hugged it to herself and walked back toward Inaba.

Others in the extended family spoke, as did friends of the family.

"My friends," spoke Jaime with assurance, holding out her arms to include all the group. "I leave you with this charge, one which I believe Daniel in his few years had already fulfilled: Accept the adventure that is your life. Drive on with gusto, and without fear of what might lay ahead. Be slow to anger, quick to forgive, and live to the fullest each moment God has granted you."

As she said these words, she couldn't help but think what a challenge they would be for her own life.

Then she finished the end of the printed service, each word resonating inside: "Let us pray. Give us faith, Lord, to see in death the gate to eternal life, so that in quiet confidence we may continue our course on earth until, by your call, we are reunited with those who have gone before us."

After the benediction, the little congregation split into groups. Eric broke away from his father to pull Zeke Derry aside and speak with him privately. Jaime could see Zeke nodding and almost smiling as Eric's hand motions betrayed the intensity of his storytelling.

Ryan and his parents were reading the long inscriptions behind the Roosevelt statue, and Inaba and Jimi spoke quietly together, possibly saying their farewells before parting to go their separate ways.

Jaime caught Abe's eye and nodded her head toward a pathway that led along the river. She couldn't help but notice how much he had aged, and how it seemed some of the great zest for life was muted from behind his eyes, even given his perspective.

They came to a bench that overlooked the river and sat facing the water, neither one able to make eye contact with the other.

"I am so sorry," Jaime finally broke the silence. "Can you ever forgive me?"

"Forgive you?" Abe was incredulous. "For what?"

"One step different, one less delay, five minutes here, or even a minute there, Daniel would be alive right now."

"You don't know that." He was almost angry now. "You don't know how one slight difference in the chain of events might have altered things, maybe for the worse. There were many people who did a lot of evil things here, who deserve at least some share of the blame, but not you. Certainly not you."

They were quiet for a while, at a loss for where to go next.

"How old are you? Really?" Jaime blurted out suddenly.

Taken aback, Abe said, "Gardeners who come to raise a family in the Terris world are usually young, somewhat equivalent in age to their counterparts here. I'm fifty-eight, which is only a few years older than my peers in the Army. Why do you ask?"

"I'm sorry; I needed to know. And forgive me if it's too personal, but do you now regret that you and Eirene chose to have, and raise, a family here in the Terris world? Things would be so different if you'd stayed in Eden."

"Jaime, we're not here to live long, uneventful lives. We're here to make a difference. Daniel might be dead, but four children are alive who might otherwise be dead. There's also a teenage girl who will never again doubt she's worth loving. And I hope my other children, and Eirene and I also, will continue to have an impact on the lives of those around us.

"And now, with the foundation to run, I know that will help Eirene."

An anonymous donor, whom both Jaime and Abe knew to be Geri Allende, had given a large bequest to start a charitable foundation in Daniel's name. Their first donations would be to the children in the orphanage run by An Bao's parents and to the African hospice headed by Inaba.

"But this isn't really about us, is it? Are you having doubts yourself, Jaime?"

"There's so much I don't know, so much that's been kept from me." Jaime looked at the river, not at Abe, when she continued. "You see, sir, I've resigned. I'm not an Operative any longer. I couldn't handle it. I'm not the right kind of person."

"Oh," he said.

"I'm still Army, and I'll do everything in my power to be the best chaplain I can possibly be. I know now that's my calling, and I'll do my best."

"It was Daniel's death that led you to this decision?"

"That, and other things."

Together the friends sat, side by side. "Life's hard," Jaime said finally.

"And then you die," agreed Abe.

"Yeah, but that's the good part," Jaime responded.

"It is indeed," Abe agreed, and put his arm around his former chaplain. "It is indeed. This year here, next year in the New Jerusalem."

This time it was her old commander who was looking off in the distance. "Here's the thing. When push came to shove, my boy, he stood up. He took risks. He did it so all those other kids could live. He did it so Zeke and Sarah would know they had it in them, too. He didn't do it so you could stand down, Jaime. He didn't do it so I could, either.

"I know you, Chaplain. I think you know that life is good, despite all you've been through. Or maybe because of it. So here's my question to you: Are you sure you quit?"

Jaime looked up, surprised. That wasn't the question she expected.

"Because, you see," said Abe, taking a chain with a small pendant out of his pocket, "this is for you. From Clement. It's your next assignment."

The general put it on her palm and closed her hand around it.

"From one simple gardener to another, Godspeed," he said.

And he walked back to join the others.

ACKNOWLEDGMENTS

We would like to express our gratitude to the following people, without whom this book would not be the same. First to our editor, Jennifer Enderlin, whose belief in Eden brought this story to life, and whose keen insights brought it into focus; to Susan Cohen, agent and friend; Sara Goodman, who keeps the ship on even keel; our copy editor Barbara Wild, who knows the difference between toward and towards so we don't have to; and Bill DeSmedt, fellow thriller-writer and all-around brilliant guy, for the final catches.

FROM SHARON: Thanks to James Shanahan, A, D.O. for continuing medical advice. We certainly tried to avoid that intercostal artery! Thanks also to anesthesiologist Tomi Prvulovic for information on how to correctly dope someone up ineffectively.

Thanks to: Deb Holton-Smith, Colleen Larsen, MaryAnn O'Roark, and Robert Owens Scott for early readings of the manuscript that led to substantial additions to the story. Thomas Mattingly and Stacey Chisholm for such important continued support. Barbara Rossing and Jurgen Moltmann for revelations on how one's view of the end of the world influences your day-to-day life, and to Bob Scott and Mark Richardson, Jamie Calloway and Jim Cooper for organizing a life-changing Trinity Institute conference on the topic. With gratitude also to Pam Heatley and the Ladies of Newport Writing Circle (who are neither from Newport or necessarily ladies) for their company during the solitary days of writing.

Thanks to Bob for living for months at a time with a wife who was under the gun and far from the mop; to Jonathan for being so thoughtful, funny, and creative, and for understanding the times I groused about helping with homework or didn't make it to the soccer game; to Linnéa for being so self-possessed and creative and for learning to tack her own horse; and to my parents for their continuing encouragement.

Last but not least, thanks to B.K. for decades of friendship, the perfect research delivered in a timely fashion even when she was deployed, for making trips to Europe to write so much fun, for skilled writing, and generally being the other half of a creative team.

FROM B.K.: Living and working in a place like Iraq does not make one an expert on all things related to it. So, recognizing my own limitations, I am grateful for people whom I consider to be the real experts, and who provided input for this book with great flair. Howard Cordingly, you were not only a talented Staff Weather Officer, but you found some really cool Google Earth satellite photos! Steve Powell, your insight was very helpful, and I appreciate that you didn't tell me so much that you had to kill me. Ed Moschella, James Griffith, Mike Doyle, you offered great insight into the military medical system.

I am also thankful for the opportunity to work with a very unique command team the likes of which may never be seen again: Becky Halstead, you taught me about compassionate leadership; Sue Sowers, you were such a diligent prayer partner; and Sharon Duffy, you always kept our feet on the ground. Whose week is it to buy the pizza?

To my sister Linda and her husband Mark, I guess I finally got something in return for all those years of being your ground crew with radio in hand. Thanks for a helpful "pilot's-eye view."

For Jim Mercer, Andrea Pfaff, and Bill Webber . . . your collective abilities to be pastors and yet real, down-to-earth people helped a young woman seeking God's direction for her life understand that you don't have to lose yourself to find your calling.

Finally, I am eternally grateful for a special friend and role model who is no longer with us, Bennett Basore. You were never too busy to help someone in need, whether an individual in distress or an entire community responding to disaster. You introduced me to the dedicated work of the Stillwater Amateur Radio Club and the thrilling activity of tornado spotting. But most of all, I will never forget returning home after a long day at church to find you mowing my lawn. You will always be the truest example of a "gardener."

FROM BOTH: Thanks to our readers who gave us a reason to write. Godspeed.

Sharon and B.K., Memorial Day, May 2007,
Villers-Agron, France

SHARON LINNÉA is the author
of the new mystery *These Violent Delights*
as well as the three Eden Thrillers. She
has also written award-winning biogra-
phies of Raoul Wallenberg and Hawaii's

Princess Kaiulani. She lives outside New York City with her family.
Visit her at SHARONLINNEA.COM

B.K. SHERER holds a Master
of Divinity degree from Princeton
Theological Seminary and a Doctorate
of Education from Oklahoma State
University. A Presbyterian minister, she
currently serves on active duty as a chaplain in the U.S. Army.

The authors first collaborated on a play about the French Underground
for their 6th grade talent show in Springfield, Missouri, and have been
friends ever since.

EDENTHRILLERS.COM

A portion of the proceeds of this book will go to the Wounded Warrior
Project, (**WOUNDEDWARRIORPROJECT.ORG**) which supports soldiers
and the families of soldiers who have been severely wounded in the service of their country.

Read on for an excerpt from

TREASURE
OF EDEN

BY

SHARON LINNÉA
AND
B.K. SHERER

PROLOGUE

IT WAS THE END of a long day and the CIA Political Officer working with the Geneva Terrorism Task Force was ready to go home, grab some dinner and a Belgian beer. But first he picked up a new file that had been left on his desk earlier in the day.

Frank McMillan was just back from three years as Chief of Station in Tunisia. Three long years. Suffice it to say some of the higher-ups had not been pleased with his performance as Chief of Station of Kuwait City during the early days of Operation Iraqi Freedom. Nor had they been pleased that certain items he'd procured for them had been found to be less than authentic.

Ah, well. Another assignment. A fresh start.

His time in Iraq had piqued his interest in the black-market trade of antiquities. Even though it had nothing to do with his official duties, Frank had one of his assistants tasked to monitor all known venues for newly available items. The folder before Frank was half an inch thick with printouts and Xeroxes of the current crop of antiquities being offered for sale illegally. He opened it and thumbed through the papers under the circular pool of illumination from his desk lamp.

Nothing especially interesting.

Until, tired as he was, one item toward the bottom of the stack caused an intake of breath. He sat up, running his hand through his thick brown hair, feeling his adrenaline surge. He grabbed for his reading glasses, closed the folder, and put the printed paper in the center of his desk. It read:

eBay Item Number: 150 126643 1598

Realistic Jewel Cask Prop From '50s Classic Movie *Jenii*

Starting Bid: $50.00

End Time: Jan-27-07 00:30:00 PST

(3 days, 12 hours)

Shipping Costs: E-mail seller before making bid

Ships to: Worldwide

Item Location: Classic Props Warehouse

Description: This is it, the jeweled treasure box at the heart of the classic film *Jenii,* set in the mountains of the Judean wilderness. This box has been guarded carefully since the 1954 production, no nicks or scratches. Six realistic gems: ruby, carnelian, turquoise, lapis, jade, mother-of-pearl. Cask itself is heavy, measures twelve inches long, ten inches wide, and six inches deep, and comes with a lifetime Certificate of Authenticity. This is a fantastic blue-chip investment piece and was acquired directly from the prop maker. One of a kind. Only time available. Don't miss this once-in-a-lifetime chance to own a piece of film history!

Seller: Classic Props

Feedback: 100% Positive

Member: since Aug-04-01 in United States

Frank put his hands over his face and leaned back in his leather desk chair.

This was it. What he'd spent the last four years waiting for. A clue.

It wasn't a prop, of course. He'd become well versed in the language of the black market and knew the entire listing was code. It was an ancient box found in the Judean wilderness in 1954. Furthermore, in this auction, every dollar bid was $1,000.

He turned his computer back on, went to eBay, and pulled up the auction. He clicked on the photo to enlarge it. It was exquisite. The gold leaf on the outside of the box, the black onyx interior. He moved through the series of photos. Incredible. The hinges, too, were the right kind for Judea of 2,000 years before.

But what had caught his attention were the jewels: ruby, carnelian, turquoise, lapis, jade, mother-of-pearl. This was a rare instance when it was possible that even the canny dealer might not fully understand the significance of what he had.

Frank McMillan was aware that many of his compatriots thought he'd gone to Iraq a pragmatist and returned an obsessed man. He had been dealing there with two powerful men, both of whom believed that the place called Eden actually existed. Both men had died in their quest.

If, by any stretch of the imagination, it was true—if Eden did exist— the implications were staggering. One of his partners, Coleman Satis, claimed his own mother had been born there. She had told him stories of Eden's incredible wealth, of jewels so abundant they were used for home décor. More to the point, she'd told Satis of an advanced society with a wealth of technological and medical advances that would be worth billions to the outside world. And she said they had no army at all. No defense. Anyone with power who found this hidden society could walk in and take over. The ramifications of being that person were enormous.

There was a saying that Satis' mother had passed along to him, a saying that had driven Satis, who was already one of the most powerful men on earth: *Who Rules Eden Rules the World.*

Sounded like a worthy job description, at least to Frank.

Satis' mother had been so persuasive that Coleman Satis—the ultimate pragmatist—had been willing to risk everything, including his life, to find and conquer this place.

Now Satis was dead.

Frank himself wasn't completely convinced it actually existed. But there were loose ends. Unsolved mysteries. And he was not a man who could tolerate loose ends or the feeling of being thwarted.

He'd come back from Iraq knowing two things. One was that these six jewels—ruby, carnelian, turquoise, lapis, jade, mother-of-pearl—were connected with the mystery. They were the jewels listed in the book of Genesis as jewels plentiful in Eden. He still didn't know how they figured into whatever the hell happened in Iraq, but he knew they did.

At the heart of the incident had been a bracelet worn by an Arab girl with those six jewels.

The other thing he knew but could not explain was that a female American Army chaplain, Jaime Lynn Richards, who'd been involved in the secret Eden operation, had disappeared off the face of the earth, from Iraq, for three years. Then she had returned as mysteriously as she'd left, and reassumed her duties, seemingly without anyone in the Department of the Army batting an eye.

Which was impossible. All the Army knew how to do was bat eyes.

The new post-9/11 policy of data sharing between agencies was extremely helpful to Frank on this score. It had enabled him to keep tabs on Jaime Richards since her return, to at least know where she was and what she was up to. Her file said she was five foot seven; from his interview with her four years ago, he knew she had piercing green eyes that saw straight through him, that seemed able to read his thoughts. At least it felt that way at the time. Obviously, she hadn't read them well enough.

Frank pulled out her file and looked at the current photo. Her blond hair was a shade lighter, undoubtedly bleached by the desert sun. She was still in good shape, and had even acquired some pleasing curves. Frank had buffed up in Tunisia; now his biceps and quads were like iron. He laughed softly. Jaime Richards and Frank McMillan, versions 2.0.

According to Frank's information, Richards had missed a promotion board while she was away. At the next board, later this month, her Officer Record Brief—which listed where and when every officer was assigned—claimed that for those three years she was attached to the Office of the Chief of Chaplains in D.C. Frank understood that the Army wouldn't keep her listed as in Iraq—why give someone three years of combat pay when they didn't have to? But there was no explanatory note that she was kidnapped, only that she was on "duty elsewhere." And her personnel microfiche had three single pages labeled "classified" where evaluation reports should be.

What did that mean? In this particular case, what the hell did that mean?

Where had Jaime Richards been? And what did it have to do with Eden and the six jewels?

If there was a chance—the smallest chance—that she'd been in Eden, that she knew about Eden, that she could get there again, Frank had to find out.

From Tunisia, all he'd really been able to do was hear (although several months after the fact) that she'd reappeared and be kept apprised of her location. Now he was back, he was in Geneva, in a situation where he had mobility. He had been waiting for something to turn up, for another ticket into the mystery that was Eden.

This box was it. It had the key jewels, the jewels that to those in the know, signalled "Eden."

Did it have a direct connection to Jaime Richards? There was one way to find out. He'd follow the box, and see who else was following it, too.

He would also keep very close watch on Jaime Richards.

He already had a man on it. His last name was Maynard and he was undercover in Iraq as a Department of the Army civilian working for Army Material Command.

Frank took out his BlackBerry and e-mailed him: *Anything to report?*

The response took only two minutes: *Nothing. She spends most of her time in her office counseling, working in their operations center, or visiting soldiers in the hospital. Although she won't stay put. I spent Christmas Eve dodging mortars because she was climbing frigging guard towers to hang out with the guards. However, no apparent nonmilitary activity. No contact with anyone of interest. She's going on mid-tour leave tomorrow. Good riddance. Let our guy in Germany sit outside her place.*

Frank stared at the words. Just stared at them.

The box had appeared, and Richards was on the move.

Was the timing coincidence? Or could the eBay listing and the chaplain's leave be connected?

Frank's response to Maynard was flagged as urgent: *Wherever she's going, you're going, too. See to it.*

It was all he could do not to add: *you moron.*

Ah. Frank was back, and the hunt was on.

WEDNESDAY

JANUARY 24, 2007, 12:10 A.M.

(3 DAYS, 11 HOURS, 20 MINUTES UNTIL END OF AUCTION)

LOGISTICS SUPPORT AREA ANACONDA

BALAD, IRAQ

JAIME RICHARDS HAD twenty hours. Twenty hours to fly from Balad, Iraq, to Tallil—make a pickup—and continue on to Ali Ah Salem, Kuwait; Frankfurt, Germany; and deliver her package safely in Switzerland.

She couldn't even count the number of things that could go wrong. She was officially taking her mid-tour leave, and soldiers knew the plane they were on to start the journey out of Iraq could leave today, tomorrow, or, God forbid, a week from today. Or they could get stuck in Kuwait. Last time Jaime's boss had flown out on leave, the emir of Kuwait died, and the whole country—including the airfields—had shut down for three days.

Jaime had twenty hours.

She was packing her bags in the trailer that served as her hooch when she got a call. A COSCOM (Corps Support Command) soldier from one of her subordinate units was critically injured and was being rushed into surgery. It was a classic chaplain's dilemma. She needed to continue packing, there was no way she could miss her flight, and she desperately needed a couple of hours of sleep before the start of her new mission.

But there was a boy, and he was badly hurt.

To her mind, there really was no choice.

She headed for the operating room in the series of large interconnected tents that comprised the hospital, to observe the surgery and pray for the young soldier while the neurosurgeon worked on his damaged skull, which had been split wide open when the Humvee tire he was inflating exploded in his face. The rim had caught him on the forehead, right at the hairline about two inches above his eyes.

"Michael, are you with us?" Once the surgery was complete and Jaime knew she wouldn't get in anyone's way, she stepped up to the patient's side.

He had begun to stir, and squeezed Jaime's hand, on which she wore a disposable purple latex glove. She was amazed that someone could wake up and be aware of his surroundings after having his brain exposed only minutes before.

The young man was lucky to be alive, and even luckier that his skull had taken most of the impact, protecting the brain housed within.

"Doc," she said over her shoulder to a man who was making notes on the patient's clipboard. "That wire mesh you put in his forehead molds perfectly. You can hardly tell this guy had a piece of his skull broken out."

"I told you," he responded. "I'm the best."

She could see him smile beneath his mask but knew that he wasn't kidding.

If I ever need neurosurgery, she thought, *I want someone with that kind of confidence working on me!*

Still in the maroon scrubs she had donned to watch the procedure, she followed the gurney as they wheeled the young man back to the ICU for observation during his first hours of recovery. If they were certain he was stable, they might put him on the next plane for Landstuhl—the military regional medical center—later that morning.

Jaime remembered when she had taken that flight, almost a year before, after being picked up along the highway in southern Iraq. She'd been away for nearly three years. The official story went that she'd had amnesia and spent the time with Iranian goatherds. In fact, although she had spent some time with goats, most of it had been spent in the place known as Eden. While most people in the world never suspected or believed it, the place that had come to be known as the Garden of Eden still existed. It was hidden—in fact, at any given time only twelve persons, known as Swords, knew the way in and out. At the end of an unusual adventure during her first tour in Iraq, Jaime had been invited to go to Eden, and she'd accepted.

She'd found Eden to be an altruistic society, whose citizens worked to help those in what they called the Terris world. There she'd spent a year in contemplation and gardening, and she was content. Until Clement had invited her to study at the place they called Mountaintop to join those they called the Integrators. The Integrators were citizens of Eden who moved back and forth between the two worlds. They included Messengers, who lived in the Terris world and delivered messages between other Integrators; Operatives, who had received special training in how to intervene in Terris affairs; and the twelve Swords who took people back and forth between the Terris world and Eden during the rare opportunities they called door openings.

Jaime discovered she felt called to be a person of action, and had trained to become an Eden Operative. Though the required training was three years, she'd been sent back a year early on special assignment.

That was nearly a year ago. Now Jaime was back in Iraq, in her Terris job, on assignment as a chaplain with the U.S. Army.

The unit with which Jaime had originally deployed to Iraq had finished their tour while she'd been gone. She'd been stationed in Germany the previous August when one of the chaplains assigned to the 5th COSCOM HQ had become ill and was shipped home. Jaime received the "Tag, you're it!" phone call on a lazy Sunday afternoon while relaxing in her rental home in the little burg of Hochspeyer. In less than two weeks she was back in Iraq.

Jaime checked her watch as she entered the ICU. Twelve forty A.M. She needed to get to the COSCOM Operations Center and clean up a few loose ends before catching her flight to Kuwait. Her original plan was to catch a few hours of sleep before finishing up. But she was now wide awake. Perhaps she should head for the COSCOM, do what she needed to do, then see if sleep was still an option.

Confident her soldier was doing well, Jaime returned to the women's dressing room, which was in truth a storeroom with a curtain hanging over the doorway. She removed her scrubs and donned the new ACU, or Army Combat Uniform, with the gray/green digital pattern. She laced up her desert boots, and pulled her dog tags off a hook hanging above her head. Her brother Joey—Joe, now, but he'd always be Joey to her—had kept them during the three years she had been missing in action. Jaime had retrieved them on her first visit Stateside when she reappeared. She looped them over her head and her blond hair, still obediently in its French braid. As the tags dropped inside her T-shirt, the various trinkets she had added over the years jangled reassuringly. They weren't regulation, but it was comforting to know they were there.

As Jaime left the hospital compound she passed a smokers' pavilion used by the staff on breaks. It was unlit, and she could barely make out the form of a man with a large backpack at his feet, and another one shaped like a teardrop slung across his shoulder, leaning against one of its support pillars. Mortaritaville, as the soldiers called Logistics Support Area Anaconda, was not well lit at night, to make it more difficult for insurgents to find targets for their mortar rounds.

That's odd, she thought. *Why would someone bother to come all the way out here, stand alone in the dark, and not even smoke?*

As Jaime rounded the corner to walk the dark block to her headquarters, she didn't notice the man from the pavilion pick up his backpack, sling it over his shoulders, and follow her down the street.

CPSIA information can be obtained at www.ICGtesting.com
Printed in the USA
LVOW082122270912

300674LV00002B/4/P